Loose Ends

Jennifer Haynie

Cover design by Indie Designz, http://www.indiedesignz.com

ISBN:
978-1-943398-09-6

Other Books by Jennifer Haynie

Last Chance Series

Operation Shadow Box
Operation Peacemaker

Unit 28 Series

Panama Deception

The Athena Trilogy

The Athena File

Other Books

Exiled Heart
Hunter Hunted

To Steve, my beloved and my encourager.

There is a time for everything, and a season for every activity under the heavens . . . a time to keep silent and a time to speak.

—Ecclesiastes 3:1, 7b

1

The note shattered her peace.

Alex Thornton stared at the eight pieces of paper she'd taped together with Scotch tape.

I know what happened to your sister. Want to know more? Come to the Nani Kai Bar and Restaurant at four. Alone.

Which was exactly what Jabir al-Omri had done.

Someone who probably didn't have his best interests at heart insinuated that Jabir's sister, dead now for ten years, possibly lived.

Alex's heart tightened. She had to find him. Now.

Note in hand, she burst onto the front lanai of their suite at a resort in Wailea, Maui, and bolted down the stairs. Thanks to her three-inch heels, she nearly turned her ankle. She settled for a fast walk since running in heels happened only in Hollywood movies.

Any remnants of the afterglow of their first successful mission as Unit 28 contractors faded. All thanks to her boyfriend of five months wanting to play secret-agent-man on his own.

"You need to sleep. I'll be here watching basketball, so don't worry." She mimicked his words to her as she'd curled up on the king-sized bed for a nap. Her fist tightened around the note. "Yeah, right. You could have gotten me up."

She followed the covered walkway as it wound its way through the resort.

Kind of like her thoughts right then. Those twisted back to earlier in the day. They'd broken into a *yakuza* boss's house, bugged it, and then fled for their lives when the owner of the house had shown up a bit earlier than planned. A raging success by everyone's count.

And now this.

Alex arrived at the Nani Kai Bar and Restaurant. At that hour, the sun cast its rays into the open-air bar and highlighted those who had sought out the watering hole a bit early. Only four people occupied the room. A man sat with his attention totally on a tablet in front of him. A bartender leaned against a cooler and watched the Maui Classic on television as she dried glasses and shoved them into an overhead rack. At least N.C. State, Alex's favorite team, whupped up on the University of Arizona, Jabir's alma mater. Across from the man with the tablet, a couple shared drinks.

Wait. The male half of that couple belonged to her.

Jabir slouched on a bar chair over a mostly empty bottle of beer. He turned his head away from her as he chatted with a woman, who rested a shapely hip against the edge.

The white-suited witch swirled her wine. She leaned toward him as she murmured something.

Alex's eyes narrowed. *Foreign agent or foe of another type?*

The woman's gaze met hers. Those kohl-lined eyes reminded Alex of a cheetah. Becoming, beautiful.

But deadly.

A smirk curled the witch's full lips. She slid a slip of paper toward Jabir, then whispered something into his ear before setting her wineglass on the bar. She turned on her heel and strutted from the restaurant with a long-legged stride.

Jabir traced her movements with his gaze.

Alex's lips curled. No way would she have any of that follow-her-like-a-lost-puppy routine from her boyfriend. No way, no how.

Especially not with *her*.

"Jabir," she called.

He spun around as if she'd taken the silver purse she had with her and bopped him over the head. Maybe she should have. It might have beaten some sense into him.

"What are you doing here?" he blurted.

Pain shot through her jaw as she exchanged a saccharine smile for clenched teeth. "Thanks for getting me up." She jerked her chin toward where the woman had left. "Who was she?"

Jabir dipped his chin as scarlet crept up from the collar of his sail-cloth shirt. His eyes hooded, and he shrugged. "Just some woman who wanted to flirt with me."

"What'd she give you? Her phone number?" With the lightning-quick strike of a snake, her hand shot out and snatched the paper from under his nose.

He grabbed at it. "Hey! Give that back."

Alex swung away as she held it up to the light. "Justice. And a 1-800 number. Care to explain?"

He huffed out a sigh. "Okay, fine. I think she was a foreign agent."

"Who obviously had a lot to say if she met you here at four."

An eye roll answered her. "She didn't show until about five minutes ago. Now give that back."

Alex didn't relinquish the note. "And I'm to believe that?"

"Verify it with the bartender," he growled.

As if on cue, a Hawaiian beauty with her thick, black hair plaited into a long braid, approached. "Ma'am, a drink?"

"Whatever his admirer had," Alex replied. *And get out of here so I can interrogate my boyfriend.* She waited until the bartender had turned away before resuming her questioning. "So?"

With great interest, he studied the golden liquid slopping in the bottom of his bottle. "It was nothing."

3

She slammed her purse onto the bar. "Look. You don't tell me, and this evening will end before it even gets started, understand?"

The bartender approached with a goblet of dark red liquid for her. "For the record, she only showed up about ten minutes ago. That'll be twenty dollars, please."

Crap. The white-suited witch had expensive tastes.

Jabir held up his bottle. "Could I have another beer?"

The bartender cocked her head at him and raised an eyebrow. "You sure you don't want something stronger?"

"Maybe later."

"Okay," she drawled. "Your choice."

With that, she dug into a cooler and brought out another bottle of Corona.

He slid a five for his beer onto the dark, shiny teak. "Keep the change."

"With pleasure." She drifted toward the other side.

Alex settled on a stool and took a sip of wine. Okay, so while it was expensive, it was also exquisite.

Jabir's lips pressed together. Finally, he set the bottle down. "She claims that, contrary to the report Tiny got from his buddy in Saudi intelligence, Yasmin is alive."

Alex shook her head and rubbed her arms. "And you believe her? I mean, you told me Ali al-Kadir handed Tiny the full version of that report, pictures included."

He flinched.

"I'm sorry, but you know that woman lied to you." Alex lowered her gaze as she remembered his brokenness when he'd described his sister's death. Public stoning—the punishment in Saudi Arabia for dishonoring her in-laws.

Alex put her elbows on the bar and leaned closer. "Why do you think the white-suited—your lady friend—was a foreign agent?"

"When she left the note, she defeated all of the tripwires I'd set up in our suite. And she called me by my given name, not my alias."

Her skin tingled, and she gasped. Her wineglass shook as she took another sip to calm herself.

Someone had known they'd be in Maui.

"We need to call Tiny."

He shook his head. "I can handle this on my own."

"No, we need to call him."

"Alex—"

"Look." She put her hand on her hip. "We just finished our first job as Unit 28 contractors. It worked. Otto said we did a great job. I happen to like being back with them. You know that the only difference now as contractors is that we get paid a whole lot more and can work when we want to work. In other words, we still have to follow protocol. And part of that protocol is contacting Tiny if we get approached by a foreign agent."

"Alex—"

"What part of that isn't clear to you?" She shoved his phone toward him. "Call him."

"I can handle it."

"You don't call, I will. And which would you rather deal with? Tiny directly? Or having him drag your butt back to DC because you refused to follow protocol?"

Jabir muttered something. "Okay. Fine."

He grabbed his phone and pecked at it like a chicken going after feed.

Her eyes stung with tears. She swallowed hard to avoid the lump in her throat that threatened to overcome her as she followed his end of the conversation.

"Tiny, Jabir here... Sorry to call you so late... Congrats on the win. We had something pop up." Jabir glanced at her as he outlined his close encounter with the white-suited witch.

Her thoughts turned inward, and they were about as comfortable as lying down on a pin cushion. Why had he tried to lie to her? Hadn't they come a long way in five months? She'd thought so. Maybe not.

"She's tall," Jabir said in response to what must have been a request for a description from Tiny.

"Five-ten," Alex muttered. A perfect match for Jabir's height of five-eleven. Her mood spiraled further downward.

Jabir added, "She had dark eyes and short hair that was black."

"It's called a pixie cut," she added. *You clueless male.*

"Alex calls it a pixie cut. She spoke Arabic in the Saudi dialect."

Boy, this just kept getting more and more interesting.

Jabir's face fell, and she wondered if Tiny, their boss at Unit 28, chastised him. "Okay… I understand. I'll cease and desist."

He'd better.

She folded her arms and raised her chin as she kept him pinned in her gaze.

"Thanks… We'll be back in town by Monday afternoon… I'll look forward to it." Jabir carefully laid the phone on the bar. His eyes clouded, and he softly asked, "Satisfied?"

She gulped more wine and winced as it burned going down. "We followed protocol. That's all I wanted."

They sat there for a few more minutes as the clock wound down on a suddenly tight game. N.C. State won with a buzzer-beating basket.

Over the roar of the crowd, Jabir softly stated, "I'm sorry."

For which part?

Let him sweat it out.

She kept silent.

"I'm sorry if it seemed like I was being unfaithful to you." He turned and took her hands. "I promise I wasn't."

That stupid lump refused to go away. She dumped more wine down her throat.

His dark eyes pleaded with her. "Forgive me?"

It took faith, this learning to trust him again. She whispered, "I do."

He bowed his head, then kissed her gently before whispering, "I love you."

Her resolve to resist him totally melted. But then the woman's image returned. She pulled back. "I love you, too. But that doesn't mean I trust you to leave this alone. So for now…" She took the slip of paper his hand had begun inching toward, folded it, and stuffed it down the front of her dress. "I'll take this for safekeeping."

His face visibly fell.

The rat.

She slid off her stool. "Now let's go before something else happens."

Saturday, November 18, 2017, 2100 hours Hawaiian Standard Time, Wailea, Maui

No doubt about it, Jabir had singlehandedly ruined the evening.

Her silence told it all.

As he leaned against the refrigerator and gazed at his love, his heart ached. Once they'd left the bar, she'd barely said a word, not over supper, not during a long walk on the beach and through the resort, and not even when he'd closed and locked the front door behind them. And no kiss either due to his errors earlier that evening. With phone in hand, she'd kicked off her heels and wandered onto the lanai overlooking the beach.

It was a nice way to mess things up by trying to hide something from her. And by tarnishing what Otto, their mission leader, had deemed as a raging success.

Any hope of romance had vanished like the November sun into the Pacific while they'd dined in silence.

With his gaze, he traced her figure.

Hope always sprang eternal in him, but nothing with Alex Thornton was ever easy. He thought he'd lost her four years ago before they reunited this past June. Then her distrust of him—for good reason—had nearly torn them apart. Except that months before, his deception had kept them alive.

He needed to make it up to her.

Fast.

He'd start with Chardonnay provided by the resort as a thank you for dumping a wad of cash into their pockets. An apology would help as well. Then maybe they could romance some since they were officially finished with the mission.

7

Jabir straightened. In search of a wine opener, he began opening drawers and came to those in the suite's granite island.

A slip of paper caught his eye. It sat on the end beside her purse, almost directly above her heels. She must have dropped it there upon their arrival.

It would be so easy. Dial the number. Get to the bottom of things with Justice, like why she'd use such an obvious lie to get him to do her bidding.

He closed his eyes. He shouldn't. Tiny had made it very clear that he was to cease and desist. And if he didn't? He would wind up in detention until they resolved the issue. Still…

He committed the number to memory, then stashed the paper in his back pocket.

Now the evening belonged to him and Alex alone.

Once he'd poured them goblets of the golden liquid, he stepped from the den to the lanai of their open-air suite created by pushing back the glass walls. He held one in front of her. "Wine for the lady?"

That finally elicited a smile, something he'd missed that evening. "Thanks."

He leaned his hip against the railing. "Want to sit down?"

"Sure."

He led her to a double chaise lounge, where she perched on the edge as if she waited for a medical procedure rather than a kiss from him.

Heart echoing in his ears, he knelt in front of her, set her glass aside, and took her hands. A lump filled his throat as he said, "I'm sorry about earlier. I was foolish. I should have trusted you. I guess…" He stared at the tile of the lanai's floor. "I guess I was so desperate to believe her—that Yasmin was alive—that I didn't trust you with the information."

"Tiny made it clear that she's not, right?"

"As clear as day." His heart ached. "She toyed with my hope, gave me everything I needed to throw caution to the wind when it came to believing that Yasmin could be alive. I guess I have so many questions, like why she'd even approach me."

Alex drew him upward until he sat beside her. She wrapped her arms around his shoulders. "Forgiven." They tightened. "Promise. And Tiny will figure out things. I mean, it sounds like he immediately knew who she was."

Oh, yeah. Tiny did. His boss had focused on her description like a sight hound on a lure.

She sampled the wine. "Hmmm. Very good. Where did you get this?"

"Compliments of the resort since we've been here for two weeks."

She interlaced the fingers of her other hand with his.

He could sit there all night in that inky blackness of a new moon with the lullaby of waves hitting the coral reef.

Alex rested her head on his shoulder. "I don't want there to be any secrets between us. Goodness knows, with working as contractors for Unit 28, we have to keep secrets from others. I don't want it to be that way with us."

If she only knew. Jabir's stomach began churning. He closed his eyes. He wouldn't think about that. Not now. He needed a distraction. "C'mon. Let's just sit here for a bit and enjoy our last night."

He eased back and tugged on her to join him.

For several minutes, they sat side by side. Gradually, her body relaxed. Her perfume tickled his nose in a melody of hibiscus with other scents in harmony. He inched closer.

Alex rewarded him with a nuzzle against his cheek.

All wasn't lost, after all.

"Sometimes, I wish we didn't have boundaries," she murmured.

"I know." Oh, did he ever. Once more, he envisioned that massive king bed, the shower large enough to accommodate two, and the hot tub outside with a privacy latticework. Perfect for honeymooners.

Too bad they weren't.

At least their no-romance rule had expired once Otto had told them to take it easy tonight.

He seriously considered cajoling her into crossing those boundaries.

Completely oblivious to his thoughts, she continued, "But we want to wait."

Forget plying her with more wine. It would dishonor them both. "With both of our experiences, we need to. And I'm glad we are."

"I know." She released a deep sigh. "You're such a voice of moral reason."

If only you knew.

"But I do want to come back here. Maybe for our honeymoon after we get married?" She playfully nudged him.

"Is that a challenge?"

"Maybe." She rested her chin on his shoulder. Into his ear, she murmured, "I know you love challenges."

"Oh?" Now his nose fairly quivered at her perfume.

"Of course. Take me up on it?" She pressed closer.

Cheeks flushing, his heart began hammering. With one finger, he turned her face toward his and kissed her long and deep. Oh, boy. His resolve to keep those boundaries began crumbling as surely as if he'd taken a pickax to an old stone wall.

Forget her phone and the wineglasses. He'd get those later.

He rose and extended his hand.

She took it, and he pulled her into his embrace. He kissed her again and ran his hand down her back. Collar of dress. Skin left bare by dress. Silk of dress. Zipper.

He drew her inside. His fingers sought out the bobby pins holding her hair in a twist. He pulled those loose and dropped them onto the floor before threading his fingers through those thick locks.

She ran her hands up and down his back.

He began calculating how to cajole her into bed.

With a shuddering gasp, she pulled back. "We'd… we'd better stop."

That had been close, too close, only mere seconds away from blowing straight past those boundaries. He scrubbed his hands through his hair. Through almost gritted teeth he admitted, "You're right. But boy, you turn me on."

Another beguiling smile rewarded him.

He moved toward her, but she stepped back. "I'll head to bed now. In the meantime," she brandished the slip of paper he'd pocketed earlier, "I'll take this for safekeeping."

He stared. What? How had she stolen it?

Of course. She'd used her feminine wiles and her pickpocketing skills, just like a well-trained Unit 28 agent.

Alex stepped toward the bedroom portion of their suite. As she reached for the Japanese shoji doors, she smiled. "Oh, and one more thing. Tiny texted and told me they got that number Justice gave you disconnected so you can't call her. And he's flagged all of your aliases so you can't leave the country without setting off alarms everywhere."

His heart dropped.

"So in other words, you're shut down no matter how much you want to pursue this. I love you, and I'll see you in the morning."

With that, she blew him a kiss and closed the doors.

Jabir stared at the translucent panes framed in mahogany.

The lights on the nightstands flashed on. In their soft, golden glow, Alex did exactly what Jabir had wanted to do. She undid the zipper to her dress. It slid from her, revealing her figure. She pulled on a nightshirt. A moment later, the lights switched off.

It served him right.

As he located the sheets and pillow he'd been using in the closet, he shook his head. Tiny had thwarted him for good reason.

And Alex?

She'd thrown down the gauntlet.

Could he answer her challenge regarding marriage?

Time would tell.

2

Tim "Tiny" Daniels strolled down the tree-lined concrete sidewalks near DuPont Circle in Washington. He passed painted homes ranging from cream to pale blue to red brick. All very well-kept, classic dwellings. He noted the addresses until he stopped at a gray, three-story structure with a turret as part of the roof. Window boxes with pansies of purple, yellow, and red decorated the front, as did pots on the small stoop.

Had Sasha al-Kadir suspected why he'd called up and asked to have tea with her after work? She probably thought he was stopping in to check on her as he and his wife, Jonna, had done ever since her husband had died two years before.

With the slightest of hesitations, he rang the doorbell.

A moment later, two deadbolts on the door slid back. It opened, revealing an older lady with sparkling brown eyes and an infectious smile. "*Ahlan wa sahlan*, Tiny."

Welcome.

Sasha shook his hand and led him inside. "So good to see you. Come on in. May I take your coat?"

He shed the trench coat that had kept him warm during his trek from the nearest Metro station. "Thanks."

13

She hung it on a peg, and he set his messenger bag that served as a briefcase underneath.

"Come on up. I have hot water all ready for tea."

He followed her and crossed hardwoods as elegant as the exterior. Rather than turn left and head into a room behind French doors, he followed Sasha upstairs to the second floor, which opened onto a large space that served as a kitchen and sitting area.

The tangy scent of spaghetti simmering on the stove tickled his nose. "I hope I wasn't interrupting supper preparations."

"No, no." She chuckled as she stepped behind a counter of dark granite. "The nice thing about spaghetti sauce is that the longer it simmers, the better. You're more than welcome to stay if you like."

After he finished his business, he doubted her daughter would appreciate that. "Thank you, but I'll have to take a pass on that tonight. Jonna's expecting me home."

"Tea's on the shelving there, as is the hot water."

"Thanks." He offered a smile and stepped to a shelving unit of elegant wrought iron and glass. He chose a mug hanging from a hook and found a bag of English Breakfast Tea in a tin. As he dropped it into the mug and added water, he said, "So sorry to call you suddenly, but it was urgent that I speak to Leila about a case. I thought it was best that we talked outside our offices."

"No worries." She smiled as she fixed her own tea and drifted to a sleek recliner. "Trust me when I say I'm used to such shenanigans. Ali would pull them all of the time."

Tiny followed her into the living room. He settled on a low couch and placed his mug on a hand-hammered brass table from Saudi Arabia. "What's it been since I've been here? Three or four months?"

"Not since you and Jonna came by in June. A long time." Sasha's eyes clouded, and she blinked as if suddenly stung by tears. "You two have been so good to me." She set her tea on a side table and picked up a picture. A sad smile crossed her face as she ran her finger down the glass. "Last week I realized that I went for a couple of days without crying.

And I told myself it was time to visit his grave once a week rather than every day."

She set the picture aside.

Tiny noticed it was of Sasha and Ali al-Kadir together, most likely at some formal function.

"It must be nice to have Leila back in the area."

"Oh, it is."

What lay behind her too-quick response? His internal radar pricked. "When did she arrive?"

"Early August or so. I think she's ready for her own place."

"Is she looking?" He studied her face.

"Not yet." She touched her lips and shook her head slightly. "She says she likes being with me, though it's not like I'm an exciting person." She shifted and faced him. "Catch me up on Jonna and the girls. How are they?"

Even he could take the hint. For the next few minutes he filled her in on the lives of his interior-designer wife and two college-age daughters.

"And how about you?" he asked.

"Hmm. Where to start?" She sipped her tea. "As you know, being home has helped. Thank goodness that Ali insisted that I get a job when we lived here. What did you call him? A liberated Saudi?"

Tiny smiled as he remembered the way he'd joked with Ali about the fact that he allowed his wife more liberties than any other Saudi he knew. "Something like that."

"I've been working for the District ever since we arrived, and it was a lifesaver, not only for the income but also for the visa."

"Did you ever regret giving up your citizenship?"

"At first, no, because I had to give it up to marry Ali. Oh, the foolishness of youth. It didn't take me long to realize what I'd done. When those radicals murdered him outside the embassy, I almost immediately applied for a green card with the District as my sponsors. You remember I got it about six months ago."

He grinned. "I do."

"And it's a good thing I chose to stay here."

"Oh?"

A real smile peeked through the sadness. "In July, I started going to church again. It's good to be back among family, and I'm not just talking about blood family."

"I know what you mean."

"I returned to the faith, which means I can't go back. Not that I would want to since Ali's family never accepted me because of my being black."

"I'd say Ali chose well."

Another soft smile curled her lips. "Why, thank you, kind sir."

The alarm panel beeped, signaling the door downstairs opening. A moment later, a rich female voice called, "Mama, who's over? I saw a coat... oh."

A younger version of Sasha joined them. She had her mother's height, and Tiny had to look up to meet her gaze, something he hated to do regardless of the person. The leggings and hoodie she wore only emphasized her stature.

Sasha rose and joined her daughter. "Leila, you remember Tiny Daniels, don't you?"

Tiny smiled and extended his hand. "Leila, how are you?"

Her gaze bounced between the two of them as she shook.

A firm grip, so very different from many of the women from the Middle East. Her father had taught her well. "I'm sorry, but why are you here?"

Tiny glanced at Sasha. "I need to speak with you about work, Leila. Do you have a few minutes?"

Leila gazed at her mother as if pleading with her to say that no, supper would be served immediately.

Sasha made shooing motions with her hands. "Supper will be in half an hour, so go on."

With a half-hearted shrug and muttered word under her breath, Leila nodded. "Let's go downstairs."

Tiny briefly took Sasha's hands. "It was good seeing you. I'll let myself out when we're finished."

Leila dropped her bag in the foyer and opened the glass French doors. She hit a switch, and recessed lighting lit the room in a soft glow. "Mama let me have the den as my own space." She approached a bar of white quartz. "I just got back from the gym, so I'm parched. You want some water to drink?"

"I'm good with my tea. Thanks."

She rubbed her short, black hair, and small droplets shot out.

"Tough workout?"

"Tough but good. It keeps me sane." She plopped onto a recliner in front of a flat screen television and turned on a small air filter. After setting her bottle on a coaster, she pulled a cigarette pack from her purse and shook one out. Eyes never leaving him, she cupped her hands around it and lit it with a silver lighter. She took a puff. The filter only captured part of the smoke. "Sorry to light up, but I've been aching for one since work, and this is the only place where Mama lets me smoke. Why are you here? It's not like we're working any cases together."

He let that one hang in the air for a moment. Never breaking his gaze, he asked, "Are we?"

With her foot, she pushed the recliner back and forth. "I'm not sure I follow."

"You tell me."

She yawned.

Tiny put his elbows on his knees, clasped his hands, and tapped his fingers on his chin. "You know what Unit 28 does, right?"

"Of course. Observe, collect, and protect. Isn't that your motto? You work to gather information in the form of human intel." A smile curled her lips. "And you've also been known to involve your agents in direct action missions aimed at protecting the homeland."

He'd counted on her doing her homework before taking any action with Jabir, and she hadn't disappointed. "Correct. When I find out from one of my agents that you approached him when he was on the job, I get concerned. Do you care to tell me why you did that?"

She took another drag and exhaled smoke through lips that still retained dark red lipstick. "We can cut to the chase. I approached Jabir al-Omri because I need his help."

"Why him?"

"Because he has history related to Samir Kamil. When everything happened in Panama last June, it rippled across the intelligence community."

It took all of his willpower not to react to that. She was right. While on loan to the CIA, Jabir had been intimately involved with the CIA's plot to take down a money laundering ring for Jihad of Light. The CIA had put a tight lid on things once they'd learned that one of their own had turned. There must have been a leak or something he hadn't known about. Focusing on her face, he asked, "How did you know that he was working under an alias on Maui?"

She didn't flinch, didn't look startled at all. Instead, she blinked in a way he knew would make most men salivate.

He wasn't one of them. He, too, was well-versed in the dark arts of intelligence gathering.

She stubbed out her cigarette and tucked one foot underneath her. "I have my ways." She rubbed the back of her neck. "And my sources because I know you're going to ask how I got his name."

"Why do you need his help? And why did you have to drag his sister into this?"

"I needed a hook. Otherwise, he would have told me to pack sand, as you Americans can say." She toyed with one of the tendrils curling around her face.

She'd probably done the same thing when speaking to Jabir. No wonder he'd been willing to do anything for her.

"I planned to string him along," a smile curved those full lips of hers, "and pass bits of information to him until he got what I needed to nail Tarek al-Hassan to the wall for what he did."

He tensed, and heat rushed into his chest. She had nerve. Too bad he viewed Sasha as a dear friend; otherwise, he would have hauled her butt to headquarters for more questioning. "You know breaking protocol and directly approaching one of our agents borders on illegal."

She shrugged. "I don't care. Obviously, you've heard of Samir Kamil."

"Indirectly, he nearly cost Jabir his life. He's the grandson of the founder of Kamil International. Corporate counsel at the company. Suspected of running a money laundering scheme through the company." *And lapdog of Tarek al-Hassan. And a target for CIA interrogation. Let's not forget whipping boy for Jihad of Light.*

"You can add murder victim to that list."

"Since when?" He cocked his head. Clearly, CIA had tightened the lid way down on their internal investigation of what went down in Panama that summer.

"He was murdered in late June."

"Do the National Police and Interpol have a suspect?"

"Officially, that remains to be seen. Unofficially?" A scowl curled her lips. "Tarek al-Hassan, his supposed best friend and a suspected leader of Jihad of Light along with his brute of a brother, Hashim."

Tiny raised his mug, frowned, and set it down. "How do you know that?"

"Samir's sister, Noor Kamil-Sultan, suspected him. She confronted him at Samir's funeral."

"I take it that was a mistake."

Leila nodded. "A big one. He dismissed her as hysterical. I was there, Tiny. I saw the way he arrogantly brushed her off. I knew I'd made a mistake when he was murdered because I had not posted guards with him. I promised her I would bring justice for Samir." She tapped her fingers on the arm of the recliner as she stared at something only she could see. Maybe her past? "The following week, I confronted Tarek at his office. I offered him leniency."

"You offered him leniency?" He rubbed his chin. "And you as an Interpol agent could do that? I thought only the Lebanese National Police could do that."

She crumpled her bottle. "I understand. I overstepped."

Whew, she'd not only overstepped but had done so by a long shot. "Should I even ask what happened?"

She rolled her eyes. "My supervisor found out. He threw me off the case. Then, when I asked him if Tarek had him in his pocket, he told me I had two choices—resign immediately or take an immediate transfer."

She'd done more than overstep; she'd cratered her career. "So you took the transfer."

She shrugged as if making such accusations were an everyday occurrence for her. "Returning to DC has been good for me." She sighed and leaned her head against the cushion. "Look. I did all of those things because I am a just person. I want to make up for my mistakes, and I want to put Tarek behind bars. I am also concerned about those who may be a liability to him."

"I get that, but this is the National Police's territory."

"So the inspector, Haresh Mansour, told me. Do you know what happened that led to Samir's undoing?"

Tiny nodded. "You told me. Apparently, Tarek al-Hassan, his supposed best friend, didn't take too kindly to his turncoat ways if you think he murdered him."

"Noor convinced him to contact the National Police. When he did, Chief Inspector Mansour called me when he realized the way it crossed international boundaries. We got his confession on video, and he agreed to testify against Tarek."

"Which put him in danger."

"Much danger. Your government offered a safe house, and I arranged transport for him to get out of the country."

"But someone got to him."

"Exactly. That someone being Tarek. When I left him that night, I told Samir to lock all of his doors. He missed one, and Tarek murdered him."

He sat back. "Theoretically."

She folded her arms and glared at him. "He was murdered atop his kitchen table, and it was not pretty. Noor discovered him."

"Okay," he drawled.

She leaned forward, and her hands tightened on the arms of the chair. Her gaze hardened. "I want justice for what happened. I want to make up for the mistakes I made. Can you not see that? Jabir has history with this case in that he knew much about Samir and JOL. That is why I needed his help."

"After the way you approached him, why should I even consider letting him help you?"

"Noor needs closure. Not to mention, JOL has ties everywhere, including the United States, and if I remember correctly, Hashim turned one of the CIA, the mission leader in Panama. This is your golden opportunity to get enough evidence on their leader to put him away."

If only she knew. Tarek al-Hassan's brother, Hashim, worried him more—and for reasons only he and Jabir knew. Tiny stuffed down his worries. But she was right. Bringing justice could serve two purposes. "Maybe I'll agree to work with you."

"I can give you a running start." Leila rose and opened a door to a closet across from the bar. Metal scraped on metal. Then a file drawer clacked shut. She placed an accordion file in his hands. "This is what I have on the case."

Tiny shook his head at its thickness. She'd definitely done a lot of work on the case. "I take it that it was legal to make this copy?"

She shrugged. "Maybe."

He nearly laughed. The woman had nerve. He had to give her that. "I'll take this case on two conditions."

"Those would be?"

"First, I have to get approval. Second, you are to have no contact with either Alex or Jabir."

She nodded. "I agree."

"This is mine to keep?"

"It is."

"I'll be in touch, then." He rose and put his hand on the handle of the French doors.

Jabir's voice when he'd talked to him two nights before echoed in his ears. Not the words. The emotion, his irrational hope.

He turned. "Tell me something."

"What?" She raised an eyebrow.

"Is Jabir's sister really dead?"

This time, she smirked. "Of course. I read the report from the Saudi police. They stoned her. I saw the pictures myself."

What a… Forget the having nerve part. She played dirty. "And when were you planning on telling him that?"

"After he did my bidding."

She played very dirty, just like any other spook, including him in his younger days.

"I see. I'll be in touch. *As-salaam 'alaykum*, Leila." Peace be upon you.

"*Wa 'alaykum salaam*." Upon you be peace. Her response was automatic.

With that, he let himself into the foyer, dropped the folder into his messenger bag, and pulled on his coat.

As he opened the front door to leave, he glanced to his right.

Leila stood behind the glass. She raised her chin as if daring him to do what she wanted him to do. That smirk played about her lips as she turned away.

A piece of work, that woman.

Tiny's mind whirled as he headed down the sidewalk toward the Metro. Leila's recklessness bothered him, as did her reticence about how she'd gotten Jabir's alias. And why had she been so brazen as to operate outside the jurisdiction of Interpol when her former supervisor had clearly told her to cease and desist? He needed information, and what better place to start than with Unit 28, his agency and one of the best at getting information? He dialed a number on his phone.

"Research, this is Sadie," a woman drawled in a fine, Charleston accent.

"Why, Sadie Callahan." He grinned as he matched that accent. "So good to hear your voice."

She laughed. "Same to you, Tiny. What can I do for you?"

"Are you headed home?"

"Not 'til after I help you."

"I need you to pull data on a name and send it to my e-mail account."

"Will do. Who's on your radar tonight?"

Tiny paused at a corner, turned, and faced the direction of the al-Kadir townhouse. Under the clear white glow of a streetlight, he barely picked out those pansy boxes and dwelling concealing more secrets than he realized. "A woman named Leila al-Kadir."

3

Jabir sat glued to the black leather of his white Subaru WRX. He stared at the back door of the Thornton house as he contemplated the way the next half hour would change his life—for better or worse. He took a deep breath. Time to do it. Otherwise, Alex's father would come to the door and ask him why the heck he'd dressed nicely, driven all the way out into the country, and sat in his car for forever.

Uh, to ask for his blessing to marry his oldest child, the apple of his eye, Daddy's little girl.

He climbed from the warmth of the car into chilly air that nipped at his cheeks and signaled the approach of winter. A low set of steps led to a deck and entrance to the biggest challenge of his life.

David Thornton grinned as he opened the door. "Jabir, hey there. I saw you pull into the driveway."

Had he witnessed him sitting there as he debated his next move?

"I, uh, happened to be in the neighborhood and wanted to drop by." Where had such a bone-headed statement come from? The idiot side of him, for sure. Heat started in his cheeks. "That was lame."

"But it was good." David chuckled and clapped him on the shoulder. "Come on in. I was just taking in some reading I hadn't done in a bit."

The former Congressman strolled to the kitchen. "You want some wine? Roya picked up a bottle of Merlot from the grocery store."

"Sounds good." Jabir took a deep breath to steady his sudden attack of nerves. "Um, is she around?"

David paused from opening the bottle. "Yep. She's upstairs getting ready for your mama to come and stay with us over Thanksgiving. Hold on just a second." He stepped into the foyer and called, "Roya, honey? You up there?"

A cheery female voice replied, "In the guest bedroom."

"Jabir's here to see us. Can you come down for a few?"

"I'll be right down." Flatness tempered her answer.

Jabir's breath caught. Not the best start to his plan.

David handed him a glass and led the way into the den where a cheery fire crackled in the wood stove. "When she called after you got home today, Alex said y'all had a good time in Maui."

"It was work." He unconsciously reached toward where he'd stashed a small jeweler's box in an interior pocket of his jacket. Not yet. Not until Roya had joined them. As an avoidance mechanism, he shucked his jacket and laid it across one of the arms of the couch.

David settled on a wingback chair and swung his feet onto an ottoman. "I take it Unit 28 was happy."

A petite, slender woman dressed in jeans and an N.C. State sweatshirt joined them.

All Jabir had to do was gaze at Roya Thornton to know that Alex would retain her beauty into middle age and beyond.

"Jabir, hi." She smiled what Alex had always called a political smile, one that didn't reach her eyes. To those who didn't know her well, it conveyed warmth and caring, but to those she loved, it signaled distance. For sure, she hadn't forgiven him for confronting her in August. She curled up on a recliner of soft black leather. "What brings you here on a chilly Monday evening?"

Sweat began building on Jabir's palms. His carefully planned words faded from his mind. "Um, contrary to what I told David, I, uh, wasn't just driving through the neighborhood."

He met her gaze, then switched to David.

His future father-in-law didn't blink. Instead he propped his chin on his hand as if waiting for Alex's prospective husband to get his act together.

Here went nothing. Go big or go home.

One more heartbeat, then two. *Let's do it.* "Actually, I came over to discuss Alex."

Her father cocked an eyebrow.

His pulse echoed in his ears. Was that a faint buzzing in his head? "I love your daughter very much." He forgot to breathe. He'd better get on with it before he passed out. "So much so that I'm planning on proposing to her soon." With trembling hands, he extracted the jeweler's box. "I know that because she's been on her own for many years, I don't need to ask your permission. But I would like your blessing."

Rather than say anything, David stared him down like he probably had a Soviet spy during his CIA days in Afghanistan.

Uh-oh. Jabir had totally misread the situation. Big time. Alex's father hated his guts. Time to chill out. Or bug out. But where had he put his keys?

"Do you promise to love her sacrificially?" David asked.

"I do," Jabir squeaked like he was a junior high kid instead of a man of the mature age of thirty.

"Do you promise to see to it that Christ is the head of your marriage, and if and when you have children, the head of your family?"

"I do."

"Are you willing to die for her as Christ died for the church?"

Alex's face floated before him. He almost felt her soft hair brush his cheek. Through the lump that had formed in his throat, he choked out, "I do. I mean, I will."

David smiled. He glanced at Roya.

Her gaze remained steady on Jabir's face.

She nodded.

David focused on him again. "Then you have our blessing. It'll be an honor to have you as part of our family."

Oozing to the floor and lying there would have been great. Instead, he flipped open the box and handed it to his future father-in-law. "This is what I got her in October." He was so proud of the marquis diamond, especially since he'd picked it out all on his own. "I need to size it, but I figured I could get her ring size when we go shopping on the pretext of looking for rings."

David whistled. "I'd say you done good for yourself, son. She'll love it. Honey, check it out."

He leaned over and placed it on the ottoman in front of Roya's chair.

She didn't pick it up, didn't even look at it. No response at all.

Yep, the ice remained between them.

David's cell phone began ringing. He sighed as he checked the number. "Sorry, but that's one of my buds calling. Let me take this."

With that, he rose and stepped into the sun room where they kept a baby grand piano. He shut the glass pocket doors behind him.

Without a word, Roya rose and retreated across the open room to the kitchen. She reached into a glass-fronted cabinet for a wineglass.

Jabir had admired her ever since he'd met her eight years before, so much so that he thought of her almost as a surrogate mother. Not anymore thanks to this distance that had begun in August.

She removed the cork from the Merlot bottle, and the dark red liquid tumbled into the goblet. "I think it's funny how Davie calls his fellow Congressmen buds."

He approached the slab of gray quartz that formed the island. "Somehow I sense you aren't as excited as your husband is about this."

"I am excited." She regarded him over the rim of her glass. Cool and confident as always. "You've always cherished Alex, and I appreciate that."

"God brought us together in Panama for a reason. I don't know if you know this, but it was a rocky start for us. One that had tons of layers of mistrust thanks to the nature of my mission. You remember, right?"

"How could I?" She leaned against the island. "You never bothered to tell us what happened."

Like maybe he couldn't since his mission had been classified? He took a deep breath. "I had to tell lies to keep myself and Melanie Forrest alive. That made it hard for Alex and me to start a relationship. We both agreed we would be honest with each other. And then I made that discovery about… well, about Hamid al-Hassan being her father."

A muscle in her cheek twitched as she seated herself on a bar chair. "You could have told her then that Davie was not her father. Yet you didn't."

He cast a glance toward the sun room.

David's voice rose and fell as he paced from one end of the sun room to the other.

Jabir turned his back on the doors. "Do you think she would have believed me? She was barely trusting me then and probably would have called me a liar before walking out of my life for good. Can't you see that?" He took a deep breath to calm nerves that this time threatened to spill into a voice raised in frustration. "Besides, it's not mine to tell about her father. It's yours—"

"No!" Roya popped to her feet.

Now he couldn't help himself. His volume matching hers, he blurted, "But she's your daughter. Doesn't she have a right to know?"

She braced her hands on the island. "Who's name is on that birth certificate? David's." She leaned on them as her gray-brown gaze bored into his. She jabbed her finger into the quartz as if to emphasize her point. "*He's* her father."

He didn't have to think hard to see why her nickname during her CIA days with the *mujahedeen* had been The Lioness. He took a deep breath and tried reasoning. "Look. I don't understand why sharing this with Alex is such a—"

"I have my reasons." Each word came out like a bullet. "And if you're smart, you'll keep your mouth shut."

"I gave you my word that I would." In his conscience, chains clinked. Maybe reason would help free him. He took a deep breath and tried again. "But what if someone else doesn't?"

She straightened. "What?"

"What if Hamid al-Hassan comes looking for her or attempts to make contact?"

She shook her head. "He wouldn't."

"How can you be so sure?" His chest tightened, and he clasped his hands together. "Or what if he ordered his sons, Tarek and Hashim, to kidnap her from Weatherly?"

"How could they know where she lives?"

Jabir swallowed hard. "Anything's available if you know where to look and are willing to pay."

"Then... she needs protection. Someone watching over her." Roya's response was automatic.

It rang hollow in his ears because Alex would never accept any reason other than the truth as a need for protection.

Roya rubbed her upper arms. "Couldn't you say that Hashim wanted revenge for what happened so many years before?"

Oh, come on! Didn't she see that Hamid al-Hassan could order his sons to take care of what he most likely viewed as a stain of dishonor to his family? "Would DHS see that as a reason to provide protection? They think—and probably rightly so—that Hashim would never risk losing his freedom for a simple revenge mission."

"Then there's no worry."

Not in his mind, not when Hashim surely knew Alex was his half-sister.

Her expression hardened. She picked up her wineglass and got in his face. Her glare burned into his soul. "You will honor my request." That came out low, threatening. "I expect that of you, Jabir, if you want to have any hope of remaining in good standing with me."

He chilled as to what it implied—lifelong stress in dealing with his future mother-in-law. No choice now. He swallowed hard. "You know I will. I just... we can't expect others to be so willing, others who don't have her best interests at heart."

She didn't answer, only turned on her heel and fled. Her footsteps pounded on the stairs. A moment later, a door slammed.

Jabir sighed and put his head in his hands. "Oh, Lord, what now?"

"It's hard," David said from behind him.

Alex's father was going to kick him out—after he rescinded the blessing. "I'm sorry."

"For what?" David picked up the wine bottle and poured the remainder into their glasses. "You've got nothing to apologize for. C'mon. Let's go shoot some pool."

With that, he led the way into the chilly evening air. They crossed the concrete parking pad until they reached a three-car garage. David led the way up a set of external stairs and flipped a switch. Light blazed forth. "Welcome to my man cave."

"Nice." With one swift gaze, Jabir took in the bar across from him, a desk, and a pool table, plus a sitting area that had a couch and a couple of chairs he remembered from their townhouse in Alexandria.

"It used to be two rooms when Alex was a teenager. Once the kids all graduated, we took down the wall between the rec area and my study. Now whenever someone from DC comes down, this is where we meet." He set his glass on the oak bar and removed a triangle from where it hung on its hook. "I'll rack up."

"I take it Alex learned to play here."

"You bet. Back then, when she and the others were teenagers, either Roya or I made it a point to be in the study." He placed the balls inside the triangle. "You break. Did you two play a lot in DC?"

"Sometimes. We liked to go to the pub around the corner from where you all lived. I guess you knew the owner, and he let us have free rounds when they weren't busy." Jabir lined up his shot and sent the cue ball skittering down the felt. It slammed into the pack, scattering the balls. A green solid dropped into a pocket.

"Looks like you're solids." David slid his reading glasses onto his nose and circled the table. "Tell me something. How did you find out Hamid al-Hassan is Alex's biological father?"

Jabir considered his question as the former Congressman set up his shot. "You're cleared for this?"

David gazed at him over the rims of his glasses. "Seeing that I consult on intelligence matters, yes, I am."

His shot dropped a stripe into a pocket.

"Then you know about Jihad of Light and its money-laundering scheme through Kamil International."

David nodded.

"When Melanie Forrest was kidnapped by our team, we were posing as a JOL cell." Jabir's mood sank lower as he recalled the events from almost six months before. "Ed DuBois, our team leader, turned traitor and wiped out all of our team but me as well as kidnapped Alex's three friends. The kidnappers issued a demand. Alex in exchange for her friends. That got me to thinking. Why the sudden shift from wanting the property to wanting Alex?"

"Understandable." David nodded and leaned against the bar. "Your shot."

"When Tiny told me about Orb Web, I pulled up his profile to read it." With one shot, Jabir dropped a red and blue into two pockets. "That's when I reviewed her personnel jacket."

He laid the cue stick across the bridge formed by his fingers for an easy shot.

Except that then, like a flashbulb revealing the contents of a room, his memory flashed to that rainy night in Panama when he'd stared at Alex's and Hashim's photos.

At that precise moment, his hand jerked. The stick barely brushed the cue ball. "I noticed the resemblance between the two of them."

David approached the table. "I take it one thing led to another."

"It did." Before he could stop it, the question burst forth. "Why, David? Why stray from Roya?"

Oh, boy. *Way to go, Jabir.*

David didn't slug him with his cue stick. Instead, he lined up his shot and dropped a second stripe into the pocket. "Thirty-six years ago, things were very different between Roya and me." He circled the table and sank a third stripe, then a forth. "I was so full of myself, thought I knew everything about marriage. I was wrong."

He missed.

Jabir focused on the layout of the balls. "I can't picture that."

He missed again.

"I know, son. I know. But it's true. I strayed with a CIA woman who'd come to the compound the spring after we married. I thought I was hiding it from Roya." He shook his head. "Hah. Was I ever wrong! Roya was lonely. She sought comfort with Hamid. What else can I say?"

With that, he focused on the game until only the eight ball remained. "Eight ball, corner pocket."

As he drew the cue stick back, Jabir asked, "But to lie and put your name on Alex's birth certificate? And how did you know Hamid was her father?"

"To the first, I had my reasons. To the second…" David took the shot, and the eight ball dropped into its pocket. He met Jabir's gaze with a steady one of his own. "Let's just say I knew, son, and that's that."

☆ ☆ ☆

Monday, November 20, 2017, 2030 hours EST, Weatherly, NC

Jabir's WRX rumbled down the driveway until the only sound was the peep of a few insects brave enough to endure the threatening chill.

On the deck where he watched it vanish into the night, David's breath came out in a vapor as he whispered, "Oh, Lord, where did we go wrong?"

He knew. All too well, he did.

When Roya had begged him to sign his name to Alex's birth certificate. That's when. Except that almost thirty-four years before, he would have done anything to preserve his newly restored marriage, even set into motion a lie that persisted to this day. When he'd scribbled his name on that line, never would he have imagined that his oldest child could wind up hating him or that his actions might place her in danger.

Jabir was right. If Hamid al-Hassan knew, then Alex might find out through other, less pleasant means.

"How do I set this right?" He voiced that question to the night.

Oh, he didn't want to face it.

Once inside the house, he paused.

Upstairs, a drawer slammed.

He left the wineglasses in the dishwasher, climbed the stairs, and found his beloved in the master bedroom.

Laundry lay spread across the bed as Roya worked to put away loads she'd finished earlier that day.

With his gaze, he traced her full lips, that slightly aquiline nose, and those expressive eyebrows. And those eyes. Normally, they sparkled with humor. Though he'd strayed from her shortly after they married, they'd found a new strength and happiness five children and thirty-six years later, something he'd thought to be impossible after those first two hellish years. No doubt about it, the net mood of their marriage had been joy.

A lump filled his throat as he noted the way her brow knitted and her lips turned downward.

He pushed away from the door frame. "You need some help?"

She shrugged.

He stepped all the way into the room and picked up a t-shirt from the basket. As he folded it, he said, "Good news tonight, wasn't it?"

She draped a pair of her jeans over a hangar and stepped into the closet. "Shocking."

Her flat tone worried him. He added the t-shirt to a stack and reached for another. "Oh, not so much. We knew where their dating was headed."

"Five months is too soon." She returned and picked up a pair of leggings.

"Is it? We dated for four. I imagine it'll be six months to plan the wedding. So it would be eleven months of seeing each other total. And they've been friends for years. He's a fine young man. You've said so yourself many times."

She tossed the hangar with the leggings onto the bed. "He'd better keep his mouth shut."

He stiffened. "I think he will."

"And you believe that?"

"I do." He placed the stack of his t-shirts in his drawer, shut it, and gazed in the mirror.

She stood ramrod straight behind him and glared with an intensity that would have made a normal person wilt. The fierce set of her chin told it all. Case closed. She didn't want to discuss it.

Steeling his courage, he swiveled and faced her. "You need to tell Alex."

She snatched up a set of hanging clothes. "We've been over this before. No, I don't."

"I'd be a fool not to keep asking."

"No, you're a fool to insist. You're her father. Not Hamid." She almost spat the name of their former ally. "You raised her."

"I get that, okay?" Gently, he took the clothing from her, laid it aside, and tugged on her arm until they both sat on the edge of the bed. He covered her hand with his. "Remember that God loves truth. And truth, because it's sanctioned by Him, will always come out. Far better it comes from you rather than someone else."

"Like who? Your name is on that birth certificate. Legally, you're her father."

"I know." Like he'd done over the years, he traced the lines of her palm with his finger. "But others know. Like probably Hamid and his sons."

"How could he?"

"There are ways. You as well as I know that. She favors him."

She snorted.

"Jabir's statement worries me."

She jumped up. "He was trying to scare me into confessing."

Forget any progress. When her stubborn streak appeared, there was no getting through to her. Taking a deep breath, he clenched his fists until his nails bit into the skin of his palms. In a level voice he said, "He knows a lot more than we do, and he's not someone who scares easily. For him to mention that means he's worried. What if Hamid ordered his sons to come over here and kidnap her?"

"How could they know where she lives? When Tiny visited us in August, he assured us that she was secure here." She turned away and folded her arms across her chest. "I don't understand why, when there is no immediate threat of danger, you're so worried."

He rose and leaned against one of the posts of the four-poster bed. "You're right. There's nothing imminent. Remember that anything's available at the right price, including her location. All it would take is the right person finding out, and it would be all over. I'm not going to take that chance. If you're not going to tell her, maybe I—"

"No!" She grabbed his hands.

Pain flared where her nails bore into him.

"You will not!"

"We need—"

"When we patched things up." Her eyes widened. The red that had suddenly appeared made their gray-brown color almost vibrate with intensity. "When we renewed our vows the year Josh and Marlie were born, you promised to stay faithful to me."

He cocked his head. "I have. You know that."

"If you tell her against my wishes, I'll consider that a violation of our vows. Think about that."

Roya released him and stormed from the room. A moment later, piano music, a minor tune, floated up the stairs as if to mock him for even thinking she would agree to the truth.

He hung his head. Case closed. Over and done with. There was nothing more he could say.

At least at that moment.

Maybe later. Like when hell froze over.

4

Tuesday, November 21, 2017, 1035 hours EST, Fort Belvoir, VA

"I take it this is where you come to hide out and work." Tiny grinned at Mitch Harris, his boss and the director of Unit 28.

With reading glasses and a scowl on his face, Mitch hunched over his laptop at a table in a corner of Unit 28's cafe on the first floor of headquarters and pecked at the keys. He rubbed a hand through his graying dark hair and shook his head. "It is when I have a presentation at one that I need to begin. Were you looking for me?"

"I was hunting for a cup of coffee, which I found." Tiny held up his steaming brew. "I won't keep you, but do you have a few minutes? I've got something I need to discuss."

Mitch hesitated. Then he nodded and pushed his reading glasses onto his head. "What's up?"

Tiny seated himself. Time to put together a really good brief really fast and get it right on the first try. "It concerns a contact by a foreign agent with Jabir al-Omri." He filled him in on everything that had transpired, from Leila's visit with Jabir to his own discussion with her the night before. "The long and short of it is that I'm concerned that if Alex and Jabir take this assignment, it would bring Alex into unnecessary danger."

Mitch, who'd listened with all of his being, leaned back and sipped his own coffee from a stout black mug with the words "Super Dad" and a lightning bolt on it. "Why do you say that?"

"Have you had a chance to do some back-reading on cases we've worked?"

Mitch grimaced and shook his head. "You've got to remember I've been on the job for only six months. Since we got such a late start, I hit the ground running. It's not like I can take files home for bedtime reading."

Tiny smiled. "I just wanted to make sure I didn't waste your time by filling you in on something you already knew. During the Bush administration when the War on Terror was at its zenith, CIA ran an op called Orb Web pretty much all over the world. It was huge, like over a hundred terror suspects huge. Since they lacked the manpower, they asked Unit 28 for an assist. Alex along with Sadie and another woman who's no longer with us acted as lures. I was their handler."

"Why does that place Alex in danger?"

"Our last suspect was Hashim al-Hassan. CIA placed him in Baghdad, so we went there. He had a habit of clubbing with pretty ladies. When assets placed him at a certain club, I sent in Alex. Navy SEALs would take care of Hashim's transfer to a CIA black site."

"I take it Alex got involved with his takedown."

"Very much so. He took a shine to her, and she was the one who led him out back. That's where the SEALs took over, knocked him out, and packed him into the trunk of a car." Tiny collected his thoughts as he sipped his coffee. His stomach twinged a little. "I'm worried because what Leila wants us to do for her could bring Alex in direct contact with Hashim."

Mitch rested his chin on his hand as he shoved his mouse around. "Here's a question for you. First, why are we even considering a case that is clearly in Interpol's jurisdiction?"

"Hashim and his brother, Tarek, are responsible for turning a CIA agent who murdered three of his colleagues. Then there's the worry by

DHS, CIA, and FBI that Jihad of Light may have a well-developed contact network in this country."

"No one's sure?"

Tiny sighed. "No. This is what I've gleaned from mid-level contacts I have."

"Turf battles." Mitch muttered something. "You'd think we would have learned sixteen years ago, wouldn't you?"

"Federal agencies can have painfully short memories at times. Since Jabir was intimately involved in the CIA's work in Panama this past summer and because we do have a concern about JOL, I think it falls squarely into Unit 28's territory."

Mitch groaned and rubbed his eyes. Shaking his head, he asked, "How many agents are we down?"

He'd brought up a really sore subject for Tiny. "Thanks to budget cuts in the previous administration, we've been unable to fill four positions. We just filled Jabir's with Isa Haswi, who was a late transfer up here even though he graduated last year—again thanks to budget cuts. I'm hoping to fill the others with our graduating class next month."

"From what I remember of our last regular meeting, all of your agents are at capacity or more in terms of work."

Tiny nodded. "They are."

"And since Alex and Jabir are contractors, they can more or less work at will. Give it to them. We can scratch that itch but not take a hit in terms of other work. And use Isa if you need, at least until a partner for him shows up." With that, Mitch moved his mouse.

The screen flashed to life, a sure indication he was done discussing things.

"But, sir, what about her safety?"

Mitch began typing. "She's a former Unit 28 agent, one of the best to hear you talk when you argued to bring her on as a contractor. Sounds like she can take care of herself."

If she saw the danger coming. "I think you're underestimating Hashim."

Mitch blew out a sigh. "Look. He's nowhere near here."

"He's in Beirut, which may be a destination if they take the case."

"Then tell her to watch her step. And I highly suggest that you keep this on the down-low, lest we get dinged by management for running a case for Interpol, no matter what kind of hook we have." He stared at the laptop's screen. "I'm sorry, Tiny, but I've got to get this done, and I've barely started."

"Will do, then. I'll get things underway." Tiny stuffed down his frustration. Much as he liked Mitch most of the time, he'd sensed some inexperience in the former FBI special agent. Still, when Mitch spoke, he expected his staff to carry out his wishes. Tiny wouldn't fail him on that account. What he could do would be to make Alex as aware of the danger from Hashim as possible. He'd also bring Isa into the fold.

Once back on the fourth floor, he strode through the field agent floor. True to his word, four workstations remained unoccupied, and most of the others were empty since agents were out in the field. Isa sat at what used to be Jabir's workstation before he'd separated from Unit 28 in August to become a contractor. Tiny grinned. "Knock, knock."

A smile lit the Iranian immigrant's face. "A good morning, is it not?"

Tiny chuckled. "Very good, at least for a Monday. You got a minute?"

"Of course."

Tiny pulled over a chair from the empty workstation next to Isa's "I need to meet with you tonight. You're not busy, are you?"

"Not at all."

"Then let's meet at my house at eight." Tiny rattled off the address. "I've got a case for you that I think will be of interest."

And hopefully, getting to the bottom of it wouldn't mean placing Alex in the crosshairs of the one person who probably wanted her dead.

Tuesday, November 21, 2017, 2030 hours EST, Mount Vernon, VA

"*Salam, chetori?*" Tiny greeted Isa, who stood on the stoop of the Daniels' Mount Vernon home, in Farsi. "Sorry about the cloak-and-dagger routine," he added as he led the way through the foyer and to the kitchen. "I want to keep this on the down-low as much as possible."

"Is your wife here?" His gaze sweeping the room, Isa hung his jacket across the back of a chair.

"She's at Bible study. You want something to drink? Tea? Coffee?" Tiny reached for a mug.

"Thank you very much. Black tea would be nice. I see you are having something else." Isa nodded toward the tumbler of bourbon Tiny had prepared to stave off the willies that had begun as he'd completed an in-depth review of the file Leila had given him.

Tiny started the electric teakettle. "I am. And when we finish, you might be needing an adult beverage too."

Isa cocked his head with a quizzical smile. "I do not understand that term."

Tiny grinned. "Something my girls call alcoholic beverages. Have a seat, and we'll get started." He stared at the accordion file as he considered the best way to begin briefing him on what he realized was a very complicated case. "You know that Jabir al-Omri and Alex Thornton are now Unit 28 contractors."

"I do."

"They just finished their first job weekend before last. Everything went like a charm, and they stayed behind to ensure our suspect was none the wiser. Someone approached Jabir." Tiny pulled out a photo that had come with the information Sadie had generated regarding Leila. "Meet Leila al-Kadir, an Interpol agent currently stationed here in DC at their Central Bureau."

"Was she working a case for them?"

The teakettle beeped, and Tiny poured hot water over the bag of tea. He set it before him and added the sugar bowl before resuming his seat. "That's where it gets blurry."

His gaze never leaving the photo, Isa spooned some sugar into his tea. "How so?"

"She used to be stationed in Beirut and began working with the Leb-anese National Police on a money laundering case related to a fellow named Samir Kamil. It ended with Samir's murder." He outlined the facts of the case. "She may be book smart, but you and I know there's a huge difference between being book smart and street smart."

"Being street smart keeps you and those around you alive." Isa nodded. "I assume she is not street smart."

"I'm not sure. She made several obvious mistakes on this case, the first being that after Samir had completed a video-taped confession regarding Tarek al-Hassan as the man behind the money laundering case, she left him on his own to secure his house and wait on her for an escort to the plane that would take him to a safe house. She didn't request the Lebanese National Police to guard him."

"Do you think it was intentional?"

"No. That was the first mistake, and Samir Kamil died as a result." He extracted a photo from the murder scene, the very one that had roiled his stomach. That's when he'd poured himself a tumbler of bourbon. "His sister found him."

Only a sharp intake of breath told him the photo disturbed Isa as much as it had him. "She made a second mistake?"

Tiny took it and returned it to the stack. No doubt, that image would haunt him when he tried to sleep. "She attended the funeral. I imagine she got emotionally involved, probably when Noor accused Tarek, Samir's best friend, of killing him. Then she made another mistake. She approached Tarek and offered him leniency."

"Did she have that authority?"

"No. Only the National Police could do that."

Isa shook his head. "I do not understand."

"Neither do I." Tiny sighed and shoved the folder away. "Her supervisor got wind of it and threw her off the case. She had the audacity to ask him if he were in Tarek's pocket."

Isa's jaw dropped. "That is—how do you say it?—a career-ender."

"I would say so. She had two choices. Resign or transfer. She transferred to DC at the beginning of August."

Isa rested his elbows on the table and fell silent for a few moments as he sipped his tea. "And what about the money laundering case? Would not the video testimony she and the National Police recorded suffice in Lebanese courts?"

"Her notes say that shortly after the funeral, it disappeared. She suspected Tarek has the National Police in his pocket. Someone took it."

"Why approach Jabir?"

Tiny leaned back in his chair. "She wants justice for Samir. And she's also concerned that some people may be loose ends, at least in Tarek's mind. Since we know he is the head of Jihad of Light—along with his brother Hashim—it's a concern."

"A loose end?" Isa rested his chin on his hand and kept his gaze on his boss.

"Someone who's related to the case that could land both Tarek and Hashim in jail. Think about it. The accountant who worked at Kamil International. Samir's sister, Noor Kamil-Sultan. Her parents. All of these have such knowledge."

Isa frowned. "This still seems to be a case for the Lebanese National Police."

Tiny took off his reading glasses and rubbed his eyes. "I know. I know. I tried to tell her that and thought I had her convinced until she pointed out that JOL has begun infiltrating this country. And I know Hashim al-Hassan has a bone to pick with someone." He couldn't mention Orb Web, not when it remained as Top Secret Need to Know. "I ran it up the chain and got permission to take the case. Alex and Jabir will run it for me."

Isa turned back to the photo of Leila that lay before him on the dark wood of the table. "And my role?"

"I want to trust Leila—I really do—but I'm not sure I do." Tiny rose and leaned against the kitchen counter.

"What makes you worry?"

"When Alex and Jabir were working in Maui, they used aliases. Leila approached Jabir and used his given name."

"Interesting."

"Someone gave her that information. She wouldn't tell me who. Take a look at this briefing sheet." He placed two pages stapled together before him. "I'll e-mail you the full file I got from Sadie." Tiny turned and poured himself a little more brandy. Maybe that would prevent the image of Samir Kamil, lying on his kitchen table and basically gutted, from keeping him awake.

Isa perused the first page, then flipped it over and studied the second page. When he finally raised his gaze, questions clouded his eyes. "Saudi Intelligence?"

"Believe it or not. The only woman we know of to get through the program. I knew her father, Ali al-Kadir, fairly well. Ali was their station chief here in DC, if you would. We somehow had a spook-on-spook friendship that worked. Two years ago, a Jewish radical murdered him outside the Saudi Arabian embassy. Leila's mother, Sasha, is an American who, because of Ali's status, gave up her citizenship to marry him."

"And she lives here now?"

"In the DuPont Circle neighborhood. After Ali passed, my wife and I remained close to her. She has her green card and hopes to become a citizen again soon." Tiny turned and gazed out the kitchen window. Floodlights illuminated the gardens Jonna so carefully tended. Peaceful by all intents, a place where he could retreat to gather his thoughts. Now, no place was safe. Almost to himself, he murmured, "No good's probably going to come from this case."

"I'm sorry?"

Tiny seated himself at the table. "This case worries me. On the surface, I truly understand Leila's desire for justice for Samir's murder—and to get anyone in danger to safety. Yet there's something that doesn't feel right, even if I can't put my finger on it. That's why I want you to keep her under surveillance. I know it's not glamorous and will probably be excruciatingly boring, but it'll help to hone your surveillance skills. Keep track of her from the moment she leaves her townhouse to when she comes home and settles in for the night. Take photos and keep a log like you were trained."

"Is there anything special to look for?"

"Not at the moment. I'll keep in touch, and if you need anything, Sadie Callahan in Research can help you. Have you met her yet?"

Isa shook his head.

Tiny slid him a business card. "Here are her numbers. Put those into your phone and give her a call if something comes up that needs checking. I've apprised her of the situation, so work with her and her only." Tiny gathered the entire file Leila had given him into a stack and slid it into the accordion file, which he secured with a rubber band. "I'll be scanning this and putting it on the servers, but unless you need the hard copy, I prefer to keep it secure at work. I'll send you what I have on Leila. Check in with me by e-mail at least once a day, but call if something pops."

"I will." Isa rose. "Thank you for this opportunity."

"You're up for it." Tiny smiled just as the door leading to the garage opened. Even after twenty-five years of marriage under his belt, his heart still thumped when he noted the attractive brunette stepping through. "Jonna, hi."

His wife smiled and extended her hand. "I'm Jonna Daniels."

Isa glanced at Tiny, and he nodded to assure the young man he was among friends. "Isa Haswi, meet my wife. I was just about to see him to the door."

"I understand." That was code for the fact that she got the covert nature of Isa's visit.

"Keep in touch. *Shab bekheir*." Good night. Tiny stood on the porch.

Isa waved, then started his old Honda Civic. Like an asthmatic, it wheezed to life. It rattled as he drove away.

Tiny bit back a sigh as he returned to the kitchen.

Jonna pulled a glass from the cabinet. "Long day?"

"How do you know?" He ruffled her short, dark hair and kissed her.

"Because I usually don't smell bourbon on your breath on Tuesdays. And then there's that thick file on the table with a rubber band around it." Amusement danced in her brown eyes. "No need to worry. Don't ask, don't tell."

Normally, he would have chuckled since she'd always worn her role as wife of a covert agent with a bit of humor.

She took his hand. "This must be serious if that didn't make you laugh."

"Maybe." He gathered her in his arms as he considered the monumental task before them. Why wouldn't his unease about Leila go away? At least he had Isa on it. Jabir's replacement oozed integrity and dedication. If anyone could find a rat in Leila's life, it'd be him. But in the meantime?

"I need to pray on this one. And pray hard."

5

When a cell phone warbled into the still air, the lump on the double bed stirred in the mid-morning chill of a November Beirut morning. Another blasting ring followed. Like the ground heaving, the bed covers shifted. Hashim al-Hassan lifted his head. "Go away."

He turned over.

The call went to voice mail.

That pesky ringing resumed. He stuffed his pillow over his head. The process repeated itself.

And did so again.

Finally, he shoved aside the ratty duvet and sheet. Caller ID revealed the source of the disturbance. Of course. His brother. With a great sigh, he lifted the phone to his ear.

"I need to meet with you at your apartment." Tarek al-Hassan's voice blared in his ear.

What? After only five hours of sleep? When he'd stayed up until four thanks to some patrons who wouldn't leave Tarek's club? Was he crazy? Hashim wanted to hurl the phone against the wall.

His mood?

Dark as the room where he now sat upright. His bass voice rasped as he said, "Do you know what time it is?"

"Of course I do." Too chipper for this time of day.

Hashim scrubbed a hand across his bearded face. "I need my sleep."

"This is of the utmost importance. I'll be there in an hour." A click sounded in his ear.

Hashim groaned and lay back.

Didn't the man ever sleep? Maybe he was in one of those manic spells that seemed to come more and more frequently as of late. When he was, no one could refuse him.

Not even Hashim, who was long considered to be the muscle of the two.

No matter how tempting it was to close his eyes and return to the cocoon of his sleep, he couldn't. With a grunt, he hefted himself onto his feet and shoved aside the sheet that served as a curtain. The dull gray of an overcast sky greeted him. Perfect for his mood. Figured.

He got hot water for tea going and showered. As he let the black tea steep in a travel mug, he leaned against the counter of his cramped kitchen and surveyed the wall across from him. The wall of the small dining nook held a floor-to-ceiling cork board he'd hung years before when he'd made the apartment his primary residence instead of just a safe house. Brightly colored stick pins held up photos. Many, many photos of a woman who'd consumed his attention for the past five months.

Alex Thornton.

As he normally did each morning while having his tea, he marched through each one and mentally ticked off where he'd taken it. Alex's passport photo, something he'd pilfered at a hotel in Panama the June before. Alex coming into the hotel after a run. He traced her lean figure with his eyes. At the bar of the hotel. Ones from the website for a business she co-owned with her sister-in-law.

His cheeks flushed. He ripped his gaze away before his thoughts wandered where they shouldn't. Who cared if she were his half-sister? No, she was more than that.

She was a traitor.

48

His mind flashed to his time spent in that hellish prison in Iraq ten years before. Automatically, he rubbed his bald head. Thanks to her, all of the hair on his head had fallen out due to the stress from his ensuing captivity. And did it grow back? No. Not a bit. And all thanks to that… that vixen.

Old anger began roiling in his gut.

Over the past five months, he'd imagined what it would be like to kidnap her. Problem was, he couldn't do that in the States, not if he wanted to remain a free man. He'd have to wait for his opportunity.

But first?

He had to attend to his brother. His sometimes very demanding brother.

As he left for the two-bedroom penthouse he now used as a secondary residence, Hashim locked the door of his one-bedroom apartment. His footsteps echoed down a dingy hallway badly in need of a good sweeping. The hall led to a set of stairs, and he took them four floors down rather than trust an elevator that sometimes worked and sometimes didn't. In the lobby, he glanced at the floor. Junk mail lay scattered on the scarred tile, and the owners needed to scrub the windows. From behind the superintendent's door, an Arabic talk show blared from a television. He tried to ignore the noxious smell of onions and garlic that already filled the air from the restaurant next door.

Hashim hit the street.

At the curb, several taxis waited. In a singsong voice, one of the drivers called to him. "Hey, mister, you need a ride?"

He ignored him and strode along the concrete. More out of habit than worry, he kept a constant scan going as he made his way toward the coast. Nothing strange. The food vendors selling breakfast. Laborers wandering in late to a job. And the beggars. Always beggars.

"Sir, a few pounds to spare?" a woman called.

A man took up the chorus. "Can you spare some?"

Hashim slowed. Digging into his pocket, he dug out a few bills of the Lebanese currency and stuffed them into their outstretched hands. Their thanks floated toward him as he approached a wide boulevard.

An old lady leaned on her cane as she waited for the light to change.

"*Madame*, would you like some help?"

She smiled up at him. "If you would, kind sir. The road is so wide, and I worry these old legs won't take me all the way across."

Hashim offered his arm, and they shuffled along the crosswalk. He released her, and she thanked him.

Just two more blocks. Already, the windows of the tall buildings along the coast glittered in the dull morning light. Hashim came to the coastal road. After one last check for traffic, he darted to the other side and approached one of concrete, metal, and glass. He pushed into the lobby. A doorman in full uniform nodded. "Good morning, Mr. al-Hassan."

"Good morning, Yousef. Has my brother arrived?"

"Not five minutes ago. May I ring him for you?" The elderly gentleman stepped behind a counter.

Add something else to his list. A brother who was early and then complained when he was on time. "Thank you, no. I'm headed that way. Enjoy your day."

An elevator swept him toward the top floor. As it rose, he gazed at the Mediterranean below. Under the overcast sky, it rippled between light and dark gray.

The car stopped on the penthouse level. With a ding, the doors slid open. The soles of his hiking boots remained silent on the marble floor. Hashim inserted his key into the lock, and the penthouse door swung open on soundless hinges.

Marble spilled in a shiny, almost liquid black through the foyer, down the hall, and to the living room. In front of floor-to-ceiling windows that opened onto a balcony overlooking the Mediterranean, Tarek sat on an arm chair of black leather with sleek, straight lines.

He heaved a sigh as he gazed at his watch. "You're late."

He raised a mug of coffee to his lips.

Hashim cast a look at the clock of chrome and black on a glass mantel in the shape of a prism. Ten on the nose. "I believe I am on time."

He crossed into the kitchen and yanked open the stainless steel refrigerator door.

Tarek rose and drifted toward the fireplace with a fancy abstract painting supplied by Father above it. "I don't understand why you insist on spending nights at that… that rat hole when this penthouse has so much more to offer."

Hashim's eyes narrowed. After pulling out a bottle of water, he returned to the living area. He wouldn't be baited. Not this time. "What was so important that we had to meet this morning and not tonight at the club?"

As he stroked his beard, Tarek studied the abstract, which Hashim had never figured out. He cut his eyes toward his brother. "I will not be at the club tonight. It is Tuesday, yes?"

Their night off. "True."

Tarek resumed his seat and brushed something off the arm of the chair. "I got a phone call from Leila al-Kadir."

Hashim settled on a couch that was perpendicular to the chair and covered with the same fine leather. "What did she have to say?"

"Much." He smiled. "She made contact with Unit 28. Which, as you can imagine, stirred up some dust from Father's past. Tim Daniels— Father said his nickname was Tiny—Jabir's boss, busted her."

"And that is good news?" Hashim never broke his gaze as he took a swig of water.

Tarek chuckled. "Oh, she said nothing about us. But what she did say was that he has put Alex and Jabir on the case of finding out who killed Samir."

The bottle halfway to his lips for another gulp, Hashim paused. "I'm not understanding."

"It is simple, really." Tarek crossed his legs and straightened the fabric of his silk trousers. "Think about it. We need to take care of anyone who can link us to the money laundering scheme and Samir's murder, yes? Samir was our most obvious target, of course. As was the inspector. Both are now dead. But Shafiq Rahman, an accountant at Samir's company? He has vanished. He is somewhere out there on the wind, but no one knows where."

Hashim rested his elbows on his knees and his chin on his hands. "And you think Alex and Jabir could lead us to him?"

"I do."

"What about Noor and her family?" What a jab. Hashim hid his smirk behind his fingers.

At the mention of Tarek's ex-girlfriend, who was also his nemesis, his face reddened, and his lips narrowed. He jumped up and began pacing the length of the apartment, from the living room all the way to the dining room. "She has nothing on us. Nothing! Only a bunch of rumors and suppositions. Her accusation in June that I murdered her brother insulted me."

"She was not far—"

"She has no evidence!" Tarek whipped around. His eyes had widened to where the whites showed. He stabbed his finger toward Hashim. "None, brother. None. We have Samir's confession video from the police and Interpol. We left no forensic evidence behind. And Leila?" A derisive smile curled his lips. "I have her in my service. I'm paying off that gambling debt she had the poor grace to accumulate many years ago."

"Leila al-Kadir is a fool."

"Exactly." As if a switch flipped, Tarek returned to the chair. He lifted his chin as he smiled. "It gets better."

"Oh?"

"When Leila called me early this morning, she let me know that Tiny will keep her informed of their progress, which keeps us informed as well. And the best thing? She accepted my invitation to go to our private island in the Caribbean."

Which they never should have bought, especially after Hurricane Irma had ravaged it. "I told you that was a waste of money."

Tarek slammed his hand onto the arm with such force that the sound echoed off the high ceiling of the penthouse. "You know it wasn't! It will serve a purpose."

Hashim didn't flinch. "To keep a—"

"Enough!"

Hashim refused to be fazed by his brother's mercurial moods. "My apologies."

Like a match blown out, Tarek calmed. "The point, before you so rudely interrupted, is that Alex and Jabir will probably come to Beirut sometime in the near future."

The news stoked the fire of anger that had smoldered in Hashim's gut for five months. Sweat built on his palms, and his hands trembled slightly as he lifted the bottle of water to his lips. "I want her."

This time, Tarek was the one who smirked. "Oh, I know you do. Just as Father wants her so he can erase that stain of dishonor from our family name."

Hashim began planning what he would do. A simple kidnapping. Find out where they were staying. Bribe the hotel employees for access to her room. Kill her lover. Take her. And have his way with her before he killed her.

"She is not to be taken."

In his mind, his plans jerked to a stop. "What?"

"She is not to be taken." Tarek stared him down. "At least not now. The time is not right."

"When will it ever be right?" Hashim pushed to his feet. "She will be here in Beirut, brother!" His face flushed. "We have access to wherever she will be. The resources. The manpower. What else—"

"Our focus must be to find Shafiq Rahman."

"But—"

"No. We must find Shafiq first. Then we can focus on her."

Hashim drained the rest of his water. Chest heaving, he smashed his bottle and hurled it across the room.

It bounced off another one of Father's expensive, bizarre abstracts.

"I know your desire. I know it well." Tarek leaned forward and focused on his younger brother. Soothing, as if calming an upset toddler, he said, "But sometimes, we must set aside our desires for the greater good. You understand, yes?"

Oh, how he wanted to say he didn't. But he did. "So we use Alex and Jabir to find Shafiq."

"Exactly. And once we dispose of him, then we can focus our attention on Alex."

When they had her? A snarl curled Hashim's lips. The vixen would wish she'd never, ever gone to that nightclub in Baghdad.

Friday, November 24, 2017, 0800 hours EST, Washington, DC

Strange. The word fit today's situation. Isa Haswi straightened as the front door to the al-Kadir residence opened early on the morning of the Friday after Thanksgiving. Most everyone else had taken the day off and slept in or risen at zero-dark-thirty to attend the post-Thanksgiving sales.

Unlike her humdrum routine of work, then celebrating Thanksgiving with extended family in the suburbs, she toted a suitcase behind her to the curb and waited for someone.

He rubbed his chin as he tried to figure out her plans. She was traveling. But to see whom? He tried to recall the friends she had. Precious few, if he remembered her profile correctly, at least in this country.

A yellow taxi pulled to a stop. The driver hopped out and placed her suitcase in the trunk.

As Leila climbed into the backseat, Isa snapped a picture of her with the high-powered camera he'd brought.

The taxi rumbled down the street.

Isa cranked the engine of the nameless, faceless Chevy Trailblazer he'd checked out from the Unit 28 motor pool. He followed at a safe distance. They turned onto Florida Avenue, then picked up the Potomac Parkway as they passed the Kennedy Center. After crossing the Potomac River, they headed west on I-66.

As they exited onto State Road 267, he realized their destination. Dulles. The taxi took her not to the commercial terminals but to the General Aviation facility.

Very interesting.

He slowed to a stop so a large Cadillac Escalade hid most of his SUV while still allowing him to watch the General Aviation Terminal's entrance.

The taxi wound up in front, and Leila settled with the driver before heading inside with her suitcase trundling after her like a small child.

He had to move quickly. She was obviously traveling somewhere by air, and the sooner he got a good view of the planes, the better. He put the Trailblazer into gear, backed out of his space, and found another one along the fence line. This one was exposed but seemed to be free of security cameras. He slouched in his seat to avoid attention.

A couple of pilots strolled into view and angled toward a low-wing plane. They appeared to be headed out for a fun day of flying.

Another pair headed toward a small, high-wing Cessna. An instructor and her student, perhaps.

He switched his attention to a Learjet with its stairs down. An older gentleman with a pilot's epaulets on his shoulders stood at the top.

Two women exited the General Aviation building, Leila along with a woman who wore a close-fitting dress and heels. She had to be a flight attendant.

Isa's breath hitched as the pilot took Leila's suitcase and helped her up the steps. The attendant followed. Once the door closed, the engines spun up.

The plane turned toward the runway.

He straightened and snapped pictures of the tail number.

Now he had nothing better to do than to turn his wheels toward home. He'd return each day until she showed her face again. Tonight, he needed his rest. His mind whirled all the way back to his one-bedroom, walk-up apartment near Fort Belvoir.

Lunch with a side of research would precede a good nap.

Once he'd fixed himself a pita with peanut butter, bananas, and apples sandwiched inside, he pulled his laptop to himself and accessed the servers at work. He began scanning the profile Tiny had uploaded.

She was a loner, no close friends in the States and only a few in Beirut. Would she go see them on a private jet? Most likely, no. He rechecked the information related to her family. Perhaps her in-laws, but once her husband had divorced her, they cut off all contact, as had her paternal grandparents when Ali al-Kadir died. For sure, her mother's side was well to do, but not so much as to own a private plane. An Interpol salary certainly wouldn't be enough for a trip by Learjet. Could she be on Interpol business?

Isa pondered that one as he transferred the photos he'd taken onto the laptop and updated his log. No answers came, but perhaps the tail number he had noted would yield something.

He pulled out his phone and dialed a number.

"Sadie Callahan," a voice with a lilt answered.

"Sadie, this is Isa Haswi. Tiny told me to call you if I needed information. And I do."

"Let me verify you first."

She was all business, not that he expected anything less.

"Your number?"

"One-six-zero-eight-six." He gave the ID number that would verify him as a Unit 28 agent.

"Looks like you're bona fide. What do you need?"

"Information on an airplane." He read off the tail number.

Fingers tapped on a keyboard. "Let me do some research on this, and I'll get back to you."

He could do nothing but wait. As he polished off his lunch and washed his dishes, he thought about that voice. Her accent had intrigued him. Why, he wasn't sure.

When his phone chirped, he shelved that thought.

He picked it up and read the text. "Your plane belongs to Sigmund Corporation. Flight plan to St. Maarten in the Caribbean. Due to return on Monday, November 27."

Isa set the phone aside and sat back. He smiled as he thought about Sadie. Then it dimmed as he considered the information she'd shared.

Sigmund Corporation? To the Caribbean? Who was Leila meeting? Unless she was deep undercover, she was not on Interpol business. Maybe Tiny could get an agent on the ground in the Dutch territory. He dialed his number. "Tiny, it's Isa. So sorry to bother you at home, but I have a question for you."

"What's going on?" Tiny asked. The sounds of what had to be an American football game played in the background.

Isa summarized Sadie's response to his query on the plane's number.

Silence fell as if his boss had muted the game. "I wish we could do that, but we don't have the manpower to put an agent on the ground there, and I can't get more without good reason."

Not that they had one, just a supposition. Isa sighed as he hung up. He had a dead end. He would have to wait. But on Monday, he would pick up her trail again. This new assignment was getting more interesting all of the time.

And in more than one way.

6

Welcome to Weatherly. Town of Yesterday, Today, and Tomorrow. Tiny grinned as he always did when he passed the sign leading into the heart of Alex's hometown and where Roya and David once more resided full time. Coming to Weatherly lowered his stress levels—at least most of the time. He shoved aside the worries that had driven him to hold an in-person conference rather than a Skype session with Alex and Jabir.

The town's only traffic signal at Main Street and Weatherly Road turned yellow, then red. As he surveyed the main intersection, Tiny rested his head against the seat. The warmth of the sunlight caressed his face and conjured memories of simpler times long ago when he'd studied outside in the autumn sunshine at American University in Washington. Looking back, he realized how petty his problems had been. Get a good grade. Get the next paper finished.

How things had changed. Now, he had to run a case that might bring his goddaughter into close contact with a very dangerous man who wanted revenge for wrongs that had happened to him years before.

To his right, he gazed at a flat above a store called Spin a Yarn. Alex lived there. Then he noted Jabir's flat across the street on the southeastern quadrant of the intersection. Both of them represented Weatherly's present, those who wanted to make the town their home.

The light turned green, and he continued southward along Main Street until he found a parking spot almost at the edge of downtown. When he climbed from the car, he unzipped his leather jacket and took a deep breath. The smell of wood smoke from somewhere wafted to him, as did the scent of dried leaves. When he turned his steps toward the center of town, they crunched under his feet.

Autumn had become one of his favorite seasons no matter what his mood. If only he could enjoy it! Maybe some coffee would help before he joined Alex and Jabir at 10:30.

On his left sat Memorial Park, a small park the town had created to commemorate its dead from all wars. When he arrived at the police station's fenced lot on the northern edge of the park, he crossed the street. No activity emanated from the unnamed storefront that served as Alex and Jabir's office. Maybe Jabir had stepped out for some coffee. He passed David's law offices, where a receptionist chatted with someone in the lobby. From an earlier text, he knew his old friend had taken the day off.

Next door, the window opened onto a conference room, complete with a state-of-the art conference phone, chair and tables of the most contemporary design, and a massive flat-screen television. David had reported that an Internet startup company had moved in not six months before. To Tiny, it represented the future of young people willing to invest in small towns.

When the pedestrian signal came up in his favor, he crossed Weatherly Road and pulled open the glass and chrome door to the Blue Plate Diner. Here, past, present, and future all collided. Even mid-morning, people filled the diner that Alex said was the backbone of the town. Tiny nudged through a crowd of farmers and retirees who Alex said gathered on an almost daily basis to solve the problems of the world. Maybe today's agenda related to the crisis in North Korea or the racial tensions that riddled the country.

In a corner booth sat a young man with headphones over his ears as he pecked furiously on a laptop. A novel or the latest program that could lead to an IPO?

And there, at the other end of the L-shaped counter on a stool of silver-flecked blue vinyl, sat Jabir.

Tiny muffled a smile at the way his former operative kept his back to the wall, typical for Jabir, who'd a few years before completed a highly dangerous undercover assignment and lived to tell about it. A mostly untouched ceramic mug of coffee steamed on the counter beside him. His protégé rested his head against the wall and stared into space as if seeing something in his inner world. His brow knitted. He didn't even acknowledge the presence of his boss.

That was strange. Normally, Jabir would have keyed onto him like a heat-seeking missile.

Tiny slid onto a stool beside him. "Jabir."

As if he'd zoned out, he didn't respond.

Tiny tried again, this time a little louder. "Jabir!"

The young man jumped as if he'd kicked him.

Tiny chuckled and raised his hand to catch the waitress's attention. "I didn't mean to disturb you."

"I was thinking." Jabir glanced at his phone. "I thought our meeting was at 10:30."

"It is. I thought I'd stop for a coffee first. I figured you wouldn't mind." Tiny smiled at the waitress as she sashayed to the counter.

"Welcome to the Blue Plate Diner," she announced with a classy Southern drawl. "My name's Daisy. I see you know Mr. Jabir."

Tiny chuckled. "Oh, we go way back."

She grinned and pulled out a pad and pen from her apron. "What can I get you today, hon?"

"What he's having to drink will do."

"Coming right up." She turned to Jabir. "You okay, sugar? Want a refill? Jabir!" she said a little louder when he didn't respond.

Jabir glanced up from where he manipulated his phone. "Uh, sure." He released a sigh. "I'm sorry. I'm being a jerk."

She chuckled. "Nah. You're better than some folks I see here." Her gaze flicked to Tiny. "Cream and sugar for you?"

"Yes, ma'am."

She grinned. "I like you. Coming up."

Facing Jabir, Tiny rested his elbow on the counter. Maybe humor would help. "Okay. What gives? Was your Thanksgiving weekend that bad?"

Jabir's face lit up. "No, it was great. Mama came down from DC. She adores Roya and David."

At the mention of Alex's parents, his face clouded.

"Then why the deep sigh and brooding? Is it Alex?"

"No, no. We're great." Jabir's lips curled in a smile Tiny could only call dreamy. Then he shook his head and rubbed the back of his neck. His gaze darted to his phone. He shoved it away and rested his chin on his hands as if contemplating taking Tiny into his confidence. "You served with David and Roya in Afghanistan, right?"

"Here you go." Daisy set a steaming mug of coffee in front of Tiny. She added a bowl of creamers and sugar packs.

Tiny cast a look around before answering, "Yeah, I did. Matter of fact, I've known Roya longer than David since we were at The Farm together." He opened a creamer and dumped it into the dark brown liquid. He added a pack of sugar and stirred. "Matter of fact, we posed as a honeymooning couple when we traveled to Pakistan to meet up with other CIA agents for the ride into Afghanistan. I don't know what it was, but while she drove the other men at the compound nearly ape, we had a purely platonic relationship."

"What was she like?"

"Drop-dead gorgeous, for sure. Spirited. She ignored it when a bunch of the guys had the nerve to suggest that she head home or do their cleaning and cooking."

"I'll bet she didn't like that."

"Hardly. And when one of the guys grabbed her inappropriately, he wound up on the ground with her knife to his throat." Tiny smiled at the memory. "People respected her after that."

Jabir fell silent and sipped his own brew, sans creamer and sugar. Finally, he set it down. "What about when they dated?"

"I don't think you can call being posted at an FOB dating." Tiny stared at the light brown liquid. He knew what had happened regarding Davie's affair shortly after he and Roya married. Did Jabir? Probably not. And Tiny would not be the one to share that information with him. "Hmmm. This is good stuff."

Jabir cradled his mug in his hands. He offered a tight smile. "Did you notice anything amiss?"

This was not a good twist of topic. He needed to deflect—fast. "I'm not sure what you mean."

Jabir once more stared into space. He set his mug down with a clunk. He murmured his words, almost as if he were verbalizing thoughts to work through them. "I love Alex."

Intense, especially for Jabir.

"I know you do. It's been clear as day on your face ever since you reunited with her."

"I love her so much!" That came out on the edges of a ragged whisper. Jabir's Adam's apple bobbed as he swallowed hard.

Something clearly bothered the young man so much that he swung from happy to stressed in the span of a second, which was unusual since virtually nothing rattled him. "Is something wrong, son?"

That dreamy smile returned. "No, no. Nothing's wrong at all."

It faded again.

Tiny doubted that, but unless Jabir confided in him, he couldn't do anything.

Jabir's phone chirped. He picked it up and swiped his thumb across it, then grinned as if none of the previous conversation had happened. "That was Alex. She said she had an incident of the canine variety and will be at the office by 10:45."

"Sounds like she has her hands full. What say we head on over so you can show me around?"

"That works."

Tiny raised his hand to signal the waitress. He held up his mug. "Can I have this to go, please?"

Monday, November 27, 2017, 1035 hours EST, Weatherly, NC

"I can't believe you two. I really can't." Alex scowled at her dogs as she swept up the rice and flour spilled across the floor. The broom left contrails of flour everywhere. She dumped the grains into the trashcan. "Which one of you decided that getting into the cabinets and pulling out my big bags of flour and rice was a good idea?"

Sabina yawned. In typical Basenji fashion, she made a sound as if to say, "It wasn't my idea."

She even wagged her tail.

"I'm not impressed by cuteness right now," Alex grumbled. She shoved the broom and dustpan into the kitchen pantry and snagged the hand vacuum. "Scoot. Both of you. I'll make good on the promise I made last year and install those baby locks on the cabinets."

Once she'd shooed them into the living room, she vacuumed up the flour. Mopping would have to wait until that evening. Now, she needed to meet Jabir and Tiny. "Promise that if I take you to the office, you'll be good."

Sabina spun around as if to agree.

Any remaining annoyance faded. "When you do that, you have me like putty in your paws. C'mon. Time's a'wastin'."

She led them down the steps and onto the street. As she strolled along the sidewalk to the office, she said hi to Scratch, the postman who delivered the mail to her flat, Mattie Hendrix, owner of Spin a Yarn and mayor of Weatherly, Charice, the town manager of Weatherly and Alex's next door neighbor, and Mary, who headed to her lunch shift at the Blue Plate Diner.

She crossed the east-west street of Weatherly Road, then Main Street, the north-south street. Once she arrived at their storefront, she swiped her ID badge across the pad next to the front door. The lock clicked, and she stepped into the spacious main room that served as their work area. Her desk with its computer monitor facing away from the front sat at the back right corner. "Yoo hoo!"

She released the dogs. Sabina immediately began a patrol of the perimeter and returned as if to report, "All secure, ma'am!"

"In here." With a stout mug of coffee and some cookies in his hands, Jabir stepped from a small room at the back that served as their kitchen. "Sorry. We were grabbing a snack."

"You eat all of the time." She grinned as Tiny joined them. "Good to see you, but I must say it's a long way to come for a little information."

"It's more than you think," Tiny said as he stooped and scratched Rocky behind the ears. Sabina nosed in for one as well. "Let's get started because we have a lot to cover."

Huh? Normally, their boss didn't mind chitchat. Well, he did seem a little preoccupied as if their next job worried him more than normal. She shot Jabir a glance. He shrugged and settled onto a bar chair at the large worktable that occupied the center of the room.

"Here's briefing sheets for each of you. I've put the whole file up on the servers under the number listed on the folder."

Good to know. She scribbled down the number on her notepad. After she mopped the kitchen that night, she'd peruse it.

For the next hour, their boss briefed them on the Samir Kamil case. Kamil International's general counsel brutally murdered. Vital mistakes made by Leila al-Kadir, including approaching the chief suspect. *What a...* Alex stopped the thought. She didn't like the woman any more than she had when she'd first seen her chatting up Jabir.

And Noor? Her heart ached for her. She'd lost her brother twice, first to his best friend and then to death. She tried to imagine what it would be like to lose Josh, Jake, or Jonathan to murder. Noor's instincts told her that Tarek al-Hassan had done it, yet she had no way to prove it, especially now thanks to Leila's missteps.

Tiny sat back. "What are your thoughts?"

Alex hopped up and approached the whiteboard they'd installed on the wall across from the flat-screen monitor. "We know Samir was murdered, most likely by either Hashim or Tarek." She scrawled their names and connected them to Samir's. "And we think Samir used an accountant named Shafiq Rahman to set up the accounts at Kamil International. Noor, her husband, Fadi, and her father knew enough to call for the forensic audit that revealed the money laundering." She added those names. "Raoul Chevrot, the Interpol supervisor, assigned the case to Leila, and Chief Inspector Mansour worked with her. Beirut is the common denominator in all of this."

Jabir rubbed his chin as he studied the board. "It sounds like we might need a trip there."

"So here's the loose ends we have. Samir is key to who would have gotten him and Shafiq to set up the fake accounts. Except he's gone." She scratched through his name. "What about Shafiq? We find him, we probably can get that person's name as well. He's missing." She put a question mark through his name. "And Noor and her family? They're in Beirut and may know something about who would have a motive to murder Samir."

Jabir scanned a sheet of paper. "It looks like Shafiq has a sister named Mira. She's a hairdresser in Beirut and is a couple of years younger than he. She could know something."

"She might know where he is." Alex added her name and connected it to Shafiq. "What about Chief Inspector Mansour?"

"Check him out." Tiny nodded. "But steer clear of Raoul. I talked to him when I was researching Leila. His suggestion was to run and run far away from the case. It's clear he's not interested in working with us."

Alex scratched out his name. She turned. "And Tarek?"

"He resides in Beirut." Tiny nodded.

"He's supposedly legit, right? Maybe we should talk to—"

"No!" Jabir jumped up. Eyes wide, he shook his head. "Alex, no way are we—"

"But he's a legitimate—"

"We can't. We shouldn't—"

"Jabir's right, Alex. Despite the fact that he's a prime suspect, we can't take that chance because we know Hashim al-Hassan resides in Beirut as well," Tiny said.

Alex swallowed hard. Her courage waned a bit before her desire to see the case to its end kicked in. "All the better to interview Tarek and maybe—"

"No is no, understand?" Sharp words from Tiny.

Taken aback, Alex tapped her marker on her palm. "But I thought you said we should follow all leads when we got these types of cases."

"There are always exceptions." Tiny sighed and scrubbed a hand across his face. "This is one of those."

"Why?"

He opened his mouth, closed it, and shook his head. "It's not wise right now, just as it isn't wise to approach Raoul Chevrot."

She glanced down and grimaced. Red ink now coated her palm since she'd tapped the business end of the marker against her hand. Suddenly, the red mess looked like blood to her. She shivered. Maybe she should drop the issue. "Okay. I'll cede, especially because if he did it—"

"Probably so." Tiny nodded. "And if he did, he's going to lie to you."

Jabir shoved his hands into his back pockets and paced. Was it the light, or had his face taken on a slight tinge of green?

"Jabir, what is it?" Alex glanced at Tiny.

Their boss studied Jabir as if he were an interesting specimen of something. Like anxiety, maybe? Then he sighed. "I think we need to break for lunch. You've got all of the information I needed to share behind closed doors. Let's go."

They wound up heading to The Blue Plate. Fast. Easy. Cheap. Good. That's what she said each time she described the diner. Today was no exception. Over lunch, they avoided talking about the case. Only when Daisy had cleared away their dishes and left them with refills on their drinks did the topic arise again.

Jabir shoved his ice tea glass around in circles. "I'll start working on our reservations. Hopefully, we can leave tomorrow night."

"Work with our reps to get your arrangements made. It shouldn't be a problem, but we need to make sure. That'll put you in Beirut Wednesday afternoon." Tiny nodded. "Hopefully someone has a line on what happened to Shafiq. Check in with me as well."

"Will do."

Tiny leaned forward. In a low voice, he added, "There are a couple of other things to know. First off, I'm not quite sure I trust Leila. Call it a gut instinct. I'll keep her informed, but I also have Isa Haswi keeping her under surveillance."

"Isa..." She struggled back in her memory. "Wait! That Iranian Rev Guard guy who defected?"

"The one and only. He's now with us. And the other thing?" Tiny fixed Jabir in his gaze. "I asked Leila about your sister. She unequivocally stated that Yasmin is dead. She was only going to use that information to string you along until you gave her what she wanted."

Double not liking the woman. Starts with a b and ends with an h is now what she thought of her. Alex's eyes narrowed.

Jabir visibly deflated, as if losing any hope that his sister might be alive sucker-punched him. "You trust her on that but not on the other stuff?"

"Trust but verify, which is why Isa's on the case." Tiny pulled out his wallet and tossed a couple of bills on the table to cover his tip. "She has a vested interest in justice for Samir while she doesn't in your peace of mind." He rose. "I need to get going. Alex, I want to swing by and see your folks, before I return to Raleigh. Keep in touch."

They rose and followed him into the chilly afternoon. When they passed the park, he continued south.

Eyes downcast and hand rubbing his chest, Jabir led them through the wrought iron gate and onto grass still green despite the change of season.

Alex took his hand. "I'm sorry."

Jabir sighed. He kicked a nearby lamppost and scrubbed his hands through his hair. As if questioning God, he lifted his face to the sky. His lips moved, but at first, no sound came out. "I was a fool."

"For believing her?" Alex shook her head and pulled him onto a bench beside her. "She knew how to get you to do her bidding. Toss a bone. Toss another and another until she had what she wanted. Then dump the truth on you."

He pulled a cigarette pack from his shirt pocket and lit one. For a few minutes, he didn't say a word, only stared at the ground. "Why do you think I believed her?"

She rubbed his back. "You loved Yasmin. She was your sister, almost your twin since you were so close in age. She died an unjust death. You would have liked nothing more than to believe she was alive."

He nodded and puffed away. Some response.

"May I ask you something?"

"Sure."

"Why did you react so sharply when I mentioned interviewing Tarek? And Tiny wasn't cool with it either."

Jabir didn't say a word, only took another drag on his cigarette before he leaned down and stubbed it out on the concrete of the bench's piling.

"Jabir."

"I didn't mean to overreact."

Huh? That was news to her. "Jabir, please."

"I think we need to get back. You said something about an afternoon meeting with a client, and I need to make our reservations."

"What is it with you?" *And why are you holding out on me?*

"It's nothing." He pulled her to her feet. After a quick check of traffic, they crossed.

She stopped him before he unlocked the door. "Why are you stone-walling me?"

He avoided her gaze and kissed her on the forehead. "I'm not. I'll bring the pups by tonight."

With that, he slipped inside. The lock clicked shut behind him.

Alex let him go. He hid something to the point where he lied to her. And Tiny? He hadn't said anything, but he clearly worried about her be-ing anywhere close to Tarek. She understood. But still… She heaved a sigh. Maybe her boyfriend would confide in her and Tiny would understand her need to cover all bases.

Maybe.

Monday, November 27, 2017, 1300 hours EST, Weatherly, NC

As he sped down the black ribbon of highway toward the Thornton residence, Tiny's thoughts raged. He should have voiced more to Alex regarding his concerns about Hashim al-Hassan desiring revenge. He couldn't when he had no proof that Hashim was planning something. All he had was an unfounded worry generated from a discussion he'd had with Jabir months before. As long as Alex avoided contact with either of the al-Hassan brothers when she and Jabir visited Beirut, she shouldn't have any problem. He'd been right in not broaching that topic.

What about Jabir? As woods flew by cloaked in greens going to red and gold, he pondered the young man. Something about the al-Hassan name had triggered an exceptionally strong reaction from a person normally calm under fire. Did he have the same concerns Tiny did? Probably, since he was the one who'd made the link between Alex being the lure for Hashim al-Hassan at a Baghdad nightclub.

Right now, Tiny desired to chat with David and Roya before turning his wheels toward Raleigh-Durham International Airport. He pulled into the driveway of the Thornton house and turned off the engine of the rental car. Like the old friend he was, he climbed the deck steps and tapped on the back door. He grinned. *"Salaam,* Roya."

Roya approached. *"Salaam alaikum,* Tiny." She pulled him inside and kissed him on both cheeks. "Come inside, why don't you?"

"I think I will."

"Would you like some tea?" She led the way across the den of the open downstairs to the kitchen.

"Sure." Tiny grinned at the Christmas tree standing in the corner with its white lights twinkling. Boxes of ornaments sat on the floor. "Looks like you've got an early start on decorating."

"Tiny!" David called from where he crouched beside a box of lights. He straightened and set his bundle on the granite bar. He extended his hand. "Good to see you!"

"The same to you. Caught ya, huh?"

Roya giggled as she stuffed three glasses with ice and pulled a pitcher from the refrigerator. "Davie is working on the lights for the front tree, or what we call the adults' tree since we kept it in Alexandria."

David grinned and settled at the island. "How's life up in the DC area?"

They chatted for a few minutes about the various goings on with their families. Time to take the plunge and get to the bottom of Jabir's mood swings. "When I got here, I arrived early and decided to head to the Blue Plate for some coffee. I ran into Jabir."

David chuckled. "It's one of his favorite haunts. He thinks the coffee's better than Starbucks."

"Why does that not surprise me since he's such a coffee hound? Anyway, we got to talking, and he seemed to seesaw between being really happy and really sad. I couldn't figure him out." He leaned forward. "Are he and Alex," he paused as he tried to figure out how to voice his worries, "having problems?"

David glanced at his wife. "None that I know of. Has Alex said anything to you, Roya?"

"No. She's been so happy ever since he moved down."

"He also started asking questions about our time in Afghanistan, specifically about you two."

Roya stilled, almost like she were conducting covert surveillance on someone and had been spotted. "What did you tell him?"

"How we met. That I rode into Afghanistan with you. That you two met and dated at the FOB. Nothing more," he added. "I told them nothing about your affair, David."

"You're sure? You didn't tell him where I had gone, did you?" Intensity laced Roya's words. She kept her gaze on him.

Huh? Where had that come from? "No, I didn't. Why?"

"N—no reason." Her cheeks flushed a delicate pink as David took her hand. "What kinds of Christmas parties do you have coming up?"

Time to change the subject because he could tell she would rather slit her wrists than endure an interrogation from one of her oldest friends. He changed topics to talk about the upcoming Holidays and goings on at work.

As he began the drive to the airport, he considered what he'd learned. Roya worried about something related to those tortuous few days when their affair had come into the open almost thirty-four years before. David knew something as well. Then there was Jabir. Something had triggered an ultra-protective streak in him that seemed a bit out of proportion for something that would most likely never happen so long as Alex didn't put herself into danger. Maybe it was because he knew how the young woman had a propensity to wander off the reservation.

He'd have to wait.

The answers would come out.

Problem was, he wasn't sure he'd like them when they did.

7

Monday afternoon, a lull for Isa under normal days. But not today since Leila was returning from St. Maarten aboard her private jet. Using the front of his shirt, he polished an apple and bit into it. Its crunch and sweet scent penetrated the interior of the Unit 28 navy blue Jeep Grand Cherokee. He stared at the English fiction book glowing on his tablet before flicking his gaze to the General Aviation terminal.

No sign of any activity that would reveal the arrival of a Learjet, only small planes arriving and departing. Perhaps he had misunderstood Sadie. He would call her and inquire, which would also be a perfect excuse to talk.

"Sadie Callahan," she said when she answered.

"Sadie, this is Isa."

"So good to hear from you!" Her lilting voice did more to warm him than his leather jacket. "Still on surveillance?"

"I am. Could you perhaps confirm the time Leila's plane is supposed to arrive?"

"I can." Clicking told him she checked the flight plan she'd obtained. "Should be 3:30."

"I suppose she is late."

"Let me check." More keyboarding. "From what I can see from Dulles Air Traffic Control, they're inbound as we speak."

"Thank you." Suddenly, his mind went blank as if someone pulled the power cord to a computer screen.

The silence stretched from cozy to awkward.

"Is there anything else?" she asked.

Yes, there was! His cheeks warmed. "I…"

Murmuring on her end, as if she spoke with someone, reached him. Then she said, "I've got to get to a meeting. Text me if anything else comes up. Take care."

Empty air.

"Isa, Isa, Isa, are you a fool?" he muttered to himself. Why did he get all tongue tied around her when he maintained cordial relationships with other women? He liked her. And he had not even met her yet, just listened to her voice. And he did not even know if she were married, involved, or single. Time to give it up. Married or involved, she was totally off limits. But single? Hah. She would never be interested.

His phone chimed again. Sadie, perhaps? Like her meeting had gotten canceled and she had called just to talk? He checked Caller ID and nearly laughed. Hardly. Tiny was calling.

"Isa, Tiny here." His boss's voice filled his ear. "Where are you?"

"On surveillance at Dulles General Aviation. Leila is supposed to be returning from her trip today." Isa straightened when a man in a day glow green safety vest with two wands strolled onto the concrete apron. "I think her plane is due to arrive any minute."

"Good. Listen. When it gets here, no need to follow her."

Isa drew in a sharp breath. "Why?"

"I've contacted her to set up a meeting. I had to leave a voice mail, so I hope she'll call me when she returns. After you confirm her arrival, head to Alexandria. We're meeting at a Mexican restaurant called Jefe's." Tiny rattled off the address, which he scribbled on a page of a small notebook he'd brought. "We're due to meet up at seven. Be there at 6:15, and I'll pass you the details. I'll send you the address."

"I will be there." Even though it was mid-afternoon, he would need to leave soon, lest he get stuck on the Beltway. Where was Leila? He resumed reading and glancing toward the apron.

The ground crewman now peered intently toward the runway and secured his ear protectors over his ears.

Isa set aside his tablet and picked up his camera.

A Learjet taxied into the parking area, and the crewman crossed the wands he held. The plane's engines began winding down as he chocked the wheels. The stairs lowered, and the flight attendant, the same one who'd greeted Leila the Friday before, preceded the woman down the steps.

Leila pressed some cash into her hand, took her suitcase, and headed toward the terminal. She had her phone out, and a frown crossed her face as she most likely checked her voice mail.

Isa grinned as he snapped several pictures, from her entry into General Aviation to her departure via taxi, most likely to her home where she could then catch the Metro to Alexandria.

He reached to put his camera in its bag.

A flash of movement toward the plane caught his eye.

He stilled.

A man stood at the top of the steps and surveyed the area around the plane as if he owned it.

His picture was not in any of the files Isa had received, and he would have remembered those olive tones, aquiline features, closely trimmed beard, and waves of dark hair almost to his shoulders. An unknown man to him. Perhaps he was not relevant, but time would reveal that. Isa raised the camera and snapped his picture.

The man turned. His gaze seemed to bore straight into his.

Isa shrank down in his seat as if that could hide him. He had not intended to do so, but something about the man's dark eyes sent a shiver down his spine. What was it?

They were empty. Cold.

Like those of a man who had killed before, maybe with no remorse.

Oh, did he know the type. He had worked with them, actually, in his past life in the Revolutionary Guard.

Time to go.

For once, he did not mind leaving a surveillance early.

Monday, November 27, 2017, 1815 hours EST, Alexandria, VA

"*Salam, chetori,* Isa," Tiny said to Isa as Unit 28's newest agent joined him at the bar of Jefe's.

"*Salam* my friend." Isa settled onto a bar chair. "She is coming?"

"She'll be here at seven. She didn't sound too happy, but I told her I didn't want to convey my information over the phone." He shifted so he sat with his back to the wall with his head resting against it. Tonight, it wasn't due to wariness but to weariness. He closed his eyes. He couldn't do that. Not when he still had to drive home.

Isa called for an iced tea and grinned. "You have had a long day?"

"Something like that. I've been up since five, down to North Carolina and back, and I'm famished. These aren't helping much." He nodded to the cheese sticks he'd ordered soon after he'd arrived. His stomach growled loud enough for Isa to raise an eyebrow. "Sorry. I promised Jonna I'd have supper with her tonight."

Isa undid his leather jacket. "What is my assignment?"

Tiny cleared his throat. "I want you to wait here in the restaurant. When she leaves, follow her. I want to know where she goes. Or if anything out of the ordinary happens. There's a table in the corner over there." He nodded toward a bar table under a neon sign advertising Corona. "The light will put you in shadow, yet you'll be close enough to follow her when she leaves."

"Do you want me to call you when I finish?"

"No. Record everything in your log and shoot me an e-mail in the morning." He sighed and stared at the beer, some local label the bartender had recommended. His thoughts returned to Leila. With his brain, he really wanted to believe her intentions were honest, but that whisper in his gut grew louder and louder. "I want to trust her. I really do. I feel like a scientist. I'm trying to do everything I can to disprove my theory that she's not trustworthy."

"May I help you, then." Isa rose with his drink. "I will be in touch."

He retreated to the bar table.

Tiny pulled out his phone. Jonna had texted some good news. Rachel, his younger daughter, had decided to come home for some family time to sustain her as she began finals. He tapped out a reply. "I'll be home by 7:30 or so."

With one eye on the door, he began reviewing the e-mails that had accumulated since he'd last checked right before leaving Raleigh. He responded to three meeting requests, two messages from his boss, and one from Jabir stating that all travel arrangements were in place. Perfect. He was about to put away his phone when another one caught his attention.

Reminder - Request for Decentralization Pilot Program Candidates.

What a subject line. In the message, Mitch reminded Tiny as well as his cohort in Research that he needed names of potential candidates for Unit 28 field teams that might work on a decentralized basis, much like Jabir and Alex were doing now. He replied that he'd put the word out and began composing the message to his staff.

A cold blast of air with a hint of wet on it distracted him.

Clad in a black leather jacket reaching her hips, jeans, and boots, Leila followed the air.

Almost every male head in the bar turned. If he were younger or not so in love with his wife, Tiny would have done the same. Had she used her beauty in her job with Saudi Intelligence and maybe even Interpol? For sure. He'd be a fool not to think that.

"Hello, Tiny." A tight smile flashed across her face as she slid onto the seat next to him. "So sorry I'm late."

"No, no. You're right on time. Thanks for calling me back. You said you were on vacation?" Maybe she'd reveal where she'd traveled by private jet.

"I was."

No such luck. For all of her missteps, she remained a clever quarry.

"I take it you have my back?" she asked in a low voice. She glanced around as if convinced someone eavesdropped from nearby.

Tiny muffled a smile. Her shadow observed them from across the room. "We're good. How's work?"

After ordering a margarita, she sighed and shook her head. "I miss Beirut. I had a nice life there. A good apartment. Good friends. Challenging cases. Here, I feel like a small cog in a very big wheel."

"It's a big country. Lots of problems, both domestic and international. I'm sure it's easy to feel a bit lost." He glanced up as the bartender brought her drink. "Sir, you can put that on my tab. My treat," he added when Leila started. "Probably the only time I'll buy a drink for another woman."

She took a sip. After a long moment, she cut her eyes toward him. "Your wife must be very trusting."

"I've never given her reason to doubt." *And I can't say that of you.*

The bartender drifted to the other end to tend to customers.

Satisfied they were alone, he began speaking in a low voice. "Here's where we stand. I spent today with Alex and Jabir. They're taking the case and are leaving for Beirut tomorrow night, so they're due to arrive late afternoon on Wednesday. They'll be talking to Chief Inspector Mansour, Mira Rahman, Noor Kamil-Sultan, her husband, and her father. Our biggest task is to find Shafiq and hand him over to Interpol. That's why we're talking to Mira. We're also trying to figure out if the Kamil family knows enough to endanger them."

"Probably not." She raised the glass to her lips.

"I'd rather be safe than sorry. And I want to see what else the inspector may have since the last time you spoke with him was four months ago."

She stilled, and her hands suddenly gripped the glass's stem with such force to make the tendons in them pop up. "What about Raoul Chevrot?"

"I've spoken to him. He made it very clear that he'd spurn any request for a meeting, so we won't waste our time. That's all I know."

"It is enough." She turned and stared hard at the bottles of liquor beneath the television screens. Slowly, as if confirming something to herself, she repeated, "It is enough."

Enough for what?

"Well, if you don't mind, I'm going to head on." Tiny took the receipt the bartender handed him and scribbled both a generous tip and his signature. He shoved it back to the man. "Dinner calls. I'll be in touch when I hear something new."

With that, he slid from his chair, pulled on his jacket, and headed toward the entrance. Isa remained where he'd been sitting for the past half hour. As Tiny had predicted, the red and yellow glare from the neon sign blacked him out into a silhouette.

He'd heeded his advice, a good sign for a new operative.

Tiny cast one last look at Leila. "I'll see you later."

She nodded, then gazed at him as if expecting him to reveal a double cross. He wouldn't. Without even a nod toward Isa, he strolled into the chilly night and headed toward the Metro. As he did so, he pulled out his phone. "Jonna, hey. I'm on my way. See you soon."

Monday, November 27, 2017, 1900 hours EST, Alexandria, VA

Isa remained at his table as Tiny left.

Eyes narrowed, Leila stared at the now-empty doorway before shifting her attention to her drink. Chin on hand, she seemed to be deep in thought as she fiddled with her phone.

Since Tiny had given Isa her cell number, he could get Sadie to run down anything she might have texted or accessed.

She must have lost interest because now she sipped her drink as she stared at a college basketball game on one of the televisions.

What are you thinking, you beautiful woman? Too bad she was a suspect. Otherwise, he might have garnered up the courage to flirt with her.

She snatched up her phone. Her eyes widened. Though she had only finished half of her drink, she hopped off her chair, almost threw on her jacket, and made for the door.

Isa slid off his chair.

She passed so close to him that her jasmine scent tickled his nose.

Now behind her, he stopped the door as it nearly hit him in the face. Chilly air filled his nostrils. He pushed outside to sidewalks filled with those on their way home from work and going out for the night. His breath leaving small entrails of vapor, he followed. He dialed Sadie's number.

"This is Sadie."

"It is Isa again."

"Hi, Isa." Her cheerfulness warmed his chilly heart. "Sorry I had to scoot earlier. What can I do for you?"

Leila paused at a street corner.

Most likely, she checked for tails.

He slowed and stepped into a recessed entryway of an Italian restaurant. Pretending to examine the menu taped next to the door, he peered through the glass.

Leila focused on crossing the street.

In a low voice, he said, "I need to know of any activity that just occurred on a phone. The number is two-oh-two-five-five-five-four-three-two-six."

"When?" Sadie asked.

Leila continued on her walk.

Isa joined the crowd crossing the intersection. "Within the past fifteen minutes."

"I'll get back to you."

"Thank you." He dropped his phone into his pocket and followed his subject as she turned left and headed into the King Street Metro station.

A distant rumble filled the air. He needed to follow her. With the Metro card he always carried in hand, he shoved it through the reader. The gates opened, and he bolted onto the platform just as the lights along the edge began flashing. A train heading into the District wheezed to a stop.

He boarded a couple of people behind Leila and slouched against the divider. She seated herself mid-car and pulled out a paperback. Reading? He doubted that. Most likely, she searched for the tail she suspected was there but could not place.

He knew better than to think she absorbed herself in the plot of her novel. He pulled out his phone and opened a game of Words with Friends. Using his peripheral vision, he watched her.

When the train reached the Foggy Bottom station, people shifted toward the door.

Leila passed him and stepped onto the platform.

With his phone still in his hand as if he were focused on texts, he followed.

When her feet hit tile, she hesitated as if she had realized she had gotten off at the wrong station.

The doorway lights to the train began flashing.

She jumped back on.

Isa's heart dropped. He could not follow without revealing himself.

In the car, she had seated herself at the window and resumed reading. A tiny smile curled her lips.

He wanted to force the doors open, leap onto the train, and wipe that smirk off her face.

He could not if he wanted to keep his cover intact. After all, he did not think she had made him. She had only suspected.

The train rumbled away from the station.

He had underestimated her. What would Tiny think? He would probably say he expected that.

His mentor's words from earlier in the evening echoed in his mind. "I want to trust her. I really do. I feel like a scientist. I'm trying to do everything I can to disprove my theory that she's not trustworthy."

Her actions honed that theory. Leila was not headed home. Why else would she have tried a deflective move like she had? No, she was headed to meet someone—someone clandestine. Maybe the man from the plane? He could not be certain.

He would have to be patient because she would misstep again. Her MO was too solid to disprove that.

With a sigh, Isa shifted to wait for the train bound for Alexandria. As he did so, his phone rang.

"Isa, it's Sadie." Her chipper voice comforted him.

"What do you have?"

"The text messages. The first one says, 'We need to meet.' The second one? 'Eight o'clock. You know where.' The number of the unknown person belongs to a corporation called The Cardinal Group."

"Do we know anything else about it?"

"About as much as we know about the corporation that owns the plane."

In other words, nothing. Not the way he had wanted to end the evening.

"Do you need anything else?"

Like maybe assurance that he had not completely failed? Could she give him that?

"Isa?"

"So sorry. Uh, have a good night." With that, he turned and faced the arriving train. As he settled on a seat, he realized that all was not lost. Leila did have a job. He would pick up her trail in the morning.

8

Hashim lay flat on a weight bench at his local gym in a working class neighborhood of Beirut. Over 150 kilos' worth of iron sat secured with clips on a bar. All the more for him to bench press. He nodded at Massoud, his friend and comrade in Jihad of Light. "Ready."

With that, he grasped the bar and lifted it. He began his reps and got to five before he called for assistance. Just as his friend helped him set it on the rack, his phone began buzzing. He glanced at the number.

Tarek. Calling from their island paradise near St. Maarten. In Arabic, he said, "*Marhaba*, brother."

"I have news for you."

What? He'd overdone it on the island drinks? Hashim rested his elbows on his knees as his chest muscles groaned from their workout. "I thought you were sunning yourself while on vacation."

"No, I'm visiting our relatives in DC."

So his brother had done actual work. "What do you have?"

"Some interesting news." Tarek's voice remained hushed as if he didn't want to waken his cousins—or maybe Leila. "Alex and Jabir are on their way to Beirut. They're traveling as a honeymooning couple under the aliases Allie and Jamal Malek."

Hashim's heart pounded, and it had nothing to do with the enormous amount of weight he'd just lifted. "And you found this out how?"

"I have my ways." His brother almost purred.

Yes, he'd taken Leila as his mistress. What a treasure trove of information. Most likely, she'd been the one to reveal the aliases.

Hashim's mind began spinning. So the vixen was coming to Beirut. "Do you know where they are staying?"

"No. That was not available. I do know they are due to land in Beirut around 4:30 this afternoon your time. Think about it, brother. Where would you stay if you were coming to Beirut for a honeymoon?"

His mind flashed to many years before when he'd been oh-so-briefly married. He'd dreamed of that day with Marie—and of planning a life with her. Ashes now. Not worth any more grief. He'd already done that years before and taken the necessary revenge—at least in that matter. Now, he wanted the vixen. "I will figure it out."

"I know you will."

Over the past couple of days, he'd planned the kidnapping to perfection. It'd go off just like when he'd taken a Mossad operative years before. First, he'd have to deal with her lover. That would be easy. When the cops found his body, they'd play it off like a kidnapping gone wrong. And the vixen? Laundry carts did wonders to hide someone when they were unconscious. All it would take would be a little money to—

"You are not to take Alex. Do you understand me?" A mind reader, that brother of his.

He slammed his fist onto his thigh. "I have the opportunity!"

"I know you do. Which is why I said something." Condescension, exactly as if Tarek were correcting an errant schoolboy. It did nothing to soothe Hashim's slowly building rage. "Not until we have taken care of Shafiq. Go to their room. Plant a bug in it. Perhaps we will learn of his location. And follow them."

No problem there. He needed to complete his wall with photos of the vixen.

"Let me know what you find."

Silence filled the air. Tarek had already broken contact.

"A job?" Massoud asked as he began removing the plates and sliding them onto a nearby stand.

"Yes." For a moment, Hashim sat there. *Breathe. Slowly. In. Out.* He'd get his chance. Until then, he had to wait. He mopped his face with a towel and rose. "We go now."

On their way to his penthouse, they stopped by one of the many nameless, faceless storage facilities around the city where he kept items for times like this. He retrieved what he needed—a bug so small it was barely noticeable. It had a limited battery life, but he figured the vixen and her lover would be in Beirut for a short period of time, especially if Shafiq were indeed out of the country.

As they strolled into the penthouse, Massoud asked, "How do you plan on finding out where they are staying?"

"Easy." Hashim thumped into the second bedroom he used as a study and seated himself at a glass table that served as his desk. "There are few hotels that would accommodate spoiled Americans on their honeymoon. And those hotels do not have secure servers, at least on the local level."

He hit a few keys. Nothing on the first one. The second? The Phoenician. Five stars. All sorts of services honeymooners might enjoy. And the temporary abode for one Allie and Jamal Malek. "They're at the Phoenician, though they have not assigned a room yet."

His chair scraped across the floor, and he rose. "We go now. They are due to arrive late afternoon, and we must be finished before they do."

The Phoenician was a short walk from the penthouse. By the time they climbed the steps to the lobby, he'd mapped out their plan of action in his head.

Early afternoon meant a slow time, and only a girl probably no more than twenty years old manned the registration desk. Perfect. He'd use what had been his own downfall—flirting.

After sweeping the lobby with his gaze, he whispered to Massoud, "Hang back."

His comrade meandered to a sofa next to a potted palm.

Hashim approached the girl. "Good morning."

"Or good afternoon," she piped up with a smile.

"Is it?" He tapped his watch as if it had stopped. "So sorry. My watch seems to have failed me."

Ever so slightly, he leaned toward her and smiled.

She blushed and clasped her hands on the counter. "It can happen to the best of us. How may I help you?"

"I have good friends coming in later this afternoon or evening, and I wanted to leave a gift for them. An Allie and Jamal Malek. Do you perhaps know what room they will be in? They said they would be staying here."

"I can't give out that information."

"Oh, I know you can't." He shifted his weight and softly added, "Honestly. Jamal and I actually knew each other in secondary school. I'd only wanted to leave him a welcome home bag of the finest coffee Lebanon has to offer."

"I can take it for you." She smiled as if she'd seen through his little ruse.

Just as he'd expected. Time to turn on the charm. He chuckled as if caught in the act. "I'm lying, of course." He ran his finger across the shiny black marble as he gazed at her. She really was pretty, from the black dress she wore all the way to light brown hair worn in loose waves. And he did want to see her again, if only for mere entertainment in his penthouse. "I'm sorry. I never should have lied to you, uh…"

He paused as if searching for a name badge or plate.

A faint pink tinge appeared on her cheeks. "Chantal."

"A pretty name. French, I take it?"

"My grandmother was French. I'm named after her."

He smiled as he gazed into her eyes, which were hazel. "Well, Chantal. Did anyone ever tell you that you are beautiful?"

She giggled, and the pink deepened. "Not in a bit."

"You are. Will you hear me plead my case?"

"About your friend?"

"Yes."

She hesitated.

"Please." He let his fingers skitter across the gold-flecked marble. "Jamal and I are indeed secondary school friends. I have not seen him in perhaps fifteen years. And he is bringing his bride to his home country. When he called, I was so excited. I promised to be the first friend she met. And rather than wait until tomorrow, I want to surprise them."

"Please understand that I'm not supposed to reveal that information, Mr., uh…"

"Call me Hashim. Hashim al-Hassan."

Her eyes widened slightly. The al-Hassan name was well known in Beirut. Only Tarek ran in high social circles while Hashim remained in the shadows. She obviously tried to make the connection. Did she? He couldn't tell.

"I don't know—"

"I'm sorry to pressure you, Chantal." He brushed his fingers across her hand and sighed as if disappointed.

She drew in a sharp breath.

"I will wait." He turned away, then back again. "Forgive me for being so forward, but would you have supper with me?"

She put her hand over her heart. "Me?"

As if she couldn't believe she were receiving such an invitation.

He nodded. "Perhaps we can go dancing. Enjoy ourselves. Unless you have to be up early tomorrow. Or are already taken."

"No, no. I'm not. Taken, that is." The blush returned. "And I don't have to be up early tomorrow."

"I'll call you." He turned again as if to go.

"Hashim, wait," she softly called when he'd taken two steps. A machine clicked.

"You need my number." She scribbled it onto a notepad, ripped it off, and folded it.

"Of course. Silly me." He shook his head as if his absentminded nature were an everyday occurrence. Hardly.

She slid the folded paper across the counter. "What time?"

Hashim opened it. She'd indeed left him her number. And beside it? 1514. Undoubtedly the room number for the vixen and her lover. The best yet? A key card for the room. He blew her a kiss. "Thank you. Let's meet here at 8:30. Wear something pretty."

With that, he strolled away from the registration desk as if he were the luckiest man in the world. In some ways, he was. He now had access to the vixen's room.

Massoud joined him. "What was that?"

"Perfection. And we have our room." Hashim smiled as he glanced toward Chantal. What did the Americans say? Hook, line, and sinker? And with a date tonight. He chalked the day up to a success already.

Wednesday, November 29, 2017, 1730 hours local time, Beirut, Lebanon

Bad luck and trouble, and they'd barely been in Beirut for two hours. Jabir tuned out Alex as she chatted on the phone with the salon where Mira Rahman worked. Bad luck came when Alex had called the Lebanese National Police and discovered that Chief Inspector Mansour was dead. Murder-suicide was what the new chief inspector had told her. Then came the kicker. Stay out of it. The case was closed in the eyes of the cops.

Only because the al-Hassan family had them in their pockets.

Trouble started when the gatekeepers at Kamil International told Alex that Noor Kamil-Sultan and her husband, Fadi, were out of the office indefinitely. It took revealing their true identities to garner an appointment with Farouk Kamil, president and CEO of the company. They were already down half of their potential leads after only being in-country for an hour.

"Jabir!"

"Huh?" He glanced at Alex, who sat in the passenger seat of their Toyota Camry rental.

"I have a hair appointment."

He nearly slammed on the brakes. Had he heard right? "What? A hair appointment?"

She grinned as if completely pleased with herself. "What better way to make sure our contact is present than to make an appointment with her?"

This had passed from serious to ridiculous in seconds. "You're kidding me."

"She's a hairdresser." She fingered the ends of her hair. "Besides. I haven't had a trim since before Melanie's wedding. I've got an appointment for six."

He huffed out a sigh. "It's going to take that long to get there."

They slowed in rush hour traffic and arrived at the hair salon at six on the dot. It sat at the edge of the upscale Ras Beirut district, a residential area where the old families of Beirut lived. He found a parking spot on the street and followed Alex through the misty evening air.

His eyes watered at the bright lights. The techno music assaulted his ears. The worst? The chemicals. His nose twitched, and he sneezed.

Alex glanced back. Amusement danced in those sea green depths as if she enjoyed his discomfort.

A receptionist, who'd been doodling something on her notepad, glanced up and smiled. She said something in French. At their blank looks, she switched to English. "May I help you?"

"Allie Malek for a hair appointment with Mira Rahman," Alex announced in a flat, Midwestern accent as if she had no command whatsoever of five languages.

The receptionist called something in French, most likely announcing Mira's new appointment.

Jabir surveyed the eight hairdressers. All had clients. Which one...? His eyes roved the area.

From the station closest to the counter, a client rose and headed to the receptionist to pay.

He took one look at the hairdresser and cringed. Leather pants. Black tank top. Spiked belts, choker necklace, and bracelets. And a couple of piercings to boot. Not to mention her hair. The base color was dark, but pink and green highlights streaked it. Would they glow in black light?

He retreated to a chair of black vinyl and chrome.

With a smile, Mira approached Alex. Almost instantly, the two began chattering in English.

This would probably take longer than normal. He surveyed the magazines in front of him and got up the nerve to pick one up. Oh, boy. He stared at some of the hairstyles. One, where one side was cut close and the other side was chin length, caught his eye. Alex wasn't planning to— No, she wouldn't. Would she? Or would she do another radical hairstyle? Absurd terror gripped him. He'd always liked her with long hair, which was why she was growing it out.

His gaze shifted to his girlfriend. She now sat up straight with a towel over her head and giggled at something Mira said.

No. She'd never shear those locks in a crazy style.

Hopefully.

He tossed that edition aside and picked up another as the remaining customers left. He surveyed the Arabic cover. It seemed to be a cross between the *National Enquirer* and *People* and most definitely aimed toward the female gender of the human species. Nope. Not his style. Not at all.

The receptionist tallied up that day's receipts and stuffed a deposit bag. She smiled sweetly at him and called something in French.

Mira replied. As she turned on the hairdryer, Jabir used his phone to read articles related to Chief Inspector Mansour's death. Murder-suicide was what the police had said. Like he believed that. He found some others. No one seemed to contradict that conclusion.

At the station nearest to him, Mira removed the cape she'd placed around Alex and handed her a mirror. Alex's fingers tousled the ends of the same style she'd had. It came almost to her shoulders.

He should be doing that. Jabir's mouth went dry. Sometimes, like now, he wished there wasn't a "no romance" rule while on the job.

Mira led the way to the counter. In English, she said, "Enjoy your stay in Beirut. And make sure to get a trim every eight weeks."

Alex glanced at Jabir. She turned back to the hairdresser and in Arabic said, "Mira, I called for more than a haircut."

The hairdresser's eyebrows quirked upward at Alex's change of language. She paused from ringing up the fee. "I'm sorry?"

"We need your help to find Shafiq."

Mira froze. She reached for the phone.

Alex put her hand over the receiver to stop her. "Please."

"How do I know that?" The hairdresser yanked the receiver away and started dialing.

Jabir snagged the phone cord and unplugged it. They needed to come clean with her before she created a scene that could be seen through the windows. "We know about Samir Kamil's murder. And about your brother's disappearance. We're the good guys here."

"Why should I trust you?" The quivering in her body now reached her voice.

He cast a glance at Alex. "Because if our intentions weren't good, we wouldn't tell you our true names. Jabir al-Omri and Alex Thornton. We work for US Homeland Security. And we'd escort you to someplace deserted. Instead, you pick where we go to talk since we have windows on all sides of us here."

Mira drew in a sharp breath. "There's a cafe a couple of stores down. We can talk there." With that, she turned off the music and lights and slid a leather biker jacket with zippers over her tank top. Within minutes, she led them onto the sidewalk, which was filling with pedestrians out for supper despite the fog.

They wound up at a coffee shop where people seemed to know her because they called her by name. She'd made a good choice since it was public and she was known to the staff. No way would someone commit a kidnapping at the height of supper hour.

Jabir noted the crowded interior. "Do you want to sit outside?"

"I can do that." Mira took a steaming cup of coffee and dumped in generous amounts of cream and sugar. "So sorry. It has been a long day."

They settled under a pergola with lights strung all along the crosspieces. With a sigh, she pulled out a chair. "Why is your country involved?"

"There's a connection between the suspected murderers and us. Interpol asked for our help because of that," Alex said as she sat across from her.

Jabir came down next to Alex. "We know Shafiq is missing."

Mira shrank against her chair. "I don't know where he is. I promise." She cringed as if she expected them to drag her away.

"Promise we're not with Hashim. Or Tarek," Alex said.

Jabir studied Mira.

She hunched her shoulders, most likely more from fear than the chill. That trembling he'd noticed at the salon returned.

He rested his hand across the back of Alex's chair. "Let me take a guess. You had a close encounter with either Hashim or Tarek."

She closed her eyes. Her fingers tightened around the ceramic of her mug. "I did."

"How did Shafiq know Tarek?" Alex asked.

So much for putting Mira on one line of questioning. Jabir shot his girlfriend a dirty look.

Alex avoided his gaze. "From what we understand, Shafiq is most likely on the run because he helped Samir set up accounts at Kamil International for money laundering."

"I know." Mira sighed. "Shafiq worked part-time at Beirut Moon, Tarek's bar. He was a bartender." A brief smile crossed her face. "He said it was a good way to pick up girls. I can only assume Tarek knew where he worked during the day."

"Did you know about what he did at Kamil International?"

"No." Mira shook her head. "Not at all. Shafiq never talked about work, but he seemed happy. But then he said one day out of the blue that he was changing jobs—after a two-week trip to Paris. That was last December. He never came back."

Alex cocked her head. "Was anything different about him leading up to his job change?

Mira sipped her coffee. "He was always a bit high strung. But the night before he left on his trip, he seemed upset but wouldn't tell me why. And when he left that night, he hugged me extra hard."

"When he disappeared, didn't you worry?"

"Of course! With both of our parents dead, he's all I have now. He called me three weeks after leaving and told me not to worry, that he'd had to go into hiding for a bit and would contact me when he felt like it was safe."

"Has he contacted you since then?"

She hesitated as if debating within herself if she could trust them. "He did. In September shortly after Hurricane Irma. It wasn't a long e-mail."

Jabir straightened. "What did it say?"

"That he was safe and he would stay there to help rebuild because he now considered where he was home."

"Do you still have that e-mail?" he asked.

"I do."

"Could you send that to me as an attachment?" He recited his e-mail address.

"Of course." Mira pulled out her phone and tapped something into it.

"You said you had a run-in with one of the al-Hassan brothers." Finally, Alex steered them back to his original question.

Even in the dim light, a dull flush stained her cheeks. "I—I did shortly after Shafiq vanished."

"Do you want to share something about it?" Alex softly asked.

"I'm embarrassed."

"Why?"

"I was gullible." She put her head in her hands. "I'd seen Hashim at the club, but I didn't know who he was. Using a different name, he wooed me, convinced me to have supper with him a few times. Then he took me to his apartment."

"Where?" Jabir asked.

"A penthouse not too far from here." She didn't elaborate, out of shame or fear, he didn't know. "We…we romanced. It got intense. Then ugly." Another shudder rippled through her slender frame. "He told me who he really was. And demanded the location of Shafiq. When I told him I didn't know, he slapped me around some. He said if I spoke one word about that night or if he found out that I'd lied, he'd cut me to pieces." She closed her eyes. "I believed him."

Jabir met his girlfriend's gaze. Mira knew nothing, and if Sadie couldn't get anything from the e-mail address, then Shafiq was lost to them. His phone pinged. "I got your forward. We'll take a look at it and see if we can decipher something. In the meantime, until you hear that the al-Hassan brothers have been arrested, you might want to take a vacation."

"Shafiq promised to let me know when I could join him."

Shafiq would be radioactive until they got him into hiding.

"Then lay low. I don't want Hashim to hurt you."

"I—I understand," Mira almost whispered. "If you don't mind, I need to be getting home. It's late, and it's been a long day."

Jabir agreed. The exhaustion now permeated his bones. "Take care, Mira."

As if they'd burned her, the hairdresser jumped up and fled.

"Thoughts?" Alex asked in a low voice as they rose and headed to the car.

Once inside, Jabir tapped out a quick message to Sadie and forwarded the e-mail. "She has no clue where he is besides the Caribbean. But I'm hopeful his e-mail address will help." He stared out the window. The fog had thickened. "If she doesn't come through, we may be SOL on this one. We'll see."

☆ ☆ ☆

Wednesday, November 29, 2017, 1915 hours local time, Beirut, Lebanon

The vixen's face lay squarely within the crosshairs as Hashim adjusted the focus of his camera. Her image sharpened. The shutter clicked, then clicked again. And again. Hashim huffed out a breath and forced himself to stop before he expended all of the camera's memory on her.

Like the fog whose tendrils now curled around the van where he sat across from the coffee shop, the tentacles of darkness made their way into his heart. He stared at the meeting between the vixen, her lover, and Mira Rahman.

The camera whirred some more.

The vixen brushed away a bit of hair in the same gesture he remembered so many years before. And her lover? He had his arm around her or rested his hand on the back of her chair. They sat close together as if they'd known each other for years. Most likely, he'd taken her to bed already.

This had to stop. Now.

Tarek's admonishment echoed in his ears.

Shafiq first. Then the vixen.

"We can take her," Massoud murmured from where he sat behind the wheel.

Heart echoing in his ears, Hashim finally lowered the camera. "I know."

It would be so simple. Ease to the curb. Jump out. Pop a bullet into her lover's forehead. Then grab her, throw her in the back, and speed away. The police wouldn't try to stop them.

He set the camera down.

"It would take less than thirty seconds," Massoud added as if he'd read his friend's thoughts.

Hashim gripped the pistol he'd tucked into a shoulder holster.

"You could get what you wanted."

His jaw tightened as he stared at the vixen. Oh, she was so oblivious to him. Had she lost her touch? This would be almost too easy.

From where it lay in the tray beneath the stereo, his phone chirped. He glanced at it. A text from one of his contacts he used to research people. "Chantal checks out."

His breath eased out in a ragged gasp. As he withdrew his hand from his gun, his brother's words once more echoed in his mind. At the moment, this was so much bigger than his simple desire for revenge.

He'd wait. Bide his time and plan well. He'd done so with his dead wife's father, and his planning had paid off. He'd walked away from that particular murder—er, administration of justice—without a scratch. "No, we wait."

"You are sure?"

The vixen and her lover rose and strolled in the opposite direction of Mira, who hurried through the misty evening. "I am. Shafiq first. Then her."

"And you're sure the bug we placed will work?"

"Absolutely. In the meantime," he smiled as he remembered Chantal's blush from earlier that day, "I have a date."

9

Thursday, November 30, 2017, 0100 hours local time, Beirut, Lebanon

Jabir lay on the couch of Room 1514 of the Phoenician. Alex had crashed on the king-sized bed after relegating him to the couch—again. He didn't care since he was too wired to sleep because of all of their travel.

He fantasized for a few minutes. A honeymoon with Alex on Maui. Her warmth as he held her close. The scent of her shampoo. The way he could curl his body around hers once they married. Time to stop his dreaming.

In the cold light of his phone, he settled on reviewing articles related to Kamil International so he'd be prepared for their meeting tomorrow. His watch beeped. One o'clock. He really did need to get some shuteye. After laying his phone on his chest, he closed his eyes, but his brain still spun on his thoughts.

Maybe thinking about the way he'd propose to Alex would help him sleep. He'd do it on her birthday. Did he want to take her out? Eat in with her? Maybe she should decide. But how would he actually *do* it?

Somewhere between thinking about the issues surrounding Kamil International and ways to propose to Alex, he dozed.

His phone began chirring and vibrating.

Startled, Jabir jerked. He began sliding off the couch. Oh, boy. He grabbed at the coffee table. No dice. He finished his face plant and brought the phone to his ear. "Hello?"

"Jabir, it's Sadie."

He groaned. She was way too chipper. But then again, it was past six in the evening in northern Virginia. Supper time for her. "Hey, Sadie. You got something for me?"

"I do. Sorry to be calling so late your time, but boy, this guy must be a computer geek because he knew how to hide his tracks. It took me and Otto a bit to track down the e-mail's origination. An Internet cafe on Tortola."

"Huh? Tortola?" He scrubbed a hand through his hair. "Okay. Any address for him?"

"Nope. I'm working through what I can find on any house or lease purchases on the island within the past year—even if it's no longer there thanks to those hurricanes."

"Thanks, girl."

"You bet. I'll call you if I get a hit."

"Jabir? Why are you on the floor?" Alex stood in the doorway. She wore nothing but her underwear and cami top.

Rational thought rapidly began receding, and he seriously considered violating the no-romance rule. "You, uh, mind putting on some clothes?"

"Right." She grinned and vanished into the bathroom. A moment later, she returned, this time wearing a sweatshirt and sweatpants. From romantic to frumpy within the span of thirty seconds. "That was Sadie?"

"Yeah." He hauled himself onto the couch. "She figured out the general location of where the e-mail came from. Tortola"

She rubbed her face as if trying to wake up. "As in the British Virgin Islands?"

"The one and only. She doesn't have an address yet." He began punching numbers. "We're going to need to go there."

"Right." Alex reached over and snatched up her laptop from where she'd left it on the coffee table. "I'll check the airlines."

"You still want to meet with Farouk?" Jabir listened as the phone clicked to a secure uplink via satellite. "Tiny, Jabir here."

"You have something?" Tiny asked.

He reported the results of Alex's efforts, the meeting with Mira, and Sadie's call. "We'll head to Tortola as soon as we can. Maybe tomorrow…" Next to him, Alex tilted the screen toward him and shook her head. Every reasonably direct flight was sold out. "Okay. We'll not be leaving tomorrow. But, we have an appointment anyway with Farouk Kamil. So it looks like we'll be leaving at…"

"Three Friday morning," Alex murmured.

"Late, late tomorrow night."

"Keep me posted."

"Will do." Jabir set his phone on the table. "Any luck?"

"There's a United flight. It's got six seats left. We'll go through Frankfurt, then Houston, then San Juan."

He groaned at the number of connections.

She shrugged. "It's either that or leave earlier but fly around the world through twice as many airports, only to get there at the same time."

"No, no. You're right. Book 'em, Alex."

She giggled at his reference to Hawaii Five-O. "It's a good thing I packed enough for five days and for all types of weather. And that our company credit card has an extremely high credit limit, 'cause these tickets are going to cost us a buttload of cash."

Jabir nodded. Forty more hours of travel. With luck, they'd be able to fly home on Sunday with the knowledge that Shafiq was safely in hiding. If it meant that kind of success, he was willing to do anything.

Thursday, November 30, 2017, 0200 hours local time, Beirut, Lebanon

Recklessness. Pure recklessness.

That's what Tarek would have said about Hashim's evening.

Clad only in his pants, he slouched on the chair in front of his worktable. Pictures glowing on the laptop's screen revealed the source of his foolhardiness.

The vixen.

And in the next room slept the result.

A smile crossed his face. Chantal had met him as promised at 8:30. She'd obviously taken pains with her appearance, everything from the short, short dress she'd worn to her hair, which she'd curled. He'd dined her at one of Beirut's finer restaurants. Wined her at Tarek's nightclub. They danced, and her perfume hit his nose, which conjured up memories of ten years before when the vixen had done the same thing.

Cue the recklessness. He could already hear Tarek. "What are you? A fool?"

No. He'd made sure Chantal had no deep, dark secrets. If she had?

The smile dimmed. He would have killed her.

He thought about asking her out again. Time would tell.

He selected all of the pictures of the vixen. The printer whirred, and he gazed at them as they emerged in full, glorious color. Perfect for completing his wall at the other apartment. He slid those into a folder, lest Chantal see them.

What about the vixen and her lover? He opened an audio program and recalled the file from the bug he and Massoud had placed in their hotel room. He began listening. Standard conversation. The vixen was tired. She wanted to sleep. So did her lover. Hashim almost burst out laughing when her lover said he was sleeping on the couch—again. What had happened? A spat? Then nothing once they settled down. At least until after midnight.

Hashim sat up straighter as he listened to her lover take a phone call. He frowned as the vixen joined her lover. They talked. Tortola? What? A smile fought its way loose as he replayed the conversation. It was almost too perfect. Who cared if they wanted to talk with Farouk Kamil? The gold lay in the Caribbean, not with some old man.

He accessed the airline websites. Like the vixen had said, the most direct route leaving in a few hours was full. But when she and her lover left? They'd be on the same flight with him. Hashim booked tickets for two passengers and texted Massoud. "Get ready to fly with me on a 3:30 AM flight out of Beirut early Friday morning. Details later."

Now for a phone call. He dialed Tarek's number. In a low voice so as not to awaken Chantal, he said, "Brother, I have something."

"What is that?" His older brother almost growled those words.

"Did I wake you?"

"It… has been a long day."

Of what? Sunning himself on the beach? Hashim bit his tongue. "Our friend is in the British Virgin Islands on Tortola."

Tarek muttered something as if totally put out by the news. "You're sure?"

Hashim rolled his eyes. "Very. Our friends are going to him, leaving out early Friday morning. I'm on the same flights. This is our one chance, brother."

Silence, as if Tarek were pondering the notion. "I could send the jet."

"No need. They still don't know his exact location. You have men with you?'

"Two who are available. The rest are completing repairs on the island's buildings."

"Send them to Tortola. Most likely, the fool is tending bar since that is the only trade he knows beyond accounting. Surely there are not that many bars there. They should find him but not touch him. That is my honor."

"And after this, Alex will be yours." Silence followed.

Hashim opened a file to a picture of the vixen. His eyes traced the curve of her cheek, her strong jaw. He set his phone on the table. His cheeks flushed. His focus increased. Yes, he could feel it. She would be his. He'd plan this one to perfection, if only to get the one obstacle between him and the vixen out of the way.

Shafiq would never know what hit him.

"Hashim?" a sleepy female voice asked. Chantal, her eyes half-closed, leaned against the door frame to his study. She wore his shirt from that night and nothing else.

His fingers tingled, and he shut his laptop. "I didn't mean to wake you."

She approached him and sat on his lap. Her fingers brushed his bald scalp.

Every nerve came to alert. He touched the collar of his shirt and toyed with the top button.

"Come to bed," she softly urged.

As he kissed her, he imagined her to be the vixen.

No, that was dangerous.

For Chantal, that is.

It was only a matter of time until that dream became reality.

10

Gray, gray, go away.

That rhyme played itself over and over in Alex's head as she and Jabir stopped outside Samir's house in the hills southeast of Beirut. Her baby of a headache had grown into an angry teenager, and the overcast, misty weather did nothing to improve it. Neither did the news they'd received from Farouk Kamil earlier that day.

As she gazed at the metal pedestrian door, she asked, "Why do you think Noor waited until the first of November to go into hiding?"

Jabir swept a hand through his curls. "I don't know. I'd like to think she couldn't handle the whole process of cleaning out her brother's house and putting it on the market."

"Hah. If she'd simply taken a leave of absence, her father would have known where she'd gone."

"I can't argue that point. Do you want to come in?"

"Of course." She undid her seatbelt. She winced as the headache twinged. If only the ibuprofen she'd popped at lunch would kick in.

"That's what I thought. Let's go." He climbed from the car.

Grumbling, Alex did the same. She shouldered a soft-sided briefcase that contained the crime scene photos, nitrile gloves, and booties, plus an assortment of other doodads that might come in handy. She stopped and examined the security camera that was part of the intercom box. "Seems he took his security seriously."

"I doubt that. If he had, we probably wouldn't be here."

"True." She recalled the history Farouk had shared over cups of tea earlier that day. Kamil International had indeed been a family business with brother and sister battling for who would succeed their father as CEO. Now, with Samir dead and Noor on the run, it didn't matter anymore.

Jabir brandished the key ring Farouk had handed him. "Let's hope no Dolly Do-Gooder calls the cops on us."

"That's when we pull out that letter Farouk wrote for us." Once more, she touched the briefcase where she'd stowed Farouk's get-out-of-jail letter that gave them permission to be on the premises.

"Let's hope that's enough." He turned the key, and the door opened on soundless hinges. "Wow."

"Middle East meets the South." She shook her head at the brick two-story house with Roman columns. Rocking chairs sat on the porch. The second story had a small balcony. "Or is it vestiges of the Roman Empire?"

"Well, Samir did live in the States for a bit. Maybe that's what influenced him to buy this house." He led the way to the front. Again, the door silently opened. "At least he liked to keep things in good repair."

"And he believed in security," she added as she examined the sensors on the door and frame. "Whether or not he used it on a regular basis."

They stepped into a two-story foyer with a grand, curving staircase that reminded her of *Gone with the Wind*. In alcoves along the wall were statues that appeared to be Roman gods and goddesses. The man must have oozed money. Question was, had the money come from laundering, or had Samir honestly earned it?

She pulled a photo folder from her bag. To her right, she noted the way a set of French doors stood open. They'd been closed when the cops worked the scene. "You want to start there?"

Jabir nodded. "Might as well."

"This seems to be his study," she remarked. Her gaze shifted to a set of cabinets with the doors open. An empty safe filled the space. "I take it the cops took whatever was in the safe?"

"Probably. I imagine Inspector Mansour was very thorough and got the combination either from Noor or Farouk."

"Not that it'll help us figure out where Noor went."

"Try to stay optimistic, why don't you?"

Whatever. She scowled. It was hard to stay optimistic when their one remaining lead had literally vanished along with her family. She studied the bookcases. The titles mainly consisted of legal volumes, plus books on economics and politics, even several on American politics. Some shelves didn't have books but instead contained pottery, statues, and photos.

She didn't need a crime scene photograph to notice a gap in the frames, which were aligned symmetrically on various shelves. "We're missing a picture."

"Where?"

"There." She nodded and began opening cabinet doors. Nothing.

"I found it." Jabir stooped and pulled a frame out of the trash. He brushed glass shards from the front. It showed Samir holding up a martini glass with a young, bearded man. "Looks like someone didn't take too kindly to Samir hanging out with this guy. Do you think he's Tarek?"

"Could be." Alex nodded. "Maybe Noor did that?" A theory began jelling in her mind. "I mean, Leila's file said there's no love lost between the two, even to the point where Noor publicly accused Tarek of murdering Samir."

"I doubt the murderers took the time to do it. Do you see anything else?"

"No." Alex continued her scan of the bookcases. A gap on the lowest shelf behind the massive mahogany desk caught her eye. "I might have something."

"What?"

She sorted through the photos of the study. "There's a book here." She squinted. "I can't read the title."

"Let me see it." Jabir laid it down and turned on a desk lamp. "Do you have a magnifying glass on you?"

"Here." She pulled one from her bag and handed it to him.

He studied the crime scene photo. "It looks like the title may be *Black Beauty*. And it looks old."

"An original?"

"Maybe."

"Strange." She slid her notepad from her bag and scribbled down that bit of information.

"Let's check the rest of the house."

Alex followed him into the foyer. Using the information the police had collected via pictures as well as her memory of Leila's file, she began theorizing what happened that terrible night. "Leila said she warned Samir to get packed. He must have because the pic shows suitcases in the foyer. I wonder where those are now."

"Maybe upstairs. We'll check."

She flipped to the next one. "Something must have happened. My gut says he was freaked out because he was going into hiding after betraying his best friend. Maybe he grabbed a drink to soothe himself. They must have surprised him." She turned and studied the small wet bar tucked into an alcove. Three crystal tumblers sat on a tray underneath glass shelving containing liquor bottles. "Want to bet the shards of crystal on the floor in this picture are from the missing tumbler?"

"Agreed there." Jabir had his tablet out and flipped through what must have been a scanned copy of Leila's file. "They found marks indicative of a taser on Samir's body."

"You think they tasered him at this point?"

"Maybe they did it to subdue him. Then they stripped him."

"They left his clothing in a pile over there." She nodded toward a spot on the floor next to a console table that framed the back of the couch. "All but his underwear."

She raised her gaze and stared at the back wall, which were floor-to-ceiling windows that could be pushed aside to let in the breeze coming off the Mediterranean. "Why do you think they opened the windows? I mean, I don't think after Leila had warned him to keep everything locked up that he would have opened them simply to enjoy the breeze."

Jabir paused from his reading. He rubbed his chin. "I think you're right because I imagined that his death was quite… noisy."

Alex shuddered.

"My gut says the murderers did it as a way to point out that they'd won. The notes from the inspector say the light of the sunset was quite strange that night. Red quickly going to black with a crazy wind from Africa coming in."

"Almost like the world mourned." She shook herself and swallowed hard when she saw the subject of the next photo. Samir spread-eagled on the table. A massive slit in his belly and his intestines hanging out. Copious quantities of blood had spilled from his body onto the floor. *God, what kind of people do such things?* "Noor found him, right?"

"Yeah. She apparently fainted before calling the cops."

"I don't blame her." Her chest tightened. If it were the last thing she did, Alex would see to it that the murderers were brought to justice. "I take it Noor had a forensic cleaning company take care of things once the cops were done."

"I'm sure. Farouk said she didn't garner the courage to make it inside until the last day of October."

"The day before her family disappeared. Why?" Had something during Noor's visit spooked her to the point where the entire family fled?

"You got me."

Alex focused her attention on the butcher block, which sat to the right of a five-burner gas stove. "A knife's missing. Looks like it was the murder weapon."

Another photo showed the knife stuck in Samir's abdomen.

"The cops probably have it."

And the kitchen table and chairs? Not the colonial style that Samir seemed to favor but instead a square, contemporary style along with complementary chairs, most likely supplied by an interior designer to fill the space.

She studied a half-wall separating the breakfast nook from the family room. Wait. What was different? She shuffled through the photographs. Chief Inspector Mansour's men hadn't missed a thing. She found a photograph of the half-wall. "Hey, I may have something here."

He edged closer. "As in?"

"This half-wall. The pic shows two vases and some sort of a box. But they aren't here."

"That's because the vases seem to be shattered on the floor." He knelt and held up a shard of dark blue ceramic. "Since they're now shattered but not in the photos, it must have happened after Samir's murder."

"And if the cleaning team didn't sweep them up, then it happened after they did their work as well." Alex peered at the shards. "I don't see any box."

"Let's make a note of that."

No problem there. The mystery seemed to grow with each oddity they found. Alex drifted toward the laundry room, the point of entry for the murderers. She studied the exterior door. According to the file, they'd picked the lock because Samir had forgotten to throw the deadbolt. Could one lock have prevented his death? Maybe. They'd never know. She undid the deadbolt and studied the exterior portion. Scratches were evident on the door frame and the navy blue paint of the door.

One small mistake had cost Samir his life. What a way to go. As she rejoined Jabir, that cold anger in her gut returned. "However misguided her motives, I now understand Leila's anger."

"C'mon. Let's check the upstairs and be done with this."

That didn't take too long. They found empty drawers in the bedrooms and others with clothing thrown around helter-skelter, as if Samir had been in a panicked state while packing. His suitcases now resided in the master bedroom. Everything seemed to be there save for his laptop, wallet, and other personal items. The police must have taken those for further investigation.

She was so done with this. All she had was a theory, nothing workable.

Or maybe it was.

"I'm going to the car," she stated as they returned downstairs.

"Are you not feeling good?"

She thought back to the photo of Samir's body. "Not really. And I want to think on this."

With that, she retreated to the Camry. For a minute or so, she sat in the passenger seat, eyes closed, head against the seat as she willed her headache to subside and her mind to clear.

Slowly, as if a fog finally lifted, she came to a conclusion.

"The key rests with the box that's not there anymore," she announced when Jabir slid into the driver's seat.

"What do you mean?"

"The day before Noor and her family disappeared, I think she finally got up the courage to go inside. Something spooked her. What, I'm not sure. But somehow, those vases and the box got knocked off the half-wall. My money says the box broke as well. Maybe something was inside that scared her. I mean, her coming by the house and then leaving the country less than forty-eight hours later strikes me as strange. But what would spark that much fear?"

"Maybe a video camera?"

"Huh?" She stared at him.

"What else would do that? Until then, she was simply a grieving sister. Now she could be someone who knows what happened. A loose end Tarek and company would want to tie up."

"Hmmm." Alex closed her eyes again as she thought about that one.

"Oh, there's something else. When I was waiting for you at the hair salon, I did some research into Chief Inspector Mansour's death. He died the night of October thirty-first."

She shuddered as it all came clear. "The same day she came over to the house. You think they were going to hand whatever she found over to the inspector the next day?"

"Maybe."

Suddenly, the ramifications of what they'd discovered slammed into her. "She could be in a lot more danger than she realizes."

"Oh, I think she realized it." He cranked the engine. "Let's head to the Kamil-Sultan house and get Farouk to meet us there."

An hour later, those questions yielded no answers as Farouk unlocked the Sultan house for them. "The box was a family keepsake box given by my father to Samir when he graduated law school. Samir put it there when Noor helped him redecorate after his divorce."

Answers begot more questions. Alex mulled that bit of information over in her mind as she searched the house with Jabir. No box, only empty spaces where suitcases had been and empty hangars indicating the family had planned for an extended absence.

Finally, they turned to Farouk.

Jabir shook his hand. "Sir, thank you for your assistance. Please. If Noor calls, tell her we wish to speak with her." He handed him a card. "My number is there. We want to help her, truly help her by putting the murderer behind bars."

"Thank you," Farouk whispered. Tears pooled in his eyes. "All this old man wants is for his daughter and son-in-law to return home. Allah go with you. May you bring these killers to justice."

Oh, yeah. Alex wanted nothing more. But until they heard from Noor, they could only theorize that something had scared the family enough to vanish in the middle of the night to someplace known only to them.

11

Three people ahead of Hashim, the vixen and her lover strolled hand in hand through the wide concourse toward the baggage claim of the Terrence B. Lettsome International Airport on Tortola. He followed so closely that her scent filled his nostrils. He could kidnap them both, make her lover watch as he exacted his revenge.

His gut tightened. He could do nothing right then thanks to the swarms of British soldiers arriving to participate in the island's recovery from Hurricane Irma. Forget it. They had no time now. He'd settle his account with Shafiq in a couple of hours, then deal with her.

The vixen continued to the rental car counter while her lover stopped in baggage claim.

Good. Hashim and Massoud had no checked luggage. The better to get a few minutes' start on them. With a nod, he led Massoud into a bathroom. Once in a stall, he removed his wig of dark, messy hair and dropped it into a bag he'd bought in Houston. The toilet took care of the brown contacts he'd used to hide his aquamarine eyes. And his heavy, shapeless blazer? He left that for someone else. When he emerged, it would take a few minutes for the vixen to recognize him—if she saw him.

No worries on his end. She remained in the car rental line, which didn't seem to have moved at all. Her lover had joined her, and she gestured as if venting her frustration to him.

The men continued toward the exit. Almost as soon as Hashim stepped outside the terminal, the hot Caribbean sun began burning his bald scalp. He grimaced and slapped his bush hat onto his head. All the more reason to take care of Shafiq. Then he could get his hands on the vixen. Maybe he'd shave her head. Or he'd torture her, like he'd been tortured, until her hair fell out from the stress of it. Bald for the rest of her life. Just like him. What an image. Maybe then she'd understand the depths of the humiliation he'd suffered.

Beside him, Massoud grumbled about the humid heat and swiped at his brow.

A white Land Rover pulled up, and Ali, one of Tarek's men, hopped from the driver's seat. In Arabic, he said, "*Salaam*, my friend. It is good to see you."

Hashim opened the door to the front passenger's side. "What do you have?"

"Much." Ali took their backpacks and tossed them into the cargo compartment. "We came over yesterday and blended in while helping with the relief effort. We showed his picture to people. A young woman who worked as a waitress at a bar that got destroyed knows him."

Hashim muttered under his breath. "Do you think he is still on the island?"

Ali grinned as he started the Land Rover. "We found him quite quickly."

"Oh?" Hashim peered at him. "How is that?"

"The woman told us several restaurants pooled resources and created one main tent where people can eat at low cost. He was serving yesterday evening when we received our supper. After he quit for the night, we followed him to his house. This morning, Rami followed him from his house back to the tent. He's been there since."

"Excellent work. You came by speedboat?"

"We did." Ali nodded as he guided them out of the airport, over a bridge, and onto Tortola proper. All around them, blue tarps dotted the terrain, as did piles of rubble and debris towering beside the road. "We're docked at an abandoned house that had an empty slip." He grinned, revealing two gold teeth. "Shafiq has no idea we are here."

The fool had let his guard down. Terrible for him but not surprising at all. He thought he was safe hiding in the Caribbean.

Hashim's lips curled as the last bit of his plan slid into place. "Call Rami. Tell him that when Shafiq leaves the tent, he is to notify us, return to the speedboat, and ready it for a quick departure. Emphasize that time is of the essence."

Ali raised an eyebrow. "Why is that?"

"The Americans are here. They were on our flight and are maybe a half hour behind us."

They wound their way into hills brown from destruction until they drove along a ridge before descending a bit. Downed trees and other debris lined the sides of the road to the point where they almost towered over the Land Rover. Ali cranked the wheel to the left, and they turned onto a dirt road rutted from the most recent rainfall. They headed deeper into the morass of the hurricane's destruction. More blue tarps peeked from between trees stripped of their leaves. The houses seemed to be tens of meters apart, many with ruined furniture in the yards. Some had windows blown out and appeared abandoned. All the better for what he had planned for the former accountant. "Is there space around back?"

"There is." Ali turned into the driveway of a bungalow at the end of the road. A tarp stretched over the entire surface of the roof. They stopped behind an ancient Jeep Wrangler that had been crushed beneath a fallen tree. "We should be hidden from view."

Hashim wasted no time. He slid from the vehicle and surveyed the road. So perfectly isolated. He stepped onto the porch and tried the door. Locked. Maybe the fool hadn't lost all common sense. He checked for signs of an alarm. Nothing. "You have what I requested?"

Ali pulled a duffel from the Land Rover and placed it at his boss's feet. "A knife and pistol."

Hashim took the holstered Beretta and slid it into his belt at the small of his back. A sheathed KA-BAR knife went beside it.

It didn't take him very long to break through the flimsy lock with the picks he found in the bag. Once inside, he drew his gun and began searching the house. The better to ensure Rami's reports weren't wrong.

The sun's glow filtered through the tarp in an eerie blue light. A smell hit him, the sharp scent of bleach as if Shafiq had scrubbed every inch of the concrete floor and concrete block walls to rid the house of any mildew.

Hashim bit back a sneeze as he checked the first bedroom. Small. No bed. Just a door over two sawhorses for a desk. He wondered if the real desk were in the pile of debris he'd noted outside. The back room? Though small, it had to be Shafiq's room. An air mattress rested on the floor since the original mattress sat in a mildewed mess outside. A ceiling fan stirred up the bleach smell to the point where Hashim's eyes watered. He came to the small kitchen with its scarred Formica counter. He noted a rectangular kitchen table for four. So perfect for his plans. Not much else anymore since the couch and television also sat outside. A ceiling fan only moved the hot, stale air around.

Hashim's lips curled. Such a complete change from the luxury to which Shafiq had grown accustomed.

He glanced at his watch. If his prey didn't leave the tent, they might be tangling with the vixen and her lover. It didn't matter since it had been clear through the conversation he'd overheard that they didn't have an indication of his address. What mattered most was Tarek's directive.

Kill Shafiq

He intended to do just that.

Ali's phone rang. He snatched it up and spoke in hushed tones for a few seconds. "Rami reported that Shafiq is getting ready to leave. He should be here in ten minutes. What do we do?"

"Silence our phones." For good measure, Hashim checked his. Then he gestured for Massoud and him to gather against the wall behind the front door. In terse words, he assigned duties to everyone before pressing himself against the wall.

114

Loose Ends

Gradually, the buzz of a motorcycle became louder until it fell silent underneath the overhang at the front door.

Shafiq cleared his throat. He began humming as the lock rattled.

Hashim nodded to Massoud.

The door swung open.

Lightning fast, Massoud jabbed Shafiq in the face.

He yelped. His keys clinked to the floor as he brought his hands up and sank to his knees. Hashim slammed the door and pounced. He flattened Shafiq to the floor and clamped his hand over his mouth. Into his ear, he hissed, "Remember me, Shafiq? It's been too long."

Shafiq tried to cry out, but his hand muffled anything he said.

Hashim hauled him upright and nodded to Ali.

Ali slapped a piece of duct tape over his mouth.

Hashim shoved him into the wall beside the door. The frame of a cheap painting of a Caribbean sunset shattered as it fell to the floor. Ali and Massoud grabbed his arms.

Hashim approached. "You thought you could run away from Tarek, eh? How foolish!" He reached up and ripped away Shafiq's t-shirt. "Get him on the table. Now."

Shafiq struggled as his men threw him on his back onto the kitchen table. Hashim took some cord from the duffel. Within seconds, he lashed Shafiq's arms and legs to the table legs so that he now lay spread-eagled.

Noises emanated from his victim, something that sounded like pleading. As if he could beg himself back into Tarek's good graces. Not to be. Not when he could spill everything related to the money laundering scheme.

Hashim approached and drew the KA-BAR knife. "So sorry, Shafiq, but Tarek wanted me to take care of you."

He laughed.

More pleading. Shafiq's eyes leaked tears. Was the accountant sobbing for his life?

Hashim turned his gaze toward his chest, which heaved with panic. He raised the knife. With no hesitation, he brought it down.

Shafiq screamed.

As his cries faded to moans, Hashim turned to his men. "He's not long for this world. Let's go."

Friday, December 1, 2017, 1500 hours AST, Tortola, British Virgin Islands

In their rented Jeep Wrangler, Alex and Jabir finally wound their way along the left side of the two-lane road into Roadtown, the provincial capital of the British Virgin Islands. At three in the afternoon, the sun burned hot on her head, which only fueled her already foul mood from over forty hours on a plane. "I still can't believe it took them over an hour to figure out our rental car situation."

Jabir shrugged as if such annoyances never ruffled him. "Tortola's a mess right now and probably will be for months. Give them a break, why don't you?"

"I will—after we find Shafiq." She stared when they pulled into the parking lot of a grocery store with a tent outside. "What are we doing?"

"Getting some water. I want to figure out our plan since we haven't heard from Sadie yet."

"You want me to call her? See where she stands?"

"That'd be great." With a quick squeeze of her hand, he hopped from the four-door Wrangler and strolled to the tent, where some volunteers from a missions organization handed out bottled water to relief workers.

Alex punched Sadie's number into her phone. Someone somewhere must have repaired the cell towers because it rang through on the other end. "Sadie?"

"Alex, hey! Let's go secure."

A few clicks later, Alex asked, "Any luck on finding Shafiq's address?"

"Finally. It came through about ten minutes ago because the guy was so good at hiding his tracks." She rattled off an address and phone number, which Alex scribbled down on her notepad. "Oh, and Lars and April are on the island. Their previous case wrapped early. Once Tiny heard y'all were getting close to Shafiq, he sent them your way. Lars just texted and said they were getting their rental car."

"Good luck with that. Do they have the information?"

"Yup. They'll meet you at Shafiq's house."

"Thanks, girl. You're the best." Alex's thumbs beat against the screen as she texted April and Lars Nordegren to let them know she and Jabir would be headed to Shafiq's house. Just as she finished, Jabir rejoined her with two icy bottles of water in hand.

"I had somewhat of a hit," he said as he swung into his seat and started the engine.

"That would be?"

"There's another tent about a block down where several restaurants are serving meals to citizens and relief workers. Shafiq finished there about half an hour ago and headed home. One of the waitresses he worked with recognized this picture." He held up his phone. Shafiq's picture from Leila's file glowed on the screen.

"And I've got an address. Lars and April are also on their way."

Jabir stilled. It was almost as if she'd frozen him into a statue with her words. Thinking. Sometimes, the boy thought way too much.

"Jabir!"

He jumped. "Sorry. Just trying to figure out a plan."

"Well, can you think and drive at the same time?"

He glanced at her and shrugged before putting the Jeep into reverse and backing out of their space.

"You're so adorkable," she muttered.

"Huh?"

She rolled her eyes. "Let's go."

They wound their way through town and to the traffic circle, which directed them in a clockwise motion before they headed into the hills behind a dump truck lumbering up the steep slope with a full load of debris. They reached a ridge, then took a right and began descending a slope that had once been green with lush vegetation. Irma had stripped away those leaves and left skeleton-like trunks in its wake.

Alex's throat tightened as she caught her first glimpse of a harbor littered with overturned sailboats. "I want to help."

"With the relief effort?"

"You bet. When we had Hurricane Matthew last year, we merely got flooded, not destroyed like the BVI did."

"Maybe once we get Shafiq into hiding, we can do that for a few days."

Alex tore her gaze away from the carnage and stared at the road ahead of her. The GPS announced their turn half a mile ahead. A white Land Rover turned right from a side street and headed toward them. It picked up speed. Thanks to her position close to the center line since Jabir drove on the left side, she noted the vehicle's occupants. Three of them. All male. Strange.

Following the GPS, Jabir turned left. They bumped down a dirt road so rutted that had Alex not been strapped in with her seatbelt, she would have flown from the Jeep and landed on her bottom in a mud puddle. They finally reached the end, where a small house with a blue tarp on the roof peeked between piles of debris. She shook her head. "I guess the work crews haven't made it this far back yet."

"C'mon." Jabir stepped through the opening for the driveway.

Alex followed. She grimaced. "Ouch regarding his Jeep." She noted the Ducati motorcycle underneath the porch roof. "At least he wasn't totally out of wheels and some nice ones at that."

Jabir knocked on the door. "Mr. Rahman?"

No answer.

Jabir knocked again and called out.

Alex listened carefully. Did she hear a noise? She tried the knob. Locked. She peered closer at the door. Scratches, just like the ones she remembered from Samir's house in Beirut. "Something's happened. We need to get inside. Now."

Jabir raised his foot and kicked the door right at the knob. The frame splintered, and the door sagged inward.

Alex's stomach dropped as she stumbled into an eerie blue light created by the tarp she'd spotted on the roof.

Shafiq lay spread-eagled on the table with his belly slit open. Blood dripped in a deep red onto the floor. He moaned.

"Jabir, he's alive!" She carefully worked the tape from over his mouth. "Shafiq, we're here to help you." She pressed her fingers to the pulse at his neck. Weak. Erratic. Oh, no. "He's going to die if we don't get help and fast."

"Don't I know it." Next to her, he punched in a string of numbers into his phone and began reporting Shafiq's condition to the provincial police.

"Shafiq, stay with us. Please!" She gripped the young man's hand. "Who did this to you?"

Shafiq's lips moved. Not sound came out, but Alex read his lips easily enough.

Hashim.

A tear dripped from the corner of his eye. Then, with one last heave of his chest, his head sagged to the side.

"No!" Alex shouted. "Shafiq, no!"

She moved to start CPR.

"He's gone." Jabir gripped her arm and pulled her back. "We were too late."

Those words rang in her ears. Chest heaving, she stared at his still form. Cold anger swooshed over her. Suddenly, it clicked. A white Land Rover turning right from this very road. Three men inside, not a family or a couple.

The murderers.

"I saw them."

"What?"

"I saw them. Give me the keys. I'm going after them."

"What?" Jabir stared at her. "Alex, we need to stay here. The police are—"

"Give me the keys." She stooped and snatched up a key ring Shafiq must have dropped. "If not, I'm going on that motorcycle out there."

Muttering something about impulsiveness, Jabir reached into his pocket.

She snatched them from his hand and dashed outside with him hot on her heels.

"You know how much trouble we're in now?"

"We can catch the murderers." She jumped into the driver's seat and cranked the big engine as Jabir buckled himself into the passenger's seat. She roared down the dirt road with such ferocity that she cut her bottom lip with her teeth when they bounced over a pothole.

"What are you trying to do? Kill us?" Jabir hollered as he gripped the roll bar.

"Trying to get us some murderers." She skidded into a right turn.

A horn blared as a truck coming from the left skidded to a stop. She offered a half-hearted wave. They barreled down the two-lane highway. She gunned the engine. "Call April and Lars. Tell them we're headed to Road Town 'cause my gut says they'll head out from there."

"What if you're wrong?"

"It's crowded there right now. Easy to blend in what with so many strangers around."

Jabir sighed and dialed.

Alex focused on driving. She swung a hard left onto the ridge road. She accelerated and wove around another dump truck. Jabir gasped as they nearly had a head-on with another car. She veered into the appropriate lane.

"You mind not killing us?" he shouted above the shriek of the wind.

"Sorry!"

"You're crazy! Absolutely crazy!"

She ignored him and at least looked this time before swinging right onto the road that would take them into Road Town.

There! Up ahead, the white Land Rover slowed as it entered town. They went almost all the way around the circle before exiting at the three o'clock position. Alex slammed on the brakes and barely avoided rear-ending a dump truck headed into town. No way to go around. Not this time as a convoy led by a British army personnel carrier rumbled up the hill.

The dump truck took the nine o'clock turn. Alex spun them around to the turn where she'd seen the Land Rover go. The road led past the private marina and toward a better part of town, at least if the gates and walls meant anything.

About a quarter mile ahead of them, barricades obstructed the end.

The Land Rover slowed.

Three men, one wearing a bush hat, climbed from the vehicle and slipped through the barricade.

Alex roared up to it. Without even turning off the engine, she jumped from the seat. She dashed toward the barricade as she swiped at the blood dribbling down her chin.

"Alex, wait!" Jabir called. "April and Lars are almost here!"

She ignored him and dashed down the road. Where had they gone? All around her were homes that were in what must have been a gated community since none had walls around them. None of them seemed to be occupied. Then it hit her. A boat. They were leaving by boat.

Alex dashed between two houses. Bingo. Docks jutted into the harbor like concrete and wooden fingers. Several had boats that had sunk at their moorings. Others had empty slots. Eight houses down, a gleaming black cigarette boat with a yellow lightning bolt on it had pulled up to a dock. One man stood on the concrete. He gestured toward someone.

"Not this time," she muttered. She vaulted a low stone wall, then another as she crossed backyards dotted with what had once been luxurious swimming pools now turned green and black since they hadn't been cleaned in three months.

The men from the Land Rover had just strode into view from between two houses.

She skidded to a stop. Before she realized what she did, she bellowed, "You murderers!"

Uh, oh. Three against one. She had not thought this one out.

The one in the bush hat yanked it off. The waning sunlight hit his eyes.

Aquamarine. Hashim.

Yep, she'd so totally not thought this one out.

Backpedaling, she turned and ran.

Snuffling told her at least one followed. She risked a glance back. Crap. All three pursued her as in the distance, the cigarette boat's engine growled to life. She reached where she'd made the turnoff. Jabir should be there. She vaulted the stone wall.

Her foot caught the top.

Pain burned across her shin as it slammed against the edge.

She tumbled in a heap onto the grass.

She staggered to her feet. Something huge, like a boulder, slammed into her. Hashim flattened her onto the weedy lawn. "You're coming with me!"

He grabbed her hair.

She shrieked and kicked at him as he snagged her arm and dragged her to her feet.

She bit him on the wrist.

He yelped.

Alex staggered forward, found no footing, and plunged into a swimming pool. She thrashed through the foul water toward the other side.

"Hashim, she has rescue!" one of his cronies shouted.

Her attacker froze. Then he smiled, blew her a kiss, and mouthed something. He turned and fled.

A bullet cracked over her head.

She whipped around.

Gun pointed at her assailants, Jabir stormed toward her with Lars, April, and a small squad of soldiers behind them.

The cigarette boat's engines roared as it blazed toward open waters and safety.

Alex hauled herself onto the tile deck and crouched. She could already feel the slime on her skin.

"Alex!" Heedless of her wet state, Jabir rushed toward her and took her in his arms. Then he held her at arms' length and shook her so hard that her teeth hit her cut lip. "Don't you ever do that to me again, understand?"

Loose Ends

He released her and stormed off. Stunned, she sank to her knees and stared at the empty dock, then down at her arm. Red marks from where Hashim had gripped her had already blossomed on her skin. She shuddered as she easily deciphered his mouthed words.

"We will meet again, Alex Thornton. And soon."

She could only hope that would never come to pass.

12

"I literally had her in my hands!" Hashim stalked onto the patio of the al-Hassan villa on Angelfish Island just a few kilometers north of St. Maarten.

"And you nearly found yourself looking down the barrel of a gun, did you not?" Tarek's question came out as a statement. "You were foolish."

He smirked as he leaned against one of the portico's marble pillars. He remained a shadow in the early evening darkness.

Hashim whipped away from him and stared at the full moon. "I had a chance. I took it."

"We had opportunity," Massoud added from where he and the two others lounged at a table overlooking the Caribbean. "We would have been wrong not to take it."

"I doubt that. Jabir al-Omri was there as well, yes? And from what Rami reported," Tarek sipped his wine, "they brought a squad of soldiers, plus backup of their own." He made a tsking sound. "At least BVI and St. Maarten remain in distinct disarray. They were unable to scramble anyone to chase you." He speared his brother with his gaze. "You could have brought the entire operation I have started here crashing down onto our heads."

125

Hashim faced him as his chest tightened. What nerve! He'd risked everything to carry out Father's wish. But no, not Tarek. He lounged around wearing the finest linen and silk with calfskin moccasins on his feet. A sneer crossed his lips. "What do you know about risk?"

"Much." A smile twitched the corner of Tarek's mouth upward. "I am a businessman, after all. In many respects. And a successful one. That success does not come without risk."

Hashim kicked one of the chairs at the table. It overturned.

His comrades jumped up and scurried a couple of meters away.

Heedless of the pain blazing in his foot, Hashim pointed to the Caribbean. "I've been out there, taken out the last one who could incriminate us, risked my life to get the vix—Alex. And this is how you thank me?"

Tarek stroked his bearded chin. His eyes narrowed as if he assessed him for any loss of mental stability. His words came out art-gallery quiet. "You forget one thing, brother. Within two weeks after the hurricane hit, I deployed men here, including Rami and Ali, to begin cleanup. Did I hear you volunteering?"

Hashim ground his teeth to avoid screaming at him.

"They worked day and night here to get the buildings repaired, the power restored, and water system up and running. When I arrived, I helped, did I not, Rami?" Tarek turned his attention to the trio.

Rami's gaze swung between Tarek and Hashim as he feared punishment if he disagreed with either of them. "Uh, yes, you did."

"And where were you, Hashim? Living in your own little world. Pursuing someone, or should I say two women? Alex and her substitute. What was her name? Oh, that's right. Chantal. Poor thing. When you slept with her, did she realize you were thinking of Alex?"

With a growl, Hashim yanked out his pistol and pointed it at Tarek's head.

His brother didn't flinch, nor did the red wine in the crystal goblet he held tremble, even though the muzzle quivered mere centimeters from his head. If anything, an even deeper calm settled over him. He simpered. "I am afraid your passion is clouding your judgment."

Hashim's finger tightened on the trigger.

"Hashim, it's not worth it." Massoud gripped the gun and thumbed on the safety as he forced it downward. He pried the gun from his fingers.

Hashim pushed out a ragged breath. "This is *my job*, brother. And I will finish it."

Tarek raised an eyebrow. "I have my doubts."

Hashim lunged at him.

This time, Rami and Ali caught him and held him back.

"I see I have struck a nerve." Tarek sipped his wine. "You think you can accomplish something beyond your reach." He strolled along the edge of the pool and studied the azure water. "When I contact Father, I will tell him that while you eliminated Shafiq, you failed to get Alex, who has now undoubtedly gone underground. He can hire mercenaries to take care of her."

"I will do this, and I will finish it!"

From the other side of the pool, Tarek paused. The lights glowing from underneath the water lit his face. "You want another chance? I will provide it. You have until the end of the year to find Alex and bring her to this island. You fail? Then you have no more chances."

With that, he dumped the remainder of his wine into the water before turning on his heel and strolling into the villa's open-air great room.

Hashim stared at the water. The wine spread like blood—Tarek's blood if he got in the way of him. He shook loose and stared at the Caribbean.

He didn't see the way the full moon sparkled on the water like sequins on a lady's dress. Instead, he strained his vision as if he could see Tortola even though tens of kilometers separated the two islands. The vixen had been so close! Next time, he would not be so impulsive.

"What do you want us to do?" Massoud quietly asked from near his right shoulder.

Hashim faced him as an idea formed in his mind. "Contact Beirut. Have them send the company plane to Havana." He rattled off a list of items he wanted included on the plane. A smile curled his lips. "In the meantime, I will contact someone who can be of the most help to us."

Friday, December 1, 2017, 2030 hours AST, Tortola, British Virgin Islands

"You're mad. I don't care." Alex stomped through the open elevator doors and down the hall to her hotel room. Her shoes, still wet from her plunge into the cesspool, squished water with each step. "I did what I had to do."

Beside her, Jabir matched her stride for stride. "Without thinking of the danger." He swiped his card through the reader for the room next to hers. "What are you? Nuts?"

"No, someone who wants to bring Hashim al-Hassan to justice for what he did to Shafiq." The light on her reader turned green. She shoved the door open. "So deal."

With that, she hauled her bag inside and heaved it onto a low dresser. Though she'd changed clothes at the police station shortly after her ordeal, she hadn't had a chance to shower. Now her hip hurt thanks to the four shots the doc had given her to counteract any vileness from her plunge into the nasty water. Her lip hurt from where her teeth had cut it. So did her shin thanks to banging it on the wall. Not to mention, her head pounded to the point where her stomach had started doing flips. Only sleep would cure a headache of this magnitude.

One bed, coming up. After her shower. A good, long, hot one that would hopefully relax her and remove the scum from her skin.

When was the last time she'd gone to bed before nine? Probably when she'd been training for Unit 28.

She reached for the zipper.

The inner door to Jabir's room banged open.

Her heart nearly seized. "Jabir! Don't do that! You nearly scared me to death."

"Like you scared me this afternoon." Arms folded across his chest, he stalked into her room. "Do you realize what could have happened?"

Her gaze slid to where the red marks left by Hashim had turned to bruises. "I had to stop them."

"How? By sitting on them?" He paced, then pawed at his shirt. A low cuss word escaped him. "Figures I'd need a smoke when I'm trying to quit." His dark eyes almost sparking, he focused on her again. "In case you forgot, Hashim's got it out for you."

She yanked on the zipper and threw open the top. "I realize that. It happened. It's done. And that's that."

He grabbed her arm.

Startled, she stared. The intensity of his grip and gaze shocked her.

"No, that's not that. We left a crime scene. It took some fast talking from April and Lars, plus a call from Tiny, to keep us out of jail. As it is, the cops want us to stay on-island until they finish their investigation."

She yanked free. "I'm not doing that."

"Alex—"

"I'm not!" She glared at him, then winced as her headache kicked up another notch. "Are you done yet? Because I'm tired. I have a bad-nasty headache. My body doesn't know what time it is, and I want to go to bed. Got it?"

"No, I'm not done." He spread his feet a little and folded his arms across his chest. "I don't think you understand the extent of the danger and what could have happened."

What a patronizing tone of voice! She lifted her chin. "Do tell me, *professor*."

He glared. "What if they'd had more men?"

"They didn't."

"What if they did? What if we hadn't been so close? What if we hadn't had the Brits backing us up? What if—"

"But *it didn't happen*, okay?" She cocked her head and studied his face.

Wide eyes. Knitted brow. Flared nostrils. What on earth? Confusion washed over her. "Why are you bringing up all of these hypotheticals?"

Without a word, he grabbed her and held her close.

He trembled, and his heart pounded against his ribcage.

She pulled back and gazed into his eyes. "Jabir?"

What could she say? Yeah, she'd acted impulsively. She probably should have stayed with Jabir. It's just that Shafiq dying on them had roused a very just anger. Okay, so he had a right to his worry.

She reached up and touched his face as she struggled to soften her tone. "Look. I know what I did to Hashim ten years ago. Whatever happened to him while he was in the custody of the CIA damaged him somehow. I get that he wants revenge." She swallowed hard at the notion of what could have happened if Hashim had succeeded earlier that day. "We're headed back to the States. He'd be foolish to pursue me there. I mean, it'd be at the risk of arrest or worse. Why the overreacting?"

Jabir almost pushed her away and paced.

Startled, she stared.

As he ran his hands through his hair, he muttered something in Arabic so low that she almost missed it. "*'Anaha la taerif.*"

She doesn't know.

"Know what?" she slowly asked.

"Nothing." Too quick.

Something chilled inside of her. She swallowed hard. "Are you hiding something from me?"

He stopped.

For a long moment, he gazed at her. Conflict raged in his eyes. His Adam's apple worked. "No, I'm not."

Liar. Hurt rose inside of her.

The nausea hit full force. Was she going to throw up?

"Listen, we, uh, have our Skype session with Tiny at nine." He bent to kiss her.

She turned her face away, and his lips landed on her cheek. She grabbed her cosmetics satchel. "Quite frankly, I'm tired. I'm tired of talking with people. I'm tired of being with people. So if you don't mind, I'm going to grab a quick shower and go to bed. Skype all you want without me."

With that, she shut the bathroom door in his face.

She turned on the shower full blast to hot.

Sitting down on the toilet, Alex put her head in her hands and cried.

Loose Ends

Friday, December 1, 2017, 2130 hours AST, Tortola, British Virgin Islands

A night rain pounded on the metal roof of the recently repaired hotel where Jabir holed up with the others. Its noise nearly drowned out Tiny's voice from the Skype conversation. He bent close and turned the laptop's volume up all the way. April sat next to him with Lars on her other side.

"I'm sorry it came to this," Tiny said.

Jabir grimaced. "I know. It's almost like they were able to anticipate our arrival. I'm beginning to wonder if someone wasn't tracking us on the plane."

Tiny adjusted his reading glasses. "Could be."

April, who sat with her knees tucked to her chest and her chin on her knees, glanced at him. "How would they have even known where to look?"

Jabir considered that one for a few minutes. "The only people to whom we revealed our true identities were to the National Police, Farouk Kamil, and Mira. All of our travel arrangements were under aliases, and those are closely guarded secrets."

"They should be." Tiny nodded. "Let me do some checking on my own. In the meantime, go ahead and fly home."

"Uh, what about the cops?" Jabir asked. "They told us to stay on the island until they were finished with their investigation."

"No worries on that end, okay? I talked with the chief, and I promised you all will remain available for questioning."

"We can do that." Lars nodded. "If that's it, we'll sign off. Once the cops finished with us, I got us an 8:10 flight. That means an early day for us."

If they could only rest! Jabir nodded. "Thanks, Tiny."

"Just write up your AAR when you feel sane. Have a safe trip home."

"Will do."

The screen went blank.

April stood. She gazed at the closed door leading to Alex's room. In a low voice, she asked, "Is she okay?"

Not after she'd heard his muttering and caught him in a lie. "She's just tired. Well, we'll be ready to go at five."

He saw them to the door. Once they'd left, he threw the deadbolt and chain lock. Hashim and company might have left the island, but he wasn't going to take any chances. Too bad he didn't have a gun anymore, just a knife from his checked baggage which was hardly any defense when he got down to it.

As he pulled out his toiletries kit, his phone began chirping.

Tiny.

Oh, he really didn't want to talk. "Hey."

"Jabir, hi. So sorry to call you, but I wanted to chat with you offline about some things."

"What things?"

"I think we may have a double agent."

It had to be Leila. April and Lars were totally trustworthy and had only been read into the case a couple of days ago. "Why? Because Hashim seemed a step or two ahead of us?"

"Exactly. I think Leila is involved, like she wasn't totally above-board when she told me she wanted justice for Samir."

"Why do you say that?"

"Because when Isa was following her, she deliberately did maneuvers to shake a tail. He lost her. She also texted a number that checks out to a shell corporation. Sadie's not been able to dig up who's truly behind it."

"She had to get our aliases to know of our travel plans. But how? Those are classified."

"I've got some ideas to work on. Stand down and return to Weatherly. Get rested. That's about all we can do. Noor's about as safe as she's going to be because if her father doesn't know where she is, chances are good that Hashim and company don't either."

Jabir thought about the way he'd almost revealed the truth to Alex. That impulse to bare his heart to Tiny remained strong. He couldn't. It wasn't his secret to tell. "Um, okay. We'll, uh, talk with you later."

"Is something else wrong?"

That urge to confess increased. Alex had scared him to death. She knew he knew something, but he couldn't tell her. Now she was angry with him. He closed his eyes and tried to think pleasant thoughts. "No, no. I'm... fine."

Another lie added on to the one he'd told earlier that evening.

"I'm here for you if you need to talk."

"I know." He stared at the door leading to Alex's room. "Thanks."

Jabir lowered the phone and stared at himself in the mirror. This trip had aged him. Was that a gray hair he saw? It had to be an illusion. He shook his head, washed his face, and left his toothbrush on the counter. Before turning in for the night, he slipped into Alex's room.

The warm glow from his room penetrated the soft tropical darkness. She lay curled on her side. Her hair fanned across her pillow in a dark curtain, and her eyelashes brushed her cheek.

Oh, how he loved her! He yearned to tell her, to come completely clean with her. He couldn't because he respected her mother too much. *Lord, this is so burdening me. I don't know what to do.* He leaned over and brushed his lips across the skin of her cheek.

As if oblivious to the events of the day, she sighed and nuzzled the pillow.

"Sleep well, love." With that, he retreated to his room but left the door between them open. How long before she knew the truth?

He wanted to say it would stay safe forever, like some long-lost treasure.

But truth was a lot like Indiana Jones, who'd persisted until he got his treasure.

Truth operated in a strange way.

It would come out.

He knew what would happen.

Alex would probably come off the rails. It was more than that. The truth had the potential to destroy not only her but her family as well.

That was his greatest fear.

13

Christmas at Miami International Airport.

Bring out the pink flamingos wearing Santa hats, the bright green, fake palms with reams of Christmas lights, and saccharine-sweet Christmas music blaring over the speakers.

Bah, humbug.

Jabir smothered his yawn. He needed sleep because being rested would put him more into the Christmas spirit. So would setting things right with Alex. On the flights to San Juan and then Miami, she'd slept and hardly said a word to him.

At least she'd laid her head on his shoulder.

He glanced toward the table where she'd set up shop. She rested her chin on her hand as she stared at something on her laptop. If she were dozing, he wouldn't be surprised.

"Coffee of the Day and grande hot chocolate," the barista called.

Jabir thanked her, picked up the drinks, and headed to the table. "Hot chocolate for your thoughts."

He set hers beside the laptop and pulled his chair around until he sat beside her. With his hand on the back of her chair, he leaned forward to gaze at her screen.

His heart nearly seized.

Hashim's prison profile picture glowed on the screen before him.

She knows.

He tried for casual. "I see you're looking at our boy."

"Yeah." She hit a few keys, and the picture vanished. She rested her elbows on the table and rubbed her eyes. "Do you remember last June?"

How could he forget? "Panama?"

"Yeah. Hashim's got memorable eyes."

"If you say so."

"If you're a girl, he does. I think I saw him at Hotel Panama when we were searching for Melanie." She ran her fingers along the edge of the laptop. "Why didn't I recognize him then?"

"Probably because it was so far out of context for you. Tell me about Orb Web."

"I thought Tiny briefed you."

"He did, but I want to hear it from you."

She sipped her hot chocolate. As she did so, her eyes grew distant as if the past became more present. "It was my first major operation. I mean, in the beginning of 2007, I'd been here and there on different missions. On this one, Sadie, Monica Chapman who was my partner, and I were the team. Tiny was our handler." She chuckled. "People called us Tiny's Angels."

"A good fit."

"Tiny certainly didn't mind it. He said it was flattering. Anyway, we were gone from May until November. I missed Thanksgiving that year but was home for Christmas. We worked all across the world and acted as pretty faces to lure terror suspects. Mooch's SEAL Team Six platoon then took care of taking them down and getting them to CIA."

At the mention of one of their old friends, Jabir grinned. "It figures Mooch would be involved."

"Of course. Hashim was our last target. CIA wanted to do a bunch of take-downs at one time and didn't have the manpower—or woman power to do so many. So they asked us to help out with Hashim."

"How hard was that?"

"Very. CIA worked their assets all fall until they established a pattern for him in terms of nightclubs."

"I take it he liked pretty women and a good time."

"Oh, yeah. Once they understood his habits, we went in on the assigned day. Assets placed him at a club. I don't know why, but he took a shine to me."

"You can be a flirt when you want." He groaned when she mock-punched him on the arm. "And you're a beautiful woman."

Her cheeks flushed at the compliment. "We got cozy. I suggested we go out back, and Mooch and his pals took it from there. We left the next day." She stared at the Word document glowing on the screen. "Why do you think his hair fell out?"

Jabir slouched on his chair and folded his arms across his chest. "I don't know. Stress, probably. Ed DuBois was the man in charge of his interrogation and that of nine others. I imagine he rode them all pretty hard."

"Why do you say that?"

"Eight died. Several of Ed's buddies got put in jail for torture. They sent him back to the States."

She powered down and shut the laptop's lid. For a moment, she stared at the silvery plastic. Only an NC State sticker marred the smooth surface. So softly that he barely heard her above the low rumble of passing people, she said, "I feel like we failed."

"How so?"

"We didn't get there in time. And then there's Mira. Samir. Farouk. Even Noor."

"I know." He rubbed his thumb across her back. "I feel that way, too. And so does Tiny. But he had a good point. Shafiq was gambling with his life. Unfortunately, he lost."

"Yeah." She stared at the crowd passing nearby. "I'm sorry I got angry with you last night. I was beyond tired."

"Me, too." He leaned forward and kissed her on the cheek. "I love you, Alex Thornton."

And I want to marry you.

She giggled.

He cleared his throat. "If I remember correctly, you have a birthday in twelve days."

That got a weak laugh, just what he wanted. "Yeah, I guess I do."

"What do you want to do? Do you want to go somewhere?"

"Honestly, no. We've been almost around the world in five days."

"Not even to Raleigh?"

"Nope."

She'd complicated his proposal plans. Then came an idea. It'd dovetail perfectly into his proposal. "How about this? Let me cook for you."

She scowled.

He chuckled. "I won't stick you with cleaning up."

"You normally do."

"Not this time. Promise, cross my heart, and hope to die." He grinned. "And how's this to sweeten the deal? I'll even wash Rocky and Sabina."

"Wow. I'm not going to pass that up." She ran her fingers along the top of his hand.

His cheeks heated. Ideas began running through his head. Lots of them, especially related to proposing. "Good. Even though we're eating in, no jeans or sweatshirts. After all, it's going to be a special night."

In more ways than one.

"No worries there." She slid her computer into her backpack, grabbed her cup, and rose. "Let's go. One more flight, then home to a good bed."

He couldn't have agreed more.

Tuesday, December 5, 2017, 1330 hours EST, near Fort Belvoir, Virginia

Tuesday afternoon, Tiny tossed his jacket across the back of one of his conference table chairs. Lunch with Jonna had passed too quickly, and now his to-do list taunted him from the glowing screen on his computer. A long list, for sure.

Prepare certificates for the 2017 graduating class of Unit 28 agents.

Attend the ceremony and reception on Friday afternoon.

On the following Monday, help his younger daughter, Rachel, move out of her dorm room since she'd be going to school in Paris for the spring semester.

Go to a Bible study Christmas party on Thursday.

And let's not forget the Unit 28 party on this Friday night and the DHS party for management on Saturday night.

He flipped to his e-mail.

There, glowing like a beacon in the dark, sat an e-mail from Mitch.

Tiny, I noticed you hadn't submitted your nominees for the pilot program. Please do so by the end of January so that we can start the selection process. I strongly suggest that you notify them now so they have time to think about it.

Now he had one more thing to do thanks to his procrastination. He tapped out the e-mail to his staff, lest he forget again.

Another e-mail, this one from Alex, contained the after-action report for their adventures. He saved the document, then printed a hard copy.

With AAR in hand, he slid over to the conference table where he tended to read through information. He scanned the Executive Summary. It contained the standard litany of their journey to Beirut and Tortola. Then he arrived at the last paragraph.

There, Alex summarized Hashim's near-kidnapping of her.

He closed his eyes as he remembered Jabir describing it to him during their Skype conversation a few days before. He thumbed forward several pages until he came to her detailed description. He took notes. Hashim had obviously seized an opportunity and acted on impulse because of the way he'd changed course. After Jabir had arrived, Hashim had mouthed something to her before blowing her a kiss as if to taunt her. They'd taken off in a black cigarette boat with a yellow lightning bolt. To where remained a mystery, and no one had pursued them thanks to the current state of disarray in that area.

Then came the question of how Hashim had anticipated their moves. Tiny flipped back several pages to the beginning of the report. Alex had captured the facts. The only three times they'd revealed their names were when they'd had to in order to establish their credibility. Hashim could have had moles anywhere, but that didn't mean he could figure out where they'd stayed since all travel arrangements had been under their aliases.

He frowned and rested his chin on his hand as he thought about that one and his conversation with Jabir Friday night.

Trouble lurked.

Hashim had left by boat, meaning he could still be in the Caribbean.

Tiny also suspected someone had provided Alex's and Jabir's aliases to Leila.

First things first. He picked up the phone and dialed a number.

"Joe Warner," a man answered.

"Joe, Tiny here."

"Hey, brother!" The bass voice of the chief of the Middle East desk boomed across the line. "What's happening? How's the family?"

Tiny endured several minutes of idle chitchat since the two went back twenty-five years. Finally, he said, "I need your help on something."

"Name it."

"Hashim al-Hassan."

Joe laughed without humor. "Oh, bad news no matter how you turn it."

"Don't I know it. He's gotten mixed up in something we're working here at Unit 28. Can you tell me if he's in Beirut?"

"Not off the top of my head, but let me do some research, see if we can't find anything on this end. Anything else that can help us?"

Tiny considered that question. For sure, it was loaded, but it would possibly help out his friend. "We strongly suspect he murdered someone on Tortola Friday afternoon. Four of our agents pursued him and his men."

"Boy, this keeps getting better and better."

"They took off in a cigarette boat. Of course, that means he could have gone anywhere. That's why I'm curious as to if he's made his way back to Beirut."

"Interesting. Let me get back to you."

"Thanks." Tiny hung up and stared at his computer. One task down, another to go. He pulled up log-in records for anyone who'd accessed Unit 28 personnel files, specifically those of Alex and Jabir, over the last six months. Jabir had in June. So had Ed Dubois. No surprise on either of those. Ed had wanted to know his foe, and Tiny remembered that rainy night in Panama when he'd discussed Orb Web with Jabir. Various people at Unit 28 had accessed their personnel jackets in July when Alex and Jabir had begun the process to work as Unit 28 contractors. Then no activity until late October when a Jeremy Whitlock had accessed their files. Tiny didn't know anyone named Jeremy Whitlock.

He did now. Whitlock had Top Secret clearance but not the Top Secret Need to Know clearance needed to access all of their personnel jackets. He checked the code Whitlock had used to go one step further. Not his.

Strange.

He dug into Whitlock's personnel jacket.

He was twenty-six with three years of DHS experience. Based upon his past and present duties, he was a perennial desk jockey with his current duty station located at the United States National Central Bureau in Washington. The code he'd used to access the TSNTK portion of the personnel jackets belonged to one of his buddies.

Heat flooded Tiny's cheeks. Someone had been careless, probably written down their code somewhere. Then Whitlock snitched it. Somehow, IT hadn't put together that it had happened. He'd check into that later. Now, his mind made the connection he hadn't wanted to make. The Central Bureau was where Interpol was housed. Did Whitlock and Leila know each other? It was a big place, but he couldn't take the chance that they were strangers.

Tiny snatched up the phone and dialed his number. His voice mail stated he was out of town on business but would be back on the following Monday. He'd have to wait until Tuesday. In the meantime, he'd do as much research as possible on the young man.

Saturday, December 9, 2017, 0200 hours EST, off the coast of South Carolina

In the early hours of Saturday morning, off the coast of South Carolina, Hashim stood on the bridge of a freighter steaming from Havana to New York. A storm had passed through the area the night before and left behind an inheritance of choppy waters and cloudy skies. Even the waning moon had failed to break through and streamed an anemic gray light across the ocean. The bridge rocked to the left and the right.

Not that it bothered him. Seasickness had never been an issue.

And the cold? His parka and knit cap kept him warm. Still, the chill teased his face and hands, the only portions of his body that weren't covered.

"You're sure about this?" the captain asked. "It's cold out there. In the forties Fahrenheit, and the wind chill…"

He shook his head as if Hashim were crazy.

Who was he to question Hashim's purpose? Hadn't he paid him enough for safe transport?

The captain went on. "It'll be rough going in that Zodiac."

Who cared? Hashim didn't. Wars weren't won by waiting on the weather but by acting in it while the enemy hunkered down. "We will leave in five minutes as scheduled."

"Note that if you capsize, we can't come back for you."

"I don't expect you to do that. If we perish, we perish. We'll be ready." With that, Hashim zipped up the parka he'd requested as part of his package that had arrived in Havana. The only other item, besides oilskins and cold-weather gear, had been a Zodiac raft with a good-sized motor. They'd pick up the rest when they made landfall.

Massoud, Rami, and Ali waited for him just inside the doorway leading to the outside. He nodded, and everyone donned the oilskins to keep out the wet. "Let's go."

They pushed into the night. Almost instantly, the wind howled around them. Cold, even for Hashim. Four sailors, similarly clad in oilskins, stood near a lifeboat rack midships. Except theirs were yellow, and they smoked in a vain attempt to stay warm.

Hashim smirked as one of them scowled at his cigarette and tossed it aside as if it offered no comfort.

They climbed into a Zodiac raft that now sat on a lifeboat rack. It began lowering toward the black water. As it did so, Rami cranked the engine. It roared to life, and he pushed it back to an idle. They hit the water. Almost immediately, the freighter began speeding up. The captain had meant business when he said he hadn't wanted to be caught with his hand in the terror cookie jar.

Rami opened up the throttle, and they sped away, lest they get sucked into the wake and killed.

"Headed toward shore," Rami reported as he turned them onto a bearing of two-seven-zero.

At the bow, Hashim hunkered down and slipped his arms through two loops to keep from getting thrown out. Spray stung his cheeks like a thousand icy needles, and they quickly numbed. Rather than freeze him, it invigorated him, made him feel more alive than he'd felt in a long time. Using his handheld GPS, he traced their progress.

Almost immediately, they crossed into the territorial waters of the United States. He peered through the darkness for signs of the coastline. Nothing yet, but then again, they were still well over five kilometers out.

They dashed over a wave and slapped into another. It reminded him of when he'd been a teenager and in love with Marie. They'd gone out on her father's boat one time in rough seas. Rather than scare him, he'd sensed a freedom that he didn't feel in the city. He'd laughed then. He did now, as if the feeling unfettered his soul, if only for a bit.

The first lights of Charleston, South Carolina, began glittering on the horizon. Five kilometers or so out now. He glanced over to his right. The running lights of an ocean freighter heading toward port gleamed. A danger if some alert sailor saw them. He turned to Rami, caught his eye, and jerked his head.

Get away from the freighter. Now.

Rami banked, and they slipped a little further away as they slowed.

Thanks to their early morning arrival, most everyone slept in their beds. As they puttered beneath the Ravenel Bridge and headed up the

Cooper River, Hashim undid his oilskin and reached into his parka. He withdrew a pair of binoculars with infrared capabilities. There. Ahead of him, a light blinked that wouldn't have been visible to the naked eye. "Beacon to our eleven o'clock."

Rami adjusted direction until the blinking light was dead ahead. They pulled up to a warehouse that seemed to hover over the water. Doors that descended into the depths began creaking open. They pulled inside and drifted to a mooring. Behind them, the doors closed, sealing them in an inky darkness.

"Creeps me out," Massoud murmured in Arabic from just behind Hashim.

Hashim smirked. Not him. He peered through the dark. Where was their host?

"Welcome to my little corner of Charleston," a male voice drawled from the shadows. A click sounded through the cavernous space. Perimeter lights switched on and provided dim illumination.

Hashim surveyed their Jihad of Light contact. Cloaked in black cargo pants, a black t-shirt, and black leather jacket, Damon Braddock stood with his feet planted shoulder-width apart and his arms folded across his chest. Behind him stood four guards with rifles at relaxed ready. The man smiled at them. "Good to see you, Hashim. Come on up and get comfortable. My boys will take care of the Zodiac later."

Hashim climbed the ladder. Relief at standing on solid ground swept over him, even though it seemed to shift as his inner ear struggled to adapt to its new environment. He shed the oilskins and left them in a dripping pile on the concrete floor. "What do you have for me?"

"Oh, more than you could imagine. Come on over here and warm up." Damon led the way away from the chilly water to a corner that had a lamp hanging over a picnic table. A space heater crackled and popped nearby.

Hashim immediately undid his parka, removed his gloves, and held his hands over the heater. Ah, warmth. Even he, who tolerated cold well, enjoyed warmth on occasion.

"When I was up in Weatherly getting pics of your favorite girl, I did some extra homework that's going to make your job a whole heck of a lot easier. Here's what I got."

He hefted a black duffel bag onto the table. "Cash. Lots of it since you'll want to buy everything in cash." He added another bag and unzipped it. "Passports. Driver's licenses. Anything you'd need for a fake identity, including disguises with colored contacts to your specifications. Sidearms." He tapped a smaller box loaded with flip phones. "All of the burner phones you could ever need, all paid for. I've got a list of their numbers in the box and a copy with me, so if you call me, I'll know it's you. You need more things like guns bigger than the pistols I provided? I'll have to get those to you. But the *coup de grace*? Intel, man. The pics I took a few days ago." He pulled a folder from the bag and spread a map onto the table. He pointed to a small town in North Carolina. "There's your destination. Weatherly, North Carolina. East of I-95. And hey, it's small as small can be."

Hashim bent over the map. Off a highway called 301. And other, smaller roads. "How small?"

"Like if you show your face on a regular basis, people start getting suspicious. So don't stay there. Stay nearby, probably on the interstate because it's easy to be anonymous there. Here's a map of the town—and folks you'll want to consider." Damon placed a satellite image on the table. "Here's the town. It's truly a one-horse town. One stoplight. Alex Thornton lives here." He pointed to a building on the northwest quadrant. "Second-floor flat. The first floor is all shops. Her man? He lives here." He pointed to the southeastern quadrant. "Same deal. Second floor. I'm sure their places are alarmed. And she's got two dogs."

Hashim rubbed his chin. Dogs would be a problem. He hated them, but he couldn't kill them, lest he put the vixen on alert. "Go on."

"And don't bother trying to kidnap her from her place. The police headquarters, plus a sheriff's outpost, are located on the southwestern corner of the intersection."

At the news, Hashim growled low in his throat.

"Her mom and dad, David and Roya Thornton." More photos landed on the table. "They live out in the country, about three miles outside of town. All of her siblings but one live in Weatherly. That one's in the Army at Fort Bragg. One's a highway patrolman, so avoid him at all costs because he can sniff out folks like you as good as any police dog. Her sister, other local brother, and brother-in-law own Hoofs, Paws, and Claws, a veterinary practice west of town. They live here. Josh lives with his wife, Diana, just on the eastern edge of town. Oh, and Diana Redbird Thornton is Alex's business partner at Personal Touch Design and Construction. Their shop is south of town off the highway, about a mile south of the town limits. Those are all places you might want to consider."

"It is good information." Hashim nodded. "Anything else?"

Damon folded the map and slid it back into the folder. "Oh, yeah. One thing about small towns. Like I said, they can get suspicious of strangers. Sure, they'll welcome you for a day or two, maybe three, but I strongly suggest you disguise yourself because the first thing they'll remember are those eyes of yours, especially the single gals. And I'd drop the beards. So far as the cops? It may be a small town, but that station's occupied twenty-four-seven. Just suggestions, but if you want to get your girl, you'll heed my advice."

"I agree." Hashim nodded. "Transportation?"

"Follow me." Damon led them away from the warmth and light near the picnic table and to an old Ford Explorer. "Don't let the dings and dents fool you. The engine's pretty new. Migrant workers drive older vehicles, and you want to blend in, right?"

"We do." Hashim noted the windows. All darkened save for the windshield.

"Weatherly's about five or so hours from here. Drive the speed limit, and don't do anything to attract attention or leave a trail." Damon helped them toss their bags into the back. "Happy travels. Call me if you need me, you hear?"

Hashim nodded. They'd be in Weatherly, or at least close to it, by mid-morning. And once they got rested? The real work would begin. He climbed behind the wheel and cranked the engine. True to his contact's word, it turned over like it was new. Ahead of him, two guards opened the warehouse doors. They pulled through and headed closer to achieving his ultimate goal—his kidnapping and taming of the vixen.

14

Tuesday afternoon, a week after he'd called Jeremy Whitlock and left him a message, Tiny sat at the Cloak and Dagger, a pub near the building where Whitlock worked. He wondered if the owner were used to clandestine meetings or if he blazed new ground here. Regardless, Tiny would not let Whitlock go until he knew the truth and until the kid, who was only slightly older than his Emily, realized the enormity of his security breach.

He laid his trench coat across the bench where he sat, placed his drink order with a cheery waitress, and waited for his quarry.

Whitlock was late, a no-no in Tiny's book. Had he truly been interviewing him for a job, an egregious error. The funny thing was, Whitlock had applied to Unit 28 already. Only his lack of experience, zero knowledge of a language other than English, and lack of recruitment by Tiny or any other Unit 28 member had resulted in his application languishing with HR. At least it had provided the perfect pretext for an interview.

His phone chirped with a text. He frowned when he read the message from Joe Warner over at CIA. "No dice yet. Still working on it."

It figured he needed that information and sooner rather than later.

"Tim Daniels?"

Tiny glanced up from his phone.

A young man with messy blond hair, glasses, and fair skin rosy from the cold stood across from him.

Tiny stood and extended his hand. "That's me. Jeremy, right?"

Whitlock shook. Weak and fishy, another no-no in Tiny's book. "Yes, sir."

"Have a seat. And tell me what's good since I've never eaten here before."

"Oh, anything. But I like their burgers the best. And their beer's not too bad either. All from breweries in the Carolinas and Virginia. How'd you find out about me?"

"I heard about you." The half-truth rolled easily off Tiny's tongue. "HR had received your application, but somehow, it got overlooked."

For good reason.

The waitress approached them and took their orders. Whitlock did his drink and entire lunch from memory, meaning he'd dined here plenty of times.

"How long have you been out of school?"

"Oh, three years or so. DHS is my first job."

"And you've been with Central Bureau the entire time?"

Whitlock fidgeted with his water. "No. I'm on a yearlong rotation that ends next month. That's why I applied to Unit 28 since I know you're working on the next class."

Tiny leaned back and rested his arm across the back of the booth. "Something like that."

"I applied back in the summer. Man, I thought I had, like, no chance of getting in."

You don't.

Whitlock rushed on. "But, wow. Here we are. How cool is that?"

Inwardly, Tiny cringed. "What do you do at Central Bureau?"

"I mainly work with Interpol agents. You know, liaise with local law enforcement across the country. We've got all sorts of agencies here. DEA. ATF. The fibbies."

"I noticed you ordered your lunch from memory. You come here a lot?"

Whitlock bobbed his head. "Lots for lunch. And sometimes at night, though I mainly prefer to stick to the 'burbs after work. You know, it's closer. But sometimes they have great bands here."

"How's your workspace set up?"

If his quarry had noticed anything strange about his question, he didn't let on. Poor guy. He was way too trusting. "Oh, you know. It's open. I mean, it's like that almost everywhere now, right?"

Was he talking to a teenager? Whitlock sounded like Rachel, who was easily five years his junior.

"I suppose it's more efficient. Do you work directly with Interpol agents?"

"Yeah. I mean, they're awesome people. And from all over the world."

"Like where?"

"Hmmm." Whitlock rested his elbows on the table as he thought for a moment. "Belgium. England. France. Japan. Man, we've got one woman from the Beirut office. She's originally from Saudi, but boy, she's hot."

He had to be talking about Leila.

The waitress approached with their food, and he thanked her before asking, "Are you two friends?"

"I guess. I mean, we talk about a lot of stuff."

If he said "I mean" one more time, Tiny would slug him.

"Tell me about her."

For the first time, Whitlock's eyes clouded. "Why?"

Tiny shrugged as he opened the ketchup bottle and dropped a glob onto his plate for his french fries. "I'm curious. You light up when you talk about her."

"Well, she's nice. We've gotten to be friends."

Tiny doubted that.

"We talk a lot. And man, she's, like, hot. Honestly?" Whitlock leaned forward as if confiding in an old buddy of his. "I have a crush on her."

Tiny's years at the CIA and now at DHS had given him a sixth sense. Crushes reveal vulnerability, and he was sure Leila had picked up on that like a shark picks up the scent of blood in the water. As he delved into his hamburger, he mentally summed up what Whitlock had revealed. Young. Single. Crushing on someone way too old for him. He loved going out with his buddies at night. He liked sports. And beer.

And he was naive to the fact that sometimes, people didn't have his best interests at heart.

Finally, the waitress cleared away their dishes. Time to tighten the proverbial screws. Tiny set aside his unused utensils and pulled out his notepad. "From what you told me, you're interested in Unit 28."

"Oh, I am." Whitlock bobbed his head, and Tiny noticed the first signs of a double chin, a sure indication he probably swilled more beer than needed and got less exercise than required to be a Unit 28 agent. "I mean, I read about you. You're like a cross between Special Operations and CIA."

"Kind of. You know we're covert, right?"

"Yeah."

Tiny kept his gaze on his target. All the more to make him squirm. "And because we are, we guard our information tightly. We operate by a code. No information about our agents gets leaked. None. It's not only vital; it's the law."

"I get it."

Tiny leaned forward. "Do you?"

Whitlock blinked as if confused. "I'm sorry?"

"I'm not so sure about that."

"I—I don't understand."

"It's come to my attention that certain folks who do not have the best interests of two of my agents at heart came across some information that is Top Secret Need to Know, a clearance you don't have." He closed the gap further. "Do the names Alex Thornton and Jabir al-Omri ring a bell with you?"

Whitlock blanched. "Uh—"

"Don't lie to me because your expression says they do. Did Leila al-Kadir ask you about them?"

Almost instantly, Whitlock deflated. He hung his head. So low that he barely heard him, he said, "I'm sorry."

"What did she offer you?" Tiny asked. "Money? Sex?"

"N—no! Nothing!" Whitlock sighed. "Okay. I thought I could score a date with her. I mean this band called the Zoids was playing, and…"

He stared at the dark wood of the table.

Tiny placed a digital recorder on top. "I'm going to record this, you understand?"

"W—why?"

"In case you don't come clean with me, it'll go to prosecutors."

"But I didn't do anything wrong!"

Tiny narrowed his eyes.

"Maybe?" Sweat built along Whitlock's hairline.

"What happened?"

Whitlock flushed, creating splotches on the fair skin of his cheeks. "Um, well, she approached me in late October and asked if I could help her out with a case she was working. She knew of two agents who could help her, but she didn't know anything about them."

"You didn't question her?"

"I thought her reasons were legit. She wanted some info about them."

"How much?"

"Just what I could find without an extensive search." He began shredding his napkin. "I told her to meet me after work at the Starbucks near our office, and I'd hand over what I could find. That's when she said to keep her request on the down-low."

"Then why, if your clearance wasn't high enough, did you make a promise you know you couldn't keep?"

Whitlock rolled his eyes.

Tiny wanted to shake him for that sign of disrespect. "Jeremy, you come clean, and maybe I can keep you from prosecution. You show disrespect, I'll do nothing on your behalf. Got it?"

He huffed out a breath. "I was crushing on her, all right? I thought maybe I could ask her for a date."

"You know she's thirty-seven."

"Yeah, I do now." Whitlock slumped in his chair. How low can you go? He took off his glasses and rubbed his eyes. "I—I wanted to impress her, okay? I mean, I would have done anything to get a date because she's hot and all. I had a buddy at work who has a TSNTK clearance."

Tiny had the guy's name memorized. "Roy Crawford."

"Right. I knew he'd written his passcode on a sticky note he kept under his keyboard. So I got it when he'd left for the day. Mr. Daniels, I thought she was totally legit. She works for Interpol and all, and I know that sometimes, they don't have access to the information we do. I mean that's what we are, right? Liaisons? I thought I was just doing my job. How was I supposed to know they were Unit 28?"

Tiny considered his words. Whitlock was doing something that was almost older than time itself and had become more and more common lately—shifting blame. He set his notepad on the table. Slowly, he took off his reading glasses and polished them with his tie. Very carefully, he set them on the table. "I want you to listen to me and listen to me good. Your actions have endangered two of my agents, understand? The fact she told you to keep it on the down-low speaks to that. Any legitimate request for information would go through proper channels."

Whitlock cowered on his chair. "I've been had?"

"Not sure yet." Tiny raised his hand to catch the attention of the waitress. "Ma'am, check please." He returned his attention to Whitlock. "What I can tell you is that you've pretty much shelled any chance you had of joining Unit 28, maybe even staying with DHS or any other agency that deals with classified information." He handed over his credit card and fixed him in his gaze. "Let me give you some free advice. If someone approaches you like that again, you run away, far away, rather than fall for a teen-aged crush. You do that, and you'll go on to have a decent career, just not one with Unit 28." He scribbled the tip and his signature on the receipt. "I appreciate your time. Keep what I said in mind, all right?"

"Yeah," Whitlock whispered.

"Have a good day." Tiny pocketed the recorder, shrugged into his coat, and headed into the brisk afternoon air. His mind raced. Maybe Leila hadn't picked up on the proper protocols in terms of requesting information. No, she'd worked with Interpol for three years. She knew each country had methods for requesting classified information, one of them being that she had to have proper clearance. Clearly, she didn't because she'd approached Whitlock.

One question remained. How did she know to ask specifically for Alex's and Jabir's personnel jackets? Someone had directed her. Who? He knew one thing. He needed to look harder at her file. Then maybe he could silence the alarm bells that had begun clanging in his head.

15

"You're sure you want the tree here?" Tiny asked as he set the tree
stand on the floor of the living room that now served as an office. "Why
not in the family room where we can enjoy it?"

Rachel set a couple of ornament tubs on the floor. "Because we have
a smaller one in there."

It looked like he was losing the battle for a less crowded office this
year. He tried one more time. "Or, we can put the little one in here. We'd
have more room."

Jonna squeezed his arm. "Sweetie, we'll enjoy it just as much in here
as in the family room because both you and I know we spend a lot of
time in here. And besides, we can shut the glass French doors. We'll still
see it, but the cats won't bother it."

"Remember the way Boscoe climbed into the tree last year?" Rachel
giggled. "Then he led Critter astray. And down went the tree!"

Tiny chuckled. The year before, he'd come home and found it on the
floor in the doorway to the living room with ornaments all over the
house. It'd taken him five minutes to stop laughing. But point taken. He
tweaked her nose. "Okay. We leave it in here."

Rachel helped him bring the tree inside. He pulled the lights from their bin and began weaving them through the branches.

His cell phone rang. He snagged it from his desk, where he'd placed it along with his work laptop. "Tiny here."

"Tiny, it's Joe. Sorry it took me so long to get back to you. Seems I have some procrastinators in my group, and I got stuck in meetings all day. I'm not interrupting anything, am I?"

Tiny grinned. "Oh, just stringing lights on the tree. Want to come over and help?"

"Pass, thanks. I already paid my dues. Listen, I got some stuff for you."

Tiny stepped into the foyer and peered down the short hall to the kitchen.

Rachel laughed at something her mom said.

He pulled back into the office. "What do you have?"

"Some interesting stuff. First off, Hashim al-Hassan hasn't been seen in Beirut since the last part of November. We've got an asset in Tarek al-Hassan's office who reports Tarek is on extended leave at the family is-land in the Caribbean. No assets there, of course."

"Not surprising."

"When you said Tortola, I let Ben know. He heads our Caribbean desk, and he put his guys on alert. One of our assets saw Hashim five days ago in Havana. Or at least they reported a bald guy with Afghani features and aquamarine eyes. Not definitive, but he's pretty distinguish-able when not trying to hide. Seems he wasn't seen again."

It was the hiding part that worried Tiny. Hashim was very adept at that.

"That's all I've got, brother."

"It's enough. Joe, thanks." As Tiny returned to his work, he mulled over what his friend had told him. Hashim had resurfaced in Cuba. Why there? Was he headed to Beirut?

Wrong, wrong, wrong!

At least, that's what his gut said. And his gut, rather than his head, had kept him alive all those years ago when he'd been deep in enemy territory in Afghanistan.

Unfortunately, he had no evidence that Hashim was headed Stateside.

"Dad, it looks great," Rachel said as she brought more boxes of ornaments into the living room.

He straightened. "I'm done. You want to take over?"

"I can do that." She opened a container. "Where are you going?"

Tiny lifted his laptop from his desk. He needed a little more privacy than being within a few feet of his daughter. "I need to check something out."

At the back of the house lay the open space of the family room and kitchen. A smaller tree with twinkling white lights gleamed from a low table between two windows. Critter already sniffed around as if trying to figure out a way to climb it.

He smiled.

It was time to find out more about Leila, like who might have wanted to know about Alex and Jabir. He settled at his typical place at the white quartz island they'd installed a few years ago. Once on Unit 28's servers, he pulled up Leila's Interpol file, something Raoul Chevrot had provided a few weeks ago. Thanks to Tiny's workload, he hadn't reviewed it.

Not anymore.

Leila's father, Ali al-Kadir, had risen to a prominent position within Saudi Intelligence and encouraged her to apply to become the first female Saudi Intelligence agent. She'd excelled in her profession and married a fellow agent, only to divorce three years ago, shortly after a radical Jewish activist had murdered her father outside the Saudi embassy in Washington. Her tenure with Saudi Intelligence ended as well, which was when she moved to Interpol.

"This is interesting." Tiny snagged a notepad from the kitchen's junk drawer and began jotting things down. He added stars beside the pertinent facts.

She'd lost her daughter in a bitter custody battle, and her ex-husband returned to Saudi Arabia with the child.

During vacation to see her mom in Washington, she headed to Atlantic City by herself, went a little crazy, and ran up a huge gambling debt.

One hundred grand.

Dang.

She consulted a loan shark, who floated her the money. Now, she was paying off the debt and was halfway through that seven-year term, which was probably why she lived with her mom.

Her loan shark? A guy named Pinky.

Tiny opened his e-mail and sent a message to Sadie asking her to look into one Pinky Salazar.

A visit to this Pinky was probably in order. Just what he wanted. Pinky was probably a high school football player gone to seed, three hundred-plus pounds, and like the bullies who'd stuffed him into his locker when he was a high school sophomore.

He cringed.

Tiny turned to Leila's work history.

She was a good, solid agent in Beirut. Maybe not standout, but then again, not everyone could be. It was as she'd said. According to Raoul, she'd had an active social life and settled well into her work. At least until June. Her one blemish was Samir Kamil's murder. A miserable failure. Raoul verbally reprimanded her.

She confronted Tarek in July, which had been a colossal mistake. Raoul had again reprimanded her, this time on paper. That's when she'd accused him of being in Tarek's pocket. Raoul issued a disciplinary action.

Way to go, Leila.

Once more, he doodled on his notepad as ideas slowly formed. Leila confronted Tarek. It ended badly. She transferred to Central Bureau, and Whitlock handed over information.

Hashim and Tarek obviously wanted to tie up loose ends to avoid arrest due to the money laundering and terrorism schemes they had going. They started with Samir, then moved to Shafiq. But how had they ascertained Shafiq's location? Tiny jabbed a question mark onto the paper.

Isa reported Leila's evasive maneuvers on her way to meet someone. Who?

Then CIA noted Hashim's presence in Havana.

Enough.

With a sigh, Tiny shut the laptop. Rachel was home. Christmas was thirteen days away. He only wanted to relax.

Jonna hummed as she bustled into the room with the creche. She shifted some pictures from the mantel to some bookshelves.

He rose and peered at one. He and Jonna with David and Roya Thornton, taken by Alex when they'd gathered at the Thornton townhouse for a Christmas celebration a few years ago: 2012 if he remembered correctly. Jabir had come over that night as well. Things had been so simple back then.

They certainly weren't now.

A week and a half ago, he'd recognized worry in Jabir's voice. At first, he'd chalked it up to Alex getting a little too close to Hashim on Tortola.

Then again, David and Roya had essentially lied to him.

Maybe digging into the past would help.

He retreated through another set of French doors, these of elegant smoked glass with clear trim that led to the only place in the house that Jonna had allowed to be in disarray—their den.

What with its see-through fireplace to the family room, they spent most of their relaxing time in here. They kept keepsakes such as scrapbooks in a cabinet underneath the television, which was where he found their wedding album and the scrapbook of his single life. Jonna had helped him put it together shortly after they'd wed.

He carried it to the island and smiled as he noted the title, done in Jonna's elegant script.

Tim's Post-College Single Years.

What years they'd been. He came to the first photo. A picture of him and Roya Thornton, then known as Roya Sayad, when they'd graduated from The Farm.

What did he see in his eyes? Innocence. Excitement. Hah. If he'd only known.

Then came another one, this one taken at the FOB shortly after their arrival. He and David Thornton over a game of chess. How typical, even today. And another, this one of David and Roya. Even thirty-six years later, he saw that look in her eyes. Hope.

"Whatcha doing?" Jonna asked as she joined him. She set clear glass cubes of Christmas lights on the counter and added a spool of ribbon. She picked up the electric teakettle and filled it.

"Reliving my glory years." He smiled wryly to show he was kidding.

She turned it on. "Afghanistan?"

"Yep. I'm thinking about how young I looked back then."

She chuckled. "How old were you?"

"Twenty-four or something like that."

"I was a senior in high school."

"Thanks, sweetie."

She laughed. "Hot chocolate?"

"That'd be great."

"Rachel, hot chocolate's going to be up in a few." Jonna leaned against the counter. "Wow. Roya looks so young."

"So does Davie."

"I take it every man there lusted after Roya."

Tiny groaned. "Most did. I think Davie won her over because he didn't—at least visibly."

Rachel placed several blue, red, and green balls in a glass bowl on the island. "What are you two talking about?" She paused when she saw the scrapbook. "Hello. What's this? Dad, is that you?" She grinned. "You look so young."

He rolled his eyes. "And I look old now?"

"You look more handsome now." She kissed him on the cheek.

"Good save, kid."

"When was this?"

"1981."

Rachel's dark hair swung in a curtain that almost brushed the white quartz. "That's Mrs. Thornton, right?"

"Yup."

"And Mr. Thornton?"

"You got it."

"I can see why she fell for him. He's gorgeous."

Tiny laughed. "I'm sure you'd flatter him if you told him that. That's where he met Roya. Matter of fact, here's a picture from September 1981, right before they headed to the States to get married."

Rachel frowned as she studied another picture, this one of everyone at the compound. "Why did she decide to come if she was the only woman?"

Sharp kid, this daughter of his. He thought about what he should tell her. Why not the truth? "You took West Asian history last semester, right?"

"Yeah."

"Roya's dad was high up in the government that fell to the communists. At that point, she was a junior in college. That summer, they told her to stay in the States, that they'd see her when they escaped. Her dad promised to call. He never did."

Rachel's dark gaze met his. "Like, they died?"

Tiny nodded. Once more, he gazed at the photo. "They did."

"She was orphaned?"

"Yep."

"Wow. I… I would have never imagined."

"I think part of the reason she joined was to utilize her skills, but I also think she wanted closure enough to endure the sexism that was rampant at the FOB."

His daughter flipped a page. "Fall 1982. This is her, right? Why is she so pensive?"

His heart caught as he studied that particular photo. He'd taken it before she'd become aware of his presence. Once upon a time, he'd considered painting her from that photo. His gaze flicked to Jonna.

His wife nodded ever so slightly. She already knew about the affair from so long ago.

"Mom, I saw that." Rachel folded her arms across her chest. "Whatever it is, I'm an adult, right? So stop treating me like a kid."

"You're right." Tiny mussed her hair. "You're an adult. And you need to know this to know how God can change lives. Back then, neither were believers. Their courtship was really, really fast and in a combat zone. In the spring of 1982, when they were newlyweds, a fresh crop of recruits joined us as the compound expanded. Two women who did clerical work were part of it. Davie ran around on Roya with one."

Rachel's eyes widened. "What? But... why?"

"Marriage is hard," Jonna said. "They didn't understand it. Their work didn't help."

"Did she," Rachel ran her finger down the photo, "did she know?"

Tiny nodded. "I think the whole compound knew. In March 1983, Davie was up to his shenanigans. Roya slipped away with the pretext of gathering information from some of our *mujahedeen* contacts. Only a snowstorm caught her in the mountains." Tiny flipped the page and studied another picture of Davie and Roya from early 1983. No intimacy whatsoever in their body language.

"Did she seek shelter with them?"

"She did. Only we didn't know it. The day after she disappeared, Davie burst into the radio room where I was translating some Russian transmissions. He demanded to know where Roya was. No one had seen her leave. We searched the FOB, then started getting ready to head into the mountains. That's when one of our guys sighted a *mujahedeen* caravan waving a white flag. She'd taken shelter with Hamid al-Hassan and his men."

"Why?"

"Later, she told me she wanted information about her parents. She never said what she found." Tiny flipped the page. There, he noted the picture taken of Hamid along with Davie and him—after Roya's departure. "Davie and Roya had it out. They must have decided to fight for their marriage because within three months, Roya was expecting Alex."

"Wow." Rachel sat back. "I admire her even more now. And them. I mean, they're so happy now."

Jonna turned, filled three mugs with hot chocolate mix and added hot water. "It's a hard-won happiness. It took a bit, but they learned about sacrificial love."

Tiny sipped some of the warm brew. "Good as ever."

"Alex is thirty-four, right?" Rachel asked as she slid onto her seat beside him.

"Yep. Or she will be in a couple of days."

Wait.

That jostled something in his memory. He sought to recall the specifics of that day when Hamid had brought Roya to the compound. The caravan approached and lined up their horses in front of Roya and Hamid's horse. The two stepped through the line, and Hamid presented her to Davie. Roya stared daggers at her husband.

Then Hamid smiled at her and nodded to Davie.

An intimate smile, one reserved for lovers.

A single guy at the time, Tiny hadn't recognized it. Now, with twenty-five years of marriage under his belt, he did.

No.

Without a word, he grabbed his laptop and bolted into his art studio off the kitchen. He pulled the door almost closed.

"Is he mad at me for pushing the issue?" Rachel's voice echoed in his ears.

He didn't hear Jonna's answer as he logged in and accessed Alex's personnel jacket. He stared at a scanned copy of her birth certificate. David was listed as her father.

He noted her DNA profile. Each Unit 28 agent, including Alex, had blood drawn in the event of their untimely demise where that was the only way to identify them. The same with David since he'd been a Congressman. Tiny would compare the two.

That would surely lay his fears to rest.

Right?

He opened the program and ran it.

No match.

Period.

Maybe Roya had strayed as well. But with whom?

He opened the record for Hashim al-Hassan. The man's penetrating aquamarine eyes stared at him as if daring him to research further. They'd drawn his blood as well, this time to identify him in case he altered his appearance so much that DNA would have been the only way to identify him.

Once more, Tiny ran the comparison program. As it crunched through the data, he paced. That long-ago look between Roya and Hamid once more flashed before his eyes.

The program beeped.

A match.

Alex and Hashim shared DNA.

"Oh, God, no." His knees weakened, and he almost fell onto his lab chair in front of the drawing table.

The naked truth glowed before him.

"Tim? What is it? Rachel's all worried about the way you suddenly bolted from the room."

Jonna.

He shut the laptop's lid.

She put her hand on his shoulder.

He covered her hand with his.

"Things aren't as they seem and will never be again." He couldn't rip that image of Roya and Hamid from his mind.

"What are you talking about?"

It was times like this when he hated his job and the barriers it formed to true intimacy with his family. "I—I can't tell you."

She didn't push since it wouldn't do any good. Without another word, she kissed his hair. The door bumped softly shut behind her.

With shaking fingers, he picked up the phone and dialed a number. When his administrative assistant answered, he said, "Leah, hey. Sorry to call so late, but I need a huge favor. I need to see Director Harris tomorrow sometime. I don't care when, but I've got to see him."

16

Late the next day, Tiny slumped on a couch in the plushly appointed office at the Unit 28 facility near Fort Belvoir. He waited on Mitch Harris to get out of his last meeting of the day.

The fallout from his discovery plagued Tiny. He's slept on the couch last night because he hadn't wanted to awaken Jonna with his tossing and turning. He'd barely eaten. A headache sprang up mid-morning. He couldn't concentrate. Each time he tried to focus, his mind wandered right back to his discovery. His headache had grown throughout the day, and he didn't have a lick of aspirin in his desk.

The door to the interior office opened. Mitch stood there, his shirt sleeves rolled up, his tie loose around his neck. His graying dark hair stood up in spikes, a sure sign of one too many meetings and not enough time to do actual work.

Tiny cleared his throat and rose. His headache kicked up another notch. "Sorry it's so late."

Mitch waved his hand. "No biggie. It's not like I ever leave here before six." He cocked his head. "Are you okay?"

"Just a headache. I barely slept. Too much excitement last night with Rachel being home." No, it was the wrong kind of excitement.

"Here." Mitch tossed him a bottle of ibuprofen and pulled some water from the mini-fridge beneath a credenza that sat along one wall. He gestured to a small conference table across from his desk and slouched on a chair next to it, elbows on the arms, his fingers steepled. "Let's talk. First off, where do you stand with recruiting folks for the pilot program?"

Uh, nowhere? "I sent out the e-mail and asked for responses by the fifteenth of January."

"Good. Alex and Jabir seem to be working out well, so maybe they're like our trailblazers."

"That's why I'm here. They just got back from Beirut a few days ago via the Caribbean." Tiny outlined what had transpired during their trip. He conveniently left out his discovery about Alex's true parentage. That wasn't his to tell. It was Roya's. "I've been trying to get a handle on Hashim al-Hassan's whereabouts. Nothing there. He's disappeared. The big worry is that I discovered we had a security breach in late October."

Mitch's feet slammed onto the floor. "What? When?"

"Yesterday. Some kid named Jeremy Whitlock, who's working for DHS at Central Bureau wanted to impress his crush, Leila al-Kadir, and he breached our TSNTK clearance with a buddy's code. He accessed Alex's and Jabir's personnel jackets. Somehow, Hashim got ahold of the aliases Alex and Jabir used and found out about their travels."

Mitch frowned and drummed his fingers on the table. "Did you write up your meeting with Mr. Whitlock?"

"Yes, I did. I sent it to you after lunch. I've already contacted his supervisor, and he's dealing with it."

"Lovely. And he did it for Leila, someone you don't trust."

"I'm worried about Alex," he blurted.

Mitch raised an eyebrow. "And not Jabir?"

"Hashim has a beef with Alex, not Jabir. She needs to be pulled off the case and have at least covert protection."

"Why?"

"Do you remember our discussion about Orb Web last month?"

Mitch nodded.

"I'm very concerned that Hashim al-Hassan is either on his way to the States or already here."

"We can put out a BOLO for him."

"That's a good idea, but he's also good at disguising himself. Ten to one, he's had help, but no one's been able to pin down who JOL contacts may be."

Mitch raised an eyebrow. Then he sighed, took off his glasses, and rubbed his eyes. "Look. I know you're concerned about Alex. I do. But right now, I also know our caseload is through the roof. You mentioned yesterday at our staff meeting that you've already put your two available agents onto another case. And," he smiled, "from what you've told me about Alex, she'd refuse to back down, at least not without an explanation."

Mitch had him there. To give an explanation to Alex would break a confidence with her mother, something he was totally unwilling to do at the moment.

"So far as covert protection, you know I'd have to run this up through management. And with no solid evidence that Hashim's in the country, they'd shoot it down. They'd also bring up that a covert agent's best defense is confidentiality."

Maybe there was hope. "Which, as I mentioned, was breached. If they have her alias, what about her home address?"

"But we have no solid evidence about Hashim's whereabouts."

"No." Tiny closed his eyes and willed the ibuprofen to start working. "I'm doing some follow-up work related to the case." He winced as he thought about his impending meeting with Pinky—if he ever got a return call from him. "I hope it'll yield the name of whoever is pulling Leila's strings."

"Do we have enough evidence to bring her in?"

"No." Tiny shook his head. "She broke protocol, but she could claim innocence on our procedures. And then there's a young man who was foolish enough to fall for a crush. We have no solid evidence of nefarious motives by her. She could claim she simply wanted to meet with Alex and Jabir in Hawaii."

Using his glasses, Mitch pointed at Tiny. "You keep a close eye on this. The second you get a clear link about her motives, you arrest her. Got it?"

"No worries there." He'd do that, especially if Hashim or Tarek were involved. "In the meantime, can't Housekeeping take Alex—"

"They're stretched too thin right now. We have more than average safe houses activated."

Tiny groaned. "What about overt? Like we take Alex to one of those houses already activated?"

"After what? You tell her why you're doing it? You said so yourself. She's secure in the idea that her information is confidential and that Hashim would never risk arrest or worse by coming to the States on a vengeance mission. And the big thing? We don't have confirmation he's here. And unless you can get me solid proof that he's on the move in the States, I'm not going to run this up the chain."

Tiny wanted to argue some more. Oh, he did. But Mitch was right. Management would say they weren't going to waste precious manpower guarding someone from a threat that hung on suppositions.

If only Alex knew the truth! Then he'd have a case. Except he knew Alex would fight him tooth and nail on going into protective custody until they found Hashim. Not that it mattered since her mother refused to divulge her secret.

With a sigh, he rose. "Thanks for your time."

Mitch walked with him into the deserted hall. "Tiny, seriously. You get me solid proof, I'll be glad to send this up to the secretary. One call is all I'll need."

"Thanks," Tiny whispered. He retreated to his office one level down. It was up five feet above the field agent floor so he could keep an eye on everything with one swift glance. The floor contained thirty-two work stations, the exact amount of agents he managed. His gaze flitted to midway down where Alex had worked until the imploded mission in 2013 that had stolen her career and nearly her life.

And Jabir. Isa had taken over his work station. Right now, it was empty since he was keeping Leila under surveillance.

The shadows seemed to close around Tiny. He leaned on the railing and whispered, "Lord, what do I do?"

Go see her.

The voice was almost audible. He glanced around the floor. Only Lars and April worked on their next case in one of the far pods of four work stations. "Huh?"

Then he realized he must have heard Holy Spirit. He knew what to do. He retreated to his office. His message light glowed.

"Hey, Mr. DHS man. Got your call. You want to talk to me? You come to my turf. Seven o'clock tomorrow night at the Royal Dunes Casino. You're late? No go."

Tiny grinned as the phone clicked in his ear. He now had a plan. He dialed a number, this time to the travel agent they used. Within an hour, he had three flights arranged, one to North Carolina, one from there to Atlantic City, New Jersey, and then from New Jersey to home. If it took all he'd have, he'd convince Roya to come clean with her firstborn.

Failing that, he was trapped.

17

Cold. Temperatures in the low twenties with highs only in the forties until the weekend warm-up.

Outside Jabir's flat, the wind ripped any remaining leaves from the branches of the trees. He shuddered. What he'd give to crawl back into bed and sleep away the morning. He couldn't even though his night-owl tendencies yearned for just that.

His early-bird girlfriend wouldn't let him.

It was time to get a move on it since she was probably already at the Blue Plate Diner. He shrugged into his leather jacket and located the birthday card he'd prepared the night before. As he tucked it inside, his phone began chiming.

"Jabir, hey." It was Sadie, a morning person who probably woke up chattering just like his beloved did. "Did I catch you at a bad time?"

"Uh, sort of. I was getting ready to meet Alex for breakfast."

"Oh, that's right! Today's her birthday. I totally forgot." She drew in a breath. "I won't keep you, but I wanted to let you know we finally had a breakthrough on the photo you sent. Do you have a moment to take a look at your e-mail?"

At least now he had an excuse for being late. A break in a case always trumped procrastination. He opened his laptop and logged in. "Sure. What do you have?"

"Don't worry about reading the message right now. What's more important is what's in the attachment. Open the first one."

He did. "It's the same picture I sent you."

"Right. Because of all of the complex shadowing, I worked with our photography expert. It was hard to separate out substance from shadows. Open the second file."

Jabir stared at the red circles. "What you circled?"

"Yep. See why it's so hard? He determined that those were most likely holes someone drilled into the side."

"Why? And why didn't the cops notice?" he blurted before he could stop himself.

"The way the pattern on the box has lots of circles, and it would be hard to tell unless you knew it was there. He had a security system, right?"

"Yeah. A monitor at the gate. Pressure sensors on the doors. A glass shatter sensor. But no cameras."

"For some reason, he didn't want anyone to know he had one. It's the only reason I can think of as to why someone would damage a family heirloom."

"It sounds like I need to do some thinking on this. And I really do need to go. Alex is waiting on me."

"Call me if you need anything." He could almost hear her smile. "Tell her I said happy birthday. Let me know if I can help some more. I love puzzles."

"Will do." With that, he hustled down the steps and into the cold.

As if she expected him, Alex sat at his favorite spot. His breath caught. In her forest green sweater and tan slacks, she personified elegance. A mug of coffee steamed in front of her as she leaned on her elbows, toyed with her gold necklace, and chatted with Dolores, one of the waitresses.

"'Bout time you joined us," she drawled as he settled on the stool beside her. She hid her mild irritation well behind a smile.

"I had good reason." He demurely kissed her and ordered his breakfast without even looking. "I'm sorry about that. Here. Will this make up for it?"

He slid her card to her.

"Oooh. You're going to stretch this out all day?"

Try a lifetime.

To distract himself, he glanced around. Those-Who-Wanted-To-Save-the-World, which is what he called the group of retired men who gathered at the far end each Thursday morning, maintained their customary place. Two strangers sat between them and the corner of the L-shaped counter. What with sweatshirts, dirty jeans, and knit caps on their heads even though they were inside, they looked like day laborers. He had to admit it was a little chilly as if the heater strained to keep up with the sudden cold snap.

"Oh, Jabir, that's so sweet." Alex's face softened, and she leaned forward to kiss him. "I can tell you put a lot of thought into it."

He smiled and kissed her again. "You're well worth it."

Once more, he surveyed the room. Everyone seemed to be involved in their conversations. He leaned toward her. "Believe it or not, I had good reason for being late."

"You didn't want to get out of bed?"

"Guilty as charged. Seriously, Sadie called. She and the photography expert finally finished with the photo of that box. It had holes drilled in it."

Her eyes widened. "Like maybe there was a camera inside?"

"Seems that way. The cops probably missed it because it was such an intricate pattern."

She rested her chin on her hands. Her brow furrowed. Then she smiled as Delores delivered their food. After a brief blessing, she dug in. "What are your thoughts?"

"We found shattered vases on the floor at Samir's house. Farouk reported that Noor went over there the night before they disappeared to start cleaning out the house. For whatever reason, vases got knocked off, maybe the box as well. She might have found the camera then."

Alex closed her eyes. "I'm trying to envision the way the box was set up."

"Where it was located, it could probably film the back of the house, plus the front door."

"Meaning it probably filmed the murder."

"My thoughts exactly." Jabir took a bite of scrambled eggs. "She probably realized what she had, called the inspector, and planned to hand it over the next day."

"Only someone murdered him." Alex's eyes darkened. "That's why they fled. It may be the only copy out there. Dynamite."

"If Tarek finds out, she's a loose end. Big time."

She visibly deflated. "We're stuck."

He nodded. "I'm afraid so. Unless Noor shows her face, there's nothing we can do. We're at a dead end."

"Which stinks."

"Maybe not."

"Huh?"

He smiled as he tucked a strand of hair behind her ear. "It's not like you don't already have enough going on. Marketing calls. Working on that house you and Diana started. Your birthday."

"Don't I know it!" She giggled. "Okay. You got me. So what will we do?"

"About the case?"

"Yeah."

"Sit tight and let things happen. Maybe Noor will drop out of thin air and tell us what happened. If not?" He shrugged. "We'll have to pray that God keeps her safe."

Loose Ends

If there were ever any minute when Hashim needed absolute control over himself, now was the time.

The vixen and her lover sat not ten meters from him.

He couldn't stare, not without raising their suspicions. Sure, he and Massoud blended well with the locals, but people felt stares.

The vixen's lover kissed her.

Hashim's gut roiled. His fingers hurt from where he clutched his mug. Damon's words suddenly echoed in his head. Small town. Strangers could wear out their welcome. The easiest way to blow his cover? His actions. He forced out a breath and loosened his grip. Breaking his gaze, he focused on the black liquid of his coffee. Pretty much the way his spirit was at that moment. Blacker than tar with his target sitting impossibly beyond reach only a few meters away.

The bell above the door chimed. David Thornton bustled in. Oh, yes. The king of Weatherly. At least if Hashim's reading on the history of the town was accurate. The Thornton clan had almost singlehandedly saved it from ruin several years ago.

The man shook hands with the old men who sat to Hashim and Massoud's right. Someone in the booths called to him, and he shifted his attention toward them before turning to his daughter. He hugged her and shook Jabir's hand.

The twins, Marlie and Josh, joined them. Then came Jake. Such a close family. Hashim wiped suddenly sweaty palms on his denim-clad legs. He glanced at Massoud, who shook his head ever so slightly. If anyone would blow their cover, Hashim would. He had to bury his angst. Now. Or the highway patrolman would notice.

Where was the queen? Roya Thornton hadn't shown herself yet.

One by one, the Thornton clan left. Like a flock of chickens, the old men followed, clucking questions at the elder Thornton.

The volume inside decreased enough for Hashim to pick up the conversation at the end of the counter.

The vixen asked, "What are your plans today?"

Her lover drained his mug and pulled out his wallet. "Errands since it's too cold to paint. And you?"

"A couple of quality calls. Then I'm meeting Mom for lunch before linking up with Marlie, Lee, and Diana at the spa in Smithfield. Don't worry. I'll be ready at seven."

Her lover tossed some bills onto the counter. "You do that, young lady."

"Oh, I will." She kissed him long and slow.

Hashim ripped his gaze away and focused on the Formica counter. He traced the swirly pattern with his gaze.

Oh, he remembered that kiss from ten years ago.

The last pleasant thing before hell began.

Her lover said, "To keep you until tonight. I love you."

"I love you, too."

The vixen's perfume hit Hashim's nose as she brushed by close enough that the air swirled around him.

Slowly, carefully, he released a shuddering breath. He needed air. Fast. The bathroom offered the safest retreat, and he stayed in a stall until his pulse and thoughts returned to normal.

During his absence, her lover had left.

Hashim stepped into the cold morning, and Massoud followed. David Thornton and the gaggle of old men had finally departed. Across the street, the vixen climbed into her yellow four-door Jeep Wrangler, backed out of her space, and rumbled southward.

Hashim strolled toward a van they'd bought for cash from a used car lot. Today, the decals indicated they were a plumbing company. Yesterday and with a different disguise for everyone, they'd been working for the local cable company. He opened the sliding door and pulled a duffel toward him. Beneath some plumbing tools were the real tools of his trade.

"Let's go." He led Massoud toward the outer door that would lead to Alex's flat above a shop called Spin a Yarn. He tried the knob. Locked but no worries. He'd snitched her neighbor's keys one day at lunch and made a copy of her apartment key, which would also allow them access through the outer door.

Hashim surveyed the narrow hall. Deserted as he expected since the town manager, who stayed in the apartment across from the vixen, was at work. They climbed the stairs. If anyone stopped them, they were plumbers headed to her neighbor's apartment to fix a leaking pipe.

Hashim peered through a narrow window next to the door. There. Her alarm pad was located on the opposite wall. Red.

She'd turned on her alarm.

"How do we do this?" Massoud softly asked.

"The joy of everything being wireless, including her alarm system. All we do is find her router's guest account." Hashim pulled out a small tablet that had come in the duffel Damon had provided. "We work our way through a back door."

He pulled up a program, connected to her guest account, and linked up using the password, something the program broke easily. From there, it wormed its way into the router's heart, which revealed all computers, printers, and other devices attached.

"I see her alarm system." He selected that device. Once more, his program tore apart the pass code for the alarm. The light on the panel changed from red to green. He stuffed the tablet into his duffel and pulled out his lock picks.

Within two minutes, he stepped into the safe haven of the vixen.

Her scent.

Even in the foyer, he smelled it.

Toenails clicking on hardwood brought him back to reality. A large dog approached and whined.

Massoud crouched. "Here, boy. Rocky, right?"

He held out his hand and softly clucked.

Hashim cringed as the dog came closer. How he hated them! His only escape was into the hall, and he wasn't going to do it, not when he'd just gained entrance into the vixen's sanctuary.

Massoud pulled a plastic bag from his jacket. Inside was a hot dog doused in sedative, enough to knock out a dog for quite some time. He held it out.

Rocky's tail wagged. He took the hot dog from his hand and wandered into a dining area.

Massoud would make sure he ate it.

Growling distracted Hashim. The vixen's other dog, a smaller black and white dog, glared at them from a crate next to the bedroom door. Her hackles had raised. She turned in circles, jumped up, and growled some more. She knew who they were.

Intruders.

Hashim smirked. "So sorry. We'll not let you out."

He drew in a deep breath through his nose.

The vixen's scent grew stronger. He ran his hand along the smooth granite of the kitchen island. She liked luxury, everything from the finishes in the room to the plush leather furniture. Suddenly, his mission's purpose faded as he penetrated further into her safety zone.

The dog snarled and slammed into the metal of the crate.

He laughed and entered the heart of her flat, her bedroom.

His pulse quickened. That flush intensified as he peered at the comforter with its pillows all neatly aligned. He closed his eyes as he remembered that kiss ten years before. He opened them. The vixen lay on the bed in nothing but a negligee. She pursed her lips and beckoned for him to join her. He scrubbed his hands across his face. She'd vanished.

Foolishness. He needed to focus.

That lasted until he stepped into the bathroom. Her scent nearly drove him mad. His fantasy turned lurid.

"Hashim," Massoud called.

He jumped. It receded.

Suddenly, he realized the way he trembled. He had to get out of there.

He joined his comrade, who asked, "Where should we place the bugs?"

"Place one behind her dresser." He stared at the bedroom.

Loose Ends

The smaller dog glared at him. Her lips curled, exposing a magnificent set of fangs.

"I'll take care of the other rooms." It was best that he not go to her bedroom again.

While Massoud went to carry out his orders, he studied the great room. It had a high ceiling. Beams crossed and offered a place for the ceiling fan to hang down. A good spot. He located a step ladder in a utility closet and placed the bug on top of the beam. It would catch all sound in that room.

As he returned the ladder to its closet, he smiled.

The larger dog now slept on a rug in front of the fireplace. He'd do so until long after they left.

In the second bedroom, which seemed to be the vixen's study, he placed a bug behind her desk. Now he'd hear anything she said, every sigh while she slept. Perfect since it would enable him to make his plans.

Massoud joined him, and they wasted no time in retreating.

"What do we do now?" he asked as they climbed into the van and headed toward the interstate. Once they passed Hoofs, Paws, and Claws, Weatherly receded behind them.

"We wait," Hashim said as he sped up. Indeed, they would.

As he had ever since his arrival in the States, he considered what he'd do with the vixen once she was in his clutches.

Really, it was simple.

She'd experience exactly what he had.

No sleep thanks to loud music and bright lights.

The denial of basic dignities like a bathroom.

Being hosed off with cold water.

And then?

He'd shave her. Completely. Let her feel the humiliation he'd felt when Ed DuBois had done the same to him.

His final act would be to have his way with her. Who cared if she were related to him? She'd tried to seduce him long before he knew who she really was.

Once he finished with her, he'd kill her.

Who cared if Father wanted that honor?
He certainly didn't.
Not anymore.

18

"Hey, man! Good to see you!" Jabir grinned as Rex Martin, his best friend from his University of Arizona days, strolled into the lobby of the gym in Raleigh where Rex worked out.

"Aren't you a sight for sore eyes," his best friend drawled in a South Carolina accent. He shook his hand and drew Jabir into a quick hug with three slaps on the back.

"I thought maybe you'd wimped out on me." Jabir scribbled his name on the sign-in sheet and presented his license.

"Nope. Just running behind. You ready to play? My buds said they'd be here at noon, so I figured we'd have some time for a game of Horse."

"Works for me."

They changed in the locker room.

"C'mon. This way." Rex led the way toward a basketball court. Once inside, he dropped his gym bag onto the floor and pulled out a basketball. "You said Alex's birthday is today."

"It is." Jabir accepted a pass and dribbled down the court. "Thirty-four. Not that she looks it."

Rex chuckled. "Not by a long shot. You start since you're the guest."

Jabir did an easy layup.

"What's on tap for her day?"

"Uh, fancy you should ask." Jabir flushed and watched his friend make the same shot.

Rex took the ball a few feet away for a simple jumper.

"I'm, um, well, I'm, uh…"

"Out with it."

Jabir dribbled the ball a few times. Oh, boy. His hands shook as he lifted it. It bounced off the rim.

"That's an H for you, young man." Rex took the ball and headed for the free throw line.

Jabir joined him. His hands had steadied, yielding nothing but net. "I'm proposing tonight."

"Wow. Hey, that's great, man!" Rex rushed his next shot, missed the basket, and shook his friend's hand. "Seriously. I adore Alex."

"Thanks." Jabir swallowed hard. The lump in his throat surprised him. Why should he be? Especially when, just one short year ago, he thought he'd lost her? "I'm, well, obviously speechless." He chuckled. "But also extremely grateful for God. Who knew she and I would see each other again? She's my world."

Rex grinned. "When you called me and told me you'd met her again, I prayed for this day. Okay, brother, shoot."

The game continued for a few more minutes, and both earned an O. The secret chaining him to silence rumbled around inside of Jabir. He so badly needed to unburden himself! And who better than the friend he considered to be his unofficial pastor? "Uh, Rex?"

"Yeah?" His buddy had moved to three-point land and lobbed one toward the basket. Swish. Tough shot.

"I have to ask this. As an associate pastor, do you counsel people?"

"Like pre-marital counseling?"

Jabir took the ball and dribbled to his location. "Yeah. That, and other stuff."

"All the time. That's why I got my Master's Degree and why the church here hired me. You want to shoot?"

Jabir took a shot that got him an R. "I need your help on something."

"Like?"

"Like when it's critical to reveal a secret." He went on and outlined everything that had transpired in June, from his discovery about Alex's true parentage to Roya's threat to keep him silent about it. Or as much as he could since some of it was classified.

By that point, they'd ceased their game. Rex stood near the bench where he'd set his gym bag. "Sorry. This takes too much concentration to talk about this and play ball at the same time."

Jabir seated himself and took a swig of water from his bottle. "Any wisdom?"

"I'm not sure."

Jabir frowned.

"Seriously. I mean, think about it. There's I guess what you could call levels of secrets. White lies are secrets, right? Like when I held a surprise birthday party for Angie. I had to keep it a secret from her so I fibbed a bit as to why we were headed where we were. Of course, you know all about occupational secrets."

Jabir winced. "Too much. But when does it tip into being wrong? At breakfast, I thought about maybe just leaving it alone. I mean, she's happy the way she is. David's her dad, the man who raised her."

"You're right."

"So I should leave it alone?"

"You should."

Jabir rolled his eyes. "But that leaves me exactly where I started. With a burden, a huge one that I'm scared will drive a permanent wedge between Alex and me."

"Still, it's Roya's to tell, not yours." Rex glanced up as four African-American men strolled into the cavernous room.

The biggest, burliest of them grinned. "Hey, man."

"Ty, hey." Rex stood and bumped fists with him. "Ty Jones, meet Jabir al-Omri. Jabir, Ty's one of the pastors in the area. We connected through an organization for pastors called Raleigh Area Concerts of Prayer."

"Good to meet you." Jabir offered what he was sure was a sick smile.

It must have been because Ty studied him for a second. "You guys need a moment?"

Rex nodded. "Give us five?"

"Sure. That'll give us time to warm up."

"His buds are from his church." Rex resumed his seat. In a low voice, he continued, "You've read Ecclesiastes, right"

Jabir nodded.

"In the third chapter, it talks about seasons. And one of those verses states that there's a time to keep silent and a time to speak."

Jabir raked his hands through his hair. "I'm not sure which time I'm in."

"At this point, it's Roya's news. And from what you've told me, she sounds like she's fighting it tooth and nail. But she's missing one big point. A huge one."

Jabir ran his towel through his fingers. "And that is?"

"God is Truth. No way around it. And because of truth with a capital T, truth with a little T always has a habit of clawing its way out of the deepest, darkest dungeons where we try to stuff it. She can deny it all she wants, but it will come out. And not from you, I know. Or from David Thornton, it seems. But it could from others."

"What do I do?" Jabir asked.

"You stay the course. Love Alex sacrificially like you are. Treasure her. Then when—note that I said when and not if—it comes out, you be there for her. Because you know she's going to need your support. Got it?"

Jabir nodded.

Rex grinned and squeezed his shoulder. "You'll get through this, and I'll be praying for you. Remember that there's a reason why Christ said to take one day at a time."

Now more than ever, Jabir understood that. As he joined Rex and the guys squared off three-on-three, he vowed to do that. Take one day at a time. And hope that when the dust settled, Alex was still speaking to him.

Loose Ends

✫ ✫ ✫

To the east of Weatherly, Tiny stopped his rental car next to the back deck of the Thornton house. Whether his stomach burned from stress, the coffee he'd drunk, or a combination of both, he didn't know. By the time this case ended, he'd probably have ulcers. Maybe he should switch to tea like Jonna had recommended.

Finally, he slid from the car and approached the back door. A shadow crossed in front of the light from the breakfast nook windows. Roya. At least she was home. And Davie wasn't since he'd recognized his car parked in front of his office on Main Street. That was good for his purposes.

Almost timidly, he knocked on the door frame.

Roya approached. She smiled. "Tiny! What a surprise. And so good to see you. Do come in."

"Thanks." He unzipped his leather jacket. "It's cold out there."

"You can lay that across the back of the couch." Roya crossed the Oriental rugs on the hardwood of the den and headed into the kitchen that opened onto the den. "I've had the fire going all morning in our wood stove."

He rubbed his arms and followed her. "This feels cozy."

Roya studied him and ran her hands down her dark ponytail. "What brings you here? Are you in Weatherly to see Alex and Jabir? For sure you still have that case going on."

"Nope." He cleared his throat, and he wiped suddenly sweaty hands on his khakis.

"No?" Her eyes twinkled, and she put her hand on her hip in a playful gesture he remembered from so many years before. "Then Davie, maybe? He told me he was handling your familial matters."

"No, again." He rubbed the back of his neck and undid the top button of his shirt. His heart jumped as she tied a bow on a gaily wrapped package. Somehow, he choked out, "Alex's birthday is today."

"It is." She grinned and fluffed the bow. "We've always had a tradition of having lunch together, even when the other kids were here. I'd either meet her in Washington, or she'd be home by that point."

He was going to throw up. He closed his eyes.

"Tiny?" Concern etched her tawny features.

"I know," he blurted before he lost his nerve.

"You know what?"

Somehow he kept eye contact. "About Alex's biological father."

"Davie is. He—"

"I know he signed her birth certificate. I saw that when Alex joined Unit 28. I know Hamid al-Hassan is her biological father."

She reeled as if he'd slapped her, but her shock lasted only for a second. "Don't you dare judge me for what I did all those years ago!"

Startled by the venom in her voice, he jumped. "I'm not, but I'm worried. If I know, who else does? Hamid and his sons could."

Roya whirled around. She gripped the kitchen counter so hard the tendons on her hands stood out. She hung her head. Seconds passed as if she contemplated her response. "It doesn't matter."

"Yes, it does." Another deep breath calmed his nerves. "How much do you know about what happened in Panama?"

Finally, she faced him. Her gray-brown eyes were all granite now, almost the same color as the island where Alex's gift sat. "How would I know anything since you refuse to keep me informed?"

He wasn't going to get baited, not this time. "Suffice it to say there was a shift in the enemy's tactics. The enemy was Hashim al-Hassan. It was a sea change because the demands came to be for her and her alone."

"He wants his revenge for whatever happened between him and Alex."

"It's more than that." Tiny ground to a halt.

"How can it be?"

"I'm not even going to venture a guess. Somehow, I think he connected the fact that not only did she bring him down to his lowest point, but she's also his half-sister. It's a perfect storm for motives."

"He'd never come here. How would he even know where here *is*?" She turned and rummaged around in the cabinet for a glass.

She didn't give him one.

Point taken.

Her hand shook as she filled it. "Isn't such information classified?"

"Absolutely." Once more, he hated the limits his job placed on his ability to share information. He couldn't tell her there had been a breach.

"Then anonymity is her best protection."

"We know Hashim al-Hassan has disappeared. And when he did so, he wasn't in Beirut. He was in the Caribbean." He clamped his jaw shut. He probably shouldn't have said even that, but he was desperate.

"You don't know if he's here, right?"

She had him there because he had no way to verify Hashim's whereabouts. And in the eyes of everyone, that meant no action needed. Still, he held out some hope that Roya would listen to him. "No, I don't, but we need her permission to take her into protective custody. I know she'll start asking questions. Please, Roya. Please tell Alex. I'm—"

"No!" She slammed the glass so hard onto the island that it shattered. Water ran all over her hand and the quartz, but she didn't notice. "I will not! She doesn't need to know."

"Doesn't she?"

"Don't you tell me how to run my life, Tim Daniels," she growled. Like her nickname from so long ago, she stalked him.

He backed up until he found himself crowded against the couch.

Eyes wide, nostrils flared, she got right in his face. "She has lived for thirty-four years without this knowledge. There is no need to start now when you can't even articulate a threat."

Courage. Keep courage here. "And what if I'm right? If Hashim al-Hassan is indeed Stateside? Then it's going to come out."

"He'd be a fool to try such a stunt."

Tiny shook his head. "And sometimes, fools emerge as victors because their opponents don't take them seriously." He tried one last, desperate ploy. "I think Jabir knows as well."

She flinched. "He told you?"

"No. I wondered why he kept shifting from extreme happiness to undeniable sadness. If we two found out, I'm very sure others like Hashim know. Please. You're my oldest friend. Alex is my goddaughter. She needs to know this from you."

"You will *not* tell her." Her voice lowered, and hardness replaced the conflict raging in those depths. "If you tell her, I will consider it to be a fatal breach of our friendship. Understand?"

Now he completely knew the bondage that had ensnared David and Jabir. Oh, the power of secrets!

"Get out of *my* house."

As he picked up his jacket and saw himself to the door, the nausea swelled, and his throat tightened. He could do nothing else. He'd warned her, tried to impress upon her the gravity of the danger that possibly lay in wait for her oldest child. He'd done all he could.

And Roya had ignored him. Why remained a mystery.

At the car, he lifted his gaze to the deck. Through the glass, did he see her leaning against the island and sobbing? Maybe. Maybe there was hope. He doubted it.

Now all he could do was pray.

Thursday, December 14, 2017, 1400 hours EST, Raleigh, NC

Tiny leaned against a concrete planter in one of Raleigh's open-air shopping centers. He checked an app on his phone. According to that, Jabir was around the corner in a store. He had just enough time to see him before he made tracks to the airport for his flight to Atlantic City.

Jabir rounded the corner with a gym bag slung over his shoulder. Cheeks ruddy and eyes hooded, he headed toward a nearby Starbucks.

Tiny pushed away from the planter. Just as Jabir reached the door, he said, "I thought I'd find you here."

Jabir jumped. "Tiny! What on—I thought you were in Washington. How did you find me? Alex?"

"Nope. She doesn't even know I'm here." Tiny smiled. "You know how I paint for relaxation and you play hoops? Well, Otto's leisure activity is creating apps. The one he wrote tells me where people are."

Jabir grinned. "Doesn't Find My Friends do that?"

"Only with permission. And it doesn't pull in photos from one's phone camera, right? I can show you this." He pulled up some pictures of Jabir and one of his friends. "Meeting an old friend?"

Jabir chuckled. "Something like that. Rex and I go way back to college."

"That's how I found you. If Otto's lucky, we might deploy that to our agents. How about some coffee before I head to the airport?" Tiny opened the door. "My treat."

"I'm never one to turn down free coffee." Once they'd settled at a small table in the corner, he asked, "Why are you here? Normally, you'd call."

The shock hadn't faded on the drive from Weatherly, and Tiny's stomach remained in a tight ball. It was time to drink the hot tea he'd ordered. "I know, Jabir."

The young man, who'd become like a son to him, didn't need any further confirmation. "About Alex's biological father."

Tiny nodded. "Your oscillating between happiness and anxiety concerned me. I started digging back into my past. Let's just say one thing led to another. I confronted Roya." A hollow laugh escaped him as he remembered her threat. "That was a big mistake. She told me exactly what she thought of my interference and said that if I told Alex, she'd consider it an irreparable breach of our friendship."

Jabir winced. "She's chained us all. You. Me. David."

"It's worse." He checked around the small interior. People were focused elsewhere. In a low voice, he briefed him on Hashim's vanishing act. "I don't have any evidence, but my gut says he's in-country. The thing is, without credible information as to his whereabouts and Alex's permission, we can't take her into protective custody. Mitch won't run it up the chain until we have something solid."

Jabir sighed. He scrubbed a hand across the stubble on his jaw. "Even if she knew, she'd probably refuse protection anyway because she's not one to run and hide."

"I agree." Tiny set aside his drink and leaned forward. "Listen. Stick to her as much as you can. You have your Glock at your place, right?"

Jabir nodded.

"Start carrying."

"I need to tell her something."

"She'd never believe you, and then you'd start down a path where you don't want to go. Read David in about Hashim. He's still got his clearances, and I know he keeps a piece."

"I will." Jabir fell silent. So softly that Tiny almost missed it, he stated, "I love her."

As if it weren't written all over his face since he'd reconnected with Alex. "I know you do."

"I—I'm proposing to her tonight."

That wasn't any surprise. "That's wonderful. Do you have the ring?"

"I got it resized and picked it up from the jeweler before I saw you." Jabir pulled out a case and flipped it open.

A marquis diamond glittered on black velvet.

Tiny softened. He knew what it meant. The promise of so many tomorrows with Alex. "She'll love it." He briefly gripped his shoulder. "Congratulations." He rose and shrugged into his jacket. "Well, I hate to run, but I've got a three o'clock to Atlantic City."

"What?"

"A lead on Leila. Best of luck with Alex. I know she'll say yes." With that, he picked up his drink and headed to the door. A blast of cold air hit him as he left. Did he feel better? Maybe. No, truly, he did. Now that Jabir was briefed, he'd guard Alex closely. Maybe that would be all they needed to keep her safe.

He earnestly hoped so.

Loose Ends

As Alex unlocked the door to the lobby of her flat, disappointment fought with elation for dominance in her heart.

Mom had texted and canceled their lunch date—after Alex had already seated herself. Migraine was what she'd said.

Yeah, Alex got that. Truly, she did since Mom occasionally came down with them. They usually sent her to bed until sleep and medication took care of them. But today of all days! They'd never broken an engagement for her birthday lunch. Even when Alex had been exhausted from pulling an all-nighter writing her senior thesis paper.

And the kicker?

No promise of rescheduling.

Get it out of your mind. You still had a good lunch, right? Sure, if she could call sitting at the restaurant by herself and reading a book on her phone fun.

No, it wouldn't ruin her mood. Hopefully. She'd had a blast with her sister and sisters-in-law at the Pretty in Pink Spa in Smithfield. Wraps. Facials. A manicure and pedicure. And tons of giggles. Her skin tingled. She held out her fingers. Glittering deep red nail polish to match the dress she planned to wear that night.

Time to get inside. After disarming the alarm, she undid the lock.

No Rocky. Usually, when he heard the beep, he was right there waiting for her.

"Rocky?" She opened the door and hung up her coat. "Rocky, where are you, boy?"

Sabina whined from her crate.

"Sabina, what is it, girl?"

She frowned when Rocky rose from the rug in front of the fireplace. "Boy, what were you doing snoozing like that? Did I wear you out that much this morning?"

He whimpered and nosed in for a scratch, as was his custom.

"Let's get Sabina out." She undid the carabiner that ensured the Basenji wouldn't lift the gate and escape.

Sabina bolted from the crate. Almost immediately, she began sniffing around the perimeter of the great room. Strange? Not really, but she only did that when coming back from being gone for a long time.

Sabina inhaled in great gusts as if trying to catch a scent.

"What is it?"

The Basenji ignored her and trotted into her bedroom, where she did the same patrol.

Alex followed. "You're worrying me. What is going on?"

The dog stopped in the doorway leading to the bathroom, lifted her head, and sampled the air.

"You are so weird," Alex muttered.

From where she'd laid it on the bar, her phone beeped. Thinking Mom had texted, she rushed over. No. Dad had.

"Just got home. Mom's still sleeping. She left a note saying she'd gotten a migraine. Wish I'd known. I would have met you for lunch."

Oh, she wished she'd known as well.

"Thanks, Dad," Alex whispered. She set the phone down.

She couldn't worry about that, not when Jabir was due to arrive in a couple of hours. Instead, she'd focus on the evening ahead. Maybe that would chase away the unsettled feeling Mom's sudden cancellation and Sabina's paranoia had produced.

19

Tiny hated casinos. Not so much for the gambling but for the food. All-you-can-eat buffets had never been his thing. Neither had gambling, hence why he'd hadn't set foot in one in years. Except now, he had to do so in order to meet with Manny "Pinky" Salazar, the loan shark who'd put Leila into bondage. No, she'd done that herself by getting rip-roaring drunk and running up a hundred grand in debt. Who in their right mind would do that? Then he remembered. She hadn't been in her right mind at all. She'd been drunk.

Tiny checked his phone.

In his text, Pinky had been specific. "Go inside to the restaurant. Go to the corner booth that is round. Seven o'clock and no later, else we have no business together."

No worries there. It was almost seven, so he was right on time. He made his way past the nickel machines that bleeped and flashed lights as if beckoning him to lose all the cash he had, all fifty dollars' worth. As if they were automatons, senior citizens stood in front of them as they slid nickels into the slots and pulled the handles. One older gentleman hooted when his machine started beeping as it dispensed a payout that he'd most likely lose within an hour.

The restaurant was midway back, between the casual gamblers with the slot machines and the more serious ones who liked to play roulette and craps. Daisy Mae meets James Bond. The buffets were up front with the tables beyond. Ah! There it was, a booth in the corner, a round one, empty of anyone, which was strange.

Pinky must have reserved it for him.

Tiny's stomach growled. Not yet. Being slightly hungry kept him on edge, alert, and maybe a little ornery. Shucking his leather jacket, he took a seat and folded his hands on the table. Seven came and went. He'd kept his part of the bargain. As 7:30 approached, he wondered if he'd been had. If he didn't leave by eight, he'd miss his flight, and as exhausted as he was, he'd be darned if he were driving home from New Jersey.

Two Oriental men approached. The suits of both men strained against their beefy frames. The one on the right, a bald man, spoke. "Tim Daniels?"

Tiny nodded.

"Come with us."

Am I going to come back? That thought crossed his mind. He nearly laughed. In his career as a field agent, he'd gone to much more clandestine, dangerous meetings than this.

They headed up a set of steps. The noise of the first floor began fading, yielding to more dignified, high-stakes gambling in the form of blackjack and poker. Groups of well-dressed men and women huddled over eight tables. Had Leila wound up here? Or had she stopped downstairs?

His escorts led him through a set of doors and down a short hall that could have passed for any hallway in an office building. At the end, the other man, this one with a dusting of short hair and a pencil-thin mustache, opened a door.

Tiny stepped into a lobby that could have been straight out of Japan. Blond wood and shoji-style doors. Low couches. Subtle lighting. Bamboo in black pots. Paper lanterns. Wait. Sadie's report had stated that Manny was of Puerto Rican descent, not Japanese. What was this all about? Mustache Man patted him down and pulled out both his cell phone and his wallet. He handed them to his pal.

"Wait here," Baldy grunted. He slipped through the doors. Just before he pulled them closed, Tiny noted a young man slumped in a chair in front of a desk. He was probably another one of Pinky's marks.

Tiny settled onto a couch and rested his elbows on his knees. If he listened closely enough, he thought he heard faint strains of Japanese music.

The doors opened, and Baldy jerked his head in silent command for him to enter.

The young man must have left through a separate door.

You have got to be kidding me. Only Tiny's training kept him from gawking. Like Baldy and Mustache, who he now realized were bodyguards, Pinky wore black, only of fine silk, everything from his suit to his shirt to the handkerchief peeking out of the breast pocket of his jacket. He'd cropped his dark hair short and—wait, was that black eyeliner he wore behind black glasses?

Using a pair of chopsticks, Pinky lifted some sushi to his mouth. He smacked his lips and sighed with contentment.

Tiny winced.

A woman done up in full geisha, from the kimono and obe all the way to pale makeup and hair, swished through another shoji door. She poured some steaming green tea into a small porcelain cup before slipping out as quietly as she'd come.

This was getting uncomfortable, ten to one intended by Pinky.

Without a word, Pinky shoved aside his sushi plate. The geisha girl darted into the room again and swept it away.

Baldy placed Tiny's cell phone and wallet on the black wood in front of him.

Pinky flipped open Tiny's wallet. His dark eyes darted to his face, then to Baldy. In a high, nasally voice, he asked Baldy, "This is the shrimp?"

Tiny now had reason number two for finishing his business and getting out of there. He hadn't heard that name since high school.

Pinky shoved Tiny's phone and wallet to the side.

Tiny stared at him. "I'd best get those back."

"There's a ninety-percent chance you will."

Had he heard him right?

Pinky leaned back. "Have a seat, Mr. DHS Man."

Tiny did.

"When you called, I thought about it. I asked myself, 'Self, why would someone from the Department of Homeland Security call me?' And I said to Self, 'It is a forty percent chance I have done something to offend him. Or twenty percent chance he simply wants to talk, or a forty percent chance he wants something.' Now, if I remember correctly," Pinky folded his napkin and laid it on the dark wood, "I have done nothing to displease you, so I eliminated that forty percent chance."

This was going to be painful.

"I'm not saying you've done anything wrong." *In our purview.* "I'm curious about one of your clients."

Pinky took a sip of tea. He blotted his lips with his napkin. "Client information is confidential."

"Understandable. What kind of clients do you normally have?"

"One hundred percent of my clients can't stop gambling."

Tiny nearly laughed at the obvious statement.

"Thirty-seven percent are old people. Eighteen percent are in their twenties and think they can beat the system. Twenty-three percent are housewives who want to escape reality by going for a weekend with their friends to Atlantic City. Seventeen percent are men who lie to their wives about a golf weekend and instead gamble. And the remaining five percent?" A devilish smile crossed his face. "Government wonks like yourself."

Tiny's chest tightened. *I will not respond. I will not respond.* Far from the ex-jock bully he'd anticipated, this guy reminded him of a nerd, one who knew he was smart, lorded it over everyone, and gave every other geek like Tiny had been in high school a bad name. As his hands curled into fists, he kept them between his knees. "How do you pick them up?"

"Simple. I wander, and I watch for the ones are who are gambling and drinking. Which I noticed while watching you on a camera, you did neither. No, you came right in here and showed no interest at all in the slot machines. You're no mark."

"Never have been. Never will be. I need to know what you know about Leila al-Kadir."

Pinky started chuckling, a high cackle that grated on Tiny's nerves. "Her? I remember her very well. What did you say, Hiroshi? She's hot?"

Baldy grinned, revealing a mouth full of gold teeth.

"He said she's really hot, like none of us have forgotten her." A sizzling sound hissed out from Pinky.

Tiny winced. He couldn't wait to leave.

"She came in here about three years ago and started off at the slots, then moved on over to roulette and craps. She drank like a fish, too. By the time she made it to the blackjack table on this floor, she was flying high. She had no business playing with those high rollers. A one hundred percent chance for a good mark, especially when she couldn't pay the hundred-grand tab she ran up. That sobered her up in a hurry."

"And you moved in."

"What can I say? The casino likes me." Pinky's chin jutted out with pride. "You could say I'm on their list of preferred loan sharks. Fifty-six percent of the money fronted to pay the house comes from me. She came to me. We worked out a seven-year payment plan. She'll pay me off in a few years, and then she can stop living with Mommy."

"If she didn't pay you?"

"Hiroshi and Norio there." Pinky nodded toward his bodyguards. "I've got five others just like him. You don't pay me, they pay you a visit. You might lose more than your shirt." He chuckled and folded his hands on his desk.

Tiny bit back his surprise. On both hands, Pinky was missing his pinkie fingers. Dang. He struggled to keep a straight face. "I see." In his mind, Tiny recalled what Sadie had pointed out from Leila's bank statements. "Yet, from what I understand, she hasn't been paying you since September."

"She's got herself a sugar daddy. He's taking care of her debt to me for the near future."

"Does this sugar daddy have a name?"

Pinky's eyes narrowed. He broke his gaze, laid his hands flat on the desk, and studied them.

A tungsten band gleamed on his left ring finger. That was good information to know in case he needed it.

Pinky almost hissed, "I don't give out names of clients. Especially to cops."

Tiny raised his hands to show no harm, no foul. "Hey, I'm no cop. And you just gave me Leila's."

"There was a ninety-three percent chance you knew her. Sorry. No can do, Mr. DHS Man."

Tiny drew in his breath, held it, and released it. Maybe then he wouldn't jump across the desk and strangle the loan shark. "It's critical to a case I'm working."

"I don't care if it's critical to anything. This interview is over." He shoved Tiny's phone and wallet toward him. "Leave here and don't come back."

Heat began making its way into Tiny's chest and neck. He'd better go before he did something he regretted. "I'll be out of your hair. But don't be surprised if I'm back, and I might not be so nice next time."

Pinky sneered at him. "Then there will be a ninety-five percent chance I will not be nice either, Mr. DHS Man. Hiroshi, you and Norio see him outside."

Tiny stuffed his wallet and phone into his jacket.

Hiroshi grabbed his arm. Norio, or Mustache Man, grabbed his other arm in a viselike grip. They propelled him into the hallway and down the steps with such speed that, had they not caught him securely between them, he would have fallen. They didn't release their grip until they marched him through the casino's sliding glass doors and into the cold night air.

Tiny turned away and adjusted his jacket. His flaming cheeks cooled as he headed down the boardwalk toward where he'd parked his car on the street several blocks away. He didn't have what he wanted, but maybe he had a hook. He'd have to think on that one.

Once he arrived at the airport, he was more than ready to get home, kiss Jonna and the girls hello, and climb into bed. Until then, he had to satisfy himself with his plan of attack related to Pinky because somehow, he knew the sugar daddy the loan shark had mentioned was the hinge to the case.

He dialed a number.

"Sadie Callahan."

"Hey, Sadie. Are you busy?"

"Nope. Just at home reading in front of my faux fireplace."

He chuckled. "I have a research project that you can either start tonight or first thing in the morning. I'm not going to be in until later, which is why I'm calling now. I need you to get more information on Manny Salazar than you gave me. Turn over whatever rocks you need to get that information. And I need to have a hook in case things head south with the Leila al-Kadir case."

"Will do. It might take some time, and I just got some other assignments."

"As soon as you can. Thanks. I'll see you tomorrow." Tiny lowered his phone. His stomach growled, and he gazed at his choices of airport fare. All bland. Suddenly, he wished for casino food, at least until Pinky's lack of pinkies floated before him.

At least he could rest in the knowledge that, if he had the need, Sadie could hand him the information needed to nail Pinky to the wall.

20

Here goes something.

Jabir stood at Alex's door. He closed his eyes and took a deep breath. With the hand that wasn't holding the cooler, he knocked.

Alex approached. "Hey, handsome."

He didn't wait. He dropped his duffel and cooler onto the floor, took her in his arms, and kissed her long and deep.

"My, my, and hello to you, too, darling." She grinned and stepped back.

His cheeks flushed as he traced her figure with his gaze. The deep red satin dress with its hem ending just above her knees outlined it perfectly. He forced his gaze upward.

"You're staring."

She'd busted him—again. He shifted to where the diamond pendant he'd given her in September hung on a black satin choker necklace. Diamond earrings, a gift from her parents upon her college graduation, glittered in her ears. Her skin practically glowed in the low light.

In a black and white streak, Sabina came flying down the hall. As if she'd pre-planned it, she put on the brakes about five feet from him and skidded into his legs. He laughed as he set the duffel on the counter and scratched her head. "Well, hello, Sabina. And Rocky."

The Coonhound mix whined as he trotted forward for his own greeting.

"Hey, you, no!" Alex snatched up the cooler from where the Basenji dog had begun nuzzling the top. "No Basenji customs inspection for you."

Jabir drank in her image. Satin, diamonds, and no shoes. Total Alex all the way and one of the things he loved most about her.

Almost immediately, he turned on the oven. "For supper, we're having salmon and vegetables. Have a seat while I cook."

"I'm not arguing with you since I'm the birthday girl. Wine?"

"Of course."

She fished in the cabinet for a couple of glasses. She snagged a bottle of Merlot from the hanging wine rack. Once she'd poured half the bottle into two glasses, she turned on the stereo to some low jazz and settled on the couch.

Jabir laid out the salmon, threw together a lemon butter sauce, and dumped out the squash, broccoli, and green beans. He washed the beans and layered them onto the salmon before cutting the squash into long strips.

Alex gazed at him. "When I got home today, the dogs were acting weird."

Jabir paused. "How so?"

"You know how Rocky always meets me at the door, right?"

"Yeah."

Alex shifted. "He was still sleeping in front of the fireplace when I got home."

"Did you run him hard this morning or something?"

"No. Just our normal walk. And Sabina seemed really upset."

His eyes narrowed, and he set down the knife. "In what way?"

"She seemed agitated when I let her out of her crate. Then she did what I call her perimeter patrol. You know, she sniffed all around the edges of the rooms like she does when she's been gone for a few days."

Slowly, he resumed his cutting. His mind churned through what he knew. Hashim had disappeared from Havana. He was a no-show in Beirut. Had he been in here? His breath quickened at the thought. "Did you see anything else out of order?"

"No. Nothing. Why?"

He opened his mouth to tell her. He couldn't. Not when Roya needed to come clean first. "Uh, just curious."

"Jabir." Doubt colored his name.

"I wanted to make sure no one broke into your flat." He added the rest of the vegetables. "But if they had, the alarm would have gone off. Also, the cold weather could have Sabina jazzed up. Did Rocky act like he felt well?"

"Come to think of it, he did seem a little off." She shrugged.

"Could be." He slid the salmon into the oven, set the timer, and braced his hands on the granite counter. He had to tell her. Matter of fact, he was surprised she hadn't questioned him further. What would happen if he confessed? Especially between him and his soon-to-be mother-in-law?

"Talk about a weird day," she murmured almost to herself.

Something else? Jabir picked up his wine and joined her. "Why? I mean, besides the pups?"

"Mom ditched me for lunch."

For a second, he stared. "What? Why?"

"She got a migraine." Alex took a sip of her wine. "You know something? That's the first time she's ever canceled on me. Ever. And she didn't even call. She texted."

"When?"

"I'd already gotten us a seat, so I didn't feel like I could up and leave."

They'd been supposed to meet at noon. Suddenly, it clicked into place. Tiny had paid Roya a visit. She'd threatened him to silence. Her reward? One massive headache that had most likely forced her to bed for the rest of the day. "Did she call afterward and reschedule?"

"She wasn't awake when Dad got home." She sighed. "He texted and told me he wished he'd known."

Roya probably hadn't wanted to tell him.

Jabir wrapped a lock of her hair around his finger. "I'm sorry."

She shrugged. "Me, too. It happened. Let's focus on the evening."

He couldn't agree more. Once the timer beeped, he served up their meal and called her over. They didn't talk much while eating, something he enjoyed about her. They could be together in comfortable silence, a true mark of a couple meant to be together. When they spoke, it was mainly about plans for Christmas. Mama would join them even though she was Muslim. For that, he was thankful.

When they carried their plates to the kitchen, Alex scowled at the aluminum foil he'd used on a cookie tray. "Cleanup? Wow! Some clean-up. Usually, you stick me with pots and pans."

He laughed. "I planned smart, didn't I? We'll have dessert later."

"That's one way to put it. Grrr! At least you have to wash the dogs." The pout turned to a smirk. "Have at it, fly-boy."

He chuckled as he retreated to the bedroom to change into the sweats and t-shirt he'd brought. Rocky was easy. He enjoyed water, so baths were always a pleasure for him. Sabina? Not so much. The black and white Basenji took one look at him and darted under the dining room table.

"Come on, you." He pulled out one of the six chairs, only to have her worm her way under another.

Alex giggled from where she sat on the couch and read a novel. "Keep trying. You'll get her eventually."

"I don't give up." He grabbed for her.

Sabina scrambled from the dining room and darted to the bedroom.

"Hah! And Basenjis think they're smart." He followed and shut the door behind him.

She dove underneath the bed, except that her rear quarters and tail remained exposed.

He grabbed for her.

She squirmed all the way under.

"Oh, come on. Don't be difficult."

Scrabbling told him she intended to make him work for his reward.

He knelt and lifted the bed skirt. "C'mon, girl. Be nice and not stubborn for once."

Her eyes almost glowed as she gazed at him.

"Sabina, here." He laid a dog biscuit in front of her. "How's that?"

No dice. She remained where she was.

He sighed, retreated to the kitchen, and opened the refrigerator. He got a few pieces of hot dog that Alex used for training. "I shall not give up."

Alex giggled.

He returned to the bedroom. The dog biscuit had vanished during his absence. He placed the treats on the floor. "Then let's try this. You like hot dogs, right?"

Ah, hot dog. The Kryptonite of Basenjis everywhere.

Nothing. Either she completely blew him off, or she contemplated the ramifications of seeking the sacred prize. Rustling reached him. Sabina darted out and seized her treat.

Jabir grabbed her. She squealed as he tucked her under his arm like a football. "See? Even wonder dogs fall for the simplicity of processed meat."

He plunked her into the water. Sabina gave him a hangdog look as he scrubbed her down. Once he finished, he dried her. She ran into the bedroom and bounced from floor to bed and back to floor again. He dried her some more and declared her fit for duty.

"Here." Jabir left a couple of more dog biscuits on the floor. "That's your reward for putting up with a bath." Once he'd dressed again in his chinos and shirt, he reached into his duffel. Good. He hadn't forgotten the ring. Or the red satin ribbon.

Sabina had briefly calmed and lay on the bed with her paws crossed as if she were royalty. She gazed at him with those Egyptian eyes of hers. He sat beside her and stroked her silky head. "Good job in taking one for the team, Sabina. Here's your assignment." He looped the ring on the satin and tied it around the Basenji's neck in a bow. "Go see Mom. Okay?"

He opened the master bedroom door. Sabina darted into the great room and began what Alex called a B-500. Terror seized him. Would the ribbon come off? He hoped not. All he could envision was it rolling into one of the air vents.

Finally, Sabina jumped onto the couch to see her mistress.

"Hi, sweetie." Alex scratched her pup on the head. "Did you have a good bath?"

"After I lured her with hot dog." Jabir ruffled her hair. "You want the towels anywhere?"

"Tossed over the bathroom door." Alex remained focused on her book.

He wasted no time. With towels properly situated, he joined his beloved on the couch.

Sabina hopped up between them. She started circling. To calm his nerves, he counted. It took the Basenji twelve times to find the precisely perfect position to curl into a ball. Over the pounding in his heart, he asked, "You want to watch something?"

Alex set aside her book. "Sure. *The Blacklist?*"

"Maybe." *Stroke her neck!* he silently begged her.

Almost as if she heard him, she reached out and ran her hand down Sabina's fur. She frowned as her fingers found the ribbon. "What's this?"

She cocked her head and undid the bow. Eyes widening, she held up the ring.

Jabir carefully took it from her. With heart hammering in his ears, he said, "Alex, first off, happy birthday. I love you, and I'm thankful God reunited us in June."

She trembled as she nodded.

"Back in 2012, I knew I loved you. Yet I hesitated. Then in 2013, I lost you for the next four years. But when we came together in June?" Sudden emotion rushed forth, and the lump in his throat choked off his words to the point where he had to whisper. "I knew I'd better not squander it again. Roya Alexandra Thornton, will you marry me?"

208

"Yes!" Her cry echoed off the high ceilings. She jumped into his arms. "Yes, yes!"

As he held her close, his heart nearly burst from joy. And fear. Joy over knowing Alex would be his for the rest of his life. And fear in knowing danger lurked in the shadows, both from family and from the enemy. All he could do was hold on and pray for comfort.

Friday, December 15, 2017, 0200 hours EST, Mount Vernon, VA

No rest for the weary, even when he badly needed it. From his favorite chair in the den, Tiny gazed as if completely mesmerized at the flames leaping and dancing in the fireplace. A cup of chamomile tea, a strong suggestion from Jonna when he'd complained—again—about his sour stomach, steamed in a mug in his hands.

On the coffee table sat his closed laptop. When Alex had called and asked to Skype, he'd placed it there so the entire family could see. She'd beamed when she announced her engagement and held up her left hand.

"Alex, I'm so happy for you," he'd told her.

Emily, his older daughter who'd arrived home from college earlier that day, almost squealed, "The ring is so beautiful!"

"When's the date?" Jonna asked.

Alex grinned. "We don't know yet. Probably in the spring."

"Sooner rather than later," Jabir added from beside her.

Tiny laughed since he fully understood the need for short engagements. "Keep us posted."

They'd promised to do so.

Now, his worry over Hashim's whereabouts and Roya's vitriol had resulted in a tender stomach and heavy heart. He also wanted to say he'd brushed off the impact of his visit with Pinky. He couldn't. Even though he'd matured from a scrawny, nerdy teenager into someone honed into good shape with a sharp mind and great confidence, it stirred up all sorts of bad memories from his early years in high school. It was funny how he'd been brought from the latter to the former—all from the words of a loan shark.

Lord, I want to rest. Just rest. That's all.

He took a sip of tea and let the mug warm his hands.

"Couldn't sleep?"

Clad in her robe, Jonna stood before him.

He sighed and resumed his contemplation of the fire. "No. Too much on my mind, I guess."

"Try me."

He considered her words. "Have you ever had a time when what someone did or said brought back some bad memories?"

"Like high school?"

"Exactly." Gratitude for his wife surged through him. He didn't want to explain. Really, he didn't.

She came over and sat down on his lap. "Yeah. For me, it's junior high. I've had a few times where I've been accidentally left off the guest list. It reminds me of when one of the most popular girls in my class intentionally left me off her birthday party guest list and made sure I knew it. That hurt. Whenever it happens, I have to tell myself I'm not in junior high anymore." She wrapped her arms around his shoulders. "There's more, right?"

He yearned to tell her about Hashim, his fears concerning Alex's half-brother, and the way Roya had threatened him into silence regarding her parentage. "I can't talk about it."

For a few moments, Jonna didn't say anything, only stroked his hair and rested her chin on his head. Her arms tightened around him, and she kissed him on the hair. "I love you, my dear man. I'll be praying. Come to bed when you're ready."

His one hope and encouragement retreated to the warm comfort of their duvet. Tiny leaned his head against the chair with a small thunk. "Lord, how did I wind up in this mess?"

Loyalties, that's how. Loyalty to Leila's mother had driven him to take the case. Loyalty to Roya and David Thornton had bought his silence related to Alex's true parentage. Loyalty to his organization had kept him from demanding that Alex be removed from the case. He couldn't ask Mitch for permission to take action. Not when Hashim's whereabouts remained a mystery.

He could only hope that when the time came, it wouldn't be too late.

21

"Oh, wow, oh, wow, oh, wow," Alex said for what was probably the
fiftieth time as she stared at the diamond ring on her finger. Focus. She
had to focus. Especially since she'd already cut three two-by-fours wrong
due to her distraction. Or was it lack of sleep? Or both?

"Some birthday present," Jazz Finley, her foreman for this particular
build, grinned. His dark eyes crinkled at the corners. "Do I get to be your
man of honor?"

Alex giggled. "Hardly. Marlie is my matron of honor. But I'm seriously considering your jazz band for the reception. And talk to Jabir
about the groom's party. Now how about handing me that measuring
tape?"

Jazz chuckled. "You're a piece of work, Alex Thornton-soon-to-be-
al-Omri. You are taking his name, aren't you?"

"You'd better believe it. I've come too far not to." Alex made a pen-
cil mark on the board, then cut it with a miter saw. "See if this works."

"Yes, ma'am." He strolled toward the house they were building and
called to one of the other guys working on the site.

Gravel crunched. An engine growled as Jabir's white Subaru WRX
rumbled onto the job site. Her cheeks warmed as she recalled the night

213

before when he'd held her after they'd Skyped with Tiny and his family. Her gaze flew to the diamond on her left ring finger. Another sappy smile spread across her face.

As he climbed from the car, she called, "Well, hello, you."

Handsome as ever, even in jeans and a sweatshirt, he joined her at the saw.

"What brings you out here?" she asked.

Without a word, he took her in his arms and kissed her.

Wolf whistles rose behind her. All in good fun.

She pulled back and grinned. "I hardly think you came all this way simply for a kiss that makes me blush."

"Maybe I needed to see you."

She stuck out her tongue at him.

He chuckled. "Mature, for an engaged woman." His brow knitted. "I've got news."

"About?"

"Our case."

Suddenly, it clicked in her mind. "Oh! Right! Sorry. I'm not firing on all six cylinders this morning. The groom-to-be kept me up too late."

"Oh?" He ruffled her hair. "I don't think the bride-to-be minded. And I thought you were an eight-cylinder girl."

She mock-punched him on the arm. "You're so adorkable."

"Huh?" He frowned.

Alex grinned. "You're cute in a dorky kind of way."

"I'll take that as a compliment."

"It is." She stepped away and folded her arms. "What's the news?"

Jabir glanced toward the house under construction. Though Jazz and the two others who worked on its front porch, he led her to the back of her Personal Touch Design and Construction pickup truck. "Noor contacted her father."

Alex's jaw dropped. "What?"

"He called a 1-800 number she'd left for their communication. This time, she returned his call. He told me he'd left a message about us wanting to talk with her."

Alex hoisted herself onto the tailgate. Wow. Totally unexpected. Her mind began whirling in all directions. She pulled and released the measuring tape she held so it slapped against the case. "Do you think she's somewhere here in the States?"

He eased down beside her and nodded. "I do. It makes sense."

"Where are we meeting her?"

"Tomorrow night in Miami. Farouk's in the States for a round of office holiday parties."

"Talk about short notice." Her mind began clicking through all they had to do. Make arrangements to fly down there. Find a hotel. Work out a protocol to—

"I'm already setting things up." He sat down beside her. "We fly down tomorrow morning. Meet with her tomorrow night. Then fly back Sunday morning."

"No Sabbath rest for us." She sighed.

"Not this weekend. Our ox is in the ditch on this one." He brushed his fingers across her cheek and hopped off the tailgate. "With luck, we can break this wide open."

"I hope so." She joined him as he walked to his car. "Is there anything I need to do?"

"Finish off the day. Our flight is at eight in the morning." He chucked her on the chin. "We'll do this. Promise on that."

She could only hope.

Saturday, December 16, 2017, 2030 hours EST, Miami Beach, FL

"What did you say the signal was?" Alex raised her voice to be heard above the blaring music that filled every nook and cranny of the hotel's ballroom.

Jabir set his beer bottle on a tray. "A waitress who winks at us. She's going to give us the time and location of the meeting."

She scowled as she stood in the massive hotel ballroom at one of Miami Beach's better hotels. Her meal of swordfish sat heavy on her stomach. Dressed in her red dress from a couple of nights before, she earnestly hoped she looked like Cinderella the princess rather than Cinderella who cleaned fireplaces, which was how she felt. That's what happened when she got up at 5:30 in the morning on a Saturday.

But, hey, if it meant breaking this case wide open, she would have gotten up at three.

At a nearby table, a woman giggled loudly. Too bad Alex couldn't exceed her two-drink limit, but she couldn't do that and keep a clear head. A guy next to her burped, and everyone standing nearby laughed. The lights flashed various colors on the dance floor, and people gyrated in time with the music. Either Farouk had already budgeted for this party, or the company must have had a sudden end-of-year surge in profits. Who cared? It gave them the cover they needed to meet Noor.

A waitress swung by with a tray of appetizers. "Fruit for the lady and gentleman?"

No wink. Okay. Not her. This was getting old already.

Alex took a pot sticker laced with pineapple, grapes, and strawberries. "Thanks."

Jabir took one of his own. He immediately chomped it down. "Yum."

She patted her stomach. "I'm already full."

"It's good for you."

She flicked his tie, a perfectly tacky one of red Santas on a green background, and rolled her eyes. "I thought you said the company took a hit."

He chuckled and smoothed it down on his black shirt. "They're projected to have a slight profit. I guess Farouk wanted to celebrate."

"Sir, a drink?" a waitress asked from behind Alex.

"Snowflake martini," he said.

She faced Alex. "And you, ma'am?"

"Rum and Coke."

"My favorite." The waitress winked. "I'll be right back."

"I take it that was the signal," Alex murmured.

He slide his arm around her waist. "Looks like it."

"Where are we meeting?"

"Patience, young grasshopper."

Whatever.

The music stopped, and Farouk stepped onto the stage. People cheered and clapped, then fell silent.

He began speaking. Yes, it'd been a tough year, but they'd pulled together. United. Worked hard. The result? 2017 would finish in the black, hence the reason for celebration. She knew he spoke through the pain of losing one child to death and the other to fear. He began running through the numbers for the Miami office.

Alex tuned him out.

"Your drinks." The waitress approached them with a martini glass filled with a white liquid and a rum and Coke. She handed Alex hers with a napkin before turning to Jabir. The cocktail napkin underneath his glass fluttered downward. "Oh! I dropped yours." She reached into her apron and pulled out another. "For you, sir. Enjoy your evening."

Farouk droned on and on. Would they just restart the music?

Alex grimaced. "This is getting old."

"Someone didn't get her beauty sleep."

She sighed. "You got that right."

Applause echoed through the cavernous room. Farouk descended a small set of steps and slipped through a side door.

Wait. Their one link to Noor had just vanished. "Great. He's gone. Are you sure we're supposed to be here?"

"I am." He unfolded his napkin. "Suite 2500. He wants us there at 9:30."

She crowded closer for a look. Someone, most likely Farouk, had scrawled the message in pen. Clever. Did he fear a mole? Unease curled within her. "This seems extremely cloak and dagger to me."

"With good reason. Being careful means staying alive."

"True." Through lowered lashes, she studied the crowd. People surged toward the dance floor. Others ordered a new round of drinks.

Jabir took her hand and leaned into her. Into her ear, he whispered, "We're slipping out of here like we're going to go and get a room. Then we'll go and see Farouk and Noor."

With that, he flirted heavily with her. His hand slid to her waist. He kissed her on the neck, then on the lips. Oh, dear. Ever since forty-eight hours before, she'd found herself desiring to push the boundaries they'd set. At least it became clear to everyone where they were headed. Like the two tipsy people they weren't, they looped their arms around each other and stumbled toward the lobby. The ride to the penthouse took only a few seconds.

Jabir tapped on the door.

It opened to reveal Farouk, still dressed in the silk suit and collarless shirt he'd worn onstage. Only now, some of the lines on his face had vanished. How much did it have to do with seeing his daughter?

"Please, both of you, come inside." He gestured for them to enter before shutting the door behind them. He even threw the security lock.

Paranoia certainly ruled the day.

"Where's Noor?" Alex blurted.

Jabir shot her a look.

Farouk led them further into the suite. "She is here. Please. Tea?"

What could she do? Refuse? Not if she wanted to see Noor. After settling on the couch, she endured the required idle chitchat. Not that she minded since most of it pertained to their engagement. No, they didn't have a date set but hopefully by June. That was a topic for later discussion with Mom. They didn't know where they would honeymoon. Personal Touch Design and Construction was thriving, and Jabir had begun figuring out what he wanted to do for a second job.

When would this end? She stared into her empty tea cup.

Seeming to sense her impatience, Farouk rose. "Would you like some more tea?"

No, what she wanted was to see Noor and head down eight floors to their room.

Jabir saved her. "Sir, I would appreciate some."

What? Oh, come on!

"Of course. Let me get some more water."

When Farouk had turned his back, Alex rolled her eyes so hard she worried they'd get stuck in her head.

A door opening caught her attention. Her jaw dropped as a woman dressed in jeans and a black, long-sleeved shirt with a ballerina neckline stepped through.

"Noor, meet Alex Thornton and Jabir al-Omri." Farouk stayed close to her side as he escorted her to two chairs. Along with the couch, those formed a conversation group near floor-to-ceiling windows overlooking the ocean below. "Alex, Jabir, my daughter, Noor Kamil-Sultan."

"Noor, it's a pleasure to meet you." Alex extended her hand.

The Chief Operating Officer of Kamil International had a firm handshake, which signified a confident woman, at least before she'd fled.

"Daughter, I believe they could help you."

"I don't see how that is possible." Noor turned her gaze, which Alex realized was almost amber in color, toward them. The lines around her eyes deepened. "Can you bring back my brother? Help him pull away from the beast who called himself his best friend? Bring Tarek to justice?"

A hard, honest charge. Not surprising.

Alex refused to let that intimidate her. "Not the first two, but maybe the third,"

"I don't see how that is possible." Noor cocked her head. "How did you get involved?"

Alex outlined their work so far and took care to present it in a concise manner to a woman who, as COO of a multinational company, was used to bullet points, conclusions, and recommendations. Noor's gaze remained blank as she focused on her to the point where Alex grew uncomfortable. As she wound down, the woman sprang to her feet and paced to the window. She stared into the darkness. Her fingers brushed the glass as if wanting to reach out and touch the brother she could no longer hold.

"Have you ever lost a brother, Alex Thornton?"

Alex swallowed hard at the implied grief. "No, I haven't. I'm sorry for your loss."

"Being sorry does not bring him back."

"I know." Alex desperately searched for something to say. "We want to help."

"How can you?" Noor turned and faced her. The prominence of her collarbones startled Alex. Samir's murder had turned Noor into a shadow of the woman who'd graced the executive team photos on the walls of Kamil International. "Samir is dead. My family and I are on the run. How, exactly, can you help us?"

Alex's mind whirled. "Due to who Tarek and Hashim are, we have the power to arrest him and see to it that he's brought to justice."

Noor snorted as if she didn't believe her. She snatched a Kleenex from its box and retreated to her chair as she dabbed the corners of her eyes. "I do not believe in justice anymore."

Alex glanced at Jabir, who nodded ever so slightly in encouragement. "We do. Very much so." She leaned forward. "When we were at Samir's house, we did some sleuthing behind the cops. One thing we discovered was that a family keepsake box was missing. We had our photo experts take a look at a crime scene photo that shows the box. They concluded it hid a camera."

Like a deer frozen in the presence of a predator, Noor stilled.

Alex had definitely struck a nerve. She pressed her advantage. "We think the camera recorded the murder."

Noor put her face in her hands and quietly wept.

Alex knelt beside her chair and rested her hand on Noor's arm. "Truly, I'm sorry. Brothers are special."

"We... we were so competitive, so caught up in who would be the one to succeed Papa." Those words came between sobs. "We finally realized our personal relationship was more important, but... but by then, it was too late."

She grabbed more tissues.

Alex didn't move, simply let her cry it out.

"I told Papa I would take care of getting the house cleaned out and put on the market. I had forensic cleaners come in, and my interior designer replaced the dinette set. It... it took me several tries to go inside the house." She lowered her hands to reveal cheeks splotchy from her tears. "At first, I didn't get out of the car. Then I got out but had my key in the gate when I lost my courage. Finally, on the last day of October, I made it inside." A brief smile crossed her face and vanished. "I went into the study first."

"Did you happen to throw a picture of Tarek and Samir into the trash?" Jabir asked from where he'd stayed seated on the couch.

Noor's face darkened. "I hate him."

Startled by the venom in her voice, Alex sat back on her heels.

"Ever since he and Samir became friends in their secondary school days, he wielded an unhealthy influence on my brother. All he had to do was snap his fingers, and Samir would do his bidding." She took a deep breath, then released it, "At least until the night he confessed to Interpol. That cost him his life."

Alex thought about that one. Had Samir known he would die? "I can only assume Tarek and his brother had no idea the camera was there."

"If they had, they would have taken it. I—I didn't know about it either until that night I went inside. I must have—what is it called?—Post Traumatic..." She shook her head. "I cannot remember."

"Post-Traumatic Stress Disorder," Alex supplied. "Why do you say that?"

"When I went to the back of the house, I relived finding him. It was... horrible." She clinched the tissues in her fist. "I panicked. All I wanted to do was leave. I heard the vases break. That's when I found the camera. I did not understand at first."

"Understand what?" Jabir asked.

"I had found something in his study, in a book."

"*Black Beauty*?" Alex asked.

Noor stared. "How do you know?"

"Good, old-fashioned sleuthing. We noticed a gap in the bookcase and took a look at the photos."

Slowly, Noor returned her gaze to Jabir. "Inside, I found a paper that I later figured out to be the name of a Cloud company. When I got home, I was able to figure out that the other set of numbers and letters was the password. It... it showed the entire murder, from the time Tarek and Hashim entered until they left."

Jabir cleared his throat. For a few seconds, he remained silent, then asked, "Does it show their faces?"

Noor's gaze hardened. "Very clearly. I knew what I had. This video was enough evidence to bring Hashim and Tarek to justice. I called the inspector and left a message." More tears began trickling down her cheeks, and she swiped at them. "He never called me back because that night, he and his wife died. The newspaper called it a murder-suicide, but I knew what happened."

"Hashim or Tarek," Alex muttered. Her gut tightened as she gazed at this woman, who'd once been so confident and sure, now brought so low.

"I worried they might have pulled the message from his phone. I got so scared. We had to leave. To live, we had no choice. That's what we did."

Alex's heart hammered, not just at the story but at the knowledge that the evidence Noor had discovered could nail Hashim and Tarek for their crimes. "Noor, do you have a copy we could have? That way, we could—"

"There is no copy." Noor jumped to her feet and returned to the window.

Alex struggled to her feet, and her joints protested. "What do you mean, there's no copy?"

"The file could not be copied, only moved. I downloaded it from the Cloud and put it on a jump drive."

"You don't have it with you?"

"No. Why should I when I am not sure I trust you?"

Alex's face flushed. She glanced at Jabir, who shook his head.

His message was clear. Don't blow it now.

One breath, two breaths, three breaths, four. Five breaths, six breaths, seven breaths, more. Her pulse settled a little. "I know it's hard to do so. Please, think about it. We have the same goal, and this will be one way to achieve it."

With that, she stepped to the couch and picked up the red satin purse she'd brought. She pulled out a business card and pen, scribbled Jabir's cell phone number on the back, and handed it to her. "There's my card."

Noor scanned it and frowned. "I thought you said you worked for the government."

"We do as contractors." Alex offered what she hoped was a conciliatory smile. "The front is my number. The back has Jabir's. Think about it. When you're ready to trust us, call us."

"Thank you for understanding. I'll be in touch." With that, Noor rose and retreated into the bedroom where she must have been staying. The door closed, signaling an end to the interview.

"I am sorry," Farouk said as he walked them to the door.

"Don't be," Alex lied. She wanted to hit something—hard.

"Sir, we appreciate it," Jabir said as he took her hand. He didn't let go as he led her into the hall. "We'll wait on her call."

Once the door shut, he practically dragged her toward the elevator.

She shook loose. "I need some time alone, if you don't mind. I'll take the stairs."

Maybe then she could walk off the need to hit something.

Sunday, December 17, 2017, 0130 hours EST, Miami, FL

What a dumb evening. For Alex the need to work off her frustration had dulled to a simple craving for rest. Hah. Hard to do when her mind refused to turn off. Why had Noor blown them off? Didn't she understand that if they got the video, they could put Tarek and Hashim away for Samir's murder? Or let Interpol do that? But no, she didn't get that.

Alex turned on her side and stared at Jabir. He lay in the other queen bed, still as death, the duvet up to his chin. How could he sleep? She closed her eyes and tried counting sheep.

That lasted three sheep before her thoughts turned to the man who would in a few short months be her husband. When Farouk had told Jabir he'd reserved a room for them, he hadn't been kidding. Maybe the old man had figured they already knew each other in the biblical sense. Why had they set up that cursed boundary?

She flipped onto her stomach. And why hadn't Mom called to talk about setting a date? No, she'd only texted and stated that she didn't want to think about it at that point.

"Alex?" Jabir pushed himself up on one elbow.

She lifted her head from the pillow. "Am I keeping you awake?"

"I'm already awake. I couldn't sleep. What's on your mind?"

She blew out a sigh. "I don't know."

"I'm sure you do."

Right. Like she was going to talk after he'd fussed at her for her mood when she'd finally gotten to their room. "Whatever."

"Alex."

Once more, she turned onto her back and gazed at him. "Sorry. I'm just very frustrated right now."

He ran his fingers along a crease in the sheet. "About?"

Did she have steam coming out of her ears yet? "Everything."

"Could you be a little more specific?"

No! Didn't he get it? "You wouldn't understand."

"Try me."

Finally, she pushed herself all the way upright and wrapped her arms around her knees. "It's a lot of stuff. This case. Our limits we set. Mom's stubbornness."

"Do you care to elaborate?"

"No." Not when his reprimand echoed in her ears.

"I don't bite. You know that."

Uh, huh. Sure. Seconds ticked by. She clamped her jaw shut.

"Beloved, you know I'm not going to judge or belittle you."

She released an audible breath. "You're right. I feel like we failed on the case—again."

He propped his head on his hand. "Because we didn't get the video?"

"Yeah."

He fell silent for a few minutes. "I'm not surprised. I mean, think about it. If you were in Noor's shoes, would you have brought the only copy of a potentially incriminating video?"

She hated it when he was right! "I guess I'm just ready for this case to end."

"I understand. But we have other things, like planning a wedding."

"Frustration number two. Mom doesn't want to talk about planning."

"What?"

She stared at her phone as if to blame it for her angst. "She texted and said she's too busy with Christmas and all. I think she's hiding something from me and keeps putting me off to avoid discussing it."

"Why do you say that?" His question followed the slightest bit of hesitation.

"Because Marlie got engaged at Christmas. I mean, on the day itself. Or at least late the night before. They had the church, reception hall, all the big stuff, done by three days after Christmas."

"That was 2013, right?"

"Yeah, so what?"

"Your mom's a little older now. Be patient with her, maybe talk to her after Christmas."

She threw her hands into the air. "But every day means that a date we want could be taken! Especially since lots of people get engaged on Christmas. And then… well, that brings me to my last frustration of the day. Sometimes, I wish we hadn't set those boundaries we did."

"We wanted to honor God."

"Stop patronizing me."

He sighed. "I'm not."

"Whatever," she mumbled under her breath, hopefully too low for him to hear.

He had. "I'm not patronizing you, Alex. We talked about it, and we both agreed on it."

"We could change that tonight." Uh, huh. She was feeling reckless.

Silenced stretched as if he were considering it. "I want to wait. It's a short period in the long scheme of things. Let's remember that."

"Okay." She dragged it out like a teenager would. Her mind swung back around to their engagement night. "A couple of nights ago when you proposed, why were you interrogating me like you did?"

"About what?"

"If someone had broken in?"

"I was… concerned."

About more than that, it seemed. "Is there anything else bothering you?"

"Nothing."

Was he lying to her again? Why did it seem like everyone was avoiding something with her? Noor avoided the case. Mom avoided talking with her and setting a wedding date. And now this. "Jabir."

"I'm good."

Liar.

She stared at him for a moment. "Okay. Fine. Be that way. It hurts that you refuse to share. And until then, I'm going to get some sleep."

With that, she put her back to him and pulled up the covers. Her fingers clenched, and her stomach knotted. Until he came clean with her, she had nothing else to say to him.

22

Once more, Tiny sat at the bar in Jefe's and waited on Leila. Except that previously, he'd trusted her. Not so much now. He wanted to know where she'd go after he revealed his latest bit of juicy information. Simply put, he wanted to experiment.

At the other end of the bar, Isa slouched with his eyes glued to the television as if he were totally involved in the basketball game between the University of Kentucky and the George Washington University. Okay, more like a slaughter of GWU by UK. At least it wasn't his alma mater, American University.

Tiny returned to his objective for the evening. He'd use the information regarding Noor as bait by providing Leila with an update but not enough that would put Noor in harm's way. The question remained as to whether or not Leila would run with it.

When he'd spoken to her on the phone earlier that evening, it hadn't seemed like she was eager.

"Tiny, honestly, I am swamped," she'd said when he'd called right after lunch. "Can't you tell me now?"

"I'm sorry, I can't," he replied. "It's pretty sensitive. Jefe's at 6:30?"

She huffed out a sigh. "Okay. Fine. I'll make up a reason for leaving work early."

"Tell them it's a case. That's a half-truth, right?" Oh, he'd loved the double meaning of that one.

Hopefully, she hadn't realized that Jeremy and his buddy had been transferred out of the Central Bureau to a desk job in some dusty, closet-sized cubicles at DHS Headquarters. At least that's what their former supervisor had said.

Tiny shivered as the opening door admitted both Leila and a blast of cold, icy air. The season's first big snowstorm was forecast to hit that evening. He definitely wanted to deliver his message and make his escape.

She slid from her wool overcoat to reveal a pantsuit and heeled boots. Without a word, she removed her beret, hung her coat over the back of her chair, and slid onto the hard wood of the bar chair next to him. She set her phone on the bar. "Perhaps I should use that line. What is it? You come here often?"

He chuckled. "Only when I have to meet with contacts."

"And your wife is fine with this?"

"She trusts me." Since he now assumed Leila to be more of a foe than friend, he didn't want to say too much. "Drink?"

"A margarita."

"Coming right up." As he signaled the bartender, his gaze crossed Isa. His operative remained fixated on the game, but he rubbed his bearded chin to show he'd seen the arrival of his quarry. "Are you pulling for GWU?"

She glanced at the television. "I'm really not a basketball person. But Mama likes them. Too bad they are not the best."

He chuckled and made more idle chitchat as the bartender prepared their drinks. As they talked, he studied her. She seemed uptight, impatient, as if she couldn't wait to get out of there. He doubted it was to get home to spend time with her mother. Once the bartender had settled his tab and left them alone, Tiny said, "I've got some news for you."

"From Alex and Jabir?"

"Yes." He shifted and leaned his elbow against the bar. "Shafiq is dead. Noor and her family are in hiding."

Her jaw dropped. "I—I don't understand. What happened?"

He gave her the Cliff's Notes version of the events on Tortola and in Beirut.

She began shaking her head. "All is lost." She closed her eyes and rubbed her temples. "The murderers will walk away."

"Maybe not."

She resumed her contemplation of her margarita and raised the glass to her lips. "What do you mean?"

"Alex and Jabir met with Noor a couple of days ago."

Leila began coughing.

He tapped her on the back as if to help her.

"So sorry." She hacked one last time and cleared her throat. "Why didn't you immediately tell me?"

"Because I didn't get the report until today." He'd gotten it yesterday, and by now, Farouk should have returned to Beirut while Noor had retreated to wherever she and her family hid. At least she was safe, and if Tiny had his way, Farouk and his wife would be in hiding by the following day. "Noor discovered a video of the murder."

"What?" Leila stared. "A video? But... how?"

"I don't know those details," he lied. He didn't want to reveal anything that might remotely endanger Noor.

"Did she hand it over to them?"

"No. She doesn't trust us." *Thanks to your errors.* "I suppose she feels let down. They left it that she would contact Alex or Jabir if she decided we were trustworthy."

"Where is she hiding?" A new intensity crept into her voice. Why did she want to know? Would she pass along the information to someone else? Someone who didn't have Noor's best interests at heart?

"She didn't tell Alex and Jabir." He held up his hands and shook his head. "Sorry, but that's all I've got. I just wanted to let you know we've made some progress. Better than the backslide we had when we lost Shafiq. I'm hoping we can get Noor to trust us enough to hand over the video and let us take her into protective custody. If it shows Tarek and Hashim murdering Samir, it would be enough for an arrest anywhere in the world, right?"

"Absolutely. We could arrest them as soon as we have that video." She toyed with her phone, and her hand shook slightly. She rubbed her nose as if it suddenly itched.

That told him enough. She lied to him about something, but what remained unclear. "That is what you want, right?"

"Of course! I want justice for Samir." She rubbed the back of her neck and suddenly focused on the game as if it were the most interesting thing in the world. "He needs to pay for his crimes."

"I agree." Now he needed to let Isa take over. "I've got to get home. Thanks for coming all the way out here. I know it wasn't an easy trek, especially with the snow getting ready to start. I'll keep you posted if Noor surfaces with the video."

"Tiny, thanks." She offered a smile but it faded too quickly for him to deem it genuine.

He shrugged into his overcoat and shoved his fedora onto his head. As he headed toward the door, he noted Isa at the bar.

The young man had pulled on his coat as if he were cold. He was ready for action.

Confident Isa would follow Leila to the end, he strolled from the restaurant.

☆ ☆ ☆

Tuesday, December 19, 2017, 1830 hours EST, Alexandria, VA

She was dirty. Isa knew it, but he had to prove it.

He would not lose her. Not this time. He remained where he was at the bar.

Leila did as well. She sucked down her drink.

Why? Probably something to do with her phone because she fiddled with it as if anticipating a call or text.

While keeping an eye on her and the game, he did as well but for a different reason. Otto, their computer expert, had installed an app on his phone that allowed him to track text conversations between different phone numbers. Now he eavesdropped with ease on her conversation. The messages flashed back and forth on his screen.

Her thumbs worked fast. "I have news. Big news for you."

The recipient's response popped up on his screen. "What news?"

Her fingers flew across her screen. "Too good to tell except in person. Shall I meet you?"

The reply flashed on his phone. "7:45. You know the place."

What place? Where she'd gone when she'd lost him on the Metro? Isa raised his gaze to the television and noted her position.

Leila finished her drink in one final gulp and winced as if it hurt going down.

He slid off his chair and looped his messenger bag over his shoulders before pulling on his knit cap.

Hopping off her chair, she threw on her coat and hat and hurried toward the entrance. Either she was tipsy or simply did not look where she was going, but she bumped into someone.

As if he were another weary commuter, Isa came up behind her fast enough to hear her mumbled apology before she pushed into the night.

The cold air nearly took his breath away. It was strange how it had been nearly sixty the day before. Winter had arrived two days early with a forecast of four to six inches of snow. He hunched further into his wool pea coat. A snowflake fluttered downward and stuck to his cheek.

Ahead of him, the heels of Leila's boots pounded on the sidewalk. She kept glancing over her shoulder as if expecting a tail.

This time, Isa maintained an even pace since he knew she headed toward the Metro. To her, he was another nameless, faceless worker who had stopped for a drink on the way home from work. He feigned a yawn to play up that image. Not too difficult, really, since he had been tailing her since seven that morning. He had definitely tired of this assignment.

Just as she had the last time, Leila turned into the King Street Metro station.

He followed. Once on the exposed platform, he shoved earbuds into his ears before pulling on his gloves. Brrr. Why could this not have happened during the summer? Music filled his ears, and he lowered the volume.

Leila stood not twenty feet from him. She wrapped her arms around herself.

Lights along the edge of the railway began blinking. A moment later, an inbound train rumbled into the station. Brakes hissed, and the doors hummed open.

Along with a gaggle of other commuters, including Isa, she stepped into a car close to the front and perched on a seat facing backwards.

Facing her, Isa leaned in the doorway against one of the dividers. He kept his phone in front of him with a game of Solitaire up on his screen to maintain the persona of a commuter. In reality, he observed her.

Nearby, Leila did the old reading-a-paperback routine. Her gaze occasionally flicked upward. It crossed over him but did not linger.

Thankfully, he had disguised himself well with his newly grown beard, pea coat, and knit cap.

The train rocked and swayed as they headed into the District. After several stops when she did not move, they slowed as they approached the Foggy Bottom station. The doors swished open with an announcement of their arrival.

Her perfume hit his nose as she passed him and stepped onto the platform.

Should he go after her? His head struggled with his gut. If he did and jumped on at the last minute with her, he would blow his cover. He took the chance and remained slouched where he was.

Leila returned just as the doors shut. She resumed her seat. This time, she did not look around as if she were confident she had no tails.

Good. He had anticipated correctly this time.

And she had gotten careless.

The train continued on its way out of the District. At the Rosslyn station, she stepped off the train again. This time, Isa was not going to lose her. He stood not ten feet away from her. She had a spring to her step as if anticipating something exciting. Whoever awaited her at her mysterious destination held some sort of sway over her.

Isa yawned again. He gazed around him at the platform. So totally a reminder of The Tube in London, including the cameras. Futuristic. Spartan. Big Brother was watching. Just in case. Little did they know they had a possible spy in their midst.

A puff of air plus flashing lights preceded the train.

Leila boarded with no glances around her. She thought she was safe. Sloppy in his mind. He wondered how she had passed the rigorous training of Saudi Intelligence. Maybe the sloppiness had been a recent occurrence. An error in judgment. Just like the one that had gotten her exiled from Beirut.

Finally, they arrived at the Ballston-MU station in Arlington. She exited, and he followed along with the other road-weary commuters. Rather than head toward a parked car, she strode through the thickening snow into a residential area several blocks away.

If he were not careful now, she would see him since the crowd had dramatically thinned. Isa hung back. The darkness and building blizzard helped, and when she turned down the walk of a townhouse, he stepped into the shadows across from it. At least the weather kept most people inside. He opened his messenger bag and pulled out a high-performance camera.

As an older couple greeted her at the door, he snapped several pictures of them. A few minutes later, the couple headed into the night and hurried down the sidewalk toward the commercial area near the station.

He waited and watched the face of the three-story structure. A moment later, a light in a third floor window flashed on to reveal a masculine silhouette. He rose. A feminine one, most likely Leila, joined him. They talked for a few minutes with the woman gesturing wildly. The man ran his hand down her hair as if to soothe her. They kissed. It grew in intensity. So embarrassing, especially for Isa, who had been taught that modesty was paramount.

He looked away.

The light turned out.

Who was Leila's lover? He tried to digest that particular new development. Snow tumbled from the sky now. The temperature dropped even further. Though he had worn long underwear for this particular venture, Isa began shivering. He tried to imagine the headline.

Unit 28 Agent Found Frozen to Death in Arlington Snowbank.

What he wouldn't do for a mug of hot chocolate. Or a cup of coffee. Better yet, some soup.

He didn't know how much time had passed. Probably a couple of hours. The door to the townhouse opened, and Leila left by herself. She hesitated, then glanced around before taking the steps off the stoop one at a time. Either she worried about falling on ice, or she did not want anyone to know she had been there for less than noble purposes. Seeing that it was closing in on nine, she most likely retreated to her house.

To him, the man held more interest.

Isa waited another agonizing half an hour. By that point, he wanted to do jumping jacks or something to warm up.

Finally, the lights on the second floor switched off. The front door opened, and a man in a trench coat and fedora pulled low locked the door behind him. He strutted down the sidewalk and waited at the curb.

Isa's breath came in shallow gasps. Slowly, ever so slowly since the man would notice fast movement, he brought the camera to his eye and snapped several photos.

As if he had seen him, the man peered in his direction.

Isa remained stock still. He did not shift the camera, rub his nose, or anything. Hopefully, the snow and the amber glow of the streetlight above the man shielded him.

A chill different from the cold snaked up his spine.

His body instinctively recognized a killer.

A taxi pulled to the curb, and the man climbed inside.

Isa did not dare move until the vehicle had turned the corner. Now, he did not waste any time. It took a bit for his numb feet to get going, but the brisk pace he kept began warming him by the time he made it to the Metro station. During the whole walk and wait on the platform, he kept an eye out for anyone watching him. As he waited, he dialed a number on his phone.

"Sadie Callahan." Her voice was hoarse.

"Sadie, it's Isa Haswi."

"Isa!" Immediately, she coughed. "Sorry. Bad cold."

"Are you still at work?" He glanced at the clock and frowned. It would be eleven before he got to the office.

"Yeah." She sighed. "Tiny wanted some information, so I'm still working on it. Where are you?"

"I am coming to the office." His weariness disappeared at the thought of having time with the redhead. "I have some photos from my surveillance. But if you are too tired—"

"No, no. I'm here to help. Bring them in, and we'll take a look."

"I will be there soon." With that, he slid his phone into his pocket and maintained subtle counter-surveillance throughout the entire ride.

After arriving at the Huntington station, Isa headed to his car. Its weak heater barely did anything to warm him up during the twenty-minute ride to Unit 28 headquarters.

Thankfully, he had warmed up. With his plain black mug and two pouches of hot chocolate mix in hand, he headed to the break room on the third floor. He found a mug that said Hot Dog Mama in a cabinet.

Sadie met him as the glass door to Research hissed open. "Hey." She smiled from behind rimless glasses before grabbing a tissue and sneezing. She turned away and blew her nose. "Sorry. I don't mean to spread germs."

"Drink?" He offered the steaming mug.

"Aren't you sweet! And with my mug. Thanks!" She smiled and took a sip. "Yum. Hot chocolate." She turned and led the way to a workstation. "Thanks for coming. I hate working late, especially when I don't feel good. I've just been so busy that I haven't been able to get to Tiny's work."

"Which is?"

"Information on a guy named Pinky. He's a loan shark."

"A what?"

"Loan shark." She grinned. "If you get into gambling trouble, you can take out a loan through him—with interest, of course. Pull up a chair and have a seat."

He found one in the cubicle next door and joined her.

She settled behind her computer. "What do you have for me?"

"Pictures from my surveillance of Leila al-Kadir." He extracted the SD card from his camera and handed it to her. "I want to identify the people in the pictures."

"We can try." She pulled them up.

As he gazed at them, Isa's spirits sank. He'd been so confident of his work, but thanks to the snow, they were almost blurry, like he'd had the lens out of focus, which he hadn't. "I thought the quality was better."

"Well, it's almost a blizzard out there. And don't worry. I can enhance it some. Which ones do you want to focus on?"

"One of a single man. And one of an older couple who I think own the townhouse."

"Coming right up." She selected the proper photos. Several clicks of the mouse lightened and sharpened the images of the couple so that they were recognizable as humans. "Who do you think they are?"

"I don't know."

"Do you have the address?"

He rattled it off.

"I'll run them through our database." She hit a button, then typed in the address. "Well, it looks like the townhouse is owned by al-Hassans. Distant cousins of Tarek and Hashim. And the photo of the guy?"

She fell silent as she loaded the photo into a program. But no matter how she tried to lighten it and sharpen it, he remained unrecognizable. Finally, she coughed and sat back. "I'm sorry, but that's the best I could do. Even though he's under a streetlight, the snow and the shadowing make it impossible to clean it up enough even to run it through the database."

He hung his head. "I failed."

"Why do you say that? I mean, look at the amount of snow falling." She gestured to a floor-to-ceiling window nearby. It was almost a total whiteout. "And, it's pitch dark out there. The only way you could have gotten a better shot was if you were standing next to him." She chuckled, which turned into a cough, then a sneeze. "But that's not a way to stay covert, exactly."

Isa shook his head. "And not a good idea with this one."

She paused from pulling another tissue from its box. "Why do you say that?"

"I think he is a killer." He shivered as he voiced his worries. "It is an instinct, nothing more."

Sadie turned back to stare at the screen. "Do you think he might have had a hand in murdering Samir Kamil and Shafiq Rahman?"

"Perhaps." He drained his mug.

"At least we know who owns the townhouse."

"And that couple let this person, whoever he is, use it for a tryst with Leila."

"Wow. The plot thickens. And, it provides maybe a lead." She coughed into her arm. "Feel better now?"

He nodded.

"Good, 'cause I'm beat." She took off her glasses and rubbed her eyes. "Matter of fact, I'm going to drop this envelope in Tiny's box and head home. Um, I have a question."

He smiled. "That is?"

"Uh, can you walk me to my car? Normally, the security guy would, but since you're here, would you mind?"

Would he? Hardly! "Not at all. I will be glad to walk you to your car."

She shut down and picked up the inter-office envelope. They headed toward the open staircase that overlooked the lobby. "Hey, have you heard about the decentralization pilot program?"

"Tiny sent an e-mail asking for candidates. How would it work?"

"They'd decentralize teams involving field agents and folks like me." She ascended the stairs one floor. "I'm actually thinking about it."

What? Before he could stop himself, he blurted, "But why? Do you not like this area?"

She shrugged as she led the way to Tiny's office. "I do. But, well, not so much anymore." She didn't elaborate but instead continued, "And I've talked with Alex. She mentioned setting up a 'pod' in Weatherly. I mean, they're contractors down there. The only difference between them and us is that they get paid a lot more and aren't gone as much. But it's a good job. How about you? There's a bonus attached to it, right?"

His mind spun. Just when he'd become interested in someone, she was contemplating moving. Would he ever be as comfortable with anyone else as he was with her? "I think so. Honestly, I had not thought about it." Maybe he should talk with Jabir. Would three agents in a pod be too many? "When is the deadline to commit?"

"The end of January." She grinned. "So you have six weeks to think about it, young man."

He laughed as she dropped her envelope into a receptacle outside Tiny's door. Together, they headed downstairs and strolled in comfortable silence from the building into the covered parking deck. She tensed, and he drew closer, almost to the point that their shoulders touched. He switched into surveillance mode again. "Are you feeling badly?"

"Oh, I'm… fine."

Then why did uncertainty echo in her voice?

They reached a white Honda CR-V. She unlocked it and turned to face him. "Isa, thanks."

He wanted to reach up and brush back a tendril of her red hair that had escaped from her knit cap. "You should call in sick. You sound like you need the rest."

"You know, I think I will." She opened her door. "See you later?"

"Is that a promise?" he blurted before he lost his nerve.

A small smile curled her lips. "If you want it to be."

With that, she climbed behind the wheel.

His heart nearly singing, he watched her leave before he retreated to his own beat-up Honda Civic ten stalls down. Yes, he would keep that promise to her. Somehow.

23

"A word with you, brother." Those words came from a lowered car window.

Hashim stopped at the door to his motel room and stared as Tarek slid from the black BMW 3 Series sedan. "What are you doing here?"

"Perhaps I have come to give you Christmas greetings." A sarcastic smile curled Tarek's lips as he shoved his fedora onto his head. He tightened his overcoat around him. "Or perhaps this is a social call."

Hashim glared at him. He needed to get inside. Thanks to the lighter weight coat he'd worn during their meal run to a restaurant, he shivered. Sleet stung his cheeks, and despite the knit cap he wore, the cold night air reached all the way to his bald scalp. "Somehow, I doubt that."

He glanced at Massoud, Rami, and Ali, who all hunched in their own jackets. "Give us some privacy, if you will."

They headed to the motel room next door where Rami and Ali bunked. Hashim turned the key in the lock and opened the door. He switched on the heater, which coughed as if it didn't want to jump into action. An acrid smell from the heating element filled the air.

Tarek placed his hat on the dresser. "What a dump."

"What did you expect? The Ritz?" Hashim asked. He shut the door and leaned against the shabby dresser. "Why did you come?"

"This madness must stop." Tarek began pacing up and down the length of the room. "It truly must stop. Based on news I received, our primary mission has changed to finding Noor. And what have you done here? Nothing. Absolutely nothing."

Hashim folded his arms across his chest. "You are wrong, brother. I have been tracking—"

"You are a fool!" Tarek whipped around and faced him. "You care about nothing except seeking vengeance against a mere woman."

"That woman destroyed my life!"

"I don't care anymore. From what you have told me, you've made no progress. None!"

"Like you have." Coldness seeped into Hashim's heart. "What have you done to find Noor?"

"I got the information, did I not?"

"And you've done nothing with it." A derisive smile curled Hashim's lips. "But with the source of that information?"

He let the barb of his insult hang in the air.

Tarek stiffened. "Leila al-Kadir means nothing to me."

"Somehow, I doubt that," Hashim muttered. That coldness inside of him spread. Would that infernal heater not warm the room? His gaze slid to the door between the adjoining rooms.

Tarek paced to the other end of the room and hissed, "This foolish pursuit of yours must end. Look where it's brought you." His nose wrinkled. He probably feared he'd catch some sort of strange, contagious disease if he lowered himself to sit on the stained bedspread. "To… this."

"We don't know where Noor is. And this is more pressing." Hashim's fists clenched. "We have as long as we need to take care of both."

"Oh?" Tarek studied him. "What is that plan, then? Do tell me."

He had him there. No plan yet, at least nothing solid. Hashim ground his teeth.

A smirk played at Tarek's lips. "Exactly what I thought. We must pull out. Turn our attention to locating Noor."

"No! I will *not* pull out. I will not!" That blackness that had invaded him when he'd almost kidnapped the vixen in Beirut returned. He took a deep breath and huffed it out. "Do you realize something, Tarek? The vix—Alex—lives not ten miles from here. She laughs. She goes about her daily routine. Yet she doesn't realize something. Her angel of vengeance lurks nearby." He hammered his chest. "I *will* have her. No matter what you say, I will."

Tarek lifted his chin and narrowed his eyes.

Hashim could almost hear his thoughts. *You are an idiot.*

Tarek sighed and shook his head. "I must say, brother, you have become rather hard of hearing. You're finished here. We have more important concerns, that of finding Noor Kamil-Sultan. You will leave here and join me in Washington. Now."

Tarek started for the door.

As he passed him, Hashim grabbed his arm. "I. Will. Finish. This."

"No, you will come with me. All of you."

Hashim shoved him.

Tarek stumbled backward into the table next to the window. His eyes widened. He charged his brother. The dresser shook as they collided, and a lamp fell to the floor. Hashim pushed back, and like two grappling wrestlers, they stumbled away from the dresser.

Tarek bumped into the corner of one of the double beds. Staggering, he thrust his arms out.

Hashim slammed into the wall next to the door to the adjoining room. With a low growl, he charged him.

Tarek fell across the bed closer to the window. Hashim's momentum carried both men onto the floor between the bed and the window.

Tarek's fist shot out.

Pain burned across Hashim's cheek. Without hesitation, he slammed a hard right into his brother's face.

Tarek yelped and scrambled toward the door on all fours.

Not so fast. Hashim drove a knee between his shoulder blades.

The breath whooshed out of Tarek. He grabbed for the lamp.

It tumbled onto Hashim.

He grasped Tarek's head. With one harsh jerk, he broke his neck.

Tarek spasmed once and went limp.

Heart pounding, Hashim remained on his knees. He shoved the lamp aside and raised his gaze.

Massoud stood in the doorway between the two rooms. Judging from his wide eyes and slack jaw, he must have witnessed the final showdown between the two brothers.

"He was going to stop me," Hashim muttered between sharp breaths. Suddenly, heat exploded across his body. He ripped off his jacket and cap and threw them onto the bed.

"What do you want us to do?" Massoud asked.

"Leave me be for a bit." Hashim refused to look between the bed and the window.

Weakness surged through him as the adrenaline from the fight faded. He grabbed the chair at the desk and sagged onto it. It groaned under his weight. On the laptop he'd brought with him from South Carolina, the sound waves from the bugs he'd placed at the vixen's flat had begun bouncing up and down. He clamped his headphones over his ears.

What was that noise? He tried to discern it. Singing. Horrible singing. Like that of lovesick cats. And from the vixen, nonetheless. A drawer thumped closed, and she chattered to her dogs like a mockingbird. Did she realize how much she revealed when she talked to them? Most of her one-way conversation was mundane, like how good it had been to gather with family for Christmas Day and to have Christmas with Jabir as her fiancé. What useless drivel.

Hashim glanced at himself in the mirror. His eyes burned with his desire for revenge, not regret over killing his brother.

He started to tune her out.

"So guess what Mom and Dad gave me?" the vixen said. "Two tickets for me and Jabir to go with them to see *The Palace Beauty Pageant* at the TAEC! Oh, I can't wait! I know Jabir doesn't like musicals that much, but I do." She sighed as if in total bliss. "I'll have to figure out what to wear."

Loose Ends

The Palace Beauty Pageant. Hashim frowned before opening a browser window. He began pecking the name into Google, but his fingers shook so much that it took him three tries.

Perfect. Almost too perfect to be true. He rubbed his bearded chin as he thought about that one. *The Palace Beauty Pageant* was the newest hit Broadway musical and was coming to the Triangle Arts and Entertainment Complex in Durham on Saturday, January 6. He pulled up the venue. A smile began playing about his lips as an idea popped into his head.

It was a risky one, for sure. If he planned well, it would work. And he would. Plan well, that is. But for this one, he'd need some extra support.

Without breaking eye contact with the screen, he reached for one of his burner phones and dialed a number. When Damon answered, he said, "I need your help. I have a potential way to kidnap Alex Thornton, but it requires extra planning and support."

"Hey, man, I'm at your service, especially if it deals with her. Explain."

Hashim outlined his idea.

Damon remained silent for a few seconds as if considering all of the ins and outs associated with such a risky endeavor. Finally, he said, "Looks like we need to meet up and hash this out in person. I've got a hunting lodge in upstate South Carolina. Meet me there, and we'll work on it." He gave the address. "Meanwhile, I'll pull up what I can. When will you be there?"

"Mid-morning tomorrow." An idea for disposing of Tarek's body flew into his head. "We have an errand to run."

"I'll be waiting. Later." With that, the line clicked.

Hashim smiled. He'd have to leave the area, which would put him far outside the range of the bugs he'd planted. No matter. He had what he wanted—a plan. He checked the route to travel to Damon's hunting lodge. Almost all woods once they were west of Columbia. Perfect for his errand.

He rose and opened the door to the other room.

The low conversation between his three men dwindled away.

He fixed each one of them in his gaze. "My brother erred one too many times and had to be dealt with. We will finish this mission all the way to the end. Understand?"

Everyone nodded.

"Pack your things. We are leaving for South Carolina right now. On the way, we'll dump the BMW and Tarek in the woods. Rami, Ali, take him and put him in the trunk. I'll drive. Massoud, you drive the van."

His lieutenant nodded.

As he watched Rami and Ali carry the body of his brother out to the car, something deep inside of him released. Finally, his patience had paid off. Just a few more days. Then the vixen would be in his hands and would wish she had never tangled with him ten years ago.

24

Enough. Enough procrastinating. Enough stonewalling. The day after Christmas, Alex gripped the steering wheel of her four-door yellow Jeep Wrangler as she bulled down the highway from Personal Touch Design and Construction to her parents' house. Already, sleet had begun sticking to the road. With any luck, she'd force the date out of Mom and make it home before it really iced up. Then maybe she and Jabir could start planning a wedding for real instead of talking about it in theory.

She turned into her parents' gravel driveway. Both Mom's Acura RL and Dad's Land Cruiser sat on the concrete parking pad. Light glowed from behind the curtains in the front. Mom must have closed them against the cold. Dad was home as well. Maybe, if Mom shut her down, he'd be there to support her in setting a date.

Alex turned off the Jeep and climbed the steps onto the back deck. Her foot started slipping. Yeah, it was getting nasty outside. Shuffling, she reached the back door. No one was in the den. Surprising since her parents liked to take it easy the day after Christmas. Also, no lights glowed from Dad's study above the garage. Maybe he was helping Mom put away the dishes from Christmas dinner.

Almost as soon as she opened the door, warmth hit her. She unzipped her leather jacket and left her scarf looped around her neck. Softly, she called, "Mom? Dad?"

No answer.

Strange.

Voices reached her. Mom and Dad. They seemed to be in the dining room. She stepped further into the den and made her way toward the hallway that led to the foyer with the dining room on one side and formal living room on the other.

The voices became more distinct, like they were fighting.

Okay, arguing. She'd rarely seen her parents fight.

"Then also a son-in-law... hadn't talked about a date yet."

Alex slowed.

"It's been too busy." Mom. She sounded like she was kneeling the way she did when she put away the fine china in the credenza.

"Just to set a date? Really?"

"For all I care, she can wait."

Alex's breath hitched.

"Roya. She wants your involvement, you know." Dad's voice had a pleading tone.

"I—I can't."

Alex peeked around the corner. With her head hung, Mom sat on her knees in front of the credenza.

Dad leaned against the door frame of the butler's pantry with all of his attention focused on his wife. He clasped his hands together in front of him as if begging. "Please, please consider telling her."

"Why? So she can hate me? She's done fine all these years without knowing. Why change it?"

"Because she's our daughter." He drew a breath. "She deserves—"

"She does not need to know. Can't you understand that?" Mom jumped to her feet as if she were a young woman in her twenties rather than in her late fifties. She didn't even notice her own daughter standing a mere ten feet away.

Alex's heart hammered. She deserved what?

"It's gone on long enough. The lies, the chaining Jabir, Tiny and me to silence. It's got to stop, baby. Please. Tell her. Because if you don't, I will. Why? I'm tired of this."

"You're her father, Davie! Not Hamid al-Hassan. He'll never—"

"Is it true?" Alex stepped into full view of them. Her stomach twisted.

Dad shifted his gaze. His eyes widened. His jaw dropped.

Tears flooded Alex's eyes. Her voice sounded too shrill as she demanded, "Is it true? Is Hamid al-Hassan my father?"

Mom stared down her husband as if she dared him to disagree with her in front of their daughter.

He hung his head and confessed in a whisper, "Yes."

Alex's mouth worked, but her voice had vanished. Heat flooded her face. Trembling started deep within her, and tears began spilling down her cheeks. Finally, she cried, "Why didn't you tell me? Why?"

Mom pushed past her. Footsteps pounded on the stairs as she escaped the scene and left her husband to pick up the pieces. A door slammed.

"Dad, why? Why didn't you?" With that, Alex turned, fled through the den, and nearly ripped the French door off its hinges as she stumbled onto the deck.

She skidded across it on a thin film of ice. Had she not grabbed the railing, she would have sailed off the stairs to a hard landing below. She cleared the steps with one jump and ran to her Jeep.

"Alex, wait!"

Dad.

She couldn't talk. She threw herself behind the wheel and cranked the big engine. Tires chirped as she shot off the concrete parking pad and blew down the driveway.

Through her tears, she barely saw Dad as he tried to follow her down the stairs and nearly fell.

Alex sobbed the entire way to her flat as Mom's words rang over and over in her head like an out-of-control bell. Hamid al-Hassan was her biological father. Not Dad. Nausea swelled. She slammed the door and burst into her flat's stairwell. Fortunately, her neighbor was on vacation and didn't witness her meltdown.

Sobbing now, she made it into her flat and kept it together long enough to release Sabina. She collapsed onto the bed and wept. Finally, she pulled her phone from her jeans pocket and dialed a number. When Jabir answered, she croaked, "Jabir, I need you here. Now."

Tuesday, December 26, 2017, 1650 hours EST, Smithfield, NC

Jabir skidded onto US 301 from the shopping center and sped toward Weatherly. He angled onto US 701 and opened up the throttle of his WRX as wide as he dared. He came upon a pickup moving sensibly on the icing roads. Stomping on the brakes, he prayed he wouldn't slam into the back of it.

He should have stayed on the line with Alex and let her talk it out. On the recorder in his mind, he replayed over and over again the news she'd forced out between sobs.

She now knew the truth.

The news drove a dagger through his heart on so many levels.

Almost all of Alex's identity had crumbled from carelessly delivered words.

He turned onto Weatherly Road and sped toward town.

Once parked in front of his flat, he dashed across the intersection of Weatherly and Main, into the stairwell, and to Alex's flat. Even from outside her door, he heard her sobs.

Lord, have mercy on us.

Jabir burst inside and found her face down on the bed in her room. Sabina sat near her head. Rocky, who almost never got on the bed, pressed against her left side. Both wore concerned expressions as if they'd never seen their mistress like that.

He had four years before when the House Intelligence Committee had almost ripped her to shreds after the failed mission that had spelled her end at Unit 28. He shooed Sabina off the bed, sat down on the edge, and ran his hand down her hair. "Alex, I'm here."

She threw herself into his arms and held on so tightly that he gasped. "Easy there."

Her grip loosened only slightly.

Finally, her sobs faded to soft cries and sniffling.

"Let me get you a washcloth." Jabir rose, got a cold, wet washcloth, and handed it to her. "Here."

She scrubbed it, leaving a ring of smeared mascara around her eyes and makeup on the white cloth.

He brushed back a lock of hair that had stuck to her damp cheek. "You scared me like that, calling like you did."

"I—I'm sorry."

"Don't be." He drew her close and kissed her hair.

After a few minutes, Alex took a deep breath. "After your mom left and you went to talk to Mattie about the paint job you were going to do for her, Diana called. The Fed Ex shipment we got had all of the flooring samples we'd requested, so we needed to organize them and meet about our end-of-year financials." Alex drew her knees to her chest and wrapped her arms around them. "I was fed up, too. I mean, Mom and I needed to set a date, so I decided to go over there on the way home."

Confusion washed over Jabir. "They just didn't out and tell you, did they?"

"Of course not." She muttered something under her breath. "You think they'd knowingly let their oldest know that the founder of JOL was her bio dad?"

"I know. Dumb question."

"I overheard them. I—I guess Dad was tired of keeping that secret. So here we are." More tears began pouring down her cheeks. "Here we are." She rested her head on her arms and cried some more.

Rocky whined from the entry hall. Jabir found both dogs standing at the front door, their eyes pleading. "Hey, the pups need to go out. Let me take them."

She'd followed him and huddled against her doorway with shoulders hunched and eyes glued to the floor as if she were a junior high kid left off the team by the popular ones.

His heart ached, and he took her in his arms again. "Are you sure you'll be okay while I'm out?"

"Can you stay here tonight?" she asked so quietly that he almost missed it.

He didn't hesitate, not when her whole world had cracked at its foundation. "Sure. Let me take them and get my stuff. It's getting nasty out there again."

He began praying for Alex in his heart as he clipped the leashes on the dogs and led them down the stairs. Even his leather jacket failed to shield him from the cold as they crossed Weatherly Road and headed to the park.

He tried to imagine Alex's agony upon overhearing a secret kept for over thirty years. He couldn't.

Jabir peered around him. No one was out. The smart ones were all tucked into their houses and sitting around fires with hot chocolates in hand.

Lord, what do I do? What? I'm at a loss right now. He reached into his jacket and pulled out a pack of cigarettes. Thanks to the events of the past couple of months, he'd started smoking again as a way to release stress, much to Alex's chagrin. He shook one out and lit it. At least the nicotine would warm him. His cell phone rang.

"Jabir, it's David." His future father-in-law's voice rang loud and clear. "I guess you heard what happened."

"I did. Alex called me a bit ago. The secret is now screeching and clawing out of the bag."

"That's one way to look at it." David sighed. "I'm sorry it happened the way it did."

"Me, too." Jabir watched as Rocky poked around a bush and began doing his business.

As if rushing to fill the void, David added, "I was going to tell her, regardless. I got tired of the threats, the way Roya wanted it to stay under wraps. Alex needed to know."

Jabir's heart chilled to match that of the weather. "Pity her own mother refused to tell her."

"She's okay, isn't she?"

"How okay is she supposed to be?" Jabir blew out a stream of smoke. "Cheerful? Happy that her mom lied to her all of her life?" He kicked a lamppost. "She's devastated. I'm worried she's lost her identity, and I'm worried about what this is going to do to her faith, okay?" Suddenly, he realized he was about to rip into Alex's father, who'd been chained to the secret just as much as he had. He blew out a sigh. "I'm sorry."

"I deserved every bit of that."

"I'm going to stay with her tonight because I don't think she should be alone right now."

"Jabir, thank you."

"For what?"

"For being there for her when her mom and I failed her in one of the worst ways possible."

"We'll be in touch." With a sigh, he continued down the street. Rocky watered a couple more lampposts, and Sabina's ears drooped. She shivered slightly. A semblance of a smile poked through his somber mood. "Girl, if you weren't a nudist, you'd be all nice and comfy in a sweater."

She turned and pulled for home. Almost reluctantly, he followed. As he did so, he wondered who had it worse, him or David. Probably David. Hopefully, their marriage would hold together. The last thing Alex needed was for that of her parents to crumble.

Wednesday, December 27, 2017, 0230 hours EST, Weatherly, NC

At the sound of scratching, Jabir's eyes snapped open. The crooked branches of the tree outside danced in time to the wind with the white glow of the street light silhouetting them. Some twigs occasionally scraped the windows of the French doors that led to a Juliet balcony.

His hearing sharpened. In the kitchen, the refrigerator hummed. Not a sound came from Alex's room since she'd finally fallen into an exhausted sleep.

Heart heavy from the sadness permeating the flat, he lay there and stared at the ceiling.

If her parents had come clean with her years before, then—

He stopped that thought as he laced his hands behind his head. It was pointless to dwell in the land of what ifs and would do nothing but stoke the flames of resentment. What was done was done. They couldn't turn back now.

"Jabir?"

He turned his head and found Alex, dressed in her flannel penguin pajamas, standing in the doorway to the study. She sat down on the edge of the futon bed.

"Hey." He pushed himself onto one elbow, reached up, and touched her cheek.

She sighed and tucked her knees to her chest. "I woke up and couldn't go back to sleep."

"I thought I was the one who was supposed to think too much." He smiled in the gloom.

"Hah. Sometimes I do, too." She twisted her engagement ring on her finger. "I guess… I realize there's no way I can plan a wedding with Mom now."

He digested that one for a moment. She was right. It would be next to impossible due to the rift between her and her parents. "Much as I hate to admit it, I agree with you."

She took his hand. "I want to elope."

"Alex?" He struggled upright. "What? Why?"

She focused on him. "How can we? Jabir, they hurt me. Can't you see that?"

"Of course—"

"There's no way I can talk to them now."

"You need to reconcile with—"

"How can I?" In the dim light, her eyes flashed with intensity. "I'm not ready. I—I'm not sure I'll ever be ready, and I'm not waiting that long. And not to mention, you're right. These boundaries suck. It's getting harder and harder to wait."

He fell silent as he considered the ramifications of elopement. He and his mom were close, and they had only each other. And Alex's siblings. They had no clue of what had happened. Alex hadn't called them. And the fact that no one had showed up banging on her door meant her parents hadn't called them either. All of this was so…

He let the thought rest. His heart ached. He knew she was right, but they had to tread carefully, else they'd wind up alienating everyone. "I know what you're saying. But you know if we do, we're denying the chance for your sibs and my mom to be there."

Her sharp intake of breath indicated she'd thought about it. "I know. I just… I don't see a way around it. Do you agree?"

"It pains me, but yes."

"Let's do it this weekend."

"Alex—"

"We're already going to be at the beach, and at least my friends can be there. Please?" She took his hand. "Look. I'll help you paint even though I wasn't planning on working tomorrow. It's not like I have anything else to do now."

Mama, I'm sorry. Heart aching, Jabir closed his eyes. *Lord, is this right?* Strangely, peace filled him. "All right, then. We do it. But only on one condition. Rex still marries us. This is still our wedding, and I don't want it to be some anonymous civil ceremony in a courtroom. I also still want us to see Rex for marital counseling—even if it's after the fact— because I want to make sure we know how to start our marriage right."

"Agreed." She smiled and kissed him. "I love you."

He reached up and ran his hand down her hair. "I want you to keep one thing in mind."

"What?"

"We take this one day at a time. I know it may take months, maybe years, but I want you to reach out to your parents, to forgive them."

Her voice shook as she said, "I—I don't see how that's possible."

"I know. And that's why we'll pray about it. Can you do that? Can you pray about it?"

Tears glimmered in her eyes. "I'm not sure I can."

A sad smile crossed his face as he wiped away one that slipped down her cheek. "I know. And that's why I'll pray."

He drew her close.

"Hold me?" she asked.

He tightened his arms. "Always, my bride-to-be."

25

Jabir dreamed. Alex stood before him in the silver silk dress she'd worn for their wedding the day before when they'd married on the strand at Myrtle Beach. Her eyes almost glowed as she spoke her vows. In sickness and in health. In happiness and sorrow. Until death did them part.

Could happiness and sorrow even dwell in the same spot?

The dream shifted to her tear-streaked face as she'd confessed what she'd overheard between her parents.

And him?

He'd been so happy to wed her, yet he'd experienced the same crushing sadness he'd felt earlier when the secret had chained him. It seemed he hadn't rid himself of that at all, only shifted the reasons for it.

"Alex," he sighed. He reached over to run his hand down his bride of a day and instead came into contact with sheets. "Alex?"

She wasn't there. Only the wind and rain of a fresh storm beat against the sliding glass doors in the bedroom of their sixteenth-floor condo. He sat up and pulled on a long-sleeved t-shirt and sweatpants.

He found her curled up in a terrycloth robe on an easy chair. She'd slicked back her hair, which was damp from her shower earlier that evening. Light from a small lamp by the sofa cast a soft glow onto her face. She stared out the window as if she could see across the ocean.

"Hey." He kissed her hair.

"Did I wake you?"

"No. I thought you'd come to bed after your shower."

"I couldn't sleep." She sighed and scrubbed a hand across her face. "Too much stuff running through my head."

"About the wedding?"

"Part of me wonders if we did the wrong thing."

His heart nearly seized. "As in getting married?"

"No! Oh, Jabir, no." She ran her fingers along the circular outline of the chair. "I guess... in eloping. Becca and I talked about it when we went walking today. She said God doesn't care if we married with just close friends present or in front of a huge crowd."

"While we were waiting for you and the ladies to join us for the ceremony, Rex said the same thing." He settled on a love seat across from a couch. "Come here."

She curled up beside him, and he draped his arm across her shoulders. "Am I sad your sibs, parents, and my mom weren't here? I am. But," he struggled for the right words, "I'm so happy, so very joyful, that we married yesterday. And I think I now understand how happiness and sadness can coexist. It's through joy. Joy at knowing we are both children of God and that Christ intercedes for us. But I realized it's almost like I interchanged two problems for..."

He crashed to a halt.

Alex cocked her head. "For what?"

Why couldn't he have kept his mouth shut? "Uh..."

"Out with it."

This was so not what he wanted to discuss on what had turned out to be their very abbreviated honeymoon. "I... I knew, Alex. I knew Hamid al-Hassan was your father."

Her face clouded. "You knew." Then her eyes widened as if she remembered something. "You and Dad and Tiny. That's what Dad said that awful night."

He hung his head and studied the carpet with great intensity. "We did."

She scrambled to her feet and backed away. "But you never even told me!"

He rose as well. "Because you wouldn't have believed me."

Alex muttered something. "Why don't you let me be the judge of that?"

Jabir raked a hand through his hair. "Think about it. Would you have believed me?"

"You know I would have."

"Back in June?"

"You've known for over six months, and you didn't bother telling me? I can't believe it!" She shoved him aside and bolted for the bedroom.

She wasn't going to slam the door on his face. Not now. Not ever—hopefully. Like a praying mantis, he caught her arm in a lightning fast motion. "Alex, hear me out."

She shook loose. "Why should I?"

He blocked her escape. "Because it's important. Please. You may not want to hear this, but you need to." He tugged her toward the kitchen, the furthest point from their bedroom. "Can you do that for me?"

Alex retreated to the other side of the granite bar and folded her arms across her chest. "I guess I don't have a choice."

"You do, but if you want to totally understand my side of what happened, you need to hear me out. Can you do that?"

"I don't know."

He had to give her honesty points. "Well, try. Do you remember when we were in Panama?"

"Of course!"

"When things went to hell, Hashim took Becca, Ellie, and Melanie as hostages."

Her gaze hardened. "Don't patronize me."

"You need to know my backstory on this. The demand came down for you in exchange for them."

"I know that. Hashim wanted to take his vengeance on me because of what I did to him at the end of Orb Web."

"I thought so, too, that Orb Web was the reason. Tiny read me in that night after we got the ransom. I wanted to know more about it, and I logged into your personnel jacket. I'd also pulled up the file on Hashim, which had his picture. Your file had yours. I thought I saw some resemblance, so I ran a photo comparison program. The results were pretty strong."

She paced a small circle in the kitchen. "But not a hundred percent."

"No. They never could be except for identical twins. But it was enough that I wanted to make sure." He took a seat on one of the bar chairs and leaned his elbows on the granite as once more, the shock of his discovery rippled over him. "I ran a DNA comparison program."

"And we matched on fifty percent of our DNA. Yeah, yeah, I know that now." Alex whirled on him. Anger radiated from her eyes. "You knew then, but you didn't tell me."

He wouldn't back down. He couldn't. With his gaze steady on her, he replied, "I wanted to tell you. You don't know how badly I wanted to do so! I even started toward the door until I realized we were too precarious for me to consider it."

She folded her arms across her chest. "I don't see what you mean."

Sometimes, she could be so stubborn. He took a deep breath as he tried to stuff down his frustration. "Think about it. We had literally just made up only hours after you wanted to rip out my throat. At that time, the trust we had was tenuous at best. How would you have reacted if I'd told you that night?"

Her lips pressed into a thin line. She lowered her head, a sure sign she knew what would have happened.

"You would have probably called me a liar and told me to get out of your life and stay out. I also realized it wasn't my secret to tell."

Her shoulders sagged. "It was Mom's."

He nodded. "I confronted her in August after Melanie's wedding. That was a big mistake. She threatened me, told me that if I didn't keep my mouth shut, she'd consider it a huge breach in our friendship."

Alex twisted the wedding band on her finger. A tear slid down her cheek. "What about Dad?"

"We talked right after you and I got back from Maui. She also threatened him. How, I don't know. Tiny too."

She turned her back on him. "Tiny? Geez, am I the only one who didn't know?"

"No, no, no. We were the only two outside of your dad. Tiny found out by looking into his own distant past and trying to recreate events. He was so worried that he came down to Weatherly and begged your mom to confess. She threatened him into silence as well."

"Worried." She frowned. "Why?"

Maybe now he could convince her to seek protection. "He thinks Hashim is in-country and coming after you, maybe to kidnap or kill you."

She began shaking her head. "He'd never do that. It's... it's too risky."

"Maybe to the average person, but he's not average. Not at all." Jabir rose and stepped around the island before taking her in his arms. "Please. We can put you into protective custody. At least until—"

"Until what? You find him?" Alex pushed him away and drifted to the sliding glass doors leading to the balcony. "What in case that never happens? What would happen then?" She turned and faced him. "I'd stay gone? I can't do that, Jabir. I can't let someone like Hashim dictate my life. I can't start over again because that would mean losing everything I love, maybe even you."

"I'd go with you."

"But my family?" Even from across the room, conflict raged in her eyes. Maybe she was considering reconciliation with her parents. She focused her attention on the blackness outside. "You know what I've learned in these past few months?"

"Tell me," he said through the rising lump in his throat.

"I'm God's kid. His child. He loves me to pieces, and He's not going to let a hair fall from my head without His permission."

In other words, Hashim couldn't touch Alex without God allowing it.

That's what scared Jabir. He honestly didn't know if he could trust God with her safety and her life.

"I understand your concerns." She crossed the room and took his hands. "Honestly. I do."

He swallowed hard. "After Shafiq's murder, CIA spotted Hashim in Havana but lost him. Tiny thinks he somehow got into the country."

"He could have retreated to Beirut."

"He hasn't been seen in Beirut since the last part of November."

"He could be anywhere." Her fingers tightened around his. Peace and defiance now beat out sadness. "You fear for my safety. I get that. But I refuse to cave to fear. I can't abandon Diana. And bad as things are, I can't leave my family and friends. Simply put," she took a deep breath, "I can't live in fear. Tiny said it so perfectly. My anonymity is my safety."

He swallowed hard. "That got breached."

Her eyes widened. "Did it?"

"We think Leila got hold of our personal information and passed it to Hashim."

"But we don't know if he's here." Alex leaned against the back of the couch. "If they spot him, if there's more concrete evidence, I'll consider it." She stood on tiptoes and kissed him. "Okay?"

"Alex—"

"Okay?" She kissed him again, this time more slowly.

Oh, boy. She knew how to weaken him, to shift his mind off such unpleasant business onto much more pleasant endeavors. He ran his hands up her arms and threaded his fingers through her hair as he deepened the kiss.

"What say we turn our attention to other topics?" she murmured against his mouth.

"I could go for a night cap." He kissed her neck.

"Good." In one smooth motion, she undid the sash of the robe and slipped it from her shoulders. She'd pulled on a negligee as if she'd planned for this occasion.

His mouth went dry. Yes, he could go for a shift in attention. Most definitely.

26

Alex's stomach knotted as she and Jabir stowed their suitcases in the attic at her flat. They had to pick up the dogs from Josh and Diana, who'd told them they'd be at Mom and Dad's for some dessert with the rest of the Thornton siblings. Usually, an occasion not to be missed since dessert consisted of hot chocolate and all sorts of leftover Christmas cookies. But tonight? She couldn't face Mom.

"Can't you go?"

Jabir shrugged into his jacket. "You need to go as well. I'm sure your sibs now know about the falling out between you and your mom, and I think they'd want to see with their own eyes that you're okay. Please? Come with me."

She huffed out a breath. "Okay. Fine. So long as I don't have to talk to Mom. With luck, she'll be upstairs with another migraine. Let's just go and get it over with."

"Yes, ma'am." He let them out and locked the door.

Alex led the way to his WRX. On the five-minute ride to her parents' house, she focused more on trying to stay warm than talking. Right then, she had nothing to say. And yes, she wondered what would happen when her sibs realized they'd eloped. Marlie most certainly would notice.

Maybe she could keep the conversation focused on Marlie's and Josette's pregnancies and not her new marital status.

"Yea, the gang's all here," she muttered as they pulled into the driveway and parked behind Jake's Suburban.

"Don't wimp out on me now." Jabir took her hand and led her onto the deck.

Everyone seemed to be in the den. Why? Normally, at least her brothers would be in the kitchen trading jokes and laughing as they cracked open beers and dug into sugar cookies, fudge, and all sorts of wicked delights. Not tonight. Dad stood next to his chair. Even from outside, Alex noted Mom's pinched mouth, folded arms, and stiff posture as she sat on her chair.

She tried to pull back and flee.

No dice because Jabir put his hand on her back.

"Did you know about this?" she hissed.

"No, I didn't. And that's the truth. Josh just said to meet him here."

She went rigid as they stepped inside. "Why is everyone here? What's going on?"

"An intervention for you and Mom." From where he stood, Dad took her hand and tugged her further into potential chaos. "Come on in and take your coats off. Have a seat."

Automatically, Alex handed her jacket to Jabir, who laid them across the back of Dad's recliner. She barely noticed Sabina as the Basenji bounced around her legs. She eased onto a stool to the right of the fireplace.

Jabir sat beside her, and then Marlie came down beside him.

Diana shot her a small smile as she held out her hand to Sabina and rubbed her ears. That smile went miles in her mind. Her sister-in-law was behind her one hundred percent.

Unlike the rest of her family, Mom hadn't stood. Her eyes stayed on her oldest child as if daring her to say a word.

Alex wouldn't. She'd hear out Dad. At least he'd wanted to tell her.

Dad remained standing. "Alex, I know you overheard things we should have told you years before. I, as your father, ask for forgiveness."

Alex glanced at Marlie. Her sister seemed to be studying Jabir's left hand.

Dad continued, "And I believe your mother—"

"Are you two married?" Marlie blurted.

Dad stopped. "What?"

"We eloped on Sunday," Alex announced. She leveled a gaze at Mom as if challenging her.

You hurt me, so I hurt you.

Pandemonium erupted. Marlie and Diana crowded around Alex.

"Wow! So cool!" Diana exclaimed.

"When did it happen?" Marlie asked.

"Who stood with you?" Again, from Diana.

The guys crowded around Jabir and offered loud congratulations.

"So you're happy, eh?" Mom almost shouted.

Like someone had pulled the plug at a rock concert, the room fell silent.

Mom had leapt to her feet. She stalked to her daughter, and both Marlie and Diana backed off as if they knew better to get in her way. She stopped a mere two feet from her. "Happy that you eloped and selfishly denied us the opportunity to be with you?"

What? It wasn't like they could have had a wedding. Alex lifted her chin. "We didn't have a choice. I mean, with the way—"

"You *always* have a choice, Alexandra."

Mom never used Alexandra with Alex unless she was furious with her. The last time had been when Mom had busted her in high school for drinking at a party.

Dad took her arm. "Roya—"

She shook him off. "You've said your piece, Davie." She trained her gaze on her oldest. "I hope this one lasts longer than the previous!"

Acute pain flashed to numbness. Then the heat of anger seared Alex's heart. She snatched her jacket up. "I'm done with this!"

With that, she fled through the French doors and slammed them so hard the pane in one of them cracked from top to bottom. She didn't care. Not now.

Forget reconciliation. It wasn't going to happen. She'd been dumb to entertain the notion.

When her bottom hit the leather of the WRX's passenger seat, Alex crumbled. Head in arms, arms on knees, she sobbed as if there would be no end to her tears.

Jabir and the pups joined her a moment later. Both dogs were subdued as if they sensed their mistress's distress. On the miserable ride back to her flat, Jabir kept his hand on her back and only removed it to shift gears. Gratitude for her groom surged through her. Had he not been in her life? She shuddered to think what would have happened.

"I've got them," Jabir told her.

On autopilot, Alex let herself into her flat and made her way to her bedroom. Not even shucking her boots, she lay down and curled into a ball. Numbness surged over her. From the shock, she was sure, which would at some point very soon melt into raw pain.

Rocky woofed his typical mealtime bark. Jabir must have been feeding them.

Maybe she'd just go to bed. Or drink herself silly. Both seemed appealing at that moment. She'd have plenty of time tomorrow to adjust to the insult Mom had hurled her way.

Someone sat down on the edge of the bed.

"I don't want to talk about it," she croaked.

"Oh, Alex."

Marlie was there.

Emotion swooped over Alex. Turning over, she practically threw herself into her sister's arms and sobbed. More arms came around her as if Marlie had grown them. She recognized Jake's Old Spice aftershave. And then the sharp scent of Josh's aftershave.

"We're here for you, Alex," Jonathan, her youngest brother, put his hand on her hair.

For several minutes, they sat in silence as Alex's tears finally dwindled away.

"Dad told us what happened," Marlie said.

Alex finally pulled back. "So I'm not your sister."

"Bull." Josh shook his head. "We don't care about bloodlines. You're family to us, always will be."

"None of that changes," Jake added.

"And I, for one, am glad I'm a member of it," Diana said.

Alex found her and Clark, Marlie's husband, sitting on the foot of the bed.

Diana, her colleague, friend, and sister-in-law, reached out and took her hand. "We're here for you. All of us. The entire Thornton gang. All the way."

Alex held on. Oh, she held on so tightly. Suddenly, she realized how true Josh's comment about bloodlines was. She was no less a Thornton now than she had been before all of this mess had begun. They were family. And the Thornton gang always stuck together.

27

"Want to go for a couple of more rounds?" Jabir asked Thursday afternoon as he dribbled the basketball. It slapped against the shiny wood of the court at Joe's Gym on the western edge of Weatherly.

Josh Thornton grinned and trotted with him. "I've got time for one more." He bent lower into a ready crouch. Sweat dripped from his chin. "Bring it on."

Jabir dribbled faster. He feinted to his right, dodged left, and drove hard down the court toward the basket. He attempted a layup, but Josh jostled him. The ball bounced off the rim. "Hey, foul!"

Josh laughed as he got the ball. "Desperate times call for desperate measures. And that was no foul. Sorry. No dice on that one." He darted away. "How's Alex?"

"Don't know." Jabir covered him as Josh bolted toward the other end. "She's barely been home since Tuesday."

Josh paused and dribbled as he looked for an opening. "We're all confused as to what got into Mom."

"Thanks for being there for Alex. Coming over probably saved her sanity," Jabir added as he thought about his bride's state of mind after her sibs had left. Though still sad, peace had radiated from her. At least she'd slept curled in his arms that night instead of pacing.

"Like we said Tuesday, the Thornton gang sticks together." Josh ducked left, then right, and darted around Jabir. He leapt toward the basket and did a reverse layup. "Two points. In style, I might add."

"Man, you're good today. Or I'm off my game."

"Or both." Josh laughed. He checked his watch. "Hey, I hate to scoot, but lunch is almost over, and I need to get cleaned up so I can get dirty again while checking on three cows, eight horses, and a dozen pigs this afternoon." He strolled to a bench where they'd tossed their duffels. He plopped down and mopped his face with a towel. "Seriously. I don't know what got into Mom. None of us do. But one thing's for sure. We're glad you and Alex married."

Jabir joined him and took a pull on his water bottle. "Thanks. She..." Thoughts of Alex and his already deeper love for her choked off his voice. "She's my world now."

"Not that I'm biased, but she's a good catch."

That did it. Jabir chuckled. "Be gone with you. I think I'm going to warm down for a bit."

"Later, dude." Josh headed for the locker room.

Jabir rose and picked up the ball. He dribbled toward the goal. Right then, he preferred to focus on the here and now, that is, the sound of hard rubber on wood, followed by the swish of net as he tossed a jumper into the basket with his characteristic precision. He took another jump shot from three-point land. This one bounced off the rim.

"Tough shot," David Thornton called.

Jabir got the rebound and turned to find his father-in-law, clad in dress pants and shirt, standing in the doorway leading to the gym's lobby. He began dribbling toward the free throw line and tossed another one into the basket. "What brings you here?"

"May I?" David gestured toward the ball.

Jabir tossed the rebound to him.

David's dress shoes clacked against the court as he joined his son-in-law. "I thought, as the husbands of the women who are estranged, we needed to talk."

"About what? I have no idea how Alex is because she's barely been home. She's been either here, at work, or with Ellie in Clayton. I'd say she's tired of talking, period."

"You're probably right." David took his own jump shot, which bounced off the rim. "I want you to know something. After Roya insulted my daughter—your bride—I felt an emotion I thought I'd never feel about my wife."

Jabir copied Josh's layup from earlier. "Which was?"

"I love Roya, love her dearly, have so for thirty-six years and counting. But two days ago, I despised her."

Jabir got the rebound and braced the ball between his arm and hip. "I'm… I'm stunned."

David shrugged. "She's already kicked me out of the bedroom. I'm sleeping in the guest room right now. Go ahead and laugh, but that night after I'd had a stiff drink to cool off, I picked the lock to our bedroom and confronted her."

Jabir didn't laugh because he imagined the ensuing fight had been one for the ages.

"I essentially told her that if she had a shred of hope of keeping any intimacy in our marriage, she'd seek counseling for wounds created all those years ago when her family died. Then she and I would go to counseling together. Surprisingly, she agreed that night. Yesterday morning, I made a call. Yesterday afternoon, we met with our counselor for two hours straight."

Jabir tossed his father-in-law the ball. "Why do you think she agreed?"

"When she insulted Alex in front of everyone, I think she realized she'd way overstepped. Our counselor gave us both homework. Hers is to apologize to Alex sooner rather than later and have it come from the heart. And sooner because if she waits, the harder it will become. My job is to make sure it happens."

"No small task since both of them are so stubborn."

"I still think we need to keep our double date on Saturday."

That was impossible, at least in Jabir's mind. "How? You think Alex is going to go?"

"You think Roya wants to?" His father-in-law shook his head as if he'd already had that discussion with his wife. "She doesn't. She's made that very clear. But our next meeting with the counselor is on Monday, and he told her he expected her to report back to him."

"You want me to get Alex there."

"Better you than me. She'll listen to you."

"Do you remember how headstrong your daughter is?"

"Oh, yeah." A smile finally poked its way through David's somber countenance. "And I remember how persuasive you can be."

"We'll see. I'll do my best. How about that?"

"That's all I can ask for." David tossed him the ball. "And it's enough."

★ ★ ★

Thursday, January 4, 2018, 1715 hours EST, Weatherly, NC

Routine. Schedule. Lifting. All great antidotes to a hurting heart. Alex slid a weight plate onto a bar for a set of back squats. She added the remaining weights and secured them with clips. What was nice about lifting? Emptying her mind of troubling thoughts and filling it with music. Lady Gaga beat anything at that point. So did simple motions. Down. Up. Down. Up. Five reps later, she eased the bar onto the squat rack and removed the clips.

As she racked her weights, movement out of the corner of her eye caught her attention. She straightened as her husband approached. "Hey. I thought you'd already had your workout."

"I did." He smiled as he leaned in for a kiss.

She shifted to another bar. "Then what brings you here?"

"Uh, maybe I wanted to see you."

She scowled and folded her arms across her chest. "Jabir."

He chuckled. "Can't I see my wife?"

"You are too funny." She turned and began adding weights for a dead lift. "Really. I'm sure you could have waited another hour for my company."

"While I was here playing ball with Josh, your dad dropped by."

She froze, her hand and the plate midway to the bar. "Why?"

"Because he still wants us to meet them at *The Palace Beauty Pageant* on Saturday."

She slammed it all the way on. "No."

"Alex."

She added the clip and yelped as it pinched her finger. "Why should I?"

"Because you love a close family. It's one of the blessings I noticed with you guys, one I appreciate since my own family is torn."

Alex paused. Oh, she knew Jabir's family history. A father who'd forced his daughter to marry too young. The same daughter had died in a faraway land for dishonoring her husband. Jabir's brothers hated him for standing up for her, and his father had divorced his mother and disowned him. Still... Mom's words echoed in her mind. "I'm not going to talk with that... that woman." She faced him, and his image shimmered in her eyes. "How can I?"

"She wants to apologize."

"No."

"Alex, please."

"No, I said." She turned to the rack and hefted another plate. "What part of that don't you understand?"

"She and your dad are going to counseling."

"Good for them. I hope they work things out." She added a smaller one and then the clip. "She made her feelings known. That's all I needed. I'm done."

With that, she centered her feet under the bar and grasped it for a dead lift.

Her phone began ringing.

"Can you get that?" she asked as she began her reps.

"Sure." He picked it up. "Private number. Strange. Jabir al-Omri." A wide smile broke across his face. "Noor?"

Stunned, Alex nearly dropped the bar. She set it on the ground with a clank. "Give it to me!"

He handed it off.

"Noor, hi." Relief surged across Alex. "How are you?"

"As good as I can be, I suppose." Noor Kamil-Sultan drew an audible breath. "Since we met in December, I have given your offer much thought. It has been a struggle, this learning who I can trust. And, I now realize I can trust you."

"What changed your mind?" Alex's heart began hammering.

"Speaking with Melanie Marks. She told me she would trust you with her life, and she has already."

Alex closed her eyes as memories from that June before when Melanie had nearly died surged over her. "I've known her since kindergarten."

"So she said. I—I want to hand the video over to you. But only to you. No one else because I only trust you and Jabir."

"That'll do." Her mind began darting in all directions. Where to meet? How to do it? "Jabir and I need to talk about this. Can we call you back?"

"No." Noor clipped her answer. "No one must know this number. I will call you back in ten minutes. If there is no solution then, it will not happen."

The line clicked.

"Talk about cloak and dagger," Alex muttered. "We need to discuss this. She has the video, and she wants to hand it over to us."

"Then we need to come up with something fast. We don't have time to get to the office." Jabir cast a look around the gym. He tugged her to an isolated corner of the weight floor. "Let's think on this. I think it needs to be a public place, preferably one with some level of security so it would be difficult for anyone following her to access and it's public enough that no one would try anything."

"But where?" She thought about the mall. No. Completely unsecure.

Jabir grinned. "*The Palace Beauty Pageant.*"

Alex stared at him. "Huh?"

"We do it at *The Palace Beauty Pageant*. We were going to be there any-way. You have to have a ticket to get in. Security is pretty tight. I mean, they actually screen people for weapons, right? And," a wicked grin crossed his lips, "you and your mom can talk."

You stinker. You absolute stinker. Alex opened her mouth to reply, found no retort, and closed it. "Okay, Einstein. Sounds like a plan. What about getting Noor's family to safety?"

"We get Tiny to launch a team as soon as she gives us the location, which I doubt she'll do until the hand off. Let me call Tiny." Jabir dialed a number and lifted his phone to his ear.

As he talked, Alex paced in circles and kept an eye on things to make sure no one came too close. Jabir relayed the plan in bits and pieces.

Her phone rang precisely ten minutes later. "Noor?"

"Do you have a plan now?"

"We do." Alex cast a look at Jabir. Time to see if Noor would totally trust them. "Do you like musicals?"

"I'm sorry?"

"*The Palace Beauty Pageant* is playing at the Triangle Arts and Enter-tainment Complex in Durham, NC. I take it you're in North Carolina?"

"Maybe."

Her tone indicated she was.

"Perfect. Do you have a laptop available?"

"I do."

"See if there's a ticket available for Saturday night."

Tapping told her Noor had begun entering information into her computer. "A few tickets are available."

"Buy one. We can do the exchange at intermission because only peo-ple with tickets can get inside. Security is pretty tight, like no weapons allowed."

A sharp intake of breath answered her. "Done. I have a ticket I will purchase."

"Text me when you get there, and I'll tell you where to meet. And Noor?"

"Yes?"

"I suggest we get your family into protective custody sooner rather than later."

"Not until I make the exchange." Steel appeared in her voice. "If something happens, no one must know their location."

Oh, she was good, really good. Probably why she was now COO and destined to become the first female CEO of a Muslim company. "Agreed." She caught Jabir's eye, and he nodded. "We've spoken with our boss, a guy named Tim Daniels. He goes by Tiny. Here's his number." She rattled it off. "Give it to your husband in case something happens to you before we can do the hand off. And afterward, we'll need to get you into protective custody as well."

"Alex—"

"Seriously. Because if this video truly shows that Tarek and Hashim killed your brother, they will come at you with a vengeance. We'll also get your parents to safety. Please," she added when silence continued.

"Agreed."

With that, Alex ended the call. Her heart hammered as she realized their case would end very soon. Then her thoughts swung to her mother. Could she do it? Could she see her? Or would Mom stonewall her? Her wounded heart rebelled, but something about Jabir's request stirred it.

She knew what she needed to do. Pray. Read Scripture, especially those verses related to forgiveness. *God, is it possible? Do I want it?* The prideful part of her screamed she didn't. Then she thought about Jabir's torn family and the way that, when he thought she wasn't looking, sadness filled his countenance.

She didn't want that to happen to hers, and she knew that if she refused to forgive her mother, bitterness would one day set in that would drive a wedge between her and the rest of her family. Maybe reconciliation could happen. But if it didn't, could she take the crushing disappointment? Of that, she wasn't sure, and she wasn't sure she wanted to find out.

28

Hashim rubbed his bearded chin as he paced around the worktable standing in the middle of the great room in Damon's hunting lodge. On top lay a large, laminated Google Earth image of the building and grounds of the TAEC. They'd outlined the route they'd pursue to isolate the vixen and take her. It would require some doing. Lots of coordination among the five-man team. Rami driving the first van. Damon driving the second. He, Ali, and Massoud would be on the ground and literally doing most of the legwork.

It all depended on everyone memorizing the layout of downtown Durham so they could account for any variations. He leaned over the table. With his finger, he traced the route they'd outlined in gold marker.

"You sure you don't want more support? My guys are discreet," Damon said from where he leaned against the door frame leading from the great room of the lodge to the laundry room.

Hashim straightened. "Infiltration is simple. To place our diversions, we use the badges we replicated from a stolen one as well as waiter uniforms. Then we cut off the vixen from the rest of the crowd."

All in a day's work, really.

He needed the crowd to panic.

They would.

Guaranteed.

He turned his attention to another map showing the exchange point between the two vans and the egress from town to a nearby airport. It would work. He knew it would. "Damon, you know what to do?"

"Get the girl and you guys. Take you to the airport outside of town, dump the vehicle, and return to my day job."

"Exactly." Hashim wandered to the cork board that held several pictures of the vixen he'd garnered over the course of his stay near Weatherly.

Damon joined him. "You got a thing for her?"

"Something like that," Hashim fibbed. "She is directly responsible for my incarceration ten years ago."

"I know what that's like." Damon frowned. "No thanks to her and her pals, I wound up in the joint for a couple of years. You got any more intel on what's going on with Alex?"

"None." Hashim shook his head. "The bugs we placed in her flat do not have the range to reach us."

"We'll wing it. Okay. Let's do it. Close up shop so we can get up there at a decent hour tonight." Damon began rolling up the map.

Hashim continued staring at his pictures of the vixen. Once more, he felt the softness of her hair as he'd sifted it through his fingers ten years before. And her perfume. Funny how it remained in his nose even after all those years. Heat rushed to his cheeks. Yes, he'd get his fill of her before killing her. He blew out a hard breath.

They'd planned well for this mission. Very well. And when they finished, he had no doubt where the vixen would be. In his hands.

Saturday, January 6, 2018, 1915 hours EST, Durham, NC

"I think I know where to meet Noor." Alex stood with Jabir in the lobby of the Triangle Arts and Entertainment Complex. Well-dressed patrons of the arts, many sporting evening finery and drinking wine,

276

swirled around them. She felt strange wearing a simple black wool dress with pearls glimmering from her neck and in her ears. Like she wasn't dressed up or something because she wasn't in silk with diamonds draped up and down her arms.

Jabir held tightly to her hand. "Where?"

"There." She nodded toward one of the conversation areas people could use even when nothing was going on. "I've noticed that right now, most people don't care about conversation."

"They care about the show."

"And wine." She surveyed a nearby coffee bar that sat near a wine bar. "But during intermission, people will be more concerned with getting drinks and chatting. I'll have to get here early."

"And a backup spot in case we have to leave the jump drive?"

"The comment box over there." She gestured to a suggestion box that sat against a nearby pillar at the base of the escalator ten or so feet from the sofa. "I'll drop it in there. Though hopefully we can simply hand-carry it out of here."

"Once we make the exchange, April and Lars will be waiting right outside the door to take Noor into protective custody," Jabir added. "Tiny's on his way down. By the time intermission arrives, he should be on the ground."

Maybe she could wiggle out of talking with Mom that way. "Can't we leave after Noor makes the hand-off?"

Nope. Jabir leaned toward her. Into her ear, he murmured, "Remember what you told me about what you'd learned regarding forgiveness? It's mandatory for the believer. And besides, you wanted to see this musical, and I'm taking one for the team since I hate musicals. We're staying for the whole thing and having coffee afterward with your parents."

He had her there.

She sighed.

Jabir smiled. "C'mon. Let's get going."

They headed up the escalator and handed their tickets to an usher, who escorted them to their seats before returning the stubs. Alex stuffed hers into her purse. The better to have it so she could return for the second half since Jabir would never believe a lost ticket as an excuse for bailing on him.

She made sure she went first. To Jabir's left, the other two seats remained empty.

"Where are they?" she muttered before she could stop herself.

"I don't know." Jabir opened his program and studied it as if it were the most fascinating thing in the world. "Have you gotten anything from Noor?"

"Not yet." Alex resisted the temptation to turn and stare at the balcony. Not that she'd see their contact anyway. She pulled out her phone and glanced at it to be sure. Nothing.

It vibrated as it notified her of a text.

Private number. A brief message. "Bingo. She's here and seated."

"Tell her where to meet," he hissed.

Alex barely heard the soft gong that signaled five minutes until the show started. Her thumbs flew across the screen. "Meet me at the couch in the conversation area beneath the escalator."

Noor replied in the affirmative.

Now maybe Alex could sit back and enjoy the show.

If Mom showed.

Still, no older couple next to them.

She'd backed out at the last minute.

Anger balled in Alex's stomach.

Just as the lights dimmed, two forms slid into the seats beside them.

Dad murmured, "Sorry we're late. Parking's a bear out there."

Alex stiffened despite her best intentions. No getting out of it now.

"We're glad you're here," Jabir replied just as the orchestra began playing.

Alex actually enjoyed the first act. She found herself enthralled with the tale of Esther being taken into the court of Xerxes and prepared for her participation in what turned out to be an ancient beauty pageant as the king chose his next wife. By the time the act ended with Esther's stating, "If I perish, I perish," she found herself totally caught up in the show.

Jabir nudged her and whispered into her ear, "Time to go. I'll be nearby on surveillance."

Mouth suddenly dry, Alex bolted up the steps toward the mezzanine. She bumped into a couple of people and earned dirty looks in the process. She could almost hear their thoughts. There went a redneck who thought she could go all fancy. She didn't care. The only thing she cared about was claiming the couch before someone else did. Rather than take the escalator, she hustled down the stairs and beat most of the crowd to the lobby.

There! One empty couch, just for her. She sat on the edge. Her knees jiggled up and down. She hopped up and paced while one hand toyed with her necklace.

Jabir, who'd finally arrived at the bottom of the escalator along with the rest of the pack, smiled and blew her a kiss as he stepped into line for some wine. He pointed to her and pantomimed drinking.

Ah, he'd get her a glass.

Or maybe three.

She nodded. She'd need it after seeing Noor to safety.

Where was she?

Nothing yet. Of course, she was probably stuck in one of the last rows of the balcony.

"Alex." Mom and her throaty voice.

Startled, Alex glanced up. Why was Mom here now? Weren't they supposed to talk after the show?

Cloaked in a long, slinky black dress with a jacket of gold, copper, and silver sequins over it, her mother strolled toward her. Elegant as always, especially with her dark hair in a twist. Only sadness in her eyes and lines at the corners of them indicated her distress.

Resentment stoked its fire inside of Alex. Despite everything, Mom looked so... so perfect, like the perfect politician's wife. Shouldn't she be rushing to her daughter, getting on her knees, and begging forgiveness?

Hah. Roya Thornton, wife of former Congressman David Thornton, didn't beg for forgiveness in public from anyone, let alone her oldest child.

Alex seated herself. "I thought we were going to talk later."

"I wanted a drink, and I saw you sitting here. What better time than now to talk?"

If only you knew.

Mom sat down a couple of feet away on the edge of the couch with knees together and purse clutched on her lap as if she waited in a doctor's office. "I didn't want to come tonight."

"Neither did I." Alex's chest tightened. *Don't say it. Don't pick a fight.* "You hurt me."

Too late. Would she ever learn? Once more, her mouth had gotten the better of her.

Mom's knuckles whitened. She offered a hard-edged smile. "Perhaps you forgot the way you hurt me as well. Running off and marrying like that. How could you?"

"And how could you keep something like that from me for my whole life?" *Way to go, Alex.* No, she was right. Her mother had lied to her, then committed a worse crime by threatening those she loved into silence.

Mom opened her mouth, but no sound came out. Her cheeks reddened as she closed it. She stared down her daughter. The gray had come out in her eyes, hard like steel. "This is pointless. I—"

"Alex?" Dressed in a pantsuit with a sequined top and her hair in a twist, Noor stood there.

Forget Mom. Alex had more important business. She jumped to her feet and extended her hands. She took those of her contact before she could run away. "Noor, I'm glad you're here."

"Who is your friend, Alex?" Mom had pasted on a perfect politician's smile. All fake and insincere though broad. And her voice? Too sugary sweet.

She'd hated her mom's politician attitude when Dad had been in office. She hated it now. Still, she had manners left somewhere inside of her. Almost automatically, she said, "Noor Kamil-Sultan, meet my mother, Roya Thornton."

"Good to meet you, Noor." Mom shook her hand.

Alex faced her contact. "Do you have the drive with the video?"

"Right here." Noor handed her a small data stick.

When she felt the shape of the jump drive in her hand, Alex wanted to do a happy dance. She couldn't. Not until she got Noor to safety and handed off the drive to Tiny. Surely Tiny was—

Flashes blinded her. Bangs knocked her off her feet. She shook her head in an effort to clear it. She lay on the ground, the drive in front of her, Mom and Noor beside her, stunned.

Smoke rose from what remained of a trashcan against the column nearest the escalator—and the comment box.

"Mom!" she shouted.

Her voice came across as muffled.

Gas spewed everywhere. Her eyes began watering.

Tear gas.

Mom pointed to her ears. Her lips moved. Somehow, Alex understood. "I can't hear you."

A roar started. The crowd. People had panicked, and they'd get trampled if they didn't stand.

The drive! Alex snatched it up. Using the couch, she pulled herself to her feet and hauled Noor upright. Mom linked arms with her, the best way to avoid getting separated.

"This way!" Alex shouted. Even then, her hearing had barely begun a comeback. She grabbed Noor's hand. "Link arms!"

Noor shook her head. Her eyes had widened to the point where the whites showed.

Alex tightened her grip. She balled her other hand into a fist around the jump drive. The comment box. Though the explosion had destroyed the garbage can, it hadn't damaged the box. With Noor and her mother in tow, she stumbled to it and dropped the drive through the slot.

Now to get out of there.

The tear gas thickened. She began coughing. "We… we've got to get to fresh air. C'mon."

At least, that's what she thought she said.

The current of the crowd carried them outside. People jostled them and nearly knocked her down. They had to get out of the middle of it.

Like a swimmer caught in rapids, Alex made her way to the side until finally, they were out of the flow and near a flagpole where the American flag snapped in the stiff breeze. Jabir would find them there since it was their designated meeting place if they got separated. Bracing her hands on her knees, she started coughing to clear her airway. "Are... you... okay?'

"F—fine." Still wide-eyed, Noor stared around her. "What happened?"

Alex tried to push thoughts through her muddled mind. Something had exploded in at least one garbage can, though judging by the amount of tear gas, it was more like several. Her hearing finally cleared. She surveyed the crowd.

Most everyone, patrons and staff, ran in a herd as they emerged from the building. Nearby, a waiter stayed on the edge as he walked out. He peered around as if looking for someone. She almost missed the small boom mike in front of his lips.

Their gazes locked.

A sneer curled his lips.

Her heart began hammering as her senses sharpened. Adrenaline electrified her as she realized he focused on her. "We've got to get out of here."

"What?" Mom stared at her. "Alex, what—"

"C'mon!" Alex grabbed her hand. She practically pulled Mom and Noor away from the TAEC building and across the grounds.

"What is going on?" Mom demanded.

"We're being targeted," Alex huffed.

"What? Impossible! By whom?"

Alex turned.

Another waiter, this one with his jacket stretched tight across his chest, had separated from the crowd.

His bald head and beard said it all.

Hashim.

Her heart raced, and she swallowed hard. Her suddenly frozen feet refused to move. "Hashim al-Hassan."

Noor whimpered.

Mom gasped. "We need to go."

That broke the spell.

Forget going toward Jabir's car, their agreed upon secondary emergency meeting place. Hashim and company blocked that route.

"We need to get out of here. Now!" Alex kicked off her heels, and they raced up a rise toward a set of railroad tracks.

Keeping a tight grip on Mom and Noor, she pulled them along the street. They staggered across a set of tracks. Gravel bit into the tender skin of Alex's feet. Her breaths came in short gasps. She couldn't stop. Not now.

Noor fell to her knees.

Alex pulled her upright.

They darted into a parking lot, which was full thanks to the show. Maybe they could lose their pursuers.

She ducked behind a car. They had to hide, had to regroup and dispel the panic that threatened to overcome her.

"What are we going to do?" Noor whispered.

"Do you have your cell on you?" Alex asked.

"No."

"Mom?"

"I lost it," Mom confessed.

Crap. She'd lost hers as well.

Alex listened.

"Where are they?" Hashim demanded in a deep, gravelly voice.

He sounded close.

Alex's breath quickened. She closed her eyes and willed herself to stay silent.

"Somewhere in this parking lot," his comrade replied. "Ali is circling."

Whatever that meant.

Oh, so carefully, she peeked over the hood of the car. Nothing thanks to a big pickup blocking her view. They could be three cars away or ten.

"Keep looking."

Footfalls came closer. Too close.

They had to leave. Now.

Alex made a gesture. Mom nodded. And Noor? Paralyzed with fear, it seemed.

Alex exploded to her feet with the two other women close to her. They raced toward another lot. Sharp pain shot through her foot. Most likely, she'd stepped on some broken glass.

They approached a street.

A van skidded to a stop in front of them.

"This way!" Alex bolted left onto soft, damp grass.

Something that felt like concrete slammed into her. She stumbled off the path and fell against a tree. Her head cracked against the trunk.

Stars danced in her vision. She sagged downward. Her attacker threw her face first onto the grass.

Noor's cry barely registered in her brain.

"I have you now, Alex Thornton."

Hashim.

Darkness covered her as he pulled something over her head.

She couldn't let him take her. Alex kicked out. Nothing but air.

Grabbing her around the chest, her assailant pinned her arms against her sides. She thrashed. She screamed. It was like ramming into a brick wall. He hefted her into the air and tossed her.

She landed hard on her left side. Pain shot up her arm. She groaned and rolled onto her back.

A huge weight landed on her chest.

Her scream faded to nothing. When she tried to draw another frantic breath, she couldn't.

Alex panicked.

Something stung her shoulder.

Almost instantly, the floor tilted. She tried once more to free herself.

Then blackness descended.

Loose Ends

"Go!" Hashim slammed the door shut. He plunked onto the floor and leaned against it.

Rami cranked the steering wheel hard to the left, and they bumped over the curb.

"Three for the price of one, eh?" From where he sat across from him, Ali's grin flashed dimly in a passing streetlight. "At least we brought extra sedative."

Hashim flicked on his red beam. What a find! Roya Thornton, queen of the Thornton clan. She lay on her side, her formerly pristine clothing now caked in mud. But the best? Noor Kamil-Sultan. Massoud pumped his fist like a hunter who'd brought down a prized lion. "A perfect ending."

"It wasn't possible without all of you." He'd planned this one well. So well. And it had netted him more than he'd anticipated.

The van slowed as it pulled into one of the downtown parking garages and wound its way to the upper level. No cars tonight since it was the weekend and too far for people seeing the show to use.

They stopped, and Hashim slid open the door.

Damon stood there, his hands hooked in his belt. "'Bout time y'all showed up." He poked his head inside. "Hey, who are those two?"

"Bonuses," Hashim grunted. "Get them transferred. I'll take care of Alex."

Without even waiting for a reply, he hopped into the van.

Massoud and Ali dragged Noor and Roya across the floor and carried them to the other van.

Hashim pulled the door almost all the way shut. As if he were unwrapping fine china, he removed the vixen's hood.

Her head lolled to one side. A lock of hair clung to her cheek. He sifted it through his fingers. Silky, the same as he remembered. He skimmed his fingertips across her cheek. Soft. Smooth. They drifted lower.

He needed to stop. Now.

Later, he'd have plenty of opportunity.

He leaned forward until his lips were mere inches from her ear. He inhaled deeply. His eyes closed as echoes of the music from that fateful night ten years ago filled his ears. Oh, yes. She wore the very same scent she had all those years before. It nearly drove him wild now just as it had then. "Just a bit longer, my little vixen. Just a bit longer."

He kissed her still lips before sliding out and dumping her over his shoulders.

Once inside, he secured her ankles and wrists with cable ties.

"We need to get out of here," Damon muttered.

"We're ready." Hashim slammed the door. "Go."

Once more, they wound down the parking garage ramp until they hit the street. No one stopped them. No one even noticed, it seemed, since all of the excitement was still at the TAEC, along with a goodly amount of cops. Because Damon had switched plates on both vans several times, it would be days before the police stopped chasing their tails.

They worked their way westward until they hit the Durham Freeway.

Only when they got up to speed did Hashim, who now sat in the front passenger seat, relax. He laced his hands behind his head. A perfect plan, precisely executed. Now all that remained was a quick flight to the Caribbean. Then the vixen would be his until he tired of her.

29

Keep cool. Go with the flow. Jabir allowed the current of the crowd to carry him along. Heedless of those around them, people charged screaming for the door. A man nearly knocked him off his feet before he bounced into a woman who tried to run in three-inch heels. She fell.

Someone stepped on her.

She cried out.

Jabir helped her to her feet. "Are you okay?"

She broke loose from him and fled.

They spewed outside. He sucked down a deep breath of cleansing air, then pulled out his cell phone and dialed Alex's number as he slowed to a walk.

He couldn't get through with his first few attempts. On his third, he got no answer, only her voice cheerfully stating to leave a message and she'd get back as soon as she could.

Tears still streaming from his eyes, Jabir stared at the crowd swarming from the building. He wiped his sleeve across his face and coughed to clear his lungs. The flash bang hadn't gotten to him. Not like the tear gas had.

Where are you? The last he'd seen of her before chaos had started, she'd been picking herself up off the floor with Noor and Roya beside her. His father-in-law had been in the auditorium. What about April and Lars? He saw no sign of them. Thanks to everyone being on their phones, the cell system had collapsed.

As if sensing his concern, his phone chirped.

"Jabir!" David's voice blasted into his ear. "Finally got through. Where are you?"

At least the crowd had thinned enough that he wasn't carried along like a leaf in a raging river. He stopped. "At the flagpole with the American flag."

"I see it. On my way."

At the top of the hill, sirens wailed and stopped. Several SWAT team vans screeched to a halt. Men in black poured out and dashed toward the TAEC building as the police began trying to make sense of that night's events.

"Jabir!"

He whipped around.

David gripped him in a brief hug. "Have you heard from Alex?"

"No. What about Roya?"

"Same thing. Did you set up a place to meet?"

"We were doing a hand off with a contact and were going to get her into protective custody with a couple of our agents right outside. Failing that, we'd meet here. The car was our emergency meeting spot. This way."

They ran through an alley and onto the American Tobacco campus. All around them, people did the same as they tried to get to the parking garage.

Jabir made a right turn. Thanks to their early arrival, he'd garnered a spot on the first floor. But still, it'd be like crossing a battlefield. Engines roared and tires screeched. People shouted at each other as they tried to back out. Metal crunched as someone backed into someone else. Cussing ensued.

David started to cross the aisle.

Jabir grabbed his arm and yanked him back before a Cadillac Escalade mowed him down.

They crossed.

Jabir's heart sank as he ripped open the door and stared at the empty interior. No women waiting for him.

He muttered in Arabic under his breath. "I'm calling Tiny." It took five tries. When his boss finally answered, he said, "We have a situation."

In terse words, he outlined what had happened.

"I'm almost to the exit," Tiny said. "Did you see April and Lars?"

Jabir shook his head. "Negative. And the cell system is jammed because so many people are using their phones."

"I'll get in contact with them. Find the police command center and meet me there." The phone clicked in his ear.

"Tiny wants to meet at the command center, wherever that is." Jabir darted across the aisle and street.

David followed.

Once they arrived back at the TAEC, Jabir stopped. His heart dropped. People were still spilling from the building, this time in a more orderly manner as the cops took over. They fled in all directions. It would take days to sort things out. "How on earth will they figure out who's missing?"

David kept up with him. "They will, but it'll take time, which we don't have."

Jabir began shivering and not just from the cold air. "We need to get that drive."

At the crest of the hill, a mobile communications unit had been set up. SWAT members ringed it.

Removing his cred pack from his pants pocket, Jabir approached. He flipped open the wallet. "DHS. We need to see the chief."

"Says who?"

"Look. My wife is missing. So is his wife. And a friend of ours."

The SWAT guy stared him down. His finger played on the trigger guard of his gun. "Dude, a lot of people are missing. No go. DHS or no DHS. Got it?"

Jabir huffed out a breath. *Think! Think!* What could get this guy to gain him entrance?

"We're concerned that there may have been foul play."

He snorted. "Ya think?"

"Let them through," a woman's voice boomed. A tall woman with stars on the collar of her jacket strode toward them. She dwarfed Tiny, who hustled next to her, by a good six inches. "Police Chief Addie Whitley. We've secured the building. Come this way."

Jabir followed them.

A squad of SWAT men ringed them as they approached the massive structure of concrete, glass, and steel.

"What do we know?" Jabir peered around him. More SWAT members had stationed themselves around the perimeter of the lobby, and canine teams now moved around inside.

Chief Whitley didn't slow down. "From what we can tell, flash bangs and tear gas cannisters went off at the same time. We haven't come across reports of severe injuries, just several related to a crowd panicking." She stopped at a set of glass doors, which were open to the outside. "Status?"

The SWAT guy guarding the entrance reported, "Teams so far have found no additional bombs. They should be finished within ten minutes."

They didn't have ten minutes to spare. Jabir asked, "May we go inside?"

She shook her head. "Not until they've completely cleared it."

"Ma'am, with all due respect, time is of essence," Tiny said. "We know the risks. We'll take our chances."

She stared at him. "Why is this so important?"

"It relates to a case we've been working. We were supposed to take someone into protective custody tonight, and the meeting place was here. We're concerned that one of my operatives, the person of interest, and another bystander may be missing."

Her gaze hardened. "Wait. You had something like this happening on my turf and you didn't bother notifying me?"

Jabir wanted to scream. He didn't have time for turf battles or semantics.

Tiny replied, "We didn't expect it to be eventful."

If they'd expected a blessing, they didn't get it. Chief Whitley folded her arms across her chest. Finally, she sighed. "We'll hash this out later. And you'd better come clean with me, Agent Daniels."

"I will. Promise."

"Be careful where you step. It's a crime scene, and I don't want anything disturbed."

"Will do." Jabir led the way inside. The shattered remains of a champagne glass crunched under his foot. Shoes lay scattered on the floor as did some scarves. Five blackened trashcans littered the lower level. There were probably more on the top level to ensure a rapid spread of tear gas. Even now with all of the doors open, its sharp odor lingered. How the attackers had planted the bombs remained a mystery for the cops to figure out.

He had more pressing matters.

Like the jump drive.

From where he stood a few feet away, Tiny glanced at Jabir. "Did you and Alex have a backup plan for the drive?"

Jabir searched for the copper box. He found it still attached to its column about ten feet from one of the mangled trash cans. "Over here."

He lifted the lid. Blessings. The jump drive sat on the bottom. He handed it to Tiny.

"I found Roya's purse," David reported as he joined them. He lowered his head and muttered something as he opened it. "And her phone. Have you seen Alex's?"

"Not yet." Jabir picked his way through more purses, shoes, and shattered glass. Wine stained the previously pristine cream marble. So did coffee as he got closer to the coffee bar near their designated rendezvous. "There!"

He stooped and picked up a black satin purse. When he opened the flap, Alex's phone and wallet slid out. He pulled up her home screen. A missed call from him. His heart sank. "Now we know why they didn't answer."

"And no trace of them," David added.

Weakness suddenly surged through Jabir, and he sank onto the couch where Alex had sat not an hour before. "What can we do?"

Tiny folded his arms. "Let the cops work. Give them complete descriptions of what they were wearing. They'll see if someone saw them."

Jabir rubbed his temples as he ran through the events of the night in his head. No problems during the first act. Intermission came. People spilled into the mezzanine and lobby during the designated time. Lines stretched long at the ladies rooms. People stood in line at the wine and coffee bars. Overall, 2,700-plus people meandered around in tight quarters. Flash bangs went off. Tear gas sprayed from cannisters. People panicked and fled in total chaos. And Alex, who knew what to do in case of precisely such a situation, had not shown up at their rendezvous. "Hashim."

Tiny faced him. "You think he's behind this?"

Jabir rose and began picking his way toward where the chief stood with one of the canine teams. "Without a doubt. If the intent had been to maim and kill, those bombs would have been a lot bigger and deadlier. Instead, they were enough to evoke panic. Create chaos. Use the chaos to cull your targets from the herd." Half an hour had passed, meaning they were already several minutes behind the kidnappers. "We've already lost too much time."

Tiny kept pace with him. "Agreed on that. That's why we're headed out of here. David, we'll keep you informed."

"Oh, no. My wife is out there as well." David set his jaw. "And in case you forgot, Tiny, I used to stare down Soviets in my younger days. I can handle a punk who wants my daughter."

"Then we'll all go. I got through to April and Lars. Give me your keys, and I'll have them drive your cars to Weatherly after they finish helping with the search. Let me chat with the chief for a moment."

A moment turned into five as Chief Whitley tried to claim her turf. "You're leaving? I need you to stay here. Since you seem to be so knowledgeable about what happened, I need your statements."

Tiny shook his head. "No time, ma'am. I promise we'll be back."

"But—"

"We're acting on a hunch, and if we don't leave now, three people may die. Here's my card." Tiny shoved a business card into her hand. "Call me whenever you need input."

With that, he left the sputtering police chief in his wake.

Jabir followed him as they trotted to a Ford Explorer with US government plates.

April and Lars waited for them.

Once he handed over his keys, Jabir climbed into the backseat with David riding shotgun.

Tiny sped onto the road. Within seconds, they were on the highway headed south.

Jabir asked, "Where are we headed?"

Tiny set his jaw. "To the airport and then New Jersey."

Saturday, January 6, 2018, 2310 hours EST, Atlantic City, NJ

Tiny's stomach roiled again as the Gulfstream began its descent into the Atlantic City airport. He tossed his empty Styrofoam coffee cup into a nearby trashcan. Within a few minutes, he'd be confronting the one man he'd never wanted to see again.

Pinky Salazar.

At least this time, he'd brought a gun to a knife fight. Sadie had done her homework, even going so far as to pose as a reporter to get the information he'd needed. *Lord, I need You. Keep me from going berserk. And bless us with the information we need.*

A name.

That's all he needed to arrest Leila.

The plane's wheels touched down. Seconds after the flight attendant lowered the stairs, Tiny crossed the damp tarmac on his way to the promised Ford Explorer. Jabir and David kept close to his heels. He would have left them behind if they hadn't.

"A man on a mission," David observed.

"You got that right." Throat suddenly dry, he cleared it and slid behind the wheel.

He gunned the engine, and they sped toward the exit. The expressway took them directly into town. Even though the city was busy, he found a parking space along the street not three blocks away from the casino. Tugging his trench coat around him, he plopped his fedora on his head and strode toward the twelve-story building.

He barely noticed the way that Jabir and David had begun shivering.

He pushed inside.

"Who is this Pinky guy?" David demanded.

Tiny needed all of his energy to focus on his impending battle. "Jabir, fill him in."

Behind him, Jabir briefed his father-in-law. Pinky Salazar. Puerto Rican turned Japanophile. Lost both pinkies in a spat with the *yakuza* in Tokyo. Hence the nickname Pinky as if to mock him for his loss. Loved to quote percentages. And dead smart, like almost hit two hundred on the IQ test.

And the very proud father of a daughter going to school at Dartmouth, one of the most prestigious liberal arts colleges in the country, on his dime alone.

A planned formed in Tiny's head.

He took the steps two at a time to the second-floor mezzanine. A poker game was in full swing while only a couple of people sat at the black jack table. They glanced up at the intruders, then back at the game as if seeing three men rush up the stairs was nothing unusual.

Hiroshi and Norio, the two bodyguards from his previous visit, blocked his way at the entrance to the hall. "Mr. Salazar will not see you."

Tiny didn't hesitate. He slammed Hiroshi to the floor with a foot sweep and then Norio with a throw across the hip. As he came up, he groped for Norio's gun. He yanked it out of its shoulder holster and pointed it at them. "One move, and I blast your head off."

He glanced toward the game tables. Everyone at the poker table had turned and faced him. Their eyes widened, and the dealer said something. They resumed the game as if nothing had happened.

Tiny imagined the dealer's remarks.

"No big deal. This happens occasionally. Play on!"

With his other hand, he reached into his pocket and brought out several zip ties. "Tie them up, will you?"

He began making his way toward the outer office.

"Do you need some help in there?" Jabir asked. He shoved Norio into the outer office and pointed to the couch. "Sit down."

Tiny barely heard him. "This is for me and me alone."

He handed Jabir Norio's gun.

David already had Hiroshi's out.

Tiny slammed open the door with such force that it rocked on its track.

"What the—" Pinky blasted to his feet as an elderly couple in front of him whipped around.

"Ma'am, sir, I highly suggest you leave," Tiny said. He didn't break eye contact as he slid the shoji door closed behind him.

The couple bolted from the office through the second door, probably to sing praises at getting away from the loan shark.

Pinky stared at him. His eyes narrowed, and his fists balled at his sides. "There is a hundred percent chance you are here because of this case you are working."

Chest heaving, Tiny glared at him. "That's right. You see, we have a situation."

Pinky smiled broadly. "And there is a hundred percent chance this situation does not involve me."

"No!" Tiny roared. "It does. All the way. I need a name."

"And there's a ninety percent chance you will not get the name. I will not give it."

"Oh, you will."

"And if I refuse?"

"You won't because you left ten percent out there." Tiny took off his trench coat. With great care, he laid it across the back of one of the chairs in front of the desk. He removed his cred pack from his pocket. Holding it by his side, he opened his hand. It fell to the floor. "Because now, I'm no longer a DHS agent. I'm just a godfather concerned about his god-daughter. And if I have to beat you senseless to get the information, I will."

Pinky began sniggering, a high, nasal sound that further stoked the fire of ire burning inside of Tiny. "You? Come after me? Hardly. You were a lot like me in high school, weren't you? A nerd. Poor little Mr. DHS man. Too smart for his own good. Got beat up by the jocks, did you? Maybe they smashed your face into your lunch tray. Or knocked your books out of your hands. Or locked you in your locker."

Tiny's fists balled.

Seeing he'd hit a nerve, Pinky continued, "Better yet, maybe you had a girl. Maybe she was cute. And they stole her." He leaned on his hands over the desk. "But there's one difference between you and me. We were both geeks. But me?" He started giggling. "I knew how to work the system. They wanted answer keys to tests? I got them. I learned a lot about statistics, you see, and I figured out how teachers picked questions. And they came to me and practically worshiped me while—"

In a lightning fast grab, Tiny gripped his collar and threw him over his shoulder in a judo throw.

The air whooshed out of Pinky. He jumped to his feet before Tiny could whip around.

An ankle sweep landed Tiny on the floor.

He groaned.

Pinky grabbed him.

Using his foot as a fulcrum, Tiny flipped him onto his back.

The man still bounced upright. He rushed Tiny, who staggered as they slammed into a wall. The chair rail bit into his lower back. Pain shot up his spine. He had to end this.

Now.

Charging, he grabbed Pinky in a reverse hip throw. As soon as his assailant hit the floor, he dropped to his knee and grabbed the man's wrist. He bent it forward.

"Ow! Ow!" Pinky squirmed. "You're hurting me!"

"Are you going to answer my questions?"

"Maybe. Ow!"

Keeping his wrist bent, Tiny hauled him to his feet and hurled him onto a chair. "You sit there. And to make sure you don't attack me…" Using other zip ties, he looped them around the man's ankles and the chair legs. "You try, and I break your wrist."

"You already did," Pinky muttered.

"Not yet, but that's always possible." Tiny rolled his sleeves as he paced in front of him.

"You at least damaged some ligaments." Pinky rubbed his wrists. "What makes you think I know anything?"

"Because you told me Leila al-Kadir has a sugar daddy. I need his name."

"I forgot thanks to the way you knocked me around."

Tiny muttered something. He folded his arms. "You're a dad, right? I noticed your wedding band."

"Why should I say anything?"

"Because one of my operatives already spoke to your daughter. Penelope."

The smirk melted from Pinky's face. "What?"

"I hear she's a sophomore at Dartmouth. And loves it there. Let me tell you a quick story." Thanks to the pain in his back, Tiny didn't dare sit lest he show weakness in front of his adversary. He settled for leaning against the desk. "Millennials are an interesting bunch. I've got two of them myself and couldn't be prouder of them. One thing I've noticed is that they love to be filmed, love to share on social media. One of my agents took it upon herself to pose as a reporter for a social media site, one that profiles women college students going into science and math teaching fields. She said Penelope was all excited to be interviewed."

Pinky's eyes widened.

For the first time, Tiny allowed himself a little bit of hope. "She has no idea what you do. What did you tell her about your missing pinkies? That the *yakuza* chopped them off because they thought you were horning in on their business?"

"Work accident."

"And she thinks that, rather than managing *yakuza* funds and bank-rolling people like Leila who get themselves into gambling trouble, you're in real estate out in Montana and Wyoming, among other places."

"She doesn't need to know what I do."

Picking up steam, Tiny continued, "She made it very clear to my operative that she loves you, thinks the world of you. She's also proud of being in college and not having any debt since you're picking up the tab. She wants to be a math teacher."

"One hundred percent chance she'll be a good one."

"If she has smarts like you, she will be." Maybe his compliment would help things along. So would a threat. "What will happen if her daddy goes to jail? She's not on any scholarships, right? You make too much for her to get any. She'd have to leave Dartmouth with maybe not even enough money to go to school, period, because it all would be spent on attorneys. You and I both know those don't come cheap. What would happen if the *yakuza* came after you? Rumor has it, they don't leave out family when settling scores."

Pinky's glare hardened, but Tiny noticed something behind it.

Fear.

Pinky growled, "You wouldn't."

Tiny shrugged. He picked at a bit of lint on his pants. "I might. I'm that desperate. You got that?"

"I am only seventy percent convinced."

It was a start. Now Tiny had to close the deal. He lifted his jacket and pulled a manila envelope from it. Sadie had prepared it and handed it to him right before he'd flown to North Carolina. "Here's the deal. This is what I have on you that I'll hand to the Feds if you refuse to cooperate. It's my only hard copy. I leave with no name, this goes into one of the many mailboxes around town. See?" He held it up to reveal an address and postage. "You may be flying underneath the radar, but if a sister agency drops evidence into the FBI's lap, they'll run with it. If I leave with a name, you keep this and do with it what you want."

Pinky remained silent. His eyes narrowed as if considering other options.

Tiny had anticipated other plans. "If you send a hit team after me or my family or sic the *yakuza* on me, I have an electronic copy all waiting to be sent to the FBI if I don't check in via phone or log into my computer at work each day."

Now he began the final push. He unfolded his arms and braced himself against the desk. "Pinky, look. I seriously have no beef with you. It's all with Leila's sugar daddy. If I get the name, then once I leave here, I'm out of your hair forever. That's all. You keep the package, and the electronic version stays with me unless something happens to me or my family. And the best thing? Penelope stays in school and continues to love her daddy. Are you willing to give all of that up for one simple name?"

"Can I trust you?"

Tiny smirked. "One hundred percent."

"You are one hundred percent sure I will not be arrested?"

"Not due to what's in the package. The rest, I can't guarantee, so it might be good to consider getting out of the business."

"Tarek al-Hassan."

Tiny's blood froze. His suspicions had been right. "Leila's sugar daddy?"

"Yes."

"That's all I needed." Tiny placed the manila envelope on Pinky's lap. He shrugged into his trench coat and groaned as he stooped to pick up his wallet, phone, and fedora. The loan shark could figure his way out of the cable tie. "Have a good life, Pinky Salazar."

With that, he joined Jabir and David.

Jabir covered Hiroshi and Norio.

David sat across from him and stared at them as if daring them to stand. He rose.

To the goons, Tiny said, "Your boss is fine. You follow me, he won't be. Jabir, leave the gun. Let's go. Time to get an arrest warrant and pay Agent al-Kadir a visit."

Sunday, January 7, 2018, 0500 hours EST, near Fort Belvoir, VA

His photos held the key to Alex's survival.

Isa stared at the prints strewn across the worktable. Ever since a frantic phone call from Sadie had brought him to the office, they had been his focus. Nothing clicked. Like a bizarre card game, he tossed some onto a discard pile and kept others.

He stared at the one of Leila returning from St. Maarten, then at the one of the mysterious man who had stepped off the plane after she had left.

His gaze shifted to the man in the blizzard. Were they one and the same?

The glass doors to their floor swished open. With her phone to her ear and talking a mile a minute, Sadie rushed inside. "Tiny, thanks. Yeah. Sorry to hear you got stuck getting the warrant." She glanced up. "Isa's here. We'll be waiting on you. And yeah, I'll check that video and follow up regarding our mystery plane to see if Pinky's statement rings true."

She seated herself at an empty workstation in his pod and logged in

"What happened?" Isa asked.

"The cops finally agreed with our assessment that what happened in Durham was a kidnapping. Someone saw three men shove three women matching the descriptions of Alex, Noor, and Roya into a van. They found it abandoned in a parking garage." Her fingers flew across the keyboard. "They got a video of the plates as it left. They'd been switched, and it took forever for them to figure out that it wound up at an airport near Sanford, about fifty miles south of Durham. And that's where video caught the women being loaded. The FBI just got ahold of it, so they're sending it shortly."

Something on her screen pinged. "Tiny transferred the video Noor handed over to us." She clicked the mouse twice. "He wants us to watch it. See if we can't definitively identify the murderers."

"Has he watched it?"

Her fingers flew across the keyboard as she transferred it to another server. "No time. He's busy trying to get an arrest warrant for Leila."

A video screen popped open. A black and white video began playing. Sadie fast-forwarded until Samir got ambushed.

With growing horror, Isa watched as Samir's assailants tasered him and stripped him to his underwear before tying him to his kitchen table.

"Oh, my…" She put her hands over her eyes as the man with a full head of hair brought the knife down for the final kill. "I think I'm going to be sick."

Isa stared. He had seen brutality in his time, so much that he worried it had scarred him. But never in his life had he seen this. Blood pounded in his ears. He wanted to hit something—or someone.

Yet they had learned something.

Sadie froze the video when she had a clear angle on the two murderers. She magnified it.

Isa peered at them. "Who are these men?"

"Noor thought the al-Hassan brothers murdered Samir." She pulled up a database. "That's Hashim in the video. And his brother, Tarek, is the one who killed him."

Wait. He knew that one from somewhere. He whipped around and stared at the worktable. There! He tossed photos aside until he finally came to the right one. He held it up. "A match."

"What?"

"The man on the plane," Isa shook the photo, " is Tarek al-Hassan."

Sadie jumped up. Her gaze jumped between photo and screen. "You're right. I need that video from the Sanford airport. I mean, they filed a fake flight plan, then dropped their transponder. Either they kept it off all the way down or turned to another code."

"Here is the tail number from the Thanksgiving plane." He rattled it off.

A rooster crowed from the computer.

"What…"

"My e-mail. Looks like the video. And something else." Her eyes flew across the screen. "Oh, my goodness."

"What?"

"This keeps getting stranger and stranger. Tiny forwarded an e-mail Mitch Harris sent to him. The South Carolina Highway Patrol found a body in the trunk of a BMW. Thanks to it being so cold, it wasn't decomposed enough that a face wasn't recognizable. It set off all sorts of alarms."

"Why?"

"It was Tarek al-Hassan. He had a broken neck." Sadie hit a button, and the printer spit out a photograph.

Isa stared at her. He blinked as he tried to comprehend what had happened.

"Let me check the video." She clicked on a file. "Perfect. It's from Sanford."

He leaned over her shoulder and peered at the screen. "I think it might be a match for Hashim."

"I think you're right." Sadie nodded and printed the image. "Leila's definitely in cahoots with Tarek—or was. Pinky was right."

Once more, the glass doors opened. Tiny, Jabir, and another man unknown to him strode through. Tiny seemed to have aged years in the span of a day, and he limped. "Isa, Sadie, do you have the photo from Mitch's e-mail?"

"I do, sir," Sadie reported. "I printed it for you."

He took it. "Strange, isn't it?"

She cocked her head. "What happened to you?"

"A run-in with a loan shark. What do you have?" He eased onto Isa's chair with a grunt.

"The same plane that took Leila to St. Maarten at Thanksgiving is the one that left the Sanford airport last night. And it's a lock that Tarek al-Hassan murdered Samir. Then someone murdered him, it seems."

The new man muttered under his breath and kicked the leg of the worktable.

Tiny put a hand on his shoulder. "I forgot introductions. David Thornton, meet Sadie Callahan and Isa Haswi."

"Nice to meet you," David grunted.

"You're Alex's dad." A vein pulsed in Sadie's temple. "Sir, we're going to get your wife and daughter back."

"And I'm going to help," he muttered.

Tiny leaned forward. Wincing and massaging his lower back, he slapped a manila envelope onto the table. "Jabir, Isa, here's the warrant we needed. Go and arrest Leila al-Kadir. Keep it as quiet as possible, understand?"

"But—" Jabir began.

"It needs to be."

"Why?"

"Contingency," Tiny muttered. He rubbed his chin and stared at the ground. "Go on."

Isa grabbed his gun and a set of handcuffs. He had been waiting for this day for a very long time.

30

Sound returned first. A sharp sound, like metal on stone in contrast to a steady beat of waves on rock. Then came sensation, that of warmth—and hardness. Her head on a pillow, Alex lay beneath a light cover. Her body ached even though she lay on a mat.

She inhaled.

Salt air.

Strange.

She tried to open her eyes. It was like she had no strength to do even that.

With almost super-human effort, she finally pushed them open a crack.

Dim light, as if she were in a room with darkness on the outside.

Without moving her head, she surveyed the room. Plaster walls. The light came from sconces. And beside the door? Hashim al-Hassan sat on a chair. He leaned against the wall with the two front legs up in the air. He sharpened a very big, very ugly knife on a whetstone.

Things couldn't get worse. Could they?

She slowly turned her head. They did.

For the moment, Mom and Noor lay on either side of her. At least they hadn't been separated.

She knew what would happen if they were.

Tarek would probably torture Noor to obtain why she'd met with Alex.

And her? Hashim would take his vengeance upon her for what she'd done so long ago. It would be brutal. She knew it would be.

What about Mom? She didn't want to think of what would happen to her.

Where were they? The salt air gave her a clue. So did the whump of waves against rock. Louvered windows let in the tangy air of dawn or dusk.

Surprisingly, no one had bound her. She raised her wrist to her face. Slightly after four. PM or AM? She couldn't tell.

The chair slammed down onto all four legs. It creaked as her half-brother rose. "I see you are awake."

"No thanks to you, dirt bag," she blurted before she could stop herself.

He chuckled. "You are a mouthy one, Alex Thornton. We'll see how long that lasts."

He opened the door. Though he'd stepped into the hallway, she easily heard his instructions in Arabic. "At least one of them is awake. Bring them to the villa at six."

With that, the door shut. A heavy bolt slid into place.

An hour and a half or so before they had no hope. She sat up.

A moan distracted her. She whipped around.

Mom stirred, as did Noor.

"Wake up, you two," she hissed.

"Where are we?" Those slightly slurred words came from Mom.

"I don't know." Alex frowned as she suddenly realized what they wore. *Shalwar kameez*, a comfortable, pajama-like garment that Pakistani and Afghan women and men wore. Meaning someone, most likely women, had changed them out of their heavy winter garb. Each wore head scarves as well.

Not wasting time, she got to one knee, then her feet. Her world spun a little, but leaning against the stone wall next to the window helped. She peered through the glass louvers. A screen and bars.

She tried to ascertain what her senses told her. Waves on rock. Salt air. Light filtering into the sky when her watch read after four. They were most likely in the lower latitudes, like the Caribbean. "We're somewhere next to the sea in a warm climate. Maybe the Caribbean? It doesn't seem like we've changed much longitudinally."

"How can you tell?" Noor asked.

"It's starting to get a little light outside." Alex turned and knelt beside them.

Noor now sat with her arms wrapped around her knees. Mom leaned against the wall next to the window.

"How are you two feeling?" Alex asked. They didn't look too worse for the wear, but she wanted to make sure.

"A bit fuzzy in the head, but okay other than that," Mom said.

Alex gestured for them to come closer. In case any guards stood nearby, she whispered, "Listen. Hashim al-Hassan is the one who kidnapped us."

Mom winced and hung her head.

Old issues, even ones angry and raw, didn't matter anymore to Alex. "We've got to get out of here because I've got a sinking feeling that once they take us to the villa, they're going to separate us, and—"

"Tarek is here, yes?" Noor's voice pitched up.

"Shhh." Alex glanced at the door. "Probably. Listen, we need to keep our heads about us."

"And do what?" A tear seeped down Noor's olive cheek. "We can't escape." She frowned when Alex began nodding. "Can we?"

"We can." Alex drew them close as if they were hugging. In her whisper, she outlined her plan. "They don't think or don't know of what we're capable. Otherwise, they would have trussed us up. And they definitely won't suspect Mom due to her age. Let's take advantage of that."

Mom began nodding. Her eyes glinted. Was this what she'd looked like during her CIA days at the compound? "We can do this."

"Noor, have you ever handled a gun?"

The brunette shook her head. "No, never."

"Then stay out of the way." So two against possibly three. Not good, but not bad either. Any more? They'd be done. Alex resumed her post at the window. She glanced at her watch. Five minutes ticked by. Then ten. Outside, dawn lit the area in a soft pink glow. She'd been right. They were somewhere in the Caribbean.

At the clomp of footsteps and rise and fall of men's voices, she straightened. She tried to distinguish them. Three distinct ones, none of them Hashim's bass rumble. Good. She'd probably not get the drop on him.

Mom resumed her position and rested her arms on her knees. Noor sat beside her.

The bolt slid back, and the door creaked open. A man said, "Get across the room, Alex Thornton."

Oh, they knew her too well.

She crossed the room and stood with her back to the opposite wall.

A guard stepped through with rifle raised and aimed squarely at her heart. "Face the wall and put your hands on it. Spread your feet."

Alex stepped to the wall beside the door and noted the way the rifle's muzzle followed her. After all, he hadn't specified which wall. "My mom's not feeling well. Whatever you guys gave her has made her nauseous."

"Is what she said true, woman?"

Mom moaned but refused to raise her head.

"She has not been right since she awakened," Noor said.

With a sigh as if they'd totally inconvenienced him, the guard slung his gun over his shoulder.

The second guard came into the room with rifle unslung but not at all up and ready.

A third stopped in the doorway.

And hopefully, no more.

While their attention focused on Mom, Alex scooted her feet close together and shifted her weight to her right leg. She glanced over her shoulder at Mom.

The first guard knelt in front of Mom. "Madam, I need you to—"

She head-butted him!

With a moan, he fell onto his back.

Alex whipped around with a roundhouse kick.

The third guard's breath whooshed out of him. As he collapsed, his finger squeezed the trigger. The bullet whanged around in the hall.

Mom snagged the first guard's pistol and pointed it at the second guard. "Don't move a muscle, or I will kill you."

In one fluid motion, Alex grabbed the second guard's pistol and slammed it onto his skull. He moaned and collapsed.

She dragged the third guard into the room. "What do they have?"

Mom was already on her knees. She undid the first one's belt and buckled it around her waist. "Lots of goodies. Guns. Knives. Radio."

"Noor, take the second one's belt. Quickly!" Alex did the same with the items from the third guard. Good. Rifle with only a bullet spent. A spare magazine. Radio. Pistol. A spare magazine for that. Binoculars. A lighter. That might come in handy. Zip ties. She handed them to Mom. "Tie them up. Quickly!"

Like an expert, Mom laced ties around two of the guards while Alex took care of the third.

What did Mom do? Practice hogtying Dad during her spare time?

Mom rose with the grace of a lioness and grabbed her rifle. She aimed it at the door. "Where to now?"

Alex stared. Who was this woman? She remembered her as the mother who'd taken her hand and walked her into ballet class when she was five, not someone who head-butted people. And hadn't Mom taught her needlework when she'd been little? Certainly not how to wield a rifle. This couldn't be.

"Alex." Mom's throaty growl returned her to the small room where their lives now hung in the balance.

Alex shook herself. "We get to the high point and see what we can see."

Mom nodded as if praising a student for the right answer. "And take the tactical advantage."

"And that." Alex took the head of the line. Lioness or no Lioness, Mom still had a few years on her. "Noor, stay between us."

Noor nodded.

With rifle held at ready, she stole from the room, down the hall, and into a large room with a kitchen. Judging by the nice furnishings, a luxury bungalow of some sort. She stepped to the door and peered outside.

A common area, seemingly deserted.

Letting the muzzle of her rifle lead, she scanned the area before slipping outside.

In the growing light, she spotted a macadam path that led from what seemed to be small guest cottages. She trotted forward. One glance back ensured that Mom and Noor followed.

The jungle quickly closed around them.

The path widened into a road that was maybe slightly wider than a golf cart. From the looks of it, a main road. It steepened as they approached a turn to the right that led upward. The other turn led downward.

A motor roared from that direction.

Nope. Not going that way.

Alex took the high road—literally.

At Hashim's shout, she broke into a run. No way would she let him catch her. Not now. Not ever. She had no desire to wind up in his clutches.

Alex's lungs burned. Her glutes and hamstrings screamed for relief. Mom and Noor huffed behind her.

Finally, they stopped on a road that ringed the ridgeline.

Alex paused and braced her hands on her knees as her sides heaved. "You… would think… that I don't… work out… six times a week."

Beside her, Mom gasped for air as well. "Or run triathlons."

"Or play tennis," Noor added.

Alex looked up. "C'mon. No time to waste."

They trotted along the road until they paused at what seemed to be the highest peak. "Let's stop for a second."

Taking care to lay flat so as not to expose her silhouette, Alex crawled to the highest point. She studied the terrain with the binoculars. The recent hurricanes had ripped off all of the green leaves and downed several trees. To the west, three peninsulas jutted into the sea. The far left one was where they'd been. The middle one had a couple of buildings. The right-hand peninsula had several smaller buildings with a fence around it. That was strange. She swung around. To the east, the slope fell away. Nothing but brown and downed trees with an abrupt drop to the ocean. The sun began rising above the water in a scarlet haze. Probably totally uninhabited on that side.

Mom had wormed her way up to lie beside her.

"What do you think?" Alex asked.

Mom shielded her eyes with her hand. "Maybe a mile wide by two miles long. It's small."

"Too small." Alex swallowed hard. Sure, they could hide, but hiding places were probably limited. She turned back to the western side. Wait. Was that a dock she saw? She peered more closely at it in the northern bay.

Bingo. A way off the island since a dock meant they had a boat. And lo and behold, two boats were tied up, one being that very same cigarette boat she remembered from Tortola. Never in her life would she forget that yellow lightning bolt along black paint. And a boat meant a chance of escape.

She lowered the binoculars as the enormity of their task hit her.

If they didn't escape? They were toast.

Sunday, January 7, 2018, 0600 hours AST, Angelfish Island, the Caribbean

"This is absolutely perfect." Hashim grinned as he surveyed the interior of one of the small shacks on the northern peninsula of the island. "For once, my brother fulfilled my request."

Massoud nodded. "As you specified."

Hashim stepped into the growing morning light and took a swig of coffee from his travel mug. Combined with the three or so hours of sleep he'd gotten on the flight to St. Maarten, the caffeine energized him, made him ready for the day and the taming of the vixen. Now, it was only a matter of time. Rami and the others should be bringing the women to the villa—

A gunshot rocketed through the still morning air.

"The vixen," Hashim muttered. He raced to where they'd parked one of four John Deere Gators next to the wrought iron gate.

He jumped into the driver's seat.

Massoud hopped in beside him. They took off as fast as they could toward the guest cottages on the southwestern part of the island.

He skidded to a halt and nearly tore the door off its hinges as he blasted inside. He turned down the hall toward the room that had once been a master bedroom. The door stood wide open.

Something had happened.

Ambush. That's what.

Rami, Ali, and a third man lay trussed up on the floor. Rami and Ali squirmed with vigor against their ties.

The other?

Not so much. Blood smeared his face like an artist had gone mad with red paint. His nose sat at an odd angle.

"What happened?" Hashim knelt beside Rami. With two deft swipes of his knife, he severed his bonds while Massoud took care of the others.

"They ambushed us." Rami's right eye had begun swelling closed. He swore as he touched it. "The older one—what is her name?"

"Roya Sayad Thornton." Hashim nearly spat the name. "Father calls her The Lioness from when he knew her in Afghanistan."

"She head-butted Fadel, probably broke his nose."

Fadel moaned and came onto all fours. More blood fell in scarlet drops on the floor. He hung his head. "Did break my nose. We were careful about Alex but not with her."

Hashim slammed the door into the wall, not once, not twice, but again and again until bits of plaster littered the floor. With a guttural roar, he literally ripped it off its hinges and threw it down. He'd erred, foolishly so. At least Tarek wasn't there to smirk at him.

A problem, once contained, now raged out of control. The island might be small, but it held plenty of hiding places. Sixteen able-bodied men might not be enough.

He stomped outside. One call on the radio summoned everyone to the cluster of lounges by the pool of the villa.

He had a mess on his hands, and he'd clean it up.

Starting now.

"Rami, you were here after the hurricane. Tell me about this island. Everything. What do you know of the trail network on it? Obviously, habitation is on the western side."

"This side is where everyone lives. There are three ring roads with connector roads running to the ridge. We cleared trees off of those roads. We have also spotted animal trails that have reformed around fallen trees."

Hashim thought through what the vixen and The Lioness might do. Escape would be first and foremost on their minds. And there was only one way on and off the island.

The dock.

He whipped around and pointed to a group of four. "You four go to the dock. Guard it well. Do not sleep, lest I kill you for negligence." He whipped around and pointed to another group of four. "You four stay here at the villa. Fan out. Same thing. If they show up, I want them alive and unharmed. Understood?"

The eight nodded.

"Rami, take Fadel upstairs and get him cleaned up with an ice pack on his face. Stay with those guards."

313

"The rest of you, we take the Gators and start patrols. Massoud, you're with me. Go now." Hashim climbed into the lead Gator and fired it up. They rumbled up the road and turned onto the one leading toward the peak.

He needed to learn the network of trails, even if it cost them precious time.

And with their only way off the island well-guarded, it would be only a matter of time before the vixen was back in his hands. Then she'd pay and pay dearly.

31

"What's Leila's normal Sunday routine?" Jabir slouched behind the wheel of a Suburban as it sat in front of a fire hydrant near Leila's townhouse.

Isa leaned forward. "Without fail, she will come out in a couple of minutes and head to a coffee shop. She stays there until a little after seven before going to the gym for a workout. Then she returns home."

"Seems you know her."

"That is what happens when I keep her under surveillance seven days a week for weeks on end." Isa cracked a smile. "A full knowledge of her routine and not much else."

"What are your thoughts about her?" Jabir asked.

"She is—how do you say it?—flaky in her work. Careless. And it is going to show... right now," Isa added as the front door to the townhouse opened. He put his hand on the handle.

"You got her?" Jabir watched as she walked away from them without a second glance back to see why an unfamiliar black Suburban sat yards from her mother's townhouse.

"Of course. The coffee shop is around the corner to the left. Approach from the opposite direction." With that, Isa pulled his knit cap down around his ears and slid from the vehicle.

Jabir passed through the intersection and rumbled down the road. On both sides, snowbanks rose up. He hung a left and found an open spot in the snow in front of another fire hydrant. He hopped out, then lingered while waiting for Leila to round the corner.

There! She wore boots, jeans and a leather jacket with a tote bag slung over her shoulder. The new operative kept close behind her. Isa had called it right. It didn't look like she'd even noticed him.

Jabir stepped onto the sidewalk and stood square in her path.

She froze. Her brow knitted. "Jabir?"

"It's been too long, Leila. We need to talk."

She gripped the handles of her bag. "Now? Why are you here?"

"Because you're under arrest."

Her hand flashed up.

He barely jerked back in time. The blow glanced off his cheek, and he staggered off balance away from her.

She bolted past him.

Isa shot after her.

Regaining his balance, Jabir followed. He leapt onto a car, thrust himself forward, and landed in front of her. He fell to his knees and covered his head. Pain blossomed in his side as she tripped over him.

Leila grunted as she fell onto the snow-covered sidewalk.

Isa pounced. He snapped cuffs on her, and Jabir Mirandized her as his partner hauled her to her feet.

Jabir led the way. "Let's get out of here."

Leila didn't go quietly. She loudly protested as Isa marched her across the street and almost threw her into the backseat.

A few other early risers cast curious glances in her direction.

"Let me go!" she hollered as they roared down the street with lights flashing and sirens blaring. She added several, more colorful Arabic words to describe them.

Jabir cranked the stereo so that hard rock drowned out her protests. They swung around on several streets before blasting onto I-395 South toward Fort Belvoir. Just a few short minutes later, they merged onto I-95, then took the exit for the fort. Unit 28 headquarters came up quickly, and he bolted onto the ramp that led to the underground parking garage where they typically unloaded prisoners. He slammed on the brakes.

"Get out," he ordered Leila.

"What? I can't hear you after all of that hard rock you blasted."

"Shut your trap." He hauled her from the backseat, pushed her inside, and marched her down a short hall. "Get in there."

Tiny met them at the door to an interrogation room. The lines around his eyes had deepened. He'd rolled up his shirt sleeves, and he cracked his knuckles as he surveyed her. With a sigh, he slowly shook his head.

Jabir shoved her onto a chair and manacled her wrists to a short length of chain connected to a bar on top of the table. He took up a post next to Isa, who leaned against the wall by a one-way window. Across the way, the power cord for a small camera high up in a corner hung loose. He gazed at his boss. Had he unplugged it?

For a few minutes, Tiny paced until he finally stopped in front of her. "You have a lot to tell us."

Leila kept her expression neutral. "About what?"

"A lot of things. Let's talk about your association with Tarek al-Hassan."

"You know that. He murdered Samir—"

"There's more."

"What?"

"I understand you visited Tarek al-Hassan in the Caribbean over Thanksgiving weekend."

"I did no such—"

"Don't lie to me!" Tiny tossed several of the photos Isa had taken onto the table. "What are these?"

"You had me under surveillance?" She glared at him. "Why? I thought we were on the same side."

"I did, too. It seems we aren't, though. My man Isa," Tiny nodded in their direction, "has had you under constant surveillance since I approached you. It seems you and Tarek were well-acquainted enough to come to Dulles *on the same private jet*. Why?"

"I want my lawyer."

Tiny froze. He backed off a step.

A smirk curled Leila's lips. She obviously thought she'd won.

Not by a long shot if Tiny's hooded gaze meant anything.

Jabir stilled.

"You want a lawyer, eh? You think you can hide your nefarious motives behind a lawyer." Tiny jerked his thumb over his shoulder toward the camera. "Guess what? That's not going to happen because officially, we're off the record right now. What happens in Vegas, stays in Vegas, right?"

"What's in it for me?" she asked.

Tiny kicked over a chair across from her. He leaned on his hands until their faces were inches apart. "How about you live if you tell me what I want to know?"

"You will so suffer for this." She blinked a slow blink of a snake. "You've arrested an Interpol agent on no grounds, then denied her due process. A fatal error, eh?"

"Oh, don't you worry about that. I have a warrant." He extended his hand, and Jabir handed him the envelope. "You tell me what I want, and I may be able to get you a good deal."

"You will never be able to take me to trial for this. Not when you've violated—"

"The moment you foolishly approached Tarek al-Hassan six months ago, you violated about every rule in the book." Tiny raised his voice to cover hers. "Isn't that why Raoul Chevrot kicked you out of Beirut? And then you used more lies to try and get Jabir to do your work for you when you'd been explicitly thrown off the case. Even after we were foolish enough to do your homework, you cozied up to the enemy."

"I was making progress by—"

"By what?" Tiny straightened and paced around the table. "By going up against Tarek al-Hassan one on one? He turned you, didn't he?"

"Of course not—"

"Then why did it seem like the al-Hassan brothers were a step ahead of us with Shafiq?" The cadence of Tiny's steps increased. "How did he know where to go? I thought about that, you know? Alex and Jabir told no one except me that information."

"Maybe you should look into your own soul."

Tiny stopped and grabbed her chin so hard that she squeaked. "No, you should look into yours."

He released her.

Leila rubbed her jaw and stared at him with narrowed eyes.

Tiny turned away from her. "What did he offer you? Sex?"

Leila kept her mouth shut.

In Jabir's mind, that was enough of an admission.

Tiny whipped around. "Was it good? Was it worth it? Because I'm pretty sure you handed over information you garnered from Jeremy Whitlock about Alex's and Jabir's aliases. Somehow, Hashim figured out where they were staying and planted bugs, which allowed him to know that Shafiq had fled to Tortola. How far off the mark am I?"

Leila remained quiet, but her hands clenched into fists.

Tiny slapped her across the face.

Jabir jumped. What had gotten into his boss?

"I'll have your head for this!" she screamed.

"Oh, no you won't! Because of you—you!" Tiny jabbed a finger in her face "Alex Thornton may die. You understand? We know you went to St. Maarten for your little tryst with Tarek. Now where did you stay?"

She began laughing.

Tiny started for her.

This time, both Jabir and Isa grabbed him and hauled him back.

"Not worth it, sir," Isa murmured. "She is not worth it."

Tiny shook them off and continued staring at her. He took a deep breath, then blew it out. "Think about what I said."

He turned toward the door.

"Where are you going?" Jabir asked.

"I'll be back. She says anything? You call me. And plug that camera back in."

He slammed the door to the room.

Isa cast a look at the door, then back at his friend.

Jabir shrugged. He'd never seen Tiny in such a state. But then again, the stakes had never been so high. He could only hope that whatever Tiny had planned would yield the results they needed.

Sunday, January 7, 2018, 0730 hours EST, Washington, DC

"Thanks. I appreciate the help. Hopefully, it won't come to that," Tiny said. With one eye on the road and his mind on the situation, he ended his call to Immigration and Customs Enforcement and made another one.

"JC speaking."

"JC, Tiny here." Only a small bit of relief unfurled as he talked to the leader of the on-call SEAL Team Six platoon.

"What's going on? Any new developments on Alex?"

"Gear up and be ready to head to St. Thomas. We think she's being held somewhere in the Caribbean near there."

"Give us the word, and we're wheels up."

"Will do." Tiny tossed his phone into the slot below the stereo and focused on his driving.

His thoughts weren't great company at the moment. He'd never hit a woman before. He'd broken probably every rule regarding the interrogation of a prisoner on Unit 28 property. And let's not forget beating up a loan shark simply because he brought back bad memories from high school.

Still, he'd do anything to get Alex back alive and well.

Anything.

Like betray a friend.

Thankfully, the DC streets remained quiet as he approached the al-Kadir townhouse. He pulled into the driveway and texted Sadie to meet him in the fourth floor conference room in fifteen minutes.

"*Ahlan wa sahlan,* Tiny. What a surprise!" Sasha al-Kadir smiled at him when she opened the door after he rang the doorbell. She wore sweats and a sweatshirt that had GWU in deep blue and gold emblazoned across the front. "Do come in. I was just getting ready to sit down for a cup of coffee before I got ready for church. Would you like to join me?"

"I need you to come with me."

"What?" Her dark eyes clouded. "Why? Is something wrong?"

"Yes, something is wrong. Very wrong. Please," he added as he refused to budge from the stoop.

She withdrew. "Does it have something to do with Leila?"

Would she stop questioning him? "Everything to do with her."

"Then let me turn off the coffeemaker. I'll be right back." She left him standing in the cold.

After she'd pulled on a heavy wool coat, he walked her down the sidewalk and settled her in the SUV. This time, he turned on both lights and siren before careening down the road.

Sasha gripped one of the handholds. "Tiny, what on earth? Can you tell me what the problem is? Why is Leila involved? What happened?"

No, no, and no. He wasn't going to say a word. He wouldn't. "I'm sorry, but I need to concentrate on driving."

He roared down the entrance ramp onto I-395. Once on the highway, he pushed the needle above a hundred. Each minute that passed meant another minute where Alex, her mother, and Noor might die.

He wouldn't let that happen.

Not on his watch.

Rather than head to the lower level of the parking garage, he pulled into a guest spot by the front door and walked her inside.

Security took only a moment since she had just her purse and keys as well as him for an escort.

"Please tell me what's going on," Sasha begged as they rode the elevator to the fourth floor.

"In just a few minutes." He led her to a conference room with glass walls.

Sadie met them with a welcoming smile. She extended her hand. "Hi, I'm Sadie Callahan."

"Sadie's going to keep you company," Tiny said as he stepped aside for Sasha to enter.

"Ma'am, would you like something to drink? Perhaps some coffee or hot tea?" Sadie asked.

Eyes still on Tiny, Sasha seated herself on a chair. "Hot tea would be great. And an explanation."

Tiny ignored her as he took Sadie's arm and led her toward the break room.

David lay asleep on the room's couch. "How long has he been here?"

"A couple of hours. I told him we'd wake him when we moved." Sadie cast a glance toward the room. "What do you want me to do?"

"Bring her in when I call for you." With that, Tiny swiped his tablet and the photo Sadie had printed for him from his desk and headed to the basement.

Nothing had changed. Leila hunched at the interrogation table. Jabir leaned against the wall beside the camera, which was now plugged in. Isa maintained his post by the door.

Tiny took a deep breath. He couldn't lose control like he had earlier. Otherwise, he'd never get what he wanted. But this time, he had an ace up his sleeve—or maybe two of them.

He righted the chair. Wincing from to the pain in his back, he eased down on the other side of the table from his quarry. Quietly, in contrast to the pounding of his heart, he began his final play. "I'll ask one more time, Leila. Where did you stay with Tarek? On St. Maarten, or on a nearby island?"

"I'll say nothing without my lawyer present." With that, Leila sat back and pressed her lips together. She refused to look at him.

Tiny set his tablet on the table. He opened the app that would show video feeds for cameras all over the building. One swipe brought up the camera for the fourth floor conference room. Sadie and Sasha sat at the table and chatted. He spun it around so Leila could see it. "Do you see this?"

Leila's eyes widened, and she gasped. "Mama?"

"That's right. I have your mom here at headquarters. She's in a conference room with one of my agents. From what she told me, she has her green card and hopes to receive citizenship soon. If you don't tell me where you stayed with Tarek in November, I'll have her deported."

She glared at him. "You wouldn't."

"Oh, yes, I would. If you don't get me what I want, she leaves the country in an hour with nothing but the clothes on her back. I've already cleared it with Immigration Customs and Enforcement. What will it be, Leila? Tarek or your mother?" He pointed to the screen. "Choose wisely. If you pick Tarek, she's gone. If you pick your mom, sure, you may go to jail, but at least she gets her citizenship. Got it?"

Her gaze darted between the screen and her hands.

Tiny noticed a ring of emeralds and diamonds on her left ring finger. From Tarek? A false show of his love and loyalty to her, especially since he now resided at a morgue somewhere in South Carolina.

She finally lowered her head. So softly that he barely heard, she said, "Angelfish Island."

"What?"

She raised her face. Tears streaked it. "Angelfish Island. He said it's called that because of its shape."

"You're sure?"

"Yes."

"Good. If I find out you lied, she gets deported. Understand?"

She nodded.

"I want you to tell me everything about this island."

Steel once more appeared in her eyes. "Why should I? I've already betrayed Tarek. Why should I do anything else to help you?"

"Because he's dead." Tiny slapped the photo down.

Leila flinched, and tears pooled in her eyes.

"Do you have any idea who might have killed him?"

"Hashim," she hissed. "He'd complained several times about his brother's obsession with Alex."

"Do you want us to arrest Hashim? Then tell me everything you know about the island." He spun the tablet around and activated a voice recorder. "Start talking."

She did. Within ten minutes, Tiny had a good, solid working knowledge of the island. He dialed Sadie's number. "Bring her down."

Leila began shaking her head. "Please. Don't tell her what I did."

"Oh, I won't. But you? You'll have all the time in the world to talk to her."

Leila gasped.

Tiny sent the audio file to JC and his team. A few moments later, beeps sounded as Sadie keyed in the code. It opened to reveal Sasha and her.

Sasha glared at her daughter. "What have you done?"

Tiny didn't waste any time and didn't care to stick around to face the fallout. He gestured to Isa, Jabir, and Sadie. "You three, come with me. Gear up. We're headed to the Caribbean and will meet the SEALs there."

32

"One way on, one way off." Alex stared through her binoculars at the bay below. Same as it had been earlier, only now, four guards with rifles unslung waited for them.

Curse their luck.

Alex knew one thing.

Hashim had realized their intentions, what they had to do.

"Thoughts?" Mom asked quietly from behind her.

Alex withdrew from the rock ledge where she'd leaned. "They're wise to us. Unless there's a submarine base I don't know about, those boats are our only route off. We need to plan."

"And get water." Mom mopped her face with her headscarf. "I thought we crossed a stream on our way to here."

At the mention of water, Alex's thirst raged.

"Could there be a spring at the top?" Noor asked.

"A pool, maybe. C'mon." Alex rose, and they retreated up one of the animal trails they'd found as they'd learned the island's trail network. All the better to avoid Hashim and his crew. She put his numbers around a dozen or so, maybe more. At least three-to-one guards to escapees. Horrible odds.

Sweat poured from her. They needed water—soon. Otherwise, dehydration would weaken them and muddle their thinking. She feared that was already happening.

They approached the highest road that ringed the island.

Alex peered both ways.

No one.

She put one foot onto the macadam.

Two Gators rumbled around the curve.

As if in shock, the guy driving the first one stomped on the brakes.

He shouted.

The three women bolted down the path they'd come.

Behind them, leaves rustled and branches snapped.

A bullet cracked past Alex's ear.

"Stop!"

No way.

Another path branched to the left. "Mom, Noor, thicket to the right. We need to ambush them!"

Mom grabbed Noor's hand. They ducked into a thicket of undergrowth, tangled vines, and branches from a fallen tree.

Alex bunched herself behind a large tree that had somehow withstood the fury of the hurricanes.

Their pursuers slowed.

"Where did they go?" one demanded.

"Perhaps down that path?" his buddy replied.

"You two go in that direction. Go!" the first one said.

More rustling. Two must have taken the other trail.

Maybe they'd pass by her hiding place. She peeked around the trunk.

One had walked by. Surely the other followed close behind.

She inched toward the trail.

Then she felt it.

A pistol muzzle.

Her captor started chuckling. "You think you are smart, Alex Thornton. Not as smart as you think, eh? Drop your rifle and put your hands on your head."

She did so.

"And now to—"

A shot echoed through the jungle. The man fell.

Alex whipped around and stared at the neat hole in his head. What the...

She turned back and found Mom standing with a two-handed grip on her pistol. Her eyes were flat gray with anger. "No one lays a hand on my daughter without my permission."

From behind Mom, the other pursuer charged toward them.

"Mom! Watch out!" Alex snatched her gun from its holster.

Mom ducked, and Alex shot him in the shoulder. He cried out and collapsed.

Noor emerged from the thicket.

More shouts from nearby told the rest. Their buddies had whipped into a U-turn and headed back up the path.

"We've got to get out of here!" Taking Noor's hand, Alex nearly dragged her new friend upward to the road.

Two empty Gators, their engines purring, sat waiting.

Alex jumped behind the wheel of the first one. "Get in!"

Noor stared. "But it's a two-seater. Where—?"

"I'll get the back," Mom jumped into the cargo area and unslung her rifle. "Get in, Noor."

Noor threw herself into the other seat.

Alex shot down the road and headed toward the northern, higher peak. A roar echoed in her ears. Why hadn't she shot out the tires or engine? "Dumb, dumb, dumb! This thirst is already getting to me."

"They're following!" Mom gripped the roll cage and shifted. "Go faster!"

Alex pushed the vehicle to the max. "I'm about as fast as I can be."

Gunfire chattered. Mom's rifle answered in return.

They crested and bounded along the ridge. She jerked the wheel to the left. Bad mistake. The pavement dramatically steepened as it headed down the eastern flank. They flew by the upper, then middle ring roads. Too much. She stood on the brakes.

Noor held on for dear life. "We're going too fast!"

"Don't I know it!" Ahead, the road teed at an intersection with the lower ring road.

She couldn't stop.

"We're going to have to jump."

"What?"

"Now!" She shoved Noor out, tossed away her rifle, and plunged from the vehicle. Macadam bit into her palms and hip. A groan escaped her as she rolled. Coming to one knee, she whipped out her pistol. She aimed and fired.

The driver of the second Gator clasped his shoulder.

His pal held on for dear life. He shouted.

Unable to stop from such high speeds on the steep slope, they whizzed past.

Trees and foliage cracked as they blasted over the cliff. Their screams faded. The Gator crashed onto the rocks below. If they'd survived, it wasn't without injury. Better odds with four down.

She holstered her gun. "Mom? Noor?"

"Here." Mom sat up. She clasped her side.

Concern unfurled within Alex. "Are you okay?"

Mom offered a smile. "Just a bad hit. I haven't jumped out of a moving vehicle lately."

At least she was okay. Alex knelt beside Noor. "How about you?"

Her friend winced but stood with her help. "I—I hurt, but nothing major, I don't think. I will be plenty sore tomorrow."

If they survived that long. At least Noor had hope.

The radio burst into life.

"I heard shots. Give me a status report." A low, gravelly voice.

Hashim.

Alex sucked in her breath.

Nothing since the four men who could update him were either dead or injured.

"Someone, give me a status report!"

"Ambush," the one who Alex had shot reported. "I am… hurt."

"The others?"

"One… dead. Not sure about the others."

"I'm on my way."

At least they'd bought themselves some more time.

Alex clipped the radio to her belt. She turned to find Mom still on the ground. She cupped her hand around her left side.

Scarlet ran between her fingers.

Alex's heart caught in her throat. "Mom, I think it's more than just landing funny. Let me look."

Mom's smile trembled. "I'm fine."

"Liar. Let me look." Alex crouched beside her.

"I'm—"

"Let me look, all right?" Alex gently pried her hand away and raised the hem of her top. A bullet had pierced her side, and blood oozed from it. She lowered her shirt and pressed Mom's headscarf over her wound. "Gunshot wound. We've got to get out of here, then tend to you. C'mon. Can you go uphill?"

With Alex's arm around her shoulders, Mom rose. She winced and kept the fabric over the wound. "We… we must."

"Noor, here. Take this." Alex handed her Mom's rifle.

"I…" She stared at it like it was a poisonous snake.

"I need you to walk point—up front. There are some rocks at the higher peak. We go there. Okay?"

"But what do I do?"

Did she have to spell it out? "You see that small switch on the trigger guard?"

"Y—yes."

"That's the safety. It's on right now. You see something, you slide it off, and then you fire."

"But—"

"Go!" They didn't have time for indecision.

Noor turned and began the steep walk uphill.

With her pistol in one hand and her other stabilizing Mom, she followed and guarded their rear flank. Mom kept up. When they crossed the middle ring road, Alex paused and checked the wound.

It still oozed blood.

"You okay?" she asked.

"Keep going." Mom took a step forward.

If it could happen, the road steepened even further.

Mom slowed.

No, not yet. They couldn't stop. If they did, they'd get captured. Alex tightened her grip on her mother. "Almost there. Hang on."

They reached the road that encircled the peak. Above it, trees ringed a jumble of rocks. Maybe they could hide there.

Mom leaned against her and panted.

Alex nodded upward. "Can you climb up?"

"I—I must." Mom winced as if the proposition daunted her.

"Lean against Noor." Alex shifted her mother, then climbed up the pile. A perfect hiding place. "Noor, help her up." The growl of an engine reached her. "Quickly!"

Alex took Mom's hand.

As her feet hit the peak, Mom collapsed.

Alex caught her and eased her down. "Easy. Easy. I've got you." She checked her wound again. The climb had increased the flow of blood. For the first time, fear began building inside of her. If she didn't get help soon, Mom would go critical. She exchanged the saturated headscarf for her own. "Keep your hand over it."

Noor's eyes widened. She raised up. "They're coming!"

Alex jerked her down. "And if you do that again, they'll see you."

"But—"

"Be absolutely still." Alex crouched and picked up her pistol.

The Gators passed below them. Hashim must have been intent on finding the missing men. They were safe—for the moment.

"Mom, when did this happen?"

"On our wild ride." Mom offered a weak smile before she winced. "Alex, you and Noor go on."

No way would that happen. "We're not leaving you." Her head spun as the burden of leadership slammed into her. She had to make decisions, ones that would impact whether the three of them would live or die. But first things first. "We need to get you out of here."

Mom winced. "You know that's not going to happen."

"What are we going to do?" Noor asked. "I mean—"

"Just... stop." Alex held up a hand. "Let me think."

She sat on her haunches and clasped her head between her hands. Sure, their only way of escape might be blocked. But she'd had some training in combat medicine. Could she get the bullet out? Then there was the issue of food and water, especially water. The enormity of their situation washed over her.

She'd been in tight spots before. What had gotten her out alive? Not panicking. Alex took several deep breaths. Her head cleared. So did her thoughts. Surely this island had some sort of medical dispensary. After all, she'd seen where they'd stayed and the other cottages on the northwestern peninsula. If not, she could swipe a First Aid kit from the villa.

Was it dangerous?

Oh, yeah.

Did she have a choice.

Nope.

Therein lay the rub, but if it saved Mom, she'd do it.

Even if it cost her own life.

Sunday, January 7, 2018, 1030 hours AST Angelfish Island, the Caribbean

On the eastern side of the island, Hashim stood with Massoud and two of his men at the edge of the cliff overlooking the rocks below. Two Gators lay smashed on the beach. As did the broken bodies of two of his men. He'd found a third off the middle ring road and as well as his injured man, who now lay moaning in the cargo area of the second Gator.

Massoud shifted nearby. "We need to bury them."

"Not now." Hashim's mind spun. Three of his men dead. Three injured. He was down to ten.

"Islamic custom dictates—"

"No!"

"But you know we must. It is required by—"

"Enough!" Hashim drew his pistol and pointed it at his lieutenant's forehead. He actually had to stop his finger from squeezing the trigger. "Say one more word, and I *will blow your head off*. Am I clear?"

Massoud didn't flinch, didn't move. He only nodded in submission. "It is as you wish, then."

Trembling, Hashim lowered his gun. What had he done? Almost killed his second-in-command. Huffing out a hard breath, he looked up and down the ring road. Wherever they were, the vixen, Noor, and The Lioness were on foot. That was the issue. They could pick off more of his men.

He needed to regroup.

Just as he was about to climb into his Gator, a splatter on the pavement caught his eye. No, puddle was more like it. He knelt and dipped his fingers into the liquid.

They came up scarlet.

He began smiling, then chuckling. One of them was wounded. Perfect. His mind whirled with new possibilities. Without saying a word, he tracked the spatters to just past the middle ring road. There, they vanished as if someone had staunched the flow. Still, it wasn't a small amount of blood.

Without a word, he returned to the Gator. "Where is the dispensary on the island?"

"The northwestern peninsula," Massoud replied. "I saw it when we were looking at the shack."

Hashim focused on the other two men with him. "It's time to put a plan of my own into play."

Ten minutes later, Hashim leapt from his Gator and nearly ripped the hinges off the door of the building that had a red cross across the front. He opened cabinets and pawed through them. Packets of gauze, sutures, and needles fell onto the counter. He found a backpack with a red cross on it and began throwing in supplies that would be needed for field treatment of a wound. He also tossed in three bottles of water.

"Ashraf and Kareem, take Omar to the villa and treat him there. Massoud, summon the guards from the boat. I'm not worried about that now. I want them here and stationed in the various buildings. Then go to the villa."

Without a word, his two men left as Massoud did what he was told.

Hashim hefted the bag and stepped into the bright morning light. Already, the sun burned his bare scalp since he'd left his bush hat at the villa. He marched to a central area covered by a tiki roof. A bar sat to one side, and several tables littered the concrete. He set the bag on a table at the edge of the shade and checked out the gate. He hit a switch on a control panel. The wrought iron gate hummed closed, and he timed it at twenty seconds.

With a satisfied smile, he raised his radio to his lips. "I know you are out there, Alex Thornton. And I know one of you is wounded. I want you to listen to me. Do you perhaps remember the movie *The Hunger Games*? I'm sure you do."

He released the button. No retorts came through.

He took another breath. "There is a part in the movie where Peeta is wounded. Katniss needs medicine, and the only way she can get it is a package left at the Cornucopia. Think about it." He let her consider that for a few seconds. "I have a similar package. First aid supplies. Which, I believe, you need. It may not solve your problems, but it will help you survive. And water. You want them?" He smiled. "They will be at the tiki bar in the center of the cottage square on the northwestern side of the island. Think about it."

"She would be foolish to come here," Malik, one of his men, muttered.

"Have some faith. One of them is wounded. And if Alex is wounded, her mother would do anything to save her. They come, we take her down." Hashim explained his plan as he opened the gate. "Now? We wait."

33

Mom had weakened.

No doubt about it. As morning had turned to afternoon, scarlet had again begun appearing on the headscarf they kept pressed over the wound.

And the thirst.

Alex grimaced. She'd managed to find a small pool of rainwater, but even sips from there hadn't slaked it. They'd soaked Noor's headscarf and dribbled some water into Mom's mouth.

Hashim's taunts from earlier echoed in her ears.

He had what she wanted.

Bandages. Sutures. Things she could use to at least close Mom's wound. And water.

He also had the upper hand and knew it.

Thing was, he hadn't realized what he'd done when he'd challenged her.

He'd stoked her competitive edge. She wanted to prove to him—and to herself—that she could get it done. She could return to Mom and save her. Right?

No doubts allowed. Tiny had drilled that into her head her first year on the job.

"I'm going." Alex began gathering her rifle and checking her magazines. Still a full one and spare one in her rifle, plus a couple she'd scavenged when they'd been ambushed. Her pistol lacked another bullet, but she had enough there.

Mom had paled. She whispered, "You cannot let him trap you."

She settled beside her mother and checked her pulse. Definitely weakening. "But if I don't, you die."

"So be it." Mom winced. "You and Noor have a fighting chance."

"Not with no way off. I have to go."

"Alex, no."

No amount of pleading would change her mind. Like Esther, she knew the risks. But doing nothing would be worst of all. *Lord, You're with me. And with Noor and Mom. You know what's best.*

She shouldered her rifle. "I'll be back in an hour, okay?"

"Alex," Mom softly called. She reached a trembling hand toward her daughter.

Alex took it.

"I'm..." Mom winced. "I'm sorry for... for all that happened."

Tears gathered in Alex's eyes. "Forgiven." She bent and kissed Mom on the forehead before crawling to the edge of their hideout. "I'll call out when I return. Noor, if anyone else approaches, shoot them."

Noor swallowed hard but nodded.

Alex slipped onto the ring road. This time, she didn't bother using animal trails since she figured they were waiting for her at the bottom. Time meant more than anything else at that point.

Once on the middle ring road, she branched onto the trail they'd used that morning. Within five minutes, she leaned on the ledge overlooking the middle and northwestern peninsulas. The image in her binoculars told it all.

A wrought iron fence ringed the cottages on the northwestern peninsula. Its gate was open, and two Gators plus two golf carts had parked in the area just outside. A pavilion lay not fifty feet from the edge of the cliff. The backpack she wanted sat on the table closest to the edge of the pavilion. A pool shaped like a kidney bean gleamed in the sun between it and the gate.

Two guards at the vehicles. And no Hashim. What about the others?

Her hope plummeted to the soles of her slippered feet.

She needed a plan—fast. Finally, as she studied the cottages and the fence, one came to her. It was risky—very risky, but it was her only option.

Alex retreated into the jungle and slowly worked her way to the lowest ring road so she came out where three roads branched off. One went to the villa, the second to the dock, and the third to the cottages.

Taking the dock road, she quickly cut into the foliage again and located a faint trail. With great care, she wove through the mess of brown vines budding with green leaves and soon came to the edge where it thinned to reveal the cottages. She peered to the right.

The parking lot and guards weren't visible.

Perfect.

She scuttled around to the back corner. No one stood outside, and she saw no movement. She examined the bars of the wrought iron fence. Climbing their six-foot height would be a long, difficult, and possibly noisy process. Could she squeeze through? She checked. Too narrow in the middle, but she hit the jackpot on the end. Whoever had installed the fence must have miscalculated because the gap between the bars nearest to the southwestern corner seemed just a bit wider.

She slid through and scurried to the back of the cottage closest to her.

A grill sat outside with a propane tank attached to it. She peered through the back door. A closed door separated the small kitchen from the front. An idea formed. Carefully, she detached the tank from the grill and hefted it into the kitchen. She turned on the valve, and it hissed as propane spewed from it.

Alex shut the door and scurried outside to the neighboring cottage. She ripped the hem from her top, located a rock, and wrapped it around so that a lengthy tail dangled from it. With the lighter she'd scavenged when they'd ambushed their guards, she lit the tail. Eying the window leading to the kitchen, she wound up and threw the flaming rock in a fast ball toward the glass.

It shattered.

Boom!

The flame ignited the gas inside the kitchen. More smoke and light than anything else, but it worked.

Guards started shouting.

With one last, deep breath, she tore between the two cottages and into the pavilion.

She snagged the pack, did a ninety-degree turn, and bolted around the pool toward the gate. It began closing.

She lengthened her stride. Almost there.

Something huge slammed into her.

Alex hit the ground and skidded on the grass.

The pack flew from her fingers as her rifle fell from her shoulders.

A few feet away, Hashim staggered upright. He must have anticipated her moves and hidden.

"No!" Alex scrambled to her feet. She reached for her pistol.

He kicked her hand and sent it flying. "None of that, Alex Thornton."

Alex groaned and reached for the pack.

He tackled her.

She jabbed her foot at him.

With a cry, he released her.

She grabbed the pack again and made for the gate, which had almost closed.

Hashim seized her arm. With a mighty pull, he swung her around hard.

Alex stumbled toward the pool. She lost her balance. For a microsecond, she hung suspended between land and water.

She landed in the water with a splash.

Hashim jumped in beside her. He slapped her across the face.

Stunned, she sagged.

His arm snaked around her waist from behind, and her belt released.

No more weapons but her wits. She reached behind her and raked her nails across his head.

He growled and shoved her underwater.

Her lungs felt like they were going to burst.

He brought her up.

She spluttered before he repeated the process.

Into her ear, he hissed, "You struggle, and I will do that again. Understand?"

Gasping for air, she nodded.

He hauled her to the steps and almost threw her onto dry land.

She lay there and coughed. Boots appeared before her.

Guards.

Once more, Hashim pulled her to her feet, this time with her arm twisted behind her until her shoulder burned in pain. He marched her to a shack that had a stout padlock on the door. He slammed her face first into the wall.

The breath whooshed from her. She struggled to draw another one.

"Malik, unlock it."

Metal clinked on metal.

His breath hot on her ear, Hashim hissed, "You and I? We have some unfinished business together, do we not?"

"We... do... not." Her words came out between frantic breaths for air.

"Oh, but we do." He kept her arm behind her. "Let me tell you a story, my little vixen. Do you remember ten years ago? We met at a night club, right?"

She refused to answer.

He whipped her around and slammed her once more against the wall.

Her head cracked against the stone. "Y—yes."

He pressed so close to her that his breath once more whispered across her cheek. She caught an iron whiff of blood dripping from the scratches created by her nails. "From what I remember, we had a good time. You flirted. I responded. When you kissed me, you started something I did not want to stop. Then you betrayed me."

He was too close to kick. The first signs of panic started rearing its ugly head. "I was never interested in you."

"I doubt that." His lips curled into a sneer. "The problem is that the last time you saw me, I had hair. You see, I spent time in the hands of your CIA. Your lover's former boss, if I remember correctly. Ed Du-Bois."

"So?"

"Malik, open the door." He returned his attention to Alex. "It fell out during my captivity. And I hold you responsible for that and the utter humiliation and destruction of my soul that I experienced. Do you have any idea what happened during my stay with him?"

Again, she refused to answer.

He grabbed her chin so hard that pain shot through her jaw. She squeaked and squirmed. "N—no."

He chuckled. "You will soon find out. Why? Because I will show you."

Keep calm. You panic, it's truly over. Problem was, she knew exactly what he talked about. CIA black sites had been nasty places.

"Do you want us to go in there with you?" one of the guards asked.

"No. This is between me and her. Stay out here and on the alert."

Alex cried out as he gripped her arm and thrust her into the interior. She stumbled and fell to her hands and knees. Behind her, the door closed, leaving them in semi-darkness with the only light coming from around the blackout curtains someone had installed. It was enough.

As her eyes adjusted, her heart dropped to the soles of her feet. Gym mats on the floor. A cooler. A smallish box. Klieg lights. A boom box. *I cannot panic. I will not panic. I will look for opportunity.* Words from her SERE training crept into her mind. Then she saw the two ropes with loops on the end hanging from pulleys in the ceiling. If he got her wrists in those, it was all over.

Hashim suddenly wrapped his arm around her chest from behind and whispered into her ear, "You and I? We're going to get well acquainted over the next several days."

He kissed her on the neck.

She cringed. She'd tried and failed. Now, she'd pay the price.

Sunday, January 7, 2018, 1300 hours AST, Angelfish Island, the Caribbean

The yacht the CIA had lent to the SEALs roared toward Angelfish Island. In the lounge, the SEAL team, Jabir, Isa, and Sadie gathered for a final briefing. Jabir studied an aerial map of Angelfish Island that had various points of interest circled.

JC, the team's commander, pointed to the video monitor. "We've had a drone circling the island ever since we got the coordinates. So far as our analysts can tell, they started out with twelve tangos against Alex, Roya Thornton, and Noor Kamil-Sultan. They're down to maybe ten now, four guards at the dock where they have two boats, four more at the villa. Two tangos died on the eastern side and one in the jungle. We think Roya's injured."

Behind them, where David and Tiny stood next to a doorway, David swore and kicked the frame.

JC continued as if he hadn't noticed. "Roya and Noor are hidden at the peak. Our drone developed engine problems, so we had to bring it down."

"So no new intel," Jabir muttered.

"We did see the dock guards shift to the staff cottages with others headed to the villa. Why, we're not sure." JC outlined his plan. The first wave of SEALs would lead in a Zodiac and come ashore in the southeastern bay. Jabir, Sadie, Isa, and the rest would follow in a second Zodiac. David and Tiny would come ashore only after the all clear. Seahawk helicopters from a nearby aircraft carrier would extract them. The platoon commander switched off the monitor. "Any questions?"

None.

"Get a move on it." JC led the team onto the stern as the yacht slowed to an idle.

Jabir risked a glance toward Angelfish Island. It rose to the west of them and would provide cover since it seemed the action was on the opposite side. He checked the safety on his gun, then slung it over his shoulder and slid into the second Zodiac. Sadie, her chin set and her eyes narrowed in anticipation, joined him, as did Isa and the second set of SEALs.

The first raft pulled away from the yacht and sped toward the cliffs of the island's eastern shore. They followed, swung southward, and hugged the coastline. Rounding the southeastern peninsula, they slowed so the engines barely purred.

The first raft beached, and the squad dispersed into a V-shaped formation.

As soon as the raft touched sand, Jabir wasted no time. He jumped ashore and joined JC. With hand signals, the commander formed up the team with their three Unit 28 guests toward the back with JC. Mooch, Jabir and Alex's friend, walked point.

Gradually, they made their way toward the villa and paused at the edge of the jungle.

The rest of the team slithered toward the villa and slipped inside. Someone shouted. Silence fell.

Jabir held his breath, then released it. They didn't have time to wait.

"Clear," Mooch whispered over the radio. "Come on up. We're on the terrace outside the master bedroom."

Jabir glanced at JC, who nodded. They dashed toward the modern, two-story structure of concrete and glass. All around them, the SEALs had taken up various guard positions. Jabir came to a set of stairs leading upward to a landing. More SEALs had taken up guard positions. He crossed the landing and passed through what appeared to be a master suite.

"Status," JC requested once they reached the second level.

Mooch nodded. "Thermal imaging from the drone showed six tangos, two of them injured. We got them. Three dead, three alive."

"Let's head downstairs and regroup." JC and Mooch turned and trotted from the room.

Jabir stayed on the terrace as he stared at the gleaming pool below. Something didn't feel right, like his instinct had begun humming a warning.

"Jabir," Isa quietly called from the doorway. "We must go."

"I know. It's just that—"

A war cry split the air.

Jabir whipped around as a figure leapt from the roof.

He slammed into Jabir, who staggered. They crashed into the marble railing.

Grabbing him around the neck, his attacker dragged him to his feet.

Jabir broke his grip. A punch sent his foe to his knees.

He recovered and charged Jabir.

Off balance, he stumbled into the railing.

The man tried to lift his legs.

He was going to throw him off.

No way would he do that.

Jabir clawed his face.

The man did the same.

Jabir had nothing but air below him. His back bent. It was going to break.

The pressure released.

With a cry, his attacker tumbled over the railing and crashed onto the stone below.

Someone yanked Jabir onto the terrace.

Isa stood there, his chest heaving as he stared below. "It was him or you. I much prefer him."

Jabir groaned and climbed to his knees. "That was close." Using the marble, he hauled himself to his feet. He called, "Is he alive?"

"Yep," JC reported. "Broken leg, but he's pissed off in all sorts of ways."

Jabir raced down the stairs.

Surrounded by four SEALs plus Sadie, the man lay moaning on the pavement. When he saw Jabir, he cussed a blue streak in Arabic.

Jabir dropped to his knees beside him and in the same language demanded, "Who are you?"

The man spat at him.

Jabir grabbed his leg at the break.

He shrieked. "M—Massoud!"

"Where is she, Massoud? Where's Alex?"

Massoud gazed at him. He smirked, then started laughing. In English, he said, "You'll get nothing from me, Jabir al-Omri."

Jabir lunged at him.

Mooch and Isa grabbed him and pulled him back. Mooch refused to release his grip. "Easy, there. It's not worth it."

Sadie pushed through the ring of SEALs. "Let me try."

"What? What can you do?" Jabir demanded.

"Something you can't. Feminine persuasion." She knelt beside their captive. "Massoud, right? Crony to Hashim?"

He winced. "You know him."

"Oh, I do. I do know him, sir. Very well." She'd turned on her Charleston accent full bore.

Jabir stared. What? He opened his mouth.

Mooch hissed into his ear, "Let her work."

"You see, I know all about you and your boys. I've studied all of you. And I know some of you aren't as pure as you like to think."

"If you think you and your routine will get me to say anything, I will not." He called her a foul name.

Sadie gazed at Massoud for a long second and shook her head with a sigh. Then she extended her hand to Isa. "Sir, if you could so kindly hand me your knife."

A smile suddenly quirked Jabir's lips.

"With pleasure." Isa handed it to her hilt first.

"Massoud, you've left many a broken body in your wake. Now it's time to pay the price. Maybe you remember hearing about a woman named Lorena Bobbitt."

"I know no such name," Massoud hissed. He winced.

"Her man assaulted her, and she took care of business by removing his... business. So unless you tell me where Alex Thornton al-Omri is, I'll ensure you pay the price. Am I making myself clear?"

"You wouldn't."

"Don't test me." Steel appeared in her voice.

"She's serious, you know," Jabir added. "She's done it before."

Massoud's eyes widened. They darted between Sadie and him. He paled. Almost in a whisper, he confessed, "A shack on the northwestern peninsula."

Jabir glanced at JC.

As if to confirm, an explosion ripped the air.

The lieutenant jumped to his feet. "Let's go!"

Jabir took off up the road. *Lord, don't let us be too late.*

Sunday, January 7, 2018, 1345 hours AST, Angelfish Island, the Caribbean

In her little shop of horrors, adrenaline exploded through Alex. She backed up, snagged Hashim's arm, and flipped him over her head.

He hit the floor with a *whoof*. But what might have knocked the wind from a mere mortal didn't faze him. He rolled to his feet in one smooth motion. "So you fight me, eh? I would have expected nothing less."

He struck out in a punch.

Alex ducked and wove around him. She slid into a karate stance. He wanted a fight? She'd give him one! The problem was, his reach was much longer than hers.

Go big or go home.

With a warlike cry that would have made her Afghan ancestors proud, she charged him with all of her might.

He stumbled off balance and landed on his rear. She fell on top of him.

Had it been anyone else, it would have been laughable. Not him.

She rolled away and caught him in the face with a kick.

He yelped and jerked back.

She scrambled on all fours toward the Klieg lights. Maybe she could pull them down on him.

Her fingers brushed the base.

He grabbed her ankle and dragged her backward.

Startled, she rolled onto her back. Wrong move. He punched her in the face.

Agony spread through her cheek.

She could only lie there as her brain tried to reconnect with the rest of her body.

Hashim grabbed her wrist. He dragged her toward the ropes. "Nice try, but your best wasn't good enough."

She struggled. She couldn't let him get her hands into those loops.

She almost had her feet under her.

He jabbed a fist into her kidney.

Sparks exploded in her vision. Moaning, she sagged to her knees.

He wrapped his arm around her chest and lifted her.

Alex struggled, but the pain raging in her back weakened her.

He forced her hand through one of the loops and tugged until it closed around her wrist. He let her go. She collapsed, and it tightened. She tried to struggle upright. He punched her in the other kidney. She went all the way down—at least as far as she could thanks to that infernal rope.

Deep breaths. She had to take deep breaths and almost relish the pain.

Gasping, she flailed. Suddenly, she stilled.

Hashim grabbed her other wrist. With one last, superhuman effort she broke loose, swung around, and jumped onto his back. She looped her bound wrist around his neck and leapt off, a move that would have made Princess Leia in *Return of the Jedi* proud.

The rope tightened.

Hashim clawed at her. He grabbed her throat.

Neck and neck. She would have laughed if she could have. She settled for wheezing.

Alex didn't give up. She kept pulling as he gasped for air.

His eyes widened. His face went a dark red. Finally, he collapsed. His hand raked down the front of her shirt and caught the neckline.

It ripped as he went limp and dangled beside her.

A moan escaped him. So did some drool.

Pain raging in her back, Alex got her feet underneath her and loosened the rope.

He collapsed to the floor.

She promptly fell to her knees. Or would have had the rope not caught her wrist. She wound up dangling in posture purgatory.

No time to rest. She had to get out of the loop and tie him up. And fast since she knew he was merely down and not out.

The noise of gunfire caught her attention. Rescue? Could Mom have mounted a rescue? Impossible! But someone else?

"Help!"

Her cry came out weak.

She tried to get her feet under her, but the burning from the blows to her kidneys kept her down. She winced and tried again. "Help! In here!"

The door slammed open.

"Alex!"

"Ja—Jabir. Over here!"

Such a precious sight.

Jabir took her in his arms and held on tightly. "Let's get you out of this."

He released her from the loop.

"He is tied up," Isa reported.

Alex opened her eyes. In the light spilling in from the outside, she noted Isa, Sadie, JC, and Mooch.

"It's… like old home week," she muttered.

"Something like that." Jabir held her tighter. "It's over."

No, it wasn't. Alex's thoughts immediately turned to those she'd left behind. "Mom and Noor! They're at the peak. Mom's hurt. She's lost a lot of blood, and we're all dehydrated, and—"

"We're on it, Alex," Sadie told her. "Stay here. We'll find her. You stay here."

"No, I'm going." She tried to rise. The pain in her back raged, and she collapsed. "I—I can't walk. He hit me in the kidneys and—"

"Alex, we've got this," Mooch said.

She tried one more time and got a foot under her before going all the way down. Her eyes filled. "I... need to go. I told Noor to shoot—"

"They'll be fine." Jabir kept his arms around her.

Her world began spinning.

"Please," she begged.

Sadie touched her shoulder. "We'll take good care of them. Promise."

The image of Sadie dashing after the SEALs blurred. She passed out.

34

Tiny sat propped up in a hospital bed. Blood streamed from his arm into a bag and would provide life to Roya Thornton as the doctors raced to save her life. He and Isa, who both had Type AB positive blood had readily stepped up to donate.

Now, a profound weariness settled over him, one brought about by too many hours awake, too many burdens on his heart, and one very angry director. Mitch Harris practically screamed at him on the phone. Tiny slid down so he rested his elbow on the bed's railing and kept the phone to his ear.

"Do you realize how many phone calls I've gotten since last night?" Mitch Harris demanded. "Do you?"

Tiny opened his mouth to answer.

Mitch blasted on before he could say anything. "Seems like a dozen! You assaulted a loan shark with no good cause. And tried to do a hand-off without local coordination."

"I didn't think—"

"Because of that, hundreds of people could have died."

"But they—"

"And then you snubbed Chief Whitley," Mitch raged on. "What did she do? She called me up and scolded me as if it were my fault!"

"I was—"

"I talked to her, smoothed the way. And what about what you did with Leila al-Kadir? From what I understand, you violated practically every reg we have regarding prisoner interrogation, including turning cameras off. What are you, Tiny? A fool?"

"I got Alex back, didn't I?" Finally, he'd gotten a word in.

That seemed to take Mitch aback. He huffed out a sigh. "Yes, you did. Would you have done the same if it had been anyone else besides your goddaughter?"

Tiny didn't hesitate. He nodded as he glanced at Isa, who sat in a neighboring bed. "Absolutely. We leave no one behind."

Mitch simmered down from a boil. "How is Alex?"

"She's resting with the help of painkillers. She has a couple of bruised kidneys that should heal over time. Jabir's with her. Roya Thornton is still in surgery." He glanced up as a nurse approached. "We're not sure about her. She's lost a ton of blood. Isa and I were able to donate, and the docs assured us they have others who are AB positive waiting to donate."

He winced as the nurse slid the needle from his arm and placed some gauze with tape over the wound. "Is there anything else, sir?"

Silence fell for a moment, followed by another sigh of a man who'd already worked too many hours. "No. I want you to rest this coming week. Then the following one, I want you and every one of your staff who was involved with this to report in person for a full debrief. I'll see what I can do to right things with the secretary."

"Thank you, sir."

Nothing. Mitch had already hung up.

Tiny placed his phone on his chest and closed his eyes. Where had he gone wrong? From the start when he'd offered to help Leila. But then came so many missteps. He should have told Alex about her parentage rather than waiting on Roya to do it. He should have forced the issue when he suspected Hashim had slipped into the country. He hadn't, and it nearly cost Alex her life and could quite possibly do so for her mother.

"I should retire." His eyes snapped open. Had he said that out loud?

He glanced at Isa. He must have because his newest agent gazed at him through dark, somber eyes. "Sir, we had no way to see what would happen. We do not have... a crystal ball, if that is the right term."

"True." Tiny shifted and winced as his back barked at him. He needed those muscle relaxants the doc had prescribed for him. His thoughts wandered to his father, who had passed away many years before. "My dad was CIA and served many years in Europe. He didn't talk much about his work. He couldn't, at least until I joined the CIA. Once when I was home on leave from Afghanistan in 1986, he told me the biggest mistake a field agent could make was to second-guess himself after a mission went wrong because it would only cause regret. He called them what ifs. What if I had forced Alex into protective custody? What if I'd told her about her biological father? I have to say Dad was right."

"Then do not ask those questions." Isa's advice was simple.

"Hard not to do when you're responsible for others." Tiny carefully rolled down his shirt sleeve and smoothed the fabric. "But you're right. You're so very right." He turned his head and gazed at Isa. "You did good work. You, Jabir, and Sadie."

"She... she was—and is—amazing. But what is it that she did?"

"I don't follow."

"When I handed her that knife, she mentioned a person by the name of Lorena Bobbitt."

A snort escaped Tiny as he started chuckling. "You'll have to ask her."

"Ask me what?" Sadie asked as she bustled into the bay.

"About Lorena Bobbitt."

"Oh, that." Her cheeks flamed. "Um, let me tell you."

She did.

When she finished, Isa's mouth dropped open. "And you have... done this before?"

"Good heavens, no!" She started giggling. "Not at all. Jabir made that up."

"I... hope so." Still, Isa regarded her through wide eyes.

"You're perfectly safe with her," Tiny said.

Sadie eased onto the foot of Isa's bed. "Boys, enough." She focused on Tiny. "I did come in here to discuss something serious."

"Which is?" Tiny asked.

"I want field status again."

Tiny studied her. Those gray eyes didn't twinkle with good humor and instead radiated sincerity. This was indeed serious. "You're sure?"

"Sure as there's water out there. Being with the SEALs—and Jabir and Isa—made me realize something. I'm ready. Ready to get back into the field."

Tiny nodded. He didn't miss the desire in her voice, something he'd hoped would return after Damon had hired people who killed her fiancé and nearly killed her almost ten years before. "All right. When we get back, let's talk further."

"And I want Isa to be my partner," she added before he could say anything else.

The door to the sick bay hissed open again. Jabir, his gaze weary and face pinched from exhaustion, joined them. Tiny struggled upright and winced as once more, pain raged through his back. "Jabir, what is it?"

A weary smile crossed the young man's face. "Roya is out of surgery. She made it. Praise God, she made it."

EPILOGUE

Saturday, April 14, 2018, 1700 hours EDT, Weatherly, North Carolina

Spring had come to Weatherly. Dogwoods bloomed. So did azaleas. Luscious April scents wafted through the open French doors of Alex and Jabir's flat. Wow. It was hard to believe she'd been married a little over three months. It was nice to have him living here, even if she'd given up half of her closet. They'd already talked about restoring an old house on the outskirts of town, similar to what Josh had done when he'd met Diana.

Alex set a vase of dogwoods and ferns on the granite island. She'd always loved the tender white blossoms and the hope they symbolized. Could it mean a new start for her and Mom? She added a good book she'd read while she and Jabir had finally honeymooned on Maui. They'd only returned a few days before.

Mom would love it. She knew she would. And what else? Oh, that's right. The bottle of wine she'd bought when she'd been at a wine store in Raleigh. She'd discovered the label in Hawaii and found it locally. Mom and Dad would enjoy the Chardonnay.

She sealed the birthday card and scribbled Mom's name on the front.

Okay. She was ready. At least physically. Mentally, she wasn't so sure. Mom's request during their conversation the night before had surprised her. Could she and Jabir come over early to Mom's birthday dinner so they could chat? If anything, it filled her with unease, especially since awkward had been the word Alex used to describe her relationship with Mom as of late. She picked up some tissue paper, fluffed it, and lined the bottom of a small wicker basket she'd gotten. Then she added the vase of flowers, wine bottle, and book. And the card.

Jabir joined her and turned his attention toward the basket as she finished with the tissue. "That's nice. For your mom?"

"Yeah." Alex bit her lip as she again thought about Mom's request.

Jabir reached up and rubbed her shoulders. "What's going on?"

"I'm wondering why Mom wanted us to come over early. She said she wanted to talk."

His hands paused. "Oh?"

"Yeah." Her stomach balled as emotional remnants from the ugliness in early January resurfaced. "I have to say I'm a little worried."

He turned her around and brushed some hair from her face. "Let's see what she has to say."

Alex nodded and accepted his kiss.

On the ride out to her parents' house, her hands tightened around the basket. Jabir seemed to sense her nervousness and pried her left one off the wicker. He held it except to change gears.

They parked beside the deck.

Dad greeted them with a smile. "Well hello, you two! Come on up. What did you bring?"

"A birthday basket for Mom." Alex set it on the table.

"Let me go get her. Y'all feel free to stay here. It's too pretty today to be inside."

Alex couldn't have agreed more. She stared at the weeping willows lining the far side of the pond. It didn't take too much imagination to envision herself lounging in their shade.

"Alex." Mom's throaty voice floated to her like the scents of the rose bushes lining the deck.

She turned.

Mom slowly made her way through the open door. It was another sign she hadn't fully recovered from her ordeal. She smiled when she saw the basket. "Oh, sweetie, this is beautiful!"

Dad grinned. "Looks like we need some wineglasses. I'll be right back."

Mom eased onto a wrought iron love seat.

"How are you feeling?" Alex asked.

"Since we last saw each other a couple of weeks ago?" Mom smiled. "Much better. Have you heard from Noor lately?"

Alex smiled as she thought about her new friend. "I did. They're returning to Beirut at the end of the month. Now that Hashim is behind bars in US custody, she says they have nothing to fear."

"Hopefully, it stays that way."

"I think it will. Tiny called yesterday." Alex smiled as she remembered the chat she'd had with her boss and mentor. "He said any thought of retirement is officially off the table. Jonna convinced him he's got a few more years left."

"I'm glad to hear that."

Jabir sat down with them. "And also, Leila al-Kadir started singing like a canary when she found out Hashim was in custody. The prosecutor offered her a deal that greatly reduces her time in prison if she comes clean."

"She took it," Alex added with a smile. She cocked her head. "Mom, have you started exercising yet?"

"Beyond physical therapy? No, no. Not yet. The therapist said soon, though, and that if I hadn't been in such good shape, I probably wouldn't be here now." She fell silent as Dad joined them.

"Wine for all." He uncorked the bottle of Chardonnay and poured everyone a glass. "Jabir, what say you and I go and shoot some pool? Leave the ladies to their talking?"

"Sounds like a plan." Jabir rose and kissed Alex on the hair before following his father-in-law to the detached garage.

Alex followed them with her gaze. She drew in a breath as the door leading to the upstairs thumped shut.

For a few moments, nothing but the sound of twittering birds filled the air. Then Mom spoke. "I think you and I need to totally clear the air."

Alex's stomach dropped. They weren't going to fight again, were they? "How so?"

"I need to tell you why I kept your parentage from you." Mom closed her eyes. When she opened them, they glimmered with unshed tears. "You know I was the oldest of three children. I had two brothers. Before my youngest brother was born, Mama was a quiet person but engaged in life. After he was born, she withdrew. She didn't socialize, didn't really connect with her children anymore. Nowadays, I know what it's called. Postpartum depression. That is the name of it. But back then? I inquired of Papa a couple of times. He rebuffed me and said it was adult business. I accepted it. And when I did so, I learned a lesson."

"What?"

"Not to talk about feelings. To accept things as they were. Perhaps that is why, when your father and I first married, I accepted his philandering for over a year. I wouldn't—no couldn't—talk to him about it. I didn't know how. But for some reason, I could talk with Hamid al-Hassan."

"Did you two talk a lot about stuff outside of work?"

"We did. We got to know each other and found out our fathers knew each other through mutual friends. That March day, when…"

She didn't need to say it. Alex knew what she was talking about.

"I'd had enough of Davie's infidelity. I was good and angry. I found my desire to know the fate of my family was enough to drive me to seek out Hamid. I thought I'd have plenty of time. Little did I know the anguish that hit me when he told me the truth. They had perished within sight of the border."

Alex winced as she considered the agony that must have rushed over her mother upon hearing the news. "I can't imagine the depths of your grief."

"I was literally unable to travel because of it. Not that it mattered. A blizzard struck. Hamid reported a total white-out and offered me shelter until the storm passed. He left me alone and approached me the next day. Then…" Mom hung her head. "It was only one time, Alex. Only once."

"But it was enough." Her own eyes filled. "Did you… did you regret it?"

"Having you? No! Oh, Alex, no! Not at all. It was like a wakeup call." Mom leaned forward and took her hands. "You see, when I returned, your father and I had the fight of all fights. At the end? We realized we needed to fight—not with each other, but together—to save our marriage. And we did." She blinked several times. "Things got better throughout that year. But I knew when I was found to be expecting that Hamid was your biological father because Davie and I… he did not approach me until after we returned to the States."

Alex lowered her head.

"Daughter, look at me." Mom lifted her chin with her finger. "When I saw you, you were so perfect. Your father agreed as well. From the top of your little head all the way down to each little toe. But I got scared, so scared because of the culture from which I came. I was afraid that if his parents found out who was your biological father, they would turn me out, or worse, kill the both of us because I had dishonored their son and the family name by straying, even if it was only once."

"Oh, Mom."

Mom swiped at a tear. "Our marriage was still so fragile at that point. I begged Davie to put his name on your birth certificate. He agreed. For right or wrong, he agreed."

Like Jabir's friend Rex had advised her when she'd begun counseling with him, she tried to empathize with her mother. What would it have been like if she'd strayed with someone? And then been forced to be apart from Jabir while she lived with her husband's parents? "Did… did you ever tell Grandma and Grandpa?"

"No, no." Mom shook her head. "They never knew. Your siblings didn't know. Davie's brothers didn't know. Just the two of us. As the years passed, I knew I needed to say something to you. Yet I was still so ashamed. Then when you hit elementary school, I was worried that telling you would accidentally lead to it getting out to your friends, and they'd make fun of you. Then when you entered junior high and high school, I worried you would hate me if I told you. By then, it simply became easier not to say a word. Sometimes, I even forgot because your father—Davie—loved you as his own flesh and blood."

Alex swallowed hard. Now, with the back story, it was easy to see why Mom had chosen avoidance.

Mom sniffled. "Many times, the truth is not the easy route. When Jabir confronted me, it brought back all of those awful memories. I felt Holy Spirit telling me to confess, only I was terrified you would hate me. I found it easier to live with threats against Jabir. Against Tiny. Even against my own husband." She lowered her head. When she raised it, more tears tracked down her cheeks. "Can you forgive me, Alex? For not telling you all these years? For the hurt I caused you? And for the way it nearly cost us our lives?"

The compassion swelling in her heart surprised Alex. It was like a clear spring of water welling to the surface. Her words came easily. "I do, Mom. I do."

She hugged her close.

Mom laid her head against her shoulder. "I love you, dear daughter. Regardless of who your biological father is, I know who your true father is. And I know you are loved by your Father in heaven."

Oh, she was. So very much loved by Him, the same one who sent His Son. She now lived by grace. And by grace came mercy before judgment. "I love you too, Mom." She pulled back and wiped away her mother's tears. "But boy, if we hadn't gotten kidnapped, I would have never seen such a side of you."

That did it. Mom chuckled. "To be honest, in a twisted way, it was fun."

Alex groaned. "Fun?"

"Until I got shot."

Alex started giggling. "Mom! I never thought I'd see you perched on the back of a Gator."

"Can we do it again? Sans guns and angry men?"

"Maybe I can convince Dad to let us careen across the meadow." Alex grinned. "Though if we can't stop, we might wind up in the water."

That got them both laughing. They were still giggling when Dad and Jabir returned from their game of pool.

"Dad, can we take the Gator and go full blast around the pond?" Alex cut her eyes to Mom, and they both chuckled.

"Uh, no." Dad grinned and mussed her hair. "Why don't you and Jabir run along? We've got a few more minutes before I need to get supper going."

"Shall we?" Jabir extended his hand to Alex.

"Of course, kind sir." She took it and rose. Hand in hand, they strolled toward the pond and the willows whose shade Alex had craved.

"I love you," Jabir whispered. He leaned over and kissed her. "How did it go?"

Alex released a breath, and any remaining weight she felt from the past winter slipped away. "Beyond all expectations."

"Praise God." He squeezed her hand. "Isa called while I was with your dad."

"What did he say?"

"He and Sadie both got word that they'd been accepted into the pilot program for Unit 28 decentralization to be part of our group."

"How cool is that?" Alex grinned.

"Way cool. They'll move down in June." Jabir fell silent and rubbed his chin as he stared at the pond.

"Where will they live?"

Silence.

Alex mock-punched him on the arm. "Jabir!"

"Sorry. I was thinking."

"As usual."

"They're coming down next weekend to look for housing. My old flat hasn't rented, so I'd be happy for him to take the rest of my lease." He smiled. "At least then, I won't have to pay rent on a place where I don't live anymore."

"Oh, I don't know." She cut her eyes at him. "Didn't you call it your man cave?"

"It's nice to have a hangout spot."

Alex snuggled up to him as relief from her chat with Mom washed over her. "I'm just thankful for no more secrets between Mom and me."

"Amen," he whispered. He nuzzled her hair. "And none between us, either."

"I'll say." She skimmed her fingers across his stubbled cheek. "I love you. Jabir al-Omri."

"Even if I'm… what did you call me a while ago?" He frowned as if searching for the right word.

"Adorkable?"

"Yeah, that."

She kissed him. "Because you're adorkable, I'll always love you."

ACKNOWLEDGEMENTS

It's hard to believe *Loose Ends* is my sixth indie-published novel. Without the support of friends and family, none of this would be possible. I want to thank Steve, my husband, for his wisdom and encouragement. With his eye for detail and his willingness not to let me get away with anything, he makes for an incredibly good beta reader. I also want to thank the rest of my family, my parents, Tom and Dee McCutchen, and my brother, sister-in-law, and niece, Quinn, Phyllis, and Avery McCutchen. Also, kudos go to the rest of my beta readers: Rich Bullock, Jenny Johnson, Amy Simes, and Pam Vashaw. Each of these readers brought good suggestions to the table. Also, many thanks to the crew of my local American Christian Fiction Writers chapter. Your encouragement and input as I worked with my cover designer, helped make it what it is. I also want to thank Dafeenah Jameel of Indie Designz. She's been my cover designer ever since I published *Hunter Hunted*. Dafeenah, you hit it out of the park with this one, and I think it's my favorite now. Last, I'm thankful to God who gave me this talent of weaving stories.

www.ingramcontent.com/pod-product-compliance
Lightning Source LLC
Chambersburg PA
CBHW071207250626
47159CB00001B/239